Praise for Anne Emery

Praise for *Counted Among the Dead*

"[Anne Emery] really is a fine writer; not just a good storyteller but a stylist as well: every word of her prose feels carefully chosen for the way it interacts with the words around it. A fine entry in a wonderful series."

— *Booklist*

"History buffs and mystery fans alike will walk away satisfied."

— *Publishers Weekly*

Praise for *Fenian Street*

"I always look forward to the next Anne Emery. They are always impeccably researched, richly atmospheric, and with a spellbinding plot that keeps me hooked until the very end. She is a true Irish treasure on both sides of the Atlantic!"

— Jim Napier, author of the Colin McDermott Mysteries

Praise for *The Keening*

"Halifax author Anne Emery has superbly blended two fascinating storylines in *The Keening*, a splendid murder mystery with characters you wish you knew."

— *Winnipeg Free Press*

Praise for *Postmark Berlin*

"Emery has twice won the Arthur Ellis Award (both for earlier installments in this series), and readers who have not yet sampled her tough-edged crime fiction are advised to rectify that immediately. A fine entry in a consistently strong series."

— *Booklist*

Praise for *Though the Heavens Fall*

"Anyone looking for a mystery series to read would be well advised to consider the Collins-Burke mystery series by Anne Emery . . . Filled with lots of suspense, a good plot and some history, *Though the Heavens Fall* is another excellent novel in this entertaining series!"

— *Hamilton Spectator*

Praise for *Lament for Bonnie*

"The author's ability to say more with less invites readers along for the dark ride, and the island's Celtic culture serves as a stage to both the story's soaring narrative arc and a quirky cast of characters, providing a glimpse into the Atlantic Canadian communities settled by Scots over two hundred years ago." — *Celtic Life*

Praise for *Ruined Abbey*

"True to the Irish tradition of great storytelling, this is a mesmerizing tale full of twists that will keep readers riveted from the first page to the last."

— *Publishers Weekly*, starred review

Praise for *Blood on a Saint*

"Emery skilfully blends homicide with wit, music, theology, and quirky characters."

—*Kirkus Reviews*

Praise for *Death at Christy Burke's*

"Halifax lawyer Anne Emery's terrific series featuring lawyer Monty Collins and priest Brennan Burke gets better with every book." —*Globe and Mail*

Praise for *Children in the Morning*

"Not since Robert K. Tanenbaum's Lucy Karp, a young woman who talks with saints, have we seen a more poignant rendering of a female child with unusual powers."

—*Library Journal*

Praise for *Cecilian Vespers*

"Emery continues to imbue her stories with a strong sense of place . . . Series readers will be pleased with the new story and character developments, as will those looking for a fresh setting."

— *Booklist*

Praise for *Barrington Street Blues*

"Anne Emery has given readers so much to feast upon . . . The core of characters, common to all three of her novels, has become almost as important to the reader as the plots. She is becoming known for her complexity and subtlety in her story construction." —*Chronicle Herald*

Praise for *Obit*

"Strong characters and a vivid depiction of Irish American family life make Emery's second mystery as outstanding as her first."

—*Library Journal*, starred review

Praise for *Sign of the Cross*

"A complex, multilayered mystery that goes far beyond what you'd expect from a first-time novelist."

— *Quill & Quire*

THE COLLINS-BURKE MYSTERY SERIES

Sign of the Cross

Obit

Barrington Street Blues

Cecilian Vespers

Children in the Morning

Death at Christy Burke's

Blood on a Saint

Ruined Abbey

Lament for Bonnie

Though the Heavens Fall

Postmark Berlin

Fenian Street

Counted Among the Dead

Declan

HISTORICAL MYSTERY

The Keening

DECLAN

A Mystery

ANNE EMERY

Published by ECW Press
665 Gerrard Street East
Toronto, Ontario, Canada M4M 1Y2
416-694-3348 / info@ecwpress.com

Series design: Tania Craan
Cover design: Jessica Albert
Cover photo: Lisa Fecker via Unsplash
Author photo: Mick Quinn / mqphoto.com

LIBRARY AND ARCHIVES CANADA CATALOGUING IN PUBLICATION

Title: Declan : a mystery / Anne Emery.

Names: Emery, Anne, author.

Series: Emery, Anne. Collins-Burke mystery series ; 14.

Description: Series statement: Collins-Burke mystery series ; 14

Identifiers: Canadiana (print) 20260115878 | Canadiana (ebook) 20260115894

ISBN 978-1-77041-677-2 (softcover)
ISBN 978-1-77852-583-4 (ePub)
ISBN 978-1-77852-584-1 (PDF)

Subjects: LCGFT: Detective and mystery fiction. | LCGFT: Novels.

Classification: LCC PS8609.M47 D436 2026 | DDC C813/.6—dc23

This book is funded in part by the Government of Canada. *Ce livre est financé en partie par le gouvernement du Canada.* We acknowledge the support of the Canada Council for the Arts. *Nous remercions le Conseil des arts du Canada de son soutien.* We would like to acknowledge the funding support of the Ontario Arts Council (OAC) and the Government of Ontario for their support. We also acknowledge the support of the Government of Ontario through the Ontario Book Publishing Tax Credit, and through Ontario Creates.

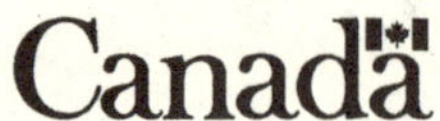

Canada Council for the Arts Conseil des arts du Canada

PRINTED AND BOUND IN CANADA

PRINTING: MARQUIS 5 4 3 2 1

PROLOGUE

"Teacups were suspended in mid-air — well, one teacup and several glasses of stronger stuff — when our oul fella made his announcement."

"Announcement?"

But Father Brennan Burke's younger brother would tell the story in his own way and time. A story apparently about their father, Declan. Terry Burke was on the phone to Brennan at the parish house in Halifax, Nova Scotia; he had rung from the family home in Queens, New York. "We were all around the dinner table. Dec and Ma, myself and Sheila, Patrick, Bridey and Larry. Bridey's kids had finished dinner and were playing outside. It was quiet for a bit and then Declan says, 'I'm going over there.' He didn't mean going to the other side of the room or to one of the other boroughs of New York. No. We'd been gabbing about the old country."

Ireland, whence the Burke family had emigrated more than forty years ago. Here they were in the middle of the 1990s and not once since their departure had the paterfamilias laid a footprint on his native soil.

Other members of the family made frequent trips to the old country. But not Declan, until now.

"What brought this on, Terry?" Brennan asked.

"All Da said was 'It's time.'"

It was long past time, in Brennan's view. Sure, Declan had been forced to leave Ireland under cover of night when Brennan was just a child, following a dispute with Declan's fellow soldiers in the Irish Republican Army. Brennan could not imagine how difficult it must have been for his father to uproot himself and the family, leave behind everything and everyone they knew, to start all over again on the other side of the Atlantic Ocean. And how painful for Brennan's mother. But Declan and Teresa Burke had managed to make a life for themselves and their six kids in New York. Declan had built up the North American arm of the family business, Burke Transport, and was doing very well at it.

In spite of all that, the midnight escape from Ireland and the conflict that gave rise to it had remained an unhealed wound in Declan. This was so even though a friend of his, Father Leo Killeen, had carried out a diplomatic mission with Declan's former brothers in arms. That had been a few years ago, and it seemed that the coast would be clear, and safe, for Declan to return to the land of his birth. Yet Declan had not made a move. Now, it was time. He was in his seventies, and this no doubt reinforced his desire to return. He had friends and family members still living in Dublin. Still living, but for how much longer? Well into his seventies he was, although his appearance, his strength, and the sharpness of his mind were those of a much younger man. Brennan tuned back in to his brother's call.

"So, of course, Bren, I said to Da, 'I'm going with you.'"

"And what did he say to that?"

"He said, 'There are scads of flights to Ireland, Terrence. You needn't be my pilot.'" Terry was a commercial airline pilot. "The expression on his face suggested more than just a determination to choose his own flight. We're well familiar with that look, Bren, the look of a man determined to go his own way."

"Especially, perhaps, on a mission like this, with old disputes and enmities to be sorted."

"Exactly. But I wasn't going to be put off that easily. Those enmities and disputes are why I don't want him heading over there alone. Who knows what he might be facing when he gets there? 'I'll be in the cockpit,' I told him, 'or beside you in the cabin, or I'll pop up in Dublin before or after your arrival, Da. One way or another, you'll be enjoying my company on your homecoming visit to Ireland.' You know the cold blue glare you get from those eyes of his."

"I know it well," Brennan agreed. "And you know *me*. What am I about to say, Terry?"

"You yourself will be joining the party."

"I shall."

"You've no direct flights from Halifax to Dublin, Bren, so —"

"I'll fly to New York via Toronto, and leave the rest up to you."

"Da wants to leave two weeks from now. Tuesday, eighteenth of June. I'll be in touch with you about the plans, and I'll reserve the flights. I can get one-way tickets; we'll decide on the return flights when we're over there. Of course, Bridey's wishing she could come along, but having seven kids puts the kibosh on that. Patrick can't make it either, as much as he would like to." Bridey was their sister, Patrick their brother.

Brennan was determined to make the trip. He had no idea what kind of reception Declan would get from the men he'd offended back in those troubled times. But, whatever it was, he and Terry were not going to let their father face it alone in the troubled times of today.

A trip to Ireland for Father Burke meant making some hasty arrangements with his pastor at Saint Bernadette's parish in Halifax, where he had been living for the past few years. Brennan travelled to Ireland from time to time, and he always arranged for a substitute to carry out his duties. He frequently took on extra work, paid work, with choirs and schools in the city to supplement his funds for his travels. His pastor and dear friend, Monsignor Michael O'Flaherty, would be bright-eyed and keen to hear about Brennan and Declan's Irish adventure whenever it was concluded. Brennan knew he might have to sanitize the story a bit for Mike, depending on how things turned out in Dublin. Some of it might not be for the telling.

Terry Burke had considerable seniority at his airline and was generally able to change his flight schedule, Dublin or Shannon instead of Frankfurt or Paris. Brennan assumed he'd met with no resistance this time round. Because on a Tuesday afternoon two weeks after their father's surprise announcement, Brennan was in New York. Their brother Patrick dropped the three of them off at JFK Airport for their flight to Dublin. Brennan thought, but didn't say aloud, that it would be even better if Patrick could join them on the trip. A loving, easygoing man like Pat — a highly regarded psychiatrist — might come in handy if things got a little rocky, a little stressful, for their da on his return to the land he'd had to flee so suddenly all those years ago. But it would be priest and pilot, not psychiatrist, on this particular mission.

CHAPTER I

Declan Burke

When more than forty years have passed since a man last set foot in the country of his birth — his true home — surely it's enough to say *It's time* to justify making that journey home. And it seemed to Declan that his simple explanation did satisfy his family as his reason to fly over to Ireland. His beloved wife, Teresa, had raised a quizzical eyebrow, but he knew that was more a matter of concern than any kind of suspicion. *It's time* was enough even to satisfy his sons Brennan and Terry. Sure, they insisted on coming with him, and God be good to them, they had his best interests at heart. They wanted to be there to look out for him in case anything from his past came back to smack him in the arse. And with a past like Declan's, that was a concern not easily dismissed. Even as much of his past as was known to the two lads would have them concerned. And they didn't know the half of it. They sure as hell did not know about the letter he had received — not at the family home, thank Christ, but at his office at Burke Transport. The letter and the tattered pieces of paper that came with it.

And now here they were, the three of them in the cabin of a Boeing 747. Brennan in the window seat, Terry on the aisle, and Declan in the middle. He could hardly have badgered Terry for a row all to himself, given that Terry had arranged the flight on this enormous jet through his airline. And Declan wasn't paying one red cent for it. It was nighttime — so late that the three of them had limited themselves to one glass of whiskey each — and all was dark outside the tiny window; the thousands of miles of ocean would not be visible for a few more hours. Declan knew the hours would seem interminable not just because of boredom but because of the tension he was feeling about his secret, the reason for this sudden flight across the Atlantic. He could feel the tension almost like a buzzing or a cloud in his head. The lads kept up a line of chatter about everything except the reason for the trip. They didn't know the reason, but that was not for want of trying. Sometimes it was Terry asking him straight out; sometimes it was merely Brennan's raised left eyebrow.

It was the letter that nearly blew his cover. Three hours into the flight, and he was wide awake. But it looked as if his sons had drifted off, both of them relaxed back in their seats, eyes closed. Declan felt that letter in his back pocket as if it were poking into his flesh. He rose slightly in his seat and reached around to pull out the letter and attached papers. Fuck! One of the papers escaped his grasp. He leaned forward to retrieve it, but not in time. Brennan was awake after all, and he got to the page before his father. He started to open it.

"Give it over, Brennan!"

"What is it, Da, that's got you on edge like this?"

"Give it!" And he reached out and snatched it from Brennan's hand. "This is nothing you have to concern yourself with. Go back to sleep."

Brennan fixed those black eyes on him for a few long seconds, but being a private man like Declan himself, he handed the paper back. Declan tried to hide the fact that his hand was shaking. His son turned his head away to stare out at the darkness.

The first stop for any of the Burkes visiting Dublin was the family bar on the city's north side. So, after landing Wednesday morning, going through the rigmarole at the airport, and freshening up in their hotel room, Declan checked his watch and announced that it was opening time. He, Terry, and Brennan walked the short distance to the iconic public house: a cream-coloured building with the name Christy Burke in gold letters set in a horizontal band of black above the door and windows. Christy, Brennan's grandfather, was long dead, but the pub was thriving under the management of Christy's son — Declan's brother — Finn. Thriving indeed; as early in the day as it was, the bar stools and several of the tables were occupied.

Brennan and Terry had stayed behind their father as he crossed the threshold of the pub for the first time in over four decades. Looking ahead, they could see Finn behind the taps, pouring a pint of Guinness. Finn often wore dark glasses, even indoors — Brennan had never asked why — but there were no glasses on him today. His grey-blue eyes looked up from the taps towards the entrance. At first, there was no reaction. Then the eyes widened, and the mouth dropped open. That provided the answer to one question for Brennan: no, his father had not given Finn any notice of his impending arrival. Declan moved slowly forward, towards the bar, towards his brother. There was a clear resemblance between the two, both strong-looking men. Finn had the same thick hair as Declan, Declan's white, Finn's mostly grey. Finn placed the pint on the bar in front of the punter who'd ordered it, took the payment, and then moved out from behind the counter and walked to meet the new arrivals.

Brennan and Terry edged their way around their father, so they could witness the long-overdue reunion.

"Declan," Finn said.

"Finn," his brother replied.

Neither man was known for dramatic gestures. Their backgrounds, their history as soldiers of the IRA, had ingrained in them a calmness, a coolness, that should never be mistaken for indifference. Declan put out his hand, and Finn took it. They stood that way for several seconds, then Finn let down his guard, put his arms around his older brother, and drew him into an embrace. Brennan gave Terry the eye, and they moved off to let their da and uncle have their moment.

A few minutes later, Finn came over to Terry and Brennan and welcomed them back to Dublin and to Christy's. "I can arrange a house for the three of yis."

"Oh, thanks, Finn," Brennan said, "but we have a hotel booked. We're not sure how long, em . . ."

"Hotel, me arse. I own a couple of properties now. Bought them a few years ago, and I'm having renovations done. One of them Conn will be living in when he moves back from London." Conn was the youngest of Finn's four sons, all grown now. Finn's wife, Catriona, had died more than twenty-five years ago. Brennan knew that Finn had not lacked for female company in the years since, but his main focus was on his sons.

"How are the boys?"

"All thriving. None of them in Dublin right now, so I've a place for yis. I'm sending you over to the Irishtown Road."

"Still called Irishtown, is it, Finn?"

"It is. Maybe by, I don't know, the year two thousand, our city planners will cop on that there's no need to single a place out as Irishtown in the middle of Ireland."

Brennan knew the history. By the thirteenth century, Dublin had become the centre of English power in Ireland. Raids by the native Irish, and increasing numbers of Irish people moving into the city, were simply unacceptable to the English occupiers. In the mid-fifteenth century, they booted the Irish out of the city. The porr oul Oirish were permitted within the city walls to do their trading during the day but had to feck off at nightfall, expelled to what became known as Irishtown. In Ireland, their own country.

Finn said, "Both the places are there. The one where you'll be staying is a fine place in a terrace of houses on the Irishtown Road near the corner with Saint Brendan's Cottages. Almost named for you, eh, Bren?"

"God has ordained it so."

"There are no tenants in it right now. I've a couple of young ones coming from Sligo for Trinity College, but the place is not quite ready for them. I've put in a shower, but I need new tiles in the jacks. I've still to put up new window blinds, some finishing touches. But it's perfectly serviceable. Beds and all the other furniture in it. Should suit the three of you for your visit here."

"That will be grand, Finn. Thank you."

Then Finn poured them each a pint and a small one — a pint of Guinness and a glass of Jameson whiskey — and signalled to Declan to join him in the backroom. Terry and Brennan found a table and settled in to enjoy the craic. There was a family taking up two tables next to them, celebrating the birth of twin boys to the family's youngest daughter, Shauna, and her husband. The new parents were home minding the babies, but the grandparents, aunts, and uncles were marking the occasion with drinks and cheers and passing colour photos of the little twins around to anyone who appeared interested. The Burkes were keen to see them and gave heartfelt praise for the two little ginger-haired infants. Brennan made the sign of the cross over the photos and gave them a blessing, for which the family expressed their thanks. One of the aunts leaned towards Brennan and Terry and whispered, "Shauna was hoping for girls, or at least one; they already have three boys!" As much as it was in character for Father Burke to give a blessing, it was in character for Terry to give a song, a story, or a recital. On this occasion, he did some quick thinking and came up with a recital, which he delivered standing with his pint glass in hand.

With a couple more lads yer one has been saddled.
Tis enough to make anyone's thinking be addled.
But it's not a bad thing to have more little boys;
There's no need to go out and buy any new toys!

And some boys turn out to be not all that bad;
Look at me and my brother, that very fine lad.
Sure, I tell tales in bars; I'm a bit of a liar,
But Father Burke here exists on a plane so much higher.

So you could have one boy who's a spinner of stories,
But another who brings you the heavenly glories.
He'll baptize and he'll marry and forgive all your sins,
So you may have good luck with Shauna's new twins!

Terry bowed in response to the laughs and applause that met his performance, and the gran got up and put her arms around him. He gave her an affectionate hug and sat at the table again. Brennan heard one of the aunts whisper to her sister, "I was foolish and made a promise to Shauna that my gift for the family would be a new camera. One of the little lads broke theirs. But now I see the price of them; I don't see how I can get one for them. Sure, I'm tempted to pretend I'm down with the flu, so I won't have to face them without the camera!" The woman's anguish was written all over her face.

Terry caught Brennan's eye; he had overheard the conversation too. "Do you know what?" he said to the woman. "I'm a nosy fucker, and I heard what you said. No, no," he assured the blushing woman, "no need to be embarrassed. Here's the thing: my daughter gave me a new camera for my birthday. And, well, I have to admit to a bit of stupidity here. I find it too complicated to use. Too many settings and adjustments; I prefer my old camera with the easy settings." This from a man who knew his way around a high-end Leica camera, not to mention the controls of a 747 jetliner. "Are you going to be here a while? I'll run out and get it for you."

The family had just ordered a fresh round of drinks, so Brennan knew they were in for the long haul.

"Ah, no, I couldn't have you do that." Brennan could see a glimmer of hope mixed in with the embarrassment.

"Of course, you could," Terry said, smiling. "Just consider it a gift for the new baby boys."

"But what about your daughter, when she finds out you don't have it?"

"I'll tell her I lost it after a night of skulling pints. She'll find that all too believable! Now, you sit tight."

It wasn't long before he was back with what he claimed was his own camera. He had in fact forgotten his own Leica in the rush to leave New York. What he had in his hand was a newly purchased camera. It was small, fitting neatly into his hand. On either side of the lens was that rough-textured black material so many cameras had, and there were dials on the top. Brennan figured Terry had bought it from one of the shops in Dorset Street and discarded all the packaging on the way back to Christy's.

"Here it is," he said to the aunt.

The woman leaned over and put her arms around him; there were tears in her eyes. "You are so kind. You shouldn't have . . ."

"Ah now, I'm just as happy to be rid of it!" Terry claimed. "There's a new film in it. I'm such a klutz, I ruined the first film I tried!"

"What did you say you are?" one of the men inquired. "A klutz?"

"That's New York talk, Yiddish, for guys like me, who keep dropping things, pressing the wrong buttons, can't follow the instruction manuals. Guys like that."

Guys who can keep several hundred passengers in a four-hundred-tonne plane in the air in a fierce bout of turbulence? Brennan's younger brother was the furthest thing from a klutz. What was the Yiddish word for "generous"? Brennan couldn't remember, but whatever it was, that was Terry Burke.

They stayed on for a couple more hours with their new friends at Christy's, enjoying a few more drinks and, in Brennan's case, a couple of cigarettes. Declan had joined them partway through the evening and was friendly with the new acquaintances. Not overly talkative, as was his wont, but an amiable addition to the group.

ᔓᔕ

The Burkes spent that night in their hotel and then, with the loan of a brand-new black Opel Astra from the other family business, the first and Dublin-based branch of Burke Transport, they drove to their new digs in Irishtown. The house was one in a terrace of two-storey red-brick houses on the Irishtown Road. There were two bedrooms, and the Burke sons took the bigger one with twin beds, granting their father a room of his own. Once they had unpacked their belongings, Terry offered to go out on a grocery run, and nobody objected; he knew the basic items his family liked for their breakfast and their tea. It was a fine sunny day, and Brennan headed out for a little walk around the neighbourhood. He peered in the windows of the big public house a stone's throw from their place, the Seapoint House, and marked the place as his new — if temporary — local. He then set out to explore the little streets with rows of attached houses, which were done in various colours of brick. The priest in him felt truly at home as he noted the saints' names given to the streets: Philomena, Magdalen, Veronica, and Oliver Plunkett. Saint Oliver, the Irish martyr, had been hanged, drawn, and quartered in England, and his head was now on display in Ireland, up the coast a bit in Drogheda. Brennan recalled the story of a Canadian friend who had come to Ireland and struck up a conversation with some locals in a bar; it somehow came up that her father's name was Oliver. Her new acquaintances reared back in their seats, obviously thinking he might have been named after that scourge of Irish history, the old war criminal Oliver Cromwell. "No, no," the visitor assured them, "he was named after Oliver Plunkett." And everyone relaxed. Brennan kept walking to the stone wall that bordered the River Dodder. He looked south to the Lansdowne Road sports stadium and north to the docks and Dublin Port, greeted the seagulls that perched upon the wall, and then returned to his new gaff.

Terry reported that Finn had come to collect their father; nothing was said about their plans or destination. But the Astra was still in place for Terry and Brennan, so they decided to do a bit of motoring down the coast, taking in the lovely seaside towns and villages south of Dublin. "I didn't think to bring my bathing costume," Brennan lamented.

"It's definitely a beach day. And you can't always say that in Ireland, can you? Let's stop and buy ourselves some shorts. What do you say?"

"Amen to that." So they found a shop, each bought a pair of swimming togs, and they parked the car at Killiney Beach. They sprinted out into the cool, bracing surf of the Irish Sea, unintentionally splashing a couple of young women standing in the water near to them, and this led to a splashing contest. Brennan mounted a defence of their boisterous behaviour: "Soon shall our wings be stilled and our laughter over and done. So let us dance on the fringèd waves!"

"I remember those lines from school!" one of the young ones said. "Who was it?"

"William Butler Yeats. May we always heed his words and his wisdom."

And they did. They danced and splashed in the waves and enjoyed a bit of banter and laughter before the Burkes returned to shore and to the city. On their way home, they found a chip shop and loaded up on fish and chips for supper. Declan returned to the house and lost no time sitting down to the meal.

"What did you get up to today, Da?" Brennan asked him.

"Finn and I talked. He suggested a couple of people I could speak to."

Brennan and Terry exchanged a glance. They would have questions for their father, but Brennan could tell that Terry shared his own view: they should allow Declan a bit of time and space before interrogating him about his sensitive mission in the country of his birth. They spoke instead of various friends and relations Declan could catch up with during their time in the city. Brennan was a fairly frequent visitor to Dublin and saw some of his cousins and old pals on those occasions, but it had been a long, long time for his father. Terry suggested that supper be followed by a visit to that grand public house on the corner for a couple of pints. So they headed out.

It had started to rain, and they were treated to one of those lovely, frequent Dublin rainbows. The Seapoint House was close enough that they didn't bother to go back inside and get their anoraks. They just hustled over to the pub and found places at the bar, facing the taps and glistening bottles of spirits, and were soon in conversation with an old couple on the stools nearby who reminisced about members of their families who had been drinking here during the earlier, and very early, decades of the century. The Burkes had a couple of pints and then said goodbye. They had noticed some other pubs in the area and were not ready to call it a night, so they thanked the barman and stepped out into the dusk. Rain was still falling.

Brennan noticed two men standing outside the west-facing wall of the pub. One was fairly tall and heavy-set, the other slimmer and shorter. They were having a smoke, their tweed flat caps pulled down fairly low on their faces. Nothing unusual about that, given the wind that was now blowing the rain sideways into people's faces. But what did strike Brennan as unusual was the men's apparent lack of curiosity. They were ignoring the three men who had just emerged from the pub. Not wondering who was there? Somebody they might know? Brennan looked over at his father and saw him observing the men too. Surely, the pair had had a glimpse of the Burkes as they came out the door. And in Brennan's experience, anyone in a close-knit community would be eyeing the blow-ins from away, curious about who had recently come to town.

But he put them out of his mind when he drew Declan's and Terry's attention to the nearby Vintage Inn. They covered the short distance in no time at all and entered the pub. It was another long-time fixture in the neighbourhood, with photos and memorabilia decorating the walls; this one had been in place since 1845. Here, too, they found people happy to make conversation with the new arrivals. No surprise there; it was well known that people in Ireland had the gift of the gab. Brennan had sat in trains for two, two and a half hours with perfect strangers, who had kept the talk going with barely a pause for breath, for the duration of the trip. One of the many aspects of life in Ireland that he cherished.

ᔕ

Brennan awoke with the morning sun streaming in through the drops of rain on his window. He'd had a relatively early night, so his hang-over was bearable. He and Declan had come home after a pint at the Vintage Inn, but Terry had not been ready to vacate his bar stool, so he'd stayed on. Brennan reached across the bed to look at his watch.

What time were the weekday Masses at Saint Patrick's, the church in Ringsend? It was only half seven now, so he'd no doubt be in time. Should he wake Terry, former altar boy that he was, and suggest that all three of them walk over to the church? Well, he'd wait to see what kind of shape his brother was in after a night on the batter. He sat up in his bed and looked across the room. The blue-and-grey patchwork quilt covering Terry's bed and the pillows were still in place, hadn't been disturbed. Nobody had slept in that bed.

CHAPTER II

Brennan

Terry Burke was a fine-looking man, with his bright blue eyes and thick chestnut-brown hair, his engaging smile that lit up many a parlour and pub. And Brennan knew of the temptations available to an airline pilot thousands of miles from home with fine-looking stewardesses for company. But, as far as Brennan was aware, Terry was not a man for playing away. It had always been Brennan's impression that Terry had remained faithful to his wife, Sheila. Had he now faced temptation in a Dublin bar? Had he fallen asleep in somebody else's bed? Not all that likely; Terry and Brennan were in Ireland to keep an eye on their father, to protect him if need be. Protect him if possible. Would Terry have so easily sloughed off the duty he had taken on with this excursion? Or had he been legless with drink, literally? Had he fallen and injured himself? What was Brennan going to say to Declan who, as Brennan could hear, was up and about in his own room?

He gave his father time to start his day — have a shower and get dressed. When Declan emerged from his room, ready for the day,

Brennan broke the news. "Terry didn't come in last night, Da. He's not here."

Declan gave him a look that was familiar to his son, a look that said *You're not making any sense*. "What are you telling me here?"

"He never came in."

Silence from his father. Then, "Incapacitated with the drink somewhere?" It was said not with disapproval but with hope.

"Possibly," Brennan replied with a similar facade of hope. "Let's go, see if he's . . . We'll ask around."

It was too early for the pubs to be open, so, after Brennan had his turn in the shower, they left the house and walked the streets of Irishtown, as if Terry might be lying injured somewhere. This proved pointless, of course, so they returned to the house and sat down to wait until the pubs opened for the day. Brennan could think of nothing to say or do until he channelled his mother and said, "Tea, Da?"

"Mm."

So Brennan brewed the tea, and they each had a cup and a smoke. It seemed like an eternity, but eventually it was late enough in the morning for the pubs to open up. They headed for the Vintage Inn, where they had last seen Terry, but the door was not open yet. Brennan peered in the window as if he expected to see, what? Terry slumped on a bar stool, a spilled pint on the bar in front of him? No, but he spotted somebody else in there, a man mopping the floor.

Brennan knocked on the window, and the man looked up. He shook his head and mouthed the words "Not open yet." Brennan mouthed, "Quick question?" And the man seemed to understand. Yes, he came to the door and opened it.

"Sorry to be bothering you. I know you're not open yet, but . . ." Brennan had to invent a story; he wished he had Terry's skill in making things up on the fly. "I don't think you were here last night?"

"I'm only here in the daytime."

"Right. Well, perhaps you can help us anyway. My brother isn't well today. We spent some time here last night, greatly enjoyed it, but my brother thinks he left something here. A little folio of pictures, of his family, his travels. He'd been showing it off, and now he can't find it at all. Would it be all right if we had a look round the place?"

The man shrugged. "Go ahead. But I didn't find anything when I came in."

"Thanks. I understand." Of course, he hadn't found anything because there was nothing to find, nor had he come upon a man passed out on the floor. But Brennan and Declan made a quick tour of the place, checked the jacks. As anyone could have predicted, there was nothing to be found. They thanked the cleaner and left the bar.

Declan said, "I wonder if he went back to the first place we were at. Seapoint House. Not likely, I suppose, but . . ." But please let it be so.

"We may as well have a look."

They made the quick walk to the Seapoint, which was open. They walked inside and saw a couple of old gents ordering their first pints of the day. Brennan caught the eye of the barman, not of course the same man who'd been on shift the night before, and gave him the same spiel he'd given the cleaner at the Vintage Inn. And heard the same response. The barman hadn't found a folder of photographs or anything of that kind.

"Would it be all right if we took a look around?"

"No bodder, go right ahead." He gestured to the other parts of the pub. It was a big place with different sections. So they made the rounds, without any realistic hope of finding their son and brother. The only things spilled on the floors were beer and a few coins. They checked the jacks, and there was nobody slumped around the sinks or toilets. They thanked the barman and walked outside.

They stood there irresolute, helpless. "Where do we look now, Da? Or do we call in the guards? My pal Shay —"

His father interrupted him. "Those men," he said.

"What men, Da?"

"That pair that were ignoring us when we came out of this place. Did you ever see such an incurious pair?"

Brennan knew that the men's behaviour had been unusual, no curious glances at the three strangers who had emerged from the Seapoint. But there could be other explanations for that; they were likely just preoccupied with matters that had nothing to do with any of the Burkes. As they walked aimlessly along the Irishtown Road, Brennan observed, "There's a Garda station, Da."

"No peelers!" It came out almost as a bark. No surprise there. Declan Burke would not want to draw the attention of the Garda Síochána, Ireland's national police force. He had never been a man who invited the attention of the police, which was not surprising, given his long history of involvement with the Irish Republican Army — designated an unlawful organization in Ireland — and his activities on its behalf.

Declan

What on earth, or the regions below, could possibly account for Terry vanishing on the second night of their excursion to Ireland? As he and Brennan walked along, Declan felt as if someone had taken a big thick rope, tied it around his head, and was pulling on it; he'd always kept quiet about these headaches, this pressure, that came upon him in times of stress. He felt weak and wanted to slump down on the ground to rest. But he had a reputation to uphold, and it wasn't of a man laid low by headaches and weakness. And if ever there was a time to focus on someone else and not himself, it was now. Terry had not passed out while on the drink or fallen injured somewhere near their lodgings or the pubs he had visited. Had he perhaps met a young one and gone off with her for a bit of the oul excitement? Would he be coming back to the house with lipstick on his collar and a look of shame about him? No disrespect meant to Sheila, Terry's lovely wife, but that would be a much more welcome explanation than whatever else might have happened, something more sinister that might explain his absence.

Who were those two men outside the bar? Declan could not imagine how Terry's disappearance could be connected in any way with the letter that had prompted Declan's hasty decision to make the trip. He hadn't even replied to it, so nobody involved with that bit of history would know that the Burkes were in Ireland. But Declan had a long and checkered past on this island, and Terry did not, at least not as far as Declan was aware. So, was this calamity not about Terry at all but about his father? If so, it was a problem to be tackled by the family. And nobody else. Declan would have to keep up his strength to handle this problem and get his son back safe and sound and full of the devil, as he'd always been.

Brennan

So. No peelers were to be involved. But when you are trying to trace the movements of a missing man, a son and brother, is it not obvious that you would do well to call on the skills and resources of the police? And Brennan was not a little boy, bound in obedience to his father. The best and only way to find Terry was to bring in the experts, and that's what he would do. Here in Dublin, Brennan knew a copper who would be more than willing to help and would be discreet while he was at it. Shay Rynne had been a pal of Brennan's for many years; he had even met Declan in New York more than twenty years ago when Shay had made a trip to the Big Apple during a murder inquiry. Whenever Brennan visited Dublin, he tried to get together with Shay. That wasn't always possible, given Shay's work schedule and Brennan's limited time in the city, but Brennan would make sure his friend was let in on what had happened. If Terry didn't turn up, he would do that in the evening without a word of it to his father.

For now, he had to help his father get through the day. The Burkes had other family, of course, in Dublin, but neither he nor Declan felt like showing up for a visit and either leaving the Terry story out of the conversation or burdening their relations with the crisis. The exception was Finn. And if, please God, Terry got away from whatever was keeping him, he would come to Christy Burke's bar if he found nobody home in Irishtown. Brennan said, "We'll go see Finn."

"Right, so. But he himself doesn't start work till the afternoon."

What would they do to pass the time until Finn came on shift? Brennan wanted something to do other than sit at home and brood over Terry's absence. All he could come up with was a little tour around the city to show Declan some of the changes his hometown had undergone in the past few decades. "How about a bus tour, Da?"

This was greeted with a roll of the eyes. "What, sit on a bus with a bunch of Yanks listening to a lot of blather about the fairies and the leprechauns?"

In spite of the dire situation they were in, Brennan had to laugh. And he needed the laugh. Declan Burke had spent more than half his life in the United States, in New York City. And he still regarded his neighbours as Yanks, a category in which he did not see himself. But fair play to him: Brennan did not see his father, did not see himself, as a Yank. They were Irishmen. The fact that they'd had to leave Ireland as the result of a conflict between Declan and some of his fellow Irishmen did not change that.

"No, Dec. But let's leave the car here and take a city bus along the quays to the city centre." Brennan knew they were both in need of distraction, even if only for a limited time during this harrowing day. "Lots to see there, even more than when you saw it last. And the best view would be from the upper deck of a bus. Maybe see our old house."

"*One* of our old houses, you mean."

"Right, Mountjoy Street. Then maybe we'll go see the other one." The Mountjoy Street house was just around the corner from the family bar.

It was a soft day, cloudy with a fine mist, so it was a good time to ride in a bus, and not all that bad for walking. They climbed to the upper deck of the bus from Irishtown to the city centre, then walked a few blocks along the quays, on the northern shore of the River Liffey. They came to O'Connell Street, one of the city's main thoroughfares. Declan was so intrigued by the changes — all the new shops, the loss of the old ones — that he took no notice of the drizzle as he walked along. Soon they were standing in front of the GPO, the General Post Office, a massive Greek Revival–style building with fluted columns across the front, topped by a triangular pediment. Declan stopped and saluted the building, not for its architecture but for its history. A salute to one of the main sites of the 1916 Easter Rising and to the men and women who had died in the fighting or were executed for their efforts to rid Ireland of British rule. Then Brennan pointed up the street and said, "Notice anything missing?"

His father snickered. Back in 1966, fifty years after the Rising, Irish republicans had blown up Nelson's Pillar, a towering granite column topped with a statue of Lord Horatio Nelson, an obvious symbol of Britain's imperial power. Declan laughed as Brennan sang the song "Up Went Nelson" by a band called the Go Lucky Four. The song had topped the charts for two months in 1966.

It wasn't all that far a walk to Christy Burke's, but now there was a steady rain falling, so they sheltered beneath the pediment of the GPO until Brennan spotted the bus they wanted. They hoofed it to the stop and boarded the bus. The route offered them a brief tour of their former neighbourhood, until they got off and walked to their old house in Mountjoy Street. They stood before the house in the brick Georgian terrace. Neither of them saw fit to comment on the name Mountjoy, a name that graced this street, the prison, and a square in another part of the city. It wasn't mentioned aloud, but a line from an old song came to Brennan's mind: "A cannon he let go. He slapped it into Lord Mountjoy, a tyrant he laid low." It was from "The Boys of Wexford," which celebrated the rebels in that county. That was one Mountjoy; an earlier tyrant by the same name had been sent over from England in 1600. He went on to destroy crops, burn houses, and slaughter men, women, and children in order to force the Irish to submit to colonial rule.

But that wasn't why the Burkes moved house when Brennan was just a child. At that time, his father had been what he and his family considered a political prisoner. Imprisoned for his activities as a member of the IRA, in its struggle against the British colonizers. The state, however, considered his activities criminal, and he was sentenced to a spell in the Joy. Mountjoy Prison. The prison was here on the city's north side, not far from their home and from Christy Burke's bar. Unbeknownst to Declan, Brennan's mother had decided to move the family farther away from all that, and she found a house on the south side of Dublin, in the Rathmines Road. A house virtually identical to the first one, a brick Georgian with a demi-lune fanlight window over the yellow door. So Teresa Burke and the two children she had at the time, Brennan and his older sister, Molly, pulled up stakes and made a new home in Rathmines. It would be understating things to say that this came as quite a surprise to Declan when he was released from the Joy. But, in time, he adjusted to his new home and did not long bear a grudge against the wife he dearly loved.

"Lots of memories here" was all Declan said now, as he turned from the house and started on the short walk to the pub.

There was no sign of Finn when they walked in; he was not in his usual place behind the bar. But they heard "Dec, Brennan!" as Finn hailed them from a table where two other men were sitting. He got up and came to meet his brother and nephew. "What's the craic?"

Declan shook his head, and Finn caught on immediately that something was wrong. "What is it?"

Declan shot a glance over to the counter, and Finn understood. For this conversation, they would go behind the bar to Finn's office. They followed him and then stood facing each other as Declan relayed the news.

"What?!"

"We have no idea where he is. He didn't ring us. We'd been to the Seapoint last night and the Vintage Inn. We got into both places this morning. No sign of him, you know, passed out or anything. We did a walk round the streets. Nothing."

"So somebody took him?" Of course. That was the idea that Brennan had been trying desperately to avoid. "Why?" Finn continued. "Why the fuck would somebody take Terry? Would anyone even know who he is?"

"They'd have seen him with me and Da."

"But," Declan interjected, "nobody knew I was coming back home to Dublin. I hadn't even told you, Finn."

"And I didn't go spreading the news around, you may be sure."

"You'd not have done that, I know, Finn."

"But there was a good-sized crowd here in the bar when you made your entrance. You and your two lads. Word obviously got around.

About you being here, and maybe about you going to stay in one of my houses."

"Right. And if someone with, well, an interest was in either of those two bars last night, they could have heard us talking to the locals. Terry's a great man for the bar chat, as you well know."

"I do. So it wouldn't take a psychic to cop on to who the three of yis are. You can be sure I'll be asking around."

"I know, Finn. And as soon as we hear anything, we'll let you know. We'll be off now."

"Mind how you go, lads."

The sun had peeked through the clouds and no rain was falling when they left the bar, so they decided on a walk. They strolled past the Hugh Lane Gallery and the wonderfully named Rotunda maternity hospital. Then Father Burke had a suggestion. "What say we take a stroll over to Marlborough Street?"

"Ceart go leor." All right. Declan would know what his son the priest was suggesting. They would stop in at Saint Mary's Pro Cathedral to say a prayer for Terry's safe return. They made the short walk to the magnificent building that was still Dublin's "provisional cathedral." Provisional because the Reformation Protestants had taken over the Catholics' "official" cathedral, Christ Church, more than four hundred years ago, and that was the situation even today. So, Saint Mary's was still provisional: "the Pro." This was another building with the appearance of a Greek temple with its pediment and fluted columns. Father Burke and his father walked up the steps and entered the building, Columns were a feature of the church's elegant interior as well. The two men made the sign of the cross and got to their knees to pray for their son and brother. Brennan also prayed for the soul and the family of his close friend Paddy Healey, who had been killed just around the corner in Talbot Street, in one of three car bombs that blew up in Dublin in May of 1974. Another bomb went off in Monaghan town the same day. More than thirty people had been killed, and more than three hundred injured. Women, men, children, babies. Brennan felt the rage come over him yet again: in all this time, nobody had been brought to law for those mass murders. That was more than twenty years ago, and none of those Northern Ireland terrorists — loyalists determined to stay united with Britain, not the rest of Ireland — had been arrested despite the fact that authorities on both sides of the border had enough information almost immediately to make some arrests. In the two decades since then, there had been peace talks on and off, ceasefires declared and broken, and the Troubles still flared up. In the words of William Butler Yeats, "peace comes dropping slow." Brennan tried to clear his mind of the atrocities, Ireland's sad history; there was a more immediate crisis to be faced.

After their moment of silent prayer, it was time to return to their most recent home. Brennan suggested that they stop to pick up something to eat for supper and then catch the bus back to Irishtown. Brennan had a plan for after supper, but he was not going to disclose that plan to his father. So, they returned to their lodgings and ate their beef-and-Guinness pies. Then came the debate about whether or not to call home, and what to say.

"Your mother will be expecting a phone call from me, telling her how I'm getting on. But I can't ring her and tell her everything's grand and glorious, and later she finds out about Terry. And I can't bring myself to tell her he's gone missing. What the fuck do I do, Brennan?"

"I know, Da. Best to put it off. We'll hope and pray that Terry comes back to us before the day's out, and he can ring Sheila at home, and you can ring Ma. And tell them everything's just fine, thank you very much."

So they decided to put off ringing New York for the time being. Then Brennan said he was going out for a drive in the car. He didn't bother to concoct an elaborate story, and Declan was clearly aware that he was up to something. But he asked no questions; maybe didn't want to know.

ᔓ

Brennan left his father alone in the house, not without regret, but he had his mind made up. He was going to consult his friend the Garda inspector, and he would fess up to his father after the fact.

Shay Rynne worked at the Store Street Garda Station on the city's north side, but Brennan, given his father's insistence on discretion, preferred to meet with Shay outside the confines of the station. Not, of course, in any of the pubs near Store Street or in Shay's adopted local, that being Christy Burke's bar. So Brennan got into the Astra and headed west, then crossed the Liffey, which was shining in the sun after another of those rapid-fire changes in the weather so familiar to Dublin. He drove through the city's north side up towards Drumcondra. He knew his way around and was soon standing at the door of the Rynne family's home, a two-storey red-brick terraced house in Fitzroy Avenue.

Shay's wife, Allie — formerly Allie Cotter — answered the door. For a moment, she stood motionless, staring wide-eyed into his face as if she wasn't quite sure who was on her doorstep. Then, "Well, isn't this a surprise! Brennan! How've you been keeping? Come in, come in!" She threw her arms around him and gave him a kiss on the cheek. Allie's ginger hair had darkened over the years to a lovely auburn; not a patch of grey to be seen. Bearing and raising five children had not worn her down; she was as quick and lively as ever. He followed her into the house. The staircase was ahead of him; to the left were square archways — was that a contradiction in terms? — framed in dark wood, leading to the sitting and dining rooms.

"Tea?" Allie asked. "Something a bit more bracing? What would you like? Shay will be home soon."

"A cup of tea would be lovely, Allie."

"Come in and sit yourself down." She led him into the sitting room, which was done up in blue and a shade of white that made Brennan think of linen. A Persian rug combined the colours in an ornate medallion pattern. And given Allie's interest and expertise in archaeology, it was not surprising to see the cream-coloured walls decorated with framed photos of ancient places and artifacts. One showed the stone "beehive" huts built on Skellig Michael as early as the sixth century. Brennan particularly enjoyed a series of colour reproductions of the ninth-century Book of Kells, the splendid book setting out the four gospels with lavish and colourful lettering and decoration. The pages chosen by Allie all depicted cats, one of which was shown chasing a rat that had in its mouth something that looked like the Eucharistic bread! One of her frames held a photo of a pair of Viking swords, another showed a piece of gold jewellery called a lunula. It was a large crescent — hence the name lunula, referencing the moon — to be worn around the neck.

"Thanks, darlin'," he said, when Allie returned with his tea and a plate of biscuits.

She had seen him looking at the gold crescent. "Aw, that's just an oul photo from the office!" Her office was the National Museum of Ireland in Kildare Street. "It's four thousand years old, one of my very favourite pieces."

"I can see why. How's the family?"

"All well and full of badness, as usual. All in their teen years now, as you know. Our middle two are off somewhere with their pals. Aisling and Maeve. The two youngest, Orla and Liam, are over with their aunt Francie today. She's sharing a flat with a friend. Not far from the old family home in Fenian Street. And Brens has, well, you know, he's finished college now and is teaching music. Loves it. He's staying in a flat with two other lads he met at UCD." Brens was the oldest boy, twenty-one years old. Brennan had never forgotten how moved he had been all those years ago when Shay asked him to be godfather to his newborn baby. Brennan had been left without words, at least momentarily, when Shay had told him the baby's name: Brennan Thomas Rynne. He had kept in touch with Brennan Thomas over the years, and he had been more than happy to offer him advice and encouragement relating to his schooling and future plans. He had just earned his degree in music from University College Dublin.

"He's at Waltons, teaching there." Waltons, the music school in the city centre.

Brennan set down his cup of tea and said to Allie, "Good man. I'm delighted to hear it. And yourself, you're still at the museum." Allie had studied archaeology in Dublin and in Norway, and Brennan knew that once her children were all in school, she had started working at the National Museum.

"I'll be at the museum until I'm *in* the museum as an exhibit. The ancient life forms of Dublin, that'll be me!"

"Ah, you've a ways to go yet, Allie."

"And how is the family in New York? I know you're in Canada yourself, but . . ."

"The family in New York is why I'm here to see Shay, but I'll explain that when he arrives, so you'll not have to hear it twice over."

"A police matter, is it?"

"It is," he said and took a sip of his tea. They chatted about the Rynne kids and about the kids at Brennan's choir school in Nova Scotia, until they heard the door opening and Shay's greeting: "Allie, have yeh got the pie in the oven?"

Allie leaned towards Brennan and whispered, "He always asks that. It's an old joke. I've never baked a pie in my life." Then to her husband, she called out, "It's all burnt with the waiting for you. But I've a surprise for you!"

Shay walked into the room and caught sight of his guest. "Brennan! You're looking right at home in here, and that's as it should be. How's the form?"

Brennan got up to shake Shay's hand. His old friend was in middle age now, as was Brennan, and there were a few silver strands in his black curls, but he was in good shape, and his dark blue eyes glinted with humour. "I'm delighted to see you here, Brennan. But has something happened? Has Christy Burke's had a fire or been closed down in the last day or so?"

"Ah, no, Christy's stands as always, an icon of Dublin life. But, yes, something has happened, and not to Christy's. Have your tea, and I'll tell you." So Shay went into the kitchen, poured himself a cuppa, and returned to the sitting room. Brennan then recounted the events of the night before and the morning after.

"Jesus! Terry has been . . . Terry's disappeared?" Shay had met Terry a couple of times over the years. He had stopped himself before completing the phrase "has been disappeared." As ungrammatical as it was, it had become a common expression for the taking of someone and making them disappear. Presumably, the person had been killed.

"Oh, God! I'm so sorry to hear it, Brennan," said Allie.

"So we're trying . . ."

Shay said, "I'll help in any way I can, Brennan."

"Thank you, Shay. Now, I have to say, well, you know my father." Shay had met Declan on a visit to New York more than twenty years ago. "So, you know he's a bit reluctant to —"

"To attract the attention of the police, in any jurisdiction where he might find himself."

"Yes, you see the problem."

"I do. But I'm no stranger to undercover work, so I could have a look around and keep my investigation off the books."

"Thank you for understanding, Shay."

"And there's no time to waste. Let's be off."

"No, no, Shay. Have your supper."

"Senior detectives in the Garda Síochána have no need of supper," Shay joked. He was a senior detective now, Detective Inspector Seamus Rynne. He was in plain clothes, a summer-weight grey blazer and white shirt. He had come a long, long way from his first days in the Garda. As a resident of the Corporation flats — the tenements — in Fenian Street, he had faced prejudice and ridicule from his fellow coppers, who slagged him about being a corner boy from the slums who would soon show his criminal side. Well, he had shown them what he was made of.

"I've some sausage rolls here," said Allie. "Take some with you. Think of it as a start on tomorrow's breakfast."

The sausage rolls smelled delicious, so Brennan grabbed a couple, not letting on that he'd already had his supper.

"Now, I've to be off," Allie announced. "Have to collect my ma in Ballsbridge."

"Attending a reception at one of the embassies, is she?" Brennan asked, smiling. Ballsbridge was a posh area of the city where many embassies and beautiful houses were located.

"Tis far from Ballsbridge *you* were reared, Allie, my love," Shay teased her.

"Ah, go on out of that, yeh oul begrudger." Then she switched to an upper-crust British accent. "My dear fellow, of course my mother is at one of the embassies, and she'll not be making a show of herself. But that sort of thing, embassy cocktail parties, it all gets tiresome after a while, doesn't it? And she doesn't want to wait for the ambassador's limo this evening, so . . ." She laughed and waved goodbye.

Shay said, "Her ma does the cleaning and some, em, personal care for a Mrs. Delahunt at her house in Ballsbridge. She's been doing that kind of work all her life, at one or another house, ever since her days in Fenian Street, trying to bring in some much-needed pounds and shillings for the family."

"Still at it? She must be of an age now, Allie's ma."

"She is. Mamie's in her seventies. But the old lady, Claudia Delahunt, relies on her. Close to ninety is Mrs. Delahunt. She loves Mamie Cotter, greatly appreciates how Mamie has cared for her over the past ten, no, more like fifteen years. Spectacular old house, she has. Lovely place. The top of it has those half timbers on the white walls. Tudor style? Well, I'm not in the know about architecture the way you are, Brennan."

"I can't claim anything other than an amateur's enthusiasm, Shay. I took another path in life, as you know."

"And you did the right thing, Father! Anyway, Mrs. Delahunt's is a large house, standing alone, not a row house. Great gardens around it. Mamie loves being there. A far cry from the tenements where the Rynnes and the Cotters were reared!" Shay shook his head then and put a hand on Brennan's arm. "I'm sorry, Brennan. Sorry to be rabbiting on like that. Our destination today is Irishtown. Our mission: to find your missing brother."

Brennan's desperate hope was that they would not only find Terry but find him with a perfectly good explanation. Perhaps, knowing Terry, a comical one. Please, God, let it be so.

"We'll start at the Seapoint, Brennan. Some of the same barmen will likely be working, and you may be sure some of the regular punters will be in their places, and may have seen something. Then we'll go to the Vintage Inn." Brennan and Declan had already been to the pubs, of course, but now the focus would be on interviewing possible witnesses.

Brennan said, "There were two men who attracted Da's notice, and mine. They were standing outside the Seapoint, and the curious thing about them was their utter lack of curiosity about who was coming and going around the bar. If they'd looked up from their own conversation, looked up at all, they'd have seen three men they'd never laid eyes on before, three blow-ins. And they showed not a flicker of interest. Have Dublin people given up all inquisitiveness about strangers in their midst, about new faces in the bars and in the streets of the city?"

Shay laughed. "They have not, as far as I have ever seen." Then he turned serious and said, "That was odd behaviour, to be sure. Can you describe them for me?"

"Couldn't see much of them, because they were both wearing flat caps and had the peaks pulled down low over their faces."

"Ah."

"One was around my height, six feet or so, and heavy. The other was a few inches shorter and thin. That's all I can recall of them."

"That should be enough to be remembered, if anyone noticed them."

They parked up and walked into the Seapoint. There was a different barman on duty tonight, but Brennan recognized a few of the drinkers who had been there during the Burkes' first visit. He discreetly pointed them out to Shay. They had decided that Shay would make it official, at least on these premises, if not at Store Street Garda Station. So Shay approached the first man, who appeared to be in his sixties, enjoying what was clearly not his first pint of the evening. Shay pulled out his warrant card and identified himself as Detective Inspector Seamus Rynne.

"I didn't do it, Detective, I've been here all day!"

Shay went along with the codology. "Ah, then, you're in the clear, sir, for today. But I'd like to ask you about last night here in the Seapoint. We are investigating the disappearance of a man, someone who was in here last night with my friend here." He indicated Brennan with a nod of his head.

"Right. I remember you and a fierce-looking older fella."

"That would be my father."

"And there was another lad, too, I remember now. He had a couple of the local girls in bits, laughing."

"My brother Terry. I'm wondering: Did you see Terry at any time later in the night, after the three of us left? Did you see him again?"

"I don't recall seeing him again, no." The man twisted around on his bar stool and looked Brennan in the eye. "Your brother's gone missing?"

"It seems that he has."

"Jaysus, I'm sorry to hear it."

Brennan inclined his head in acknowledgement, then Shay asked, "Did you see two men outside the place, with caps pulled low on their faces? One man taller than the other?"

The witness shook his head. "I don't remember seeing anybody like that."

They didn't have any luck with the other drinkers who had been present last night; nobody remembered seeing the two men outside. One thing was clear: Terry Burke had not made a second appearance in the Seapoint House. So, on to the Vintage Inn. Here, Brennan was relieved to see the same barman who had served him on his previous visit.

"Hello again. You may remember that I was in last night?"

"I do, sure."

"With my father and brother."

"I remember the three of yis."

"My brother has gone . . . is missing." The barman peered at Brennan as if he didn't quite understand. "My father and I called it a night, but Terry stayed on. He never came home, and we haven't seen him since."

"That's terrible. I'd help you if I could. But your brother stayed on for a bit after yis left, I remember, and I heard him telling another fella some story about an airplane. Having to land in a hailstorm, something like that. I went into the backroom there and when I came back out here, the other guy was still at the bar but your brother had left."

Shay took over the questioning then, after identifying himself and showing his card. "Who was the other lad Terry was talking to? Did you know him?"

"I did. I do know him. Con-David Kelly, one of our regulars here. Con wouldn't have anything to do with a man disappearing; he wouldn't hurt a fly if it flew into his breakfast."

"Where would we find Mr. Kelly?"

"I'd say you'd find him over at Clarke's. He drinks here till around four o'clock, and then goes over there to meet some mates of his for a few scoops before he heads home to the wife."

"Thanks. We'll try over there, after we're done here." Shay turned to Brennan. "Do you recognize anyone else?"

There was only one man who looked familiar, an old gent sitting by himself at a table, reading what looked like a racing form. Brennan pointed a discreet finger in his direction.

"The oul baldy fella?" Shay asked. Yes. So, they walked over to his table.

The man greeted Brennan. "Good evening to you, sir. Back for some more of the Vintage craic, are yeh? This another one of your brothers, is it?" he asked, meaning Shay.

"No, this is Detective Inspector Rynne. We're looking —"

The man's eyes widened in alarm. "Trouble, is it?"

"Brennan's brother, the man you met last night, never arrived home. We're asking around, trying to find him."

"No! Is that so? You think he injured himself, something like that?"

"We don't know what happened. Did he mention anything about somewhere he might have been going after he left here?"

"He didn't. He was after telling us a terrifying story of flying an airplane in a storm, the plane rocking back and forth and up and down. I've never been in an airplane in my entire life, and I don't think I ever will be, after hearing that. But, maybe, with him at the controls, I'd chance it. Fine man, he'd build confidence in you. Ah, sorry, sorry, I'm rabbiting on here."

"No, you're grand," Shay assured him. "So, he didn't mention a plan or a destination after his time here?"

"Not at all."

"Did he seem worried in some way? Preoccupied about something?"

"No, he was flyin'. I mean, sorry, I wasn't making a joke, I just meant he'd had a few jars and he was in great form. Said goodbye and said he'd be back again another time, and he up and left."

"Thank you, sir. One more thing. Did you happen to notice a couple of men, outside or maybe in here, one fairly tall and the other a little shorter? Flat caps on both of them."

No, he hadn't noticed them. Once again. Shay and Brennan said their thanks and left the bar. Brennan turned to Shay. "Clarke's?"

"Right so."

Clarke's was nearby on the Irishtown Road. Approaching it from the side, they saw a large square church tower looming high on the other side of it. They went in and looked around. It was a big place, the main part of the pub, and there was a separate room as well, a lounge. There were several drinkers ensconced at the bar, and two tables with several men sitting around them. Brennan headed to the closest of the tables and said, "Excuse me. Would one of you be Con-David Kelly?"

"That would be me." He was in his early forties, with curly ginger hair and a cropped beard.

"I'm sorry to be bothering you, but could we ask you a couple of questions?" Brennan introduced himself and Shay and told Kelly why they were there. Kelly gestured to an unoccupied table, so they moved over there and sat down. The man said he had enjoyed talking to Terry last night at the Vintage Inn. No, Terry had said nothing about any plans for later on, and he had shown no signs of being concerned or edgy about anything. Terry left before Kelly did. Shay then described the two men in caps, and Kelly shook his head. "Didn't see anybody standing around like that." Brennan and Shay thanked him and headed for the door. "Hold it there!" Kelly called out, and he got up and came to the door. "I did see a man I didn't recognize. He was by himself though. Or, no, he couldn't have been alone because there must have been somebody else in that old car that he was shouting at. Shouting at someone, I mean, not at the car!"

"What's this?" Shay asked. "A car? Take your time and tell us what you saw."

"I'd left to go home. And I saw a dark-coloured car, an old one from, I don't know, last decade maybe. The motor was running, and this one man, a big hefty fella, standing outside it, shouting at whoever was in the back seat. Yeah, I think he, the man outside, had a cap on his head, and he was having a row with whoever was in the car. And he kind of jerked his thumb towards the back of the vehicle and lifted his hands up, the way you might if you were saying, *What the fuck?* That sort of thing. But it had nothing to do with me, so I went off in the other direction, off towards home. I heard a door bang shut, and the motor rev up, so I think the car drove off. That's all I saw."

"Thank you, Mr. Kelly. Can you tell us anything more about the car? The colour, the make?"

"No, just a dark colour. It was dark outside by that time, near midnight, so I wouldn't be able to tell you the colour of the thing. It wasn't a boxy kind of car, more like it was long in front. Long bonnet on the thing."

"That's good. Thanks. And where was the car when you saw it?"

"In the street right across from the Vintage Inn, intersects with the Irishtown Road. Dodder Terrace, it's called."

"Right. And did you see which way the car went when it took off?"

"Sorry, no. I heard it but didn't turn to look."

Shay thanked him again, said the information might well be useful, and they left him to return to his pals, who would no doubt be curious about his questioning by a stranger and a Garda detective.

ꩰ

Brennan drove them back to Shay's house in Drumcondra, and Shay assured Brennan that he would follow up on the description of the men and the car. Brennan thanked him, then motored back to Irishtown. He saw no point in sitting in the house with his father, the two of them fearful and dejected, with no idea where to direct their anger. "Come on, Da, let's go for a walk."

"Sure, that will solve it for us. Oh, there you are, Terry, out having a walk. What a coincidence."

"We're not getting anywhere, just sitting on our arses. Up with you now."

Declan got up from his chair, reluctantly, and followed Brennan out of the house. It was a lovely warm summer evening, the sun still high and bright in the western sky. They walked around the neighbouring streets and then arrived at Ringsend Park, a large green area with a tennis court and sports pitches, and they looked on as teams of young boys played Gaelic football on a nearby pitch. One side was kitted out in green and yellow, the other in blue and white. There were shouts of joy when a tall golden-haired boy booted the ball and it flew beyond the reach of the goalkeeper's hands, ending the match three-nil for the team in blue. The victors leaped into one another's arms and ended up in a mad heap on the ground. Brennan smiled at the sight of it, but he was not distracted for long. It was time to come clean with his father.

"I went to see Shay Rynne."

"The guards!"

"Only Shay, and he'll keep it to himself." Declan seemed to relax then; he knew Shay and knew he could keep a confidence. Brennan repeated what he and Shay had heard from the punter in Clarke's, about the car and the two men arguing.

"What do you make of that?" Declan asked. "That wasn't far from the last place anybody saw our Terry."

"Shay will try to trace the car. He'll be in touch with us about that."

"I say we check in with Finn," Declan said. "See if that car, the description of those men sound familiar to him."

It was a long shot, Brennan knew. But there was no point in giving voice to that. His father knew that as well as Brennan did. So it was another trip to Christy's.

"Any word?" Finn asked as soon as he spotted them approaching the counter.

Brennan filled him in on what he had learned, as Finn pulled their pints.

"I'll ask around about that car," he said, "and about two men fitting those descriptions. It's not much to go on."

It wasn't. But Brennan knew without saying that the three of them were going on the assumption that those two men, and that car, were more than likely connected to Terry's disappearance.

CHAPTER III

Terry Burke

It was great gas talking with some of the drinkers, male and female, at the Vintage Inn; he had entertained them with a jetliner adventure, but they had so many tales about local characters and their own adventures and mishaps that Terry hardly got another word in. You know you're in Ireland when the punters out-talk Terry Burke in a bar. But Terry and Brennan were on a mission, and that might require a clear head in the morning. So Terry paid for his round, bade goodbye to his new group of friends, and said he hoped to see them again soon. He walked out of the bar and started up the street to the house. It was still raining, but he'd be home soon.

What was that? Sounded like footsteps, but he hadn't seen anybody about. Then, as quick as lightning, two figures emerged from the darkness. They both had caps pulled down over their faces. One was a big beefy-looking guy, the other shorter and slim. Both wore track suits, the big man's black, the smaller man's grey. Were they the same men he and his father and brother had seen outside? They were on him in a flash, each taking one of his arms. They pushed him forward.

"What the fuck?"

"Shut your gob if you want to keep breathing." The voice was pure Dub.

He shifted left and right, trying to shake them off. To no avail. They each had a grip on him like a vise. They frogmarched him across the road and to a car parked on a street perpendicular to the Irishtown Road. It was an old battered-looking Ford Capri. Dark blue. The smaller of the men let go of Terry. Terry raised his arm, ready to strike out. Too late. The man was ready, had pulled a gun from his pocket. The barrel of the gun was pointed at Terry's face. "Get in!"

"What? Who the fuck are you? What do you want with me? I don't get it."

"You'll get it in the back of yer head if you don't get the fuck into this car. In! Now! Front seat."

Terry's mind was racing. How could he get away? But he had no options with a gun pointed at him. He opened the passenger-side door and got in. The guy with the gun got in behind him.

The big guy was outside shouting at the gunman. "This is a fuck-up!"

And the gunman shouted back, "Shut your fuckin' mouth and get in here!"

He got into the driver's seat, started the engine, and roared away up the Irishtown Road.

There was no point in asking questions. But Terry was a navigator, whether he was soaring thirty-five thousand feet above the earth or down on the ground being jostled about in an old beater of a car. It was dark, but he tried to register what he was seeing, commit it to memory. They were going roughly north along the Irishtown Road and then they made a fast, screeching turn to the left, propelling Terry into the driver; he and his captor shrank away from each other. They came to a bridge crossing the River Dodder. After that, Terry recognized the Dublin Bus Ringsend Garage and then they were crossing water again. The Grand Canal up by the docks?

The car was racing; Terry's mind was racing. Who were these two thugs? What was going to happen? Could he remember all these turns, find his way back? Back from where? When? The car drove ahead, then lurched around a right turn, throwing Terry up against the passenger door. Going north again? The fellow in the back seat raised the gun so Terry couldn't miss it. As if being slammed against the car door was something Terry had planned; trying to wrench the door open was not an option. A bullet launched from that gun would travel a hell of a lot faster than Terry launching himself from the car. His heart felt like a hammer pounding in his chest; each breath was coming faster than the last. He tried to ignore the weapon and looked out the windows, but he could no longer make out where he was. Within seconds, though, they were driving over a bridge again, and he knew they were crossing the River Liffey. Another abrupt swerve and he was disoriented. He didn't know the names of the streets around here, but he tried to catch a street sign as they sped along. No luck. No, wait — East Wall Road. There was indeed a wall, walls on both sides of the road. The one on Terry's left was old and made of stone; the one on the right was concrete. There were a few housing terraces but a good many industrial type buildings along the route. A bridge above the road, an overpass. Then a slamming of brakes and he was propelled forward. His forehead slammed into the windscreen, causing a sharp stab of pain. The car was parked in front of a row of brick terraced houses, numbered in the forties.

The driver got out, ran around to Terry's side, and yanked him from the car. Another bang on his head, this time on the door frame; his yelp of pain came out as "Fuck!" The gunman jumped out right behind him and gave him a shove towards the door of one of the houses. Terry stumbled and fell on his right knee. Someone shouted from across the street. A witness to a man being forced into a house at gunpoint? Terry twisted around, but it was only a young guy calling out to his mate on the riverbank. So they must have been alongside the River Tolka. Next thing Terry knew, he was inside the house, after another push by the gunman. It had happened so fast that Terry had not had the chance to see the number of the house. All he knew was that it was in the middle of the terrace. It was dark in the room, no lights on inside and none shining in from the street. A glance at the front window showed why: the window was covered top to bottom by a slab of wood, presumably plywood, and it was painted black. It must have been black on the outside as well because Terry had not seen any windows with light-coloured wood outside. The slab was bolted to the wall. Nobody could see in, and nobody could see out.

The big man turned on a lamp and told Terry to sit. The light was dim but he could see a sagging couch, a couple of armchairs with the fabric worn away from the arms, a coffee table covered with newspapers, and a television in the corner at the far end of the room. He walked to the couch and sat down. The only remotely welcoming element in this place was the cabinet on the opposite side of the dingy room; it held an array of bottles and cans. Whiskey, beer, and porter. A well-stocked bar.

"Drink?" the big man said. He had taken off his cap, revealing a head of thick wavy grey hair. His eyes were a darker grey, and he had a small nose that turned up at the end.

Was this going to be a friendly visit after all? Terry doubted it, but if drink was on offer, that might be the only solace he would get. "I'll have a whiskey." His host poured him a generous helping of John Jameson and handed it to him. The man poured one for himself, and his pal cracked open a can of Guinness. Both men remained standing.

"Why am I here?"

The shorter man looked at him with narrowed eyes. The eyes were dark, as was his hair, with strands of grey. His head and face were thin, with a prominent pointy nose and thin lips. He had the look of an aggressive rodent. He said, "Your da will know why you're here when we make contact with him."

"What does this have to do with my father? Let me walk out of here, and I won't tell anyone about this . . . this episode."

"We're not finished with you yet. We've only got started. And don't get it into your head that you can get past us and get your arse out of here. I always have this!" And he lifted the gun and pointed it in Terry's face. The man's hands weren't steady; Terry had noticed that one or more of the fingers jerked upwards. Christ almighty, would that pistol go off by accident? Terry turned his eyes from it; didn't want to give the gunman the satisfaction of seeing his fear.

"Now, drink your whiskey and fuck off with the questions. If you want to speak to either of us, you'll call me Gerry and the big man here Frank.

"All right now," said Frank, "bring your glass with you while I show you to your quarters." Terry knew that Gerry still had the gun, so he followed the instructions while desperately trying to scheme a way out of there. He was led into a tiny bedroom. Frank flicked a switch and the overhead light came on. Another dim bulb. There was a narrow cot up against a window, this one boarded up on the outside. There was a grey blanket on the cot, no pillow. One wall of the room had been smashed open between the studs, the plaster jagged around the edges. Terry peered through the opening and saw a toilet and a sink with a cake of soap and a towel. "When you're out there," Frank pointed to the sitting room, "your hands and legs will be tied. You'll not be going anywhere until or unless we say so. And if you had the talents of — who's that magician fella, Houdini? If you had his talents for escaping, you'd not get past the doorstep out there because Gerry will be watching, and he'll be armed. Now, while you're in *here*" — the bedroom and the en suite bathroom without a bath — "your arms and legs will be free. Because there is no way out." So, the bathroom door must have been bolted shut as, Terry assumed, the bedroom door would be when he was in residence. In captivity. Now, how was he going to talk his way out of this?

But first, a more immediate concern. Access to the jacks during the day. "And if I have to have a slash when I'm out there?"

"You'll be able to come into your private suite from time to time during the day. Now, sit down," Frank commanded, pointing to the cot. "And don't start thinking that this will be your chance to get away. Whenever we give you these little breaks for using the jacks, Ger will know. If he's not in the house with us, I'll be giving him the signal."

Terry sat down and the cot wobbled as if it might collapse. "Listen," he said, "whatever it is that's led to this, tell me, and we'll work something out."

Ger had come into the room and scowled at him. "The only man who can *work something out* is your old man. Your fate is entirely in his hands!"

But no, it wasn't. Terry's fate was in the hands of these two gurriers who had a grudge, an agenda, Terry couldn't even guess at. He had never been short of words in any situation; what was it going to take to get himself out of here?

Ger stood and gestured to Frank, then turned to Terry. "Lock-up time. Sweet dreams." The two kidnappers left the room and quietly shut the door behind them. Terry heard them locking it from the outside. Then he heard, "Turn on the match, Frank," and the sound of the television coming on.

"Not the football. Switch to the hurling! They're showing a rerun of Kilkenny and Wexford."

His captors had something to amuse them. But what in God's name was Terry going to do? Sleep? How could anyone fall into a peaceful slumber in a situation like this? And if he couldn't sleep, what would he do? Terry had always had zero tolerance for inactivity, for boredom. Here, there were no books or magazines, no radio, no television, and, of course, no telephone. One good thing, if good things could be imagined at a time like this: smoking had never been much of a habit for Terry, and he had given up cigarettes a long time ago. So at least he wasn't craving a smoke, and his captors wouldn't have that to hold over him. The only thing for him to do was obsess over how to get himself out of here; otherwise, he feared he would go mad. Lose his mind.

CHAPTER IV

Brennan

It was a sleepless night for Brennan and Declan. They had decided not to do anything that would leave the rest of the family sleepless in New York; they would not be telling Terry's wife, Sheila, or, of course, his children. Nor would they be telling his mother, Teresa, or his brothers or sisters. Brennan made a mental reservation to that agreement; he might want to confide in his brother Patrick. But he didn't care to dwell on whatever had prompted this idea in his head, or what might occur that might give rise to the need for the assistance or consolation of a psychiatrist. Pat was more than that; he was the kindest, most understanding of men, and the family had always benefited from his compassion and good sense.

Declan could have benefited from that compassion and good sense last night. The conversation he had with Brennan could only have come from a Declan Burke with all defences down. He had a look of vulnerability about him that Brennan had never seen before. "Don't give up, Da. Whatever happened, we'll have Terry back with us again."

"This is all on me, Brennan. I'm sure Terry never dirtied his bib over here." Never behaved badly or did anything controversial. "Nobody here would have a grudge against Terry. Who would even know him here? The grudge is against *me*. And this is the revenge. Word must have got round about me being back in Ireland. Why in the fuck did I decide to come back here?"

"Because this was your home, Da. You're an Irishman; this will always be home to you, as difficult as that is to believe right now."

"This is doin' my head in. There I was, all my life, thinking nothing could be worse than the leaving of it. The leaving of Ireland."

"I could never imagine what that had been like for you, spiriting us out of Dublin in the middle of the night, speeding down to Cobh, all of us piled into the car, with a few bags of belongings, trying to get to that ship on time. The ship that was to take us three thousand miles across the Atlantic to . . . to what? You would not have known what awaited us there."

"I remember it as if it was last Tuesday! Sailing out from that beautiful coast, the coast of County Cork, not knowing if I'd ever see Ireland again. My parents, my brothers and sisters, everyone. I love this country, Brennan."

"I know you do. You were willing to die for it."

"And what it was like for your mother. I, at least, had a reason to get away." Brennan knew that Declan had disobeyed an order from his officer commanding in the IRA, and his disobedience resulted in a setback for his comrades. They lost a cache of arms; that was the truth of it, not that Declan had been directly responsible for that. He had been ordered to "eliminate" a traitor in the ranks, a man named Quinn, and for various reasons could not bring himself to do so. And the man whose life was spared went on to inform the government of the location of the weapons. Declan had never breathed a word of this story; it was conveyed to the family only a few years ago by a visiting priest. Father Leo Killeen.

"Your mother was heart-scalded at having to leave. She very nearly didn't." Brennan hadn't known that, but he could not say he was surprised. What did surprise him was his normally taciturn father opening up about this traumatic period in the family's life. "It broke her heart, but she didn't want to break up the family. She and I were both determined that we had to stay together. And that long, heaving, agonizing voyage across the sea, with everyone sicking up and . . . and all that. I know I wasn't the only one who was tempted to give up entirely and jump into the water. Put an end to it all." Brennan had been very young at the time, but he remembered feeling like doing exactly that.

"Then there we were in a new country. No home, no work. And I had a family to support. There were people I had to . . . to deal with to get anything. That poxy flat in Hell's Kitchen, all of us in two rooms. And having to drag the lot of you down that hall to the jacks. The toilets and the filthy bathtubs must have given you a complex for life. Well, you for certain, Bren!"

"Me for certain."

"Oh, God forgive me, for what I put your poor mother through. That was before I was able to set up Burke Transport, American version. Me working as a security man at a nightclub did not exactly fill the coffers with gold and silver. With that wage packet, I couldn't get us out of there."

"Until you did. We moved into the lovely brick house in Sunnyside. That enclave of New York Irish. I've never been clear on how you got the money for a place like that."

"You don't want to know." Brennan didn't know, but he was well aware of some of the shady characters his father had associated with, members of the Irish and the Italian "communities," so somewhere in there was the answer. "But I had to do something, Bren, to get us into a decent place. We heard that your ma's parents were coming over to New York. To check up on us. And Teresa didn't have to tell me, although she did in no uncertain terms, that if I didn't get us a decent place to live before they arrived, she and you children would be going back with them to Dublin. Goodbye, Declan."

That was the most forthright Brennan's father had ever been about his painful emigration and the torment he suffered during that period of his life. After that unprecedented baring of his soul, he seemed to cop onto himself, and he said, "That's enough of that. Off with you and get yourself some sleep."

ᔕ

The last Brennan saw of his father that night was him staring out the front window and spluttering with rage. When Brennan finally gave up all thought of rest, and the morning came, he got up, went into the bathroom to have a shower and brush his teeth. Didn't bother to shave. Declan's door was still shut, and that suited Brennan, because there was someone else he wanted to see. He wasn't sure whether Declan would agree or not agree with seeing Father Killeen, so Brennan would go on his own. It was just past seven in the morning, too early to arrive at the parish house but not by much. Brennan knew there was an Irish-language Mass at the Aughrim Street church in Stoneybatter, sometimes at noon, sometimes at eight in morning. And Leo was usually the priest who celebrated it. If he was on for noon, Brennan could likely catch him beforehand. If his Mass was at eight, Brennan would attend. So he dressed for Mass, not in his black clerical suit and collar but a navy blazer and light-blue shirt.

He left the house and drove to Stoneybatter, an area northwest of the city centre. He parked up and stopped in at a café for a cup of tea, a smoke, and a pastry for breakfast. Then he walked to the Church of the Holy Family, a lovely grey-stone church with twin steeples. A woman and her little daughter were heading for the door, so Brennan excused himself and asked, "Which priest is saying the Mass this morning, do you know?"

"An tAthair Ó Cillín," the daughter replied, in the native language of Ireland. Father Killeen.

"Go raibh maith agat," Brennan said in thanks, and he followed them inside. The church had some of the most beautiful stained-glass windows Brennan had seen anywhere, biblical figures in jewel-like colours of blue and red, green and gold. He chose a pew near the back of the church and knelt to pray. At eight o'clock, two altar boys emerged from the sacristy in their white surplices over black cassocks.

The boys, one with ginger hair, the other dark, appeared to be twelve or so years old. They were followed by Father Killeen in his green vestments, a black biretta on his head. They processed down the left side aisle, then to the centre and up towards the altar. Killeen was around five feet eight inches tall, lean and grey-haired with lively dark eyes. He was of an age with Brennan's father. There was a fair crowd on hand for a Saturday morning Mass, though not as big as the congregations at the Sunday Masses Brennan had attended. Any time he'd been at those Masses, he'd always been impressed by the children in the congregation, their superb command of the Irish-language responses.

Brennan would be telling Leo all about the events that had befallen the family upon their arrival in Ireland; this first meeting would be between himself and Leo. He might get more information from the man without Declan running interference during the conversation. Brennan remembered Leo's visit to New York, when it seemed the dam had burst after decades of carefully maintained discretion. Father Killeen, on that occasion, was absolutely garrulous, entertaining Brennan and his close friends Monty Collins and Maura MacNeil with tales of Declan's till-then murky past in Dublin. To be sure, Leo would not have been talking outside his limited, trusted circle of listeners; still, it was a welcome change from the air of secrecy that had always surrounded Declan Burke.

Now it was time for the homily, and Leo gave it in English. It was all about love. He quoted Saint Paul: "Faith, hope, love abide, these three, but the greatest of these is love." And he spoke with a gentleness that would inspire every person present to be as loving as Father Leo Killeen clearly was. It was a different Leo Killeen that Declan Burke had known here in Ireland decades before. Declan had known Leo not as a priest in those days but as his OC, his officer commanding, in the Irish Republican Army.

Brennan had never asked Leo whether he, like Brennan, frequently agonized over the role the IRA had been playing in the life of Ireland. Brennan's thoughts centred on the theory of a "just war." Saint Augustine wrote about this in the early fifth century, and the idea had been developed over the centuries since. There were two aspects of war to be considered. Jus ad bellum referred to the justice of the war itself: is there a just cause, a legitimate reason to go to war? Jus in bello referred to the conduct of the war: what actions are justified, and what actions are not justified, in the conduct of the war? In Brennan's view, the actions of the British during the eight hundred years of its involvement in Ireland, the discrimination and the atrocities committed by its representatives and its surrogates, especially in the North of Ireland in recent decades, justified the IRA taking up arms against it. But to state the obvious, not all the actions taken in the conduct of that war could be justified. The killing of civilians, even if not intended, was the most obvious example of what should never be allowed. But — at the risk of sounding like a child in the schoolyard — *we* didn't start it. Our lands were stolen, our people were starved, thousands were massacred by the likes of Cromwell. In the North, we did not have equal rights to jobs, to the vote or to housing; Catholics were burnt out of their homes in 1969. Yes, it was justified to fight against all this, but it had to be done "justly" by all sides in the conflict. Brennan made the sign of the cross, said a mea culpa for his distraction during the Holy Mass, and returned his attention to the sacraments.

When the Mass had ended, it was time to wait for the priest to emerge from the sacristy and bring back memories of his former role in the RA. The "Rah," the IRA. Leo was a man who might, by some obscure chance, have an idea why someone would snatch a member of the Burke family during the first visit of the paterfamilias in over forty years. And here he was now, Leo in his black clerical suit and Roman collar. Brennan stood back until the priest had finished greeting his parishioners, and then he stepped forward. The recognition was instant: "Brennan!" He moved to Brennan, put out his arms, and embraced him. They said their hellos and Leo asked, "And how's the family?"

"Is there somewhere we can go and talk, Leo?"

"Bad, is it?"

"It's bad."

Leo led Brennan over to the parochial house and into his office, poured them each a cup of tea, and, once they were seated, said, "Tell me."

So Brennan told him about Declan's decision to finally return to Ireland after his long exile. "And, of course, he was — is — planning to see you, Leo. But something's happened."

Leo's hand, with his teacup, stopped before it reached his mouth. "What's happened? Is Declan —?"

"Terry has disappeared."

"Terry!"

"You remember my brother."

"Of course. Terry the pilot."

Brennan proceeded to tell Leo about the Burkes' night out in Irishtown, Brennan and Declan going home, Terry staying out for a couple more jars and a few more tales from the bar stool. And Terry's absence in the morning. "Another thing: when the three of us left the Seapoint House, before we walked over to the Vintage Inn, we saw two men standing around outside, caps pulled down. They didn't pay us any attention —"

"But, Brennan, there's always punters standing outside a bar. Having a smoke, were they?"

"They were."

"And it's been raining, so why would a man not have a cap on?"

"I know. But what struck me as odd, Leo, was their complete lack of interest in the three of us, three strangers, and not a curious glance at all."

Leo smiled at that. "True, there's always a great interest shown among the regular punters when a new face shows up in a shebeen."

"I don't know what to think. I find it hard to believe that somebody just decided to snatch a member of our family or . . . do something to him, on Declan's second day in Ireland, his first visit since our midnight departure all those years ago. Coincidences happen, no question, but this?"

Killeen's dark eyes stared into Brennan's. He made no comment.

"And I don't think Da knows either. Or if he does, he hasn't opened up to me about it. I know, Leo, that on your visit to New York, you said the . . . the incident with Quinn was straightened out or would be straightened out. But is it possible that some animosity has lingered?

And someone from back in those days chose this method of acting out against my father?"

"I wouldn't think so, Brennan. But we're going to find out." Brennan must have looked surprised because Leo smiled, reached over, and patted his arm. "That business I told you about when we were in New York, we can check into that. Where is Declan now? Where are you staying?"

Brennan gave him the address and phone number, and Leo said he had some things to take care of in the parish, but he should be free in the early afternoon. "I'll take a drive to Irishtown and collect the two of you."

"No, we can come and collect you here, Leo." So that's the way they decided to do it.

ᔓ

It was just before two in the afternoon when Brennan and his father arrived in Aughrim Street and presented themselves at the parochial house of the Church of the Holy Family. Declan knocked at the door, and Leo appeared seconds later. Declan put out his hand for a shake but accepted and returned Leo's warm embrace. Brennan could not hear what the two men said to each other, but both were silent when they got into the car, Dec in the front passenger seat, Leo in the back. Leo instructed Brennan to drive to Dundalk. The three of them managed to chat about other things, thanks to Leo's friendly and inquisitive manner, as they drove out of Dublin and headed north to County Louth.

It took them just under an hour to get to the town, only a few miles south of the border with the North of Ireland, a border not recognized as legitimate by anyone in the car. As they drove through the lovely market town, Leo gave directions to the home of a man he identified only as Fergo, whom he described as "well up in the hierarchy" — Brennan interpreted this to mean he held a high position in the Irish Republican Army — "and one of the most feared men of his time." Meaning his time fighting the Brits as a soldier of the IRA. It was not Fergo's house they were going to but that of his granddaughter.

"That's the place," Leo said, pointing to a two-storey terraced house clad in beige stucco. Brennan parked up, and they walked to the front entrance. Leo rapped on the door, and a young woman greeted them and invited them inside.

"You're here to see Fergo," she said.

"We are."

"I'm Maisie. I'll take you up to him."

Maisie had a little girl in her arms; she looked to be about two years old. A boy a couple of years older peered from behind his mum at the newcomers. Maisie's fair hair was pulled back in a ponytail; there was no makeup on her pallid face, and the dark circles under her eyes were those of an exhausted young mother. There was a crib at one end of the sitting room, and toys and children's books were piled on the chairs and sofa. Brennan stood back and let Leo and Declan precede him up the stairs.

Maisie knocked and opened a bedroom door, and Brennan looked inside. Got his first view of the feared man of his time. Brennan knew Fergo was in his eighties, but he was not prepared for the sight of him in his chair by the window. There was a walking frame in front of the chair. The man was rail-thin, almost completely bald, his face deeply lined. He was wearing dark plaid pajamas, the right leg of which was tucked up, showing that Fergo's leg was cut off at the knee. The room reeked of stale smoke. Pale blue eyes turned to scan the visitors.

"Grandda," Maisie said, "this is Father Killeen, and Father Burke, and —"

"A thiarcais!" My goodness! "Declan Burke!"

"Fergo."

Brennan could see the effort his father made to mask his reaction. Not usually a problem for Declan, for whom a poker face was the norm.

There were no other chairs in the tiny room, just a bed, a dresser, and a makeshift rack with a few items of clothing on hangers. Maisie said, "I'll leave youse now. Only place to sit is the bed. Sorry!"

"That's fine," Brennan assured her. "No worries." And the three visitors squeezed onto the bed side by side.

"I didn't know you were here in Ireland," Fergo said.

"It's my first time back since, well, you know."

Leo spoke up then. "It's his first time back, but I've been telling him for years that he'd be welcome here. Amn't I right, Fergo?" No reply. "But now there's trouble."

Fergo barked out a laugh. "Trouble, is there? Imagine that."

"Fergo," Declan began, but his former OC, Killeen, overrode him.

"Declan arrived with two of his sons, Brennan here and Terry. The three of them went out to enjoy a few glasses on their second night in Dublin, and it seems somebody snatched Terry."

"What?!" The man's eyes were wide, and he looked from Leo to the two Burkes. "What is it you're telling me here, Leo?" His surprise was almost certainly genuine.

"Declan and Brennan knew it was unlikely that Terry was known to anyone here, to anyone who would do something like this. So, their thinking was that this relates somehow to Declan."

"Who in the hell would do this? What are they playing at?"

Declan answered. "We don't know, Fergo. We haven't a clue what's behind this."

Leo said, "Whoever they are, maybe they intended Declan as the target, but they missed a chance to get to him and snatched his son instead. We simply don't know."

"Jaysus!"

Brennan joined the conversation. "We're staying in Irishtown. The three of us had been out, having a few scoops at the Seapoint House and then the Vintage Inn. Declan and I went home at ten or so but Terry wasn't ready to call it a night, so he stayed on at the bar. We had seen two men standing around, one tall and heavy, the other quite a bit smaller, both in caps pulled down. It was raining, so that in itself was not unusual. But when we woke up in the morning and realized that Terry had not come in, we thought of those two men. Whoever they are, or whoever did this, Terry was the only one of us who was out alone. So, they may have seen him as their only opportunity. Declan was never alone."

Fergo spoke, as if to himself, in a low voice. "A big man, a smaller man, standing around."

Brennan said, "And a witness saw a man acting strangely, shouting at someone and then getting into an old dark-coloured car with a long bonnet."

Fergo shook his head. That apparently did not sound familiar.

"You and I know," said Leo to the frail old man in the chair, "that there was no reason for Declan to remain in exile, to be exiled from the country he loves and fought for. Yes, he disobeyed an order."

"To take care of Quinn."

"Quinn, yes. Quinn had betrayed us. He was a danger to us — his actions put our men's lives in danger — and he had to be taken care of. But it was my order, Fergo; I'm the man who gave Declan the order. And Declan explained to me why he hadn't carried it out."

Declan's eyes were downcast; it was clear to Brennan that he would rather be anywhere but here, reliving that traumatic time in Dublin, his last nights in the city, all those decades ago.

Leo said, "Declan had seen the man with his family. He'd seen Quinn with his wife and his children, had heard his little son singing a song. And he could not bring himself to do away with Quinn. That's the humanity in Declan here, a family man himself." Fergo was staring at Declan. "Look at me, Fergo," Leo commanded. Brennan could hear in Leo the authoritative voice that had been Leo's when he was an officer commanding in the RA. "It was my order, and I have long forgiven him for not carrying it out. I understood his reasons. As for the other . . . matters, Declan made up for that many times over, as you well know."

It took a moment, but Fergo nodded. "He did."

Brennan knew what the other matters were. This was the series of events Leo had described to Brennan during that visit to New York a few years back. When all hell broke loose — when the man Declan was supposed to eliminate had turned around and tipped off the authorities about an IRA arms dump — some suspected that Declan had been the informer who'd caused his comrades to lose their stock of guns. Declan was not, and never would be, an informer. But with feelings running high, he had seen no alternative but to take his wife and children and flee Ireland in the dark of night. He had kept one of the organization's guns for his and the family's protection. And he had taken a modest sum of money, which he needed to get the family aboard the ship and to the shores of New York. Brennan also knew that his father had repaid what he had taken, in the form of weapons obtained in the USA and sent over to Ireland.

What, though, did Leo mean by "many times over"? How long had Declan continued making reparations to his old comrades in arms? More than twenty-five years ago, the Irish Republican Army had split into two factions, the Officials and the Provisionals. The Official IRA wanted to take a political approach to the situation in the North; the Provisional IRA took the "physical force" position. The Provos believed that nothing short of force would get the British occupiers out of the North. There was no doubt in Brennan's mind where Declan's sympathies lay; he'd be a Provo through and through. Had the gun-running operation Brennan had learned of, which had been carried out during the family's early years in New York, not been the end of his involvement? Had his father continued supplying arms to the Irish rebels? If so, for how long? How long had he been putting himself in danger of being caught, arrested, and put on trial? An image flashed into Brennan's mind: his mother staring in horror at the bars of a cell, his father staring out defeated, hopeless. Brennan tried to shake off his unease. Tried not to think about other times when his father almost certainly had not been so merciful to an enemy of the Irish Republic. His mind was assailed with an image again, his father standing over a man face down in the street, a man with two bullet holes in the back of his head. He shook off the terrible visions, returned to the conversation here in present-day Ireland.

"So, given all that history, Fergo, do you think anyone from back in those times would act out now in revenge against Declan and his family?"

Fergo was shaking his head. "Wouldn't happen."

"There's no doubt in your mind?"

"None. Wouldn't happen. There's no lingering, what is the word? Anim . . ."

"Animosity?"

"No lingering animosity; nobody thinks of Declan in that way." He looked at Declan then. "Our men know that you gave as much as you could for the cause."

"As did you," Leo replied and looked at the place where Fergo's leg should have been.

"Mm," Fergo said, then leaned forward in his chair. He grimaced with pain. But his voice was strong. "So, who the fuck would have done this to the Burke family?"

"That's what we're determined to find out."

Fergo looked at Declan then and said, "It's been a long time, Declan. How is life in New York? I can't imagine myself in a city that big."

"It's surprising how quickly you get used to that, Fergo. Ah, sure, you're gobsmacked when you first see it, how huge it is, the number of people in the streets. But then you settle in. We live in Queens. A lot of Irish there."

"Right. I've heard that. And your work?"

"Burke Transport, North American division. A lot more vehicles needed there than here! So business has been good."

"And Teresa? Do I have that right?"

"You do. And she's made a good life for us, the family."

"How many do you have? In the family, like?"

"I have six. Six," he repeated, and he looked away for a moment. Oh, God, Brennan fretted, was he already thinking he had lost one of the six? Brennan didn't know. Sometimes, to understate things, his father was hard to read. Declan gave the names of his four sons and two daughters, and a few details of their work and lives. Then, "And you, Fergo? How's it been for you, with . . ." He glanced at the injured leg.

Fergo shrugged and said, "It hasn't been all bad. Lovely granddaughter, Maisie, does all she can to make life easy for me. And my two great-grandchildren keep me entertained!"

They chatted for a few more minutes, and then Leo said, "We'll leave you now, Fergo." Brennan and Declan said their goodbyes, wished Fergo well.

"Mind how you go, Leo. Lads."

Leo made the sign of the cross over him and said, "Bail ó Dhia ort." The blessing of God on you.

The Burkes knew they were seeing the "most feared man" for the last time, ever.

When they were in the car again, Brennan asked, "What happened to the man's leg?"

"He was in a gunfight in Belfast," Leo replied, "between our boys and some Brit soldiers. Fergo was shot and wounded; he fell in the street and a British Army tank ran over him. Over his leg."

"God help him!" Brennan exclaimed. "And that was the end of his days as a republican soldier."

"Ah, no, it wasn't. He got fitted with an artificial leg. Prosthetic leg? And he did his best to carry on the fight. He was a hard man, no question, but his war was against legitimate targets, paramilitaries and Brit soldiers who had been killing and maiming our people. Not civilians, no matter what foot they kicked with."

No matter which religion they belonged to.

When they got back to Aughrim Street, they thanked Leo, promised they'd let him know if and when they learned what was going on.

ଓ

When they opened the door of their house in Irishtown, Brennan started to walk in and felt something against his right shoe. He looked down and saw an envelope. It must have been slipped in under the door. He bent and picked it up. It was addressed, simply, to "BURKE."

"Oh, Christ, what's this?"

He showed it to his father. He, too, called upon the Saviour of the World. "Jesus!" Declan gripped the edge of the door, as if to keep himself upright.

"Come on inside. We'll be careful opening it in case there are fingerprints on it."

"Or a fucking explosive in it."

It was too thin for that, Brennan was sure. Almost sure. They sat side by side on the sofa, and Brennan carefully slit open the envelope and drew out the contents, holding the paper at the very edge. It was a note with a photograph taped to it. Brennan was horrified to see a photo of Terry sitting in a chair, his hands and feet bound to the chair by ropes or straps of some kind. There was a gag over his mouth, a strip of white cloth that extended to the sides of his head, presumably tied or bound in some way in the back. Terry's blue eyes were narrowed and staring at the camera. Brennan could read the rage in those eyes.

Declan peered at the image. "Fuck!"

The accompanying note was in black ink, all capital letters: "YOU WANT HIM ALIVE AND HOME AGAIN? KEEP YOUR GOB SHUT AND FUCK OFF HOME YOURSELF! GET OUT OF IRELAND!"

ര

Half an hour after that bombshell arrived, Brennan and his father were seated in Christy Burke's, smoking and fuming over Terry's disappearance, the warning note, and their inability to figure out what was at the root of this aggression against their family. By unspoken agreement, they kept their drinking to a minimum; they wanted to keep their minds sharp to deal with the crisis that had beset them. Not long after their arrival, Declan said, "I'll have a word with Finn." He approached his brother at the counter, said something to him, and the two of them went off to the office behind the bar. The young assistant barman, Sean Nugent, ably worked the taps and kept the punters happy while Finn was occupied elsewhere. When Declan emerged and returned to the table, he shook his head and said, "Finn doesn't know any more now than he did before." Doesn't know who or what was behind the kidnapping.

"You told him about the note."

"Oh, yes. He doesn't know who's doing this, but he says he has a plan for us. He — here he is now."

Finn joined them at the table. "Those scuts who have Terry, they know where you're staying. Well, they've known all along. Knew where they could find Terry. Or, more likely, it was you they wanted to find, Declan. How they knew, we can only guess. Followed you there when you arrived? Heard through the grapevine or the barley — husks? — well, you know what I mean. They got wind of it somehow. The point is, they know where to find you. So we can't have yis staying there without protection."

"Protection?" Brennan asked.

"I think I told you that I have another house in addition to the one where you're staying. The other one is in Irishtown as well. Unfortunately, it's not right next door to yours. It's a few blocks away. But it's going to be the base from which your bodyguards will operate!"

"Bodyguards," Brennan repeated.

"Your protectors, security men. I've two lads for the job. Completely reliable, the pair of them, and well able to take care of themselves in, let's say, tense or dangerous situations."

"They've experienced those kinds of situations, have they?" Brennan inquired.

"They have. I'll be offering them free rent for as long as they're needed. Right now, each of them is living with other people, sharing the rent. So, that's an incentive. They're young fellas, and they work for me in the other family business." Burke Transport. "One's a driver, the other an auto mechanic. They'll stay on the payroll, but their duties will be different for this new role for as long as they're needed."

"But, Finn," Declan protested, "you shouldn't have to —"

Finn waved away his protest. "It will all work out. They've done . . . They've helped me out in the past, and there's a financial incentive for them here. The house they'll be staying in is in Saint Magdalen Terrace. It's across the way, other side of the Irishtown Road between the road and the river. The place isn't finished yet, but it has a toilet and shower and a kitchen. I'll be moving a couple of cots in there, and a few other things."

"We should help with —"

"You should stay alive and safe, is what you should do, Dec. I know these boys will be keen to help. They'll work in shifts, and they'll have a vehicle. They'll be making regular checks on your house, and if there's any trouble, they'll be well able to handle it."

"Armed, will they be?" Brennan asked.

"That's a fair assumption to make."

Brennan wondered, but didn't ask, where they had acquired their abilities to "handle it" and to use a gun.

"Their names are Barry and Donal. Barry has short gingery curls; he looks a lot like Martin McGuinness. Donal has short black hair and a craggy face, a scar on his right cheek. Don't ask him about it! They'll be in a dark green van with white lettering: Conahan Plumbing and Heating."

"I don't know how to begin thanking you, Finn," said Brennan.

"What he said," Declan added, pointing to Brennan.

"All the thanks I'll need is Terry returned to us safe and sound, and the discovery of whoever is doing this to you."

Brennan and Declan stayed on a bit longer, then left for Irishtown. They were travelling by bus, out of an excess of caution, not knowing whether they — despite their modest intake — would still be under the legal blood-alcohol limit for drivers when it came time to leave. In fact, they were well within the limit; they wanted to stay sober and alert these days.

"So, Finn has our backs, God bless him," Brennan said as they took their seats on the top deck of the bus.

"He does. If he vouches for those two young fellas, we're in good hands."

"Now, Da," Brennan said, turning to face his father, "the note said that if you want to see Terry alive again, get out of Ireland. So —"

"I know what it said, Brennan."

"Would you be giving Terry a better chance if you, em, decided to do just that? Leave this country on the next flight out?"

"Give in to their demands? Men like that, a crowd of kidnappers? That doesn't sound like you, Brennan."

"It doesn't, I know." And it didn't. Brennan had never been the kind of man to give in when threatened or urged to do something he didn't want to do. "But if this is all they want, whoever they are, and it would mean Terry is set free . . . It doesn't sit well with me either, Da, but what are we going to do?"

"Me fleeing the country at their demand doesn't give me much confidence that those blaggards would just say, 'Off you go, Terrence Burke, have a nice day.' Terry will have seen them, be able to identify them. They'd have no guarantee that he wouldn't go immediately to the guards and set off a manhunt for their arrest."

Yes, Brennan had thought of that. "Right enough, Da. We don't know what they'd do. We don't know what we're up against here." He didn't want to think of what the kidnappers might do if they began to fret about the police, about the consequences of letting Terry go. Then he thought of something else. "Whoever penned that note to you did not kindly leave a return address. A way to contact them to say, 'All right, lads. I'm leaving on the next flight out.' So I think we can assume they have other ways of knowing whether or not you've left the country."

"Apparently so."

"Now tell me, Dec: Do you have any idea what's behind this? What's got them so exercised against you?"

Declan shook his head. "The thing that . . . I can't think of anything that could possibly explain this."

"You started to say 'the thing that.' What did you mean? You made a sudden decision to come back to Ireland. Is there some specific 'thing' you're thinking might account for this?"

"No, no. I don't know what I started to say. The nerves are going on me. And they'd be going on me even more if I fucked off out of this country not knowing whether Terry would ever be . . ."

Brennan knew his father well enough to know he'd get no more out of him if he kept on with the questions. But he was left with the distinct impression that there was some *thing* that had prompted his return to Ireland. There was more to it than just *It's time*. He remembered Declan dropping a piece of paper on the plane and snatching it back with no word of explanation. Whatever accounted for these events, it was not going to be resolved by Declan giving up and getting out of Ireland. And Brennan was no more confident than Declan was that leaving Ireland would solve the matter and inspire the kidnappers to let Terry go without any concern about the consequences of their crime.

Declan

That warning, that threat — the situation had been ratcheted up to a whole new level. And Declan's fears with it. What in the hell was going on here? He didn't see how it could have anything to do with those papers that had arrived for him at the office and sent him flying over here to Ireland. Now, on a bus rumbling its way across the city, he was barely aware of the passing streets, the buildings, the river. His thoughts were elsewhere. They're warning me to keep my gob shut. What the fuck? I've never opened my gob about that bit of history. Why would anyone think otherwise? Sure, there could be bad feelings, resentment, and who knew what other discontent arising out of those times. But a warning like this? A threat against my son? My *son*. Oh, Christ, was that it after all?

Brennan had turned in his seat and was giving him a worried look. Had Declan blurted something out? Or did he look as weak and frightened as he felt? He affected not to notice Brennan's concern. When they got back to Irishtown, Declan went into his room, shut the door, and took out the pages that had come for him in New York. The letter:

> These are two pages I found at my grandmother Althea's home after her death. They were under some rubbish in the cellar. You'll see that the notes aren't dated. (Maybe the dates were on pages before these ones.) I found a couple more pages, but they were only about her garden and a charity dinner. If this was a diary, she must have destroyed the rest of it.

Declan looked again at the two crumpled pages. One of them was done in blue ink, and the writing was slanted to the right. Maybe done in a hurry. The other page was in green ink, the letters printed, not written. They weren't done at the same time; perhaps a considerable amount of time separated the two entries. He looked again at the blue-ink page.

> *Fred was on again about Declan. He was practically shouting. "What did you say? That Burke chap? A man who tinkers with motor cars?"* [Next words illegible] *"What are you implying, you wish you'd stayed with <u>him</u>? Raised the boy with him? You say some grease monkey would have been better at this than I am?"* [Next line illegible] *"Look at the rest of them. Successes, one and all." And yes, they have done well. But he blames me for Denn. Takes no responsibility himself. Brought me back to when he learned about the time I spent with Declan. I never expected him to bring his name up again.*

Then the other page.

> *Refuses to go look for Dennison! I'll be a parent, even if he won't.* [Next words illegible] *Went searching. Seán MacDermott Street, Killarney Street. South side too. This poison is everywhere now. Needles on the pavement, men, young chaps lying in the lanes unconscious! (But breathing.) Every one of those boys someone's son. And some girls too. Daughters. Where, oh God, where is my boy?*

Declan returned to the granddaughter's letter.

> I saw your name on that page and the reference to cars. I know of the company here, fixes vehicles, loans them out. Burke Transport. I rang them, asked for Declan Burke. A young man answered. Had a foreign accent.

> Polish? He said, "You want him, you ring New York!" New York? "Yeah, our New York office!" I made some calls, found Burke Transport in New York City. Maybe you will help?!

Declan still felt gobsmacked by these words. The message here was that his long-ago relationship had produced a son! A son who ended up being reared by a man who was not his real father and who, according to these scribbled notes, had failed the boy. And the "rest of them," it seemed, were "successes." Other children born to the couple? However it went, this lad — Dennison — had apparently ended up on the streets poisoning himself with hard drugs. The granddaughter, the writer of the letter, thought that Declan, after all these decades, should step in and try to help the boy. Boy? No, a man well on in years. And maybe she was right: he should make the effort. Had others in the family tried and failed? Or had they just written him off as a lost cause? As for Declan, could it be said that he had failed a son he didn't know he had? If he had known and had scarpered, that would be something else entirely. But she had never told him.

The granddaughter mentioned Seán MacDermott and Killarney Streets; that was a rough area of the city. Neglected by the powerful in favour of the leafy suburbs south of the Liffey? Whatever the cause, he knew there were some disadvantaged people there. And he knew that whenever you had disadvantaged people, there were others who were all too ready to take advantage. Get them hooked on substances that would destroy their lives.

CHAPTER V

Terry

Terry knew his obsession with escaping captivity would keep him from sleep, but having nothing to do or watch or read would surely drive him out of his mind. The day had seemed endless. The coarse ropes that bound his wrists and ankles to the chair dug into his flesh with even the smallest movement. And his forehead felt bruised and painful where he had banged his head in the car. He had looked at himself in the bathroom mirror and seen two bumps. Were they going to grow, like devil horns?! But what disturbed him more than the pain was the feeling of utter helplessness as he was held immobile at the will of these two brutal bastards. Frank had been in the sitting room with him, and when he was not, Ger the gunman appeared like a spectre emerging from the ether. Terry wasn't easily frightened, not after twenty years of flying in sleet and high winds in a plane rocked by turbulence. He had dealt with aggressive, sometimes dangerous passengers. But Ger scared the hell out of him, with his beady little eyes squinting at his prisoner and his fingers twitching on the gun. Would he fire that weapon? Deliberately or perhaps by accident?

Terry's mind reverted from fear to boredom. The only distraction was the reruns of hurling and Gaelic football matches on the television. Sport was the only topic of conversation, the few desultory conversations Frank initiated. He refused to answer Terry's questions about why he was there and what the men were after. Being spoon-fed porridge and a bap made Terry ache with pity for all those people who were crippled and unable to feed themselves. And pity for himself. Drink was offered from time to time, and he felt even more pitiful for being so grateful for a glass of whiskey or a can of beer.

Now again for a second night, he lay on his cot, going over images of everything he had seen of the house. He knew its location, a block on the East Wall Road with houses numbered in the forties. He knew the layout of the place, the small sitting room where Frank might still be on guard. Awake, though, after all these hours? The sitting room was in the front of the house, on the road and across from the riverbank. The bank of the River Tolka. And what about Gerry? Where was he when he wasn't in the house? Out there someplace with his gun, keeping watch all night? In a car, or over on the riverbank, or maybe in one of the houses flanking this one? Even if the two men were fast asleep, there was nothing Terry could do. His hands and feet were free while in this room, but he was not free to get out. He had tried the bedroom door, the bathroom door, and the window. The doors were securely locked from the outside, and the boards nailed over the window were not for moving; they were attached on the outside.

For about the hundredth time, he made the mistake of flicking the light on and looking at his wristwatch. This did nothing but drive home how slow the hours and minutes were passing. He turned the light off. It was half three in the morning, as dark as the bottom of a coal mine, and he stared up at a ceiling he couldn't even see. He tried to think of Sheila and his children, but that only led to greater desperation. He would not be able to phone them, and what the hell would he say if he could? He tried to distract himself, to think of a film he had seen, a book he had enjoyed, a joke or two, or some of his own comic recitals. But his mind kept lurching back to his presence in a dark room with no way out, and no way he could imagine to escape the house or the gunman outside. Turned the light on again, looked at his watch. Quarter to four. Is this what eternity felt like? If so, he wanted no part of it.

When narrow shafts of light seeped around the edges of the window boards, he realized he had finally drifted off to sleep. But the nightmares of being at the bottom of a cave and of being chased by men with swords and guns were so real to him, he could hardly believe he had been asleep. He knew before he even looked at his watch that he'd had only an hour or so of sleep because at this time of year the sun rose in Dublin at around five in the morning. How in the hell — almost literally hell — was he going to get through another day? Even going to the bathroom was something to do! So he got up, used the toilet and the sink, gave himself a wash from head to toe. At least there was toothpaste, if not a brush, so he made use of that.

Now what? As dreadful as it was to be tied to a chair, that now seemed preferable to lying any longer in the cot. Even talking to his captors was something to do, such was his desperation after two nights of this. And at least they'd been giving him something to drink and to eat, as humiliating as it was to be spoon-fed like a baby. So he walked over to the door and knocked on it. No response. He hammered at it. Nothing. It was nearly two agonizing hours before the two men opened his door, allowed him to walk into the sitting room, while Ger stood with a gun pointed at him. "Sit in your chair," he commanded, gesturing to the old armchair with faded grey cushions on the seat and the back. "We have some new *accessories* for you."

Terry sat, and Frank walked over to him with a pad of paper. The top paper was blank. He gave it to Terry along with a pen and said, "Sign your name." Terry's mind flashed back to Michael Collins in 1921 when he signed the treaty ending the Anglo-Irish War, a treaty that did not provide for full Irish independence from Britain and precipitated the Irish Civil War. Collins said that he had just signed his death warrant, which indeed he had. He was assassinated eight months later. Is that what Terry was doing now, signing his own death warrant? "Sign it!" Frank barked at him, so he took the pen and paper and started to write. Didn't even finish before Frank snatched the pen and paper from him and said, "Right, so."

"Right" in two meanings of the word; Terry's captors now knew he was right-handed. And they had the new accessories to tie him up with.

Ger held the gun while Frank produced the straps that would hold their captive in the chair. The straps were brown and looked like leather, ragged along the edges as if they'd been cut from a leather coat. First to be tied was the right hand. The strap had metal loops on the ends, and Frank reached into his pocket and drew out a tiny padlock, which he fastened to the ends of the straps, and he secured Terry's wrist to the arm of the chair. Next it was his ankles. Frank used the same kind of straps for those and secured the ends together. Terry couldn't see how he did it, but it was done without padlocks. In case Terry got it into his head that his fetters would be easy to break, Frank took another one and pulled on it from end to end, to demonstrate how strong they were.

Frank stood up then and looked down at Terry's left hand. "We're not Brits. We're not going to produce a famine here. You'll have your left hand free to eat and drink. And if you think you can use that hand to free any other part of you, that won't work. Your right hand is locked, and I have the key. Your ankles are securely fastened. You'll not be able to free them. But even if you did, you'd not get far by dragging the chair with you on your way out, the chair that will be attached to your right hand until we unlock it. That sort of clamour would not escape our notice."

Before morning was out, Frank was pouring whiskey for Terry again. Were his captors being generous, or was it something else that inspired their hospitality? Were they hoping drink would loosen his lips? Terry saw an advantage in that. He would indeed become talkative after, say, two glasses of the stuff. If he played the buffoon or the naive Irish American, would this make his captors relax a bit? Maybe even make them sympathetic to this poor clown they had in chains? What else could he do but try?

So, after two generous helpings of the whiskey, he started to talk. The first scene he played was about growing up in New York with Declan Burke as a father. "I always wanted to get over here to the Emerald Isle. And the books and the movies aren't lying; the fields really are beautiful and green! I could see that flying over the country. And there's so much history here, and of course this is called the land of saints and scholars! Wonderful stories I heard at my mother's knee. I want to learn more, as much as I can. Which I will, if you let me go! Yeah, I heard fun stories, folklore and all that, from my mother. But what I really wanted to hear was what my father would say! Okay, I know he was involved in . . . the situation here. But whatever happened to the old image of the Irish having the gift of the gab?! Not our dad. You'd have to use a tire iron to open his mouth!"

"You better hope he never talked about . . . anything over here. For his sake. And for yours." Frank's lips twisted into a smirk. "You better hope he takes our warning letter seriously. Keeps his gob shut and fucks off out of Ireland!"

A bit of the tough guy coming out of Frank now, but Terry persisted. "What do you mean a letter?"

"We dropped a little note off to the house on the Irishtown Road."

These shitheads were at the house? Well, of course they knew where the Burkes were staying; how else would they have found them outside the pubs that night? Oh, Christ, would they go after Declan directly now? "Frank," Terry said now, "my father is not a talker. If you know Declan Burke, he's not a man for running off at the mouth."

"Is that so?"

Terry made a point of looking at his glass. Time to do some play-acting. "Jesus, I'd better not have any more of this, or I'll never shut up! My old man would kill me if he heard me here blabbing away! Not that I'd tell any secrets! I don't have any; sometimes I wish I did! Oh, shit, I should be more like him, the strong, silent type!"

This had the desired effect: Frank got up, went to the bar, and brought another bottle of whiskey over to Terry. Poured him a full glass of the stuff. Terry pretended to rebuff the offer, holding his free hand up to ward off the proffered drink. But, oh well, he succumbed to temptation. A couple more sips, wait a few minutes, and Terry the guy who can't handle his liquor will start blabbing again. Never know what he might say.

"I guess I won't be able to get any information out of you guys!"

Frank snickered, looked amused. He didn't offer any information about Declan or anyone else, but he told a couple of tales about some of the goofy things he had seen tourists get up to in Dublin. That was Frank. Ger was another story altogether. Whenever he was in the room, there was no amusement, and certainly no sympathy, in him. He was downright vicious in his looks, in his threats to "keep you here as long as it fuckin' well suits us."

But Terry had another angle to play when Ger was absent. Terry had noticed that Frank was nervous whenever Ger was with them, and he thought that Frank might be flattered if he was perceived to be as dangerous as Ger. So Terry, when he put on a show of sobering up, affected to be nervous in Frank's presence. Twitched in his seat when Frank drew close. He had a chance to bring this out in the open when, later on in the course of the conversation, Frank said, "You don't want to get on the wrong side of yer man Ger." And Terry replied, "I wouldn't want to get on the wrong side of *you*." This brought a smirk to Frank's face. Good. The man might think Terry would never try anything — never try somehow to escape —when it was just him with Terry in the house.

And it was interesting to note that Terry was not the only man in the room with a weakness for the strong stuff. Feigned in his case, but as Terry's confabulations escalated, Frank's weakness — genuine, in his case — began to take its toll. He began to slump in his seat; his eyes kept closing. Good to know.

But somebody else was wide awake and as sober as a Belfast Presbyterian on a Sunday afternoon. Ger was in the room. When did he come in? How? And when not in the room, where was he? Outside the house the whole time, an armed sentinel at his post? Or did he come and go, on and off the premises? Terry wished he knew.

ᔕ

Later in the day, the situation changed. Ger, wherever he was lurking outside or next door, hadn't come inside for a couple of hours. And Frank was passed out, slumped over in his chair, his drink spilled on the carpet. Now! This was Terry's chance. The phone was nine or ten feet away. It was on a table on Terry's side of the room, at the other end of the sofa that was beside his chair. Could he get to it, with both feet and one hand locked to the chair? It was a cheap wooden chair, didn't weigh much. Drag it over to the table? How much noise would it make? The floor was covered with a thin, worn carpet. He could use his free hand, grab on to the sofa, and pull himself along, grab the fabric of the sofa, keep pulling like that. Stop overthinking it! Go for it, before Frank comes out of his stupor.

He reached out and grasped the nearest cushion of the sofa and pulled. His chair moved forward a few inches. If it had been a linoleum floor, the chair would have moved faster, more smoothly. But with more noise, Terry was sure. He grasped the sofa again, moved a bit farther. He avoided looking at the carpet, such as it was, in case the legs of the chair had made a visible indentation, evidence of the path of the chair legs. He kept going. Christ! What was that? The slam of a car door? He turned his head, but of course the window was boarded up. He started again, dragged the chair. He was halfway down the length of the sofa. Three-quarters, almost there.

"Unnhh!" Terry started at the sound. He turned to look and saw Frank's head come up. Terry had made it so close to the phone, so close to a call for rescue and now . . . Frank's head flopped forward again. And Terry pulled himself to the table, to the phone. He picked up the receiver and laid it on the table, so he could punch in the number of the Irishtown house. He prayed to God that Brennan and Declan were home. If not, he'd try Christy Burke's, but how much time would he have? How many seconds before Frank woke up or Ger came in? He pushed the numbers and heard the ringing at the other end. Ring, ring. Come on, Bren! Come on, Da!

"Hello?"

CHAPTER VI

Brennan

"Hello?"

"Brennan!" It was Terry, though Brennan could hardly hear him, his voice was so soft.

"Terry! Jesus, where are you? Are y'll right? That note, it nearly put the heart crossways in —"

"I'm tied to a chair, one hand free. They think I'm passed out drunk. Can't leave house, gunman outside. Call Garda! Use caution! Terraced house, numbers in the forties —" Brennan heard a crack. Something falling? Then "Fuck!" And the phone went dead.

"God Almighty!" Brennan prayed. "Please, please God, don't let him get punished for this!" He looked over at his father, who was gripping the edge of the kitchen counter as if without it he would collapse. His face was nearly grey, and he stared ahead, not speaking.

Brennan told him what Terry had said before being . . . before the call ended. Brennan tried desperately to think of something to do. But what could they do? Terry had started to give them his location, the address where he was being held. A terraced house: that could be anywhere in or around Dublin. Or farther away. House numbers in the forties, same thing. Could be anywhere. So, there wasn't a hope of finding him. But he had made a phone call. What might happen to him because of that? It didn't bear thinking about. Brennan tried to take something positive from this.

"Phone calls can be traced, Da. The guards —"

But Declan was shaking his head. "I don't know, Bren. This is Finn's property, and he might not —"

He might not want the police tracking calls to the house. Was it, or had it been, a safe house perhaps? A place where IRA men on the run could hide out? But let's get our priorities straight here. "There may have been calls to this house that Finn might not want the guards knowing about, Da. But this is Terry, for Christ's sake. Held captive in a house somewhere with a gunman outside!"

His father's face reddened. "D'you think I've forgotten that? My son kidnapped? We'll go and have a word with Finn and get this sorted."

They left the house, got into the car, Brennan at the wheel. They sped through the city on their way, once again, to Christy Burke's. Brennan's mind was reeling, trying to see each step ahead in the effort to find his brother. "Let's take the most optimistic view," he said. "The guards are able to trace the call and we get the address of the place where they're holding him."

"Then we take it from there, me and you."

As if the guards would say, *Ah, sure, we'll trace a call for yis*. And otherwise show no interest in a kidnapping case. "How the fuck are you and I supposed to handle it, Da? Some shower of shites, armed with a gun or guns, are holding Terry, but the grudge is against you. What are you going to do, walk up to the door and knock? Say *God bless all in here. You're holding my son. I'd be much obliged if you'd let him go.*"

Brennan glanced sideways and was treated to his father's icy-blue glare and to an explanation in a faux-patient tone of voice meant to convey an obvious truth to someone too thick to have figured it out. "Brennan. They are holding Terry to get to me. They must have missed a chance to grab me, didn't find me alone, so they took my son. They have done this because of something I have done or said, or something I know about, which they don't want revealed. Their stated aim is to force me to keep my gob shut and get the fuck out of Ireland. Whatever has set them off, I don't know. And I sure as hell do not want the peelers to know it, whatever it is. I want Terry released, unharmed, to state the glaringly obvious! We should be handling it ourselves, within the family. If we can."

When they arrived at Christy's and went inside, Finn saw them and motioned them into his office. So, there they were again, trying to figure out what they had to do to spring Terry Burke from captivity. Declan relayed Terry's message, the message he was not able to complete. "He's being kept somewhere in a house numbered in the forties."

"Forties," Finn repeated, his face showing no animation. "That doesn't get us anywhere. And what the hell happened —"

Brennan silently finished the thought: What the hell happened to cut off the call? To Finn he said, "Phone calls, of course, can be traced."

Quick intake of breath when Finn heard that. But he kept his thoughts to himself, his thoughts about what a phone trace on one of his properties might reveal.

"That would give us the address," said Brennan, once again stating what was obvious.

"It would," Finn agreed. Then, God bless him, "There's nothing for it but to give it a try."

"We'd better get on it then, Finn. I'm going to check with Shay Rynne. Come on, Da." Finn had long been acquainted with Garda — now Detective Inspector — Seamus Rynne, as Seamus had long been a regular at Christy Burke's bar.

ꕤ

Next stop, Store Street. It was getting late in the afternoon. Would Shay still be there? They'd know soon enough. Brennan drove in an easterly direction through streets of shops and pubs and, yes, terraced houses. Then he turned south and cruised along until he was in the area of the bus station, the train station, and the Store Street Garda Station. He found a place to park and looked over at his da. Declan was gripping the sides of his head with his two hands.

"Headache, Da?"

Brennan did not get the kind of smart-arse reply he would often get from his father, such as *Go on with yeh. Yeh sound like your mother*. No. Declan looked over at him with none of the cold defiance Brennan usually saw in his eyes. What he saw now was sadness. Fear.

"Brennan, this has me feeling as if my head's going to blow up. Or cave in on me. I can well believe I did something to deserve some form of retribution, but we can be sure Terry did nothing to deserve it!"

"I know, Da. I'm feeling much the same way. And we're going to do everything we can to bring an end to this hell. Come on. Out with you now." The two of them got out and walked up to the three-storey red-brick building. Brennan asked the garda at the desk if Detective Inspector Rynne was available. DI Rynne had just radioed in that he'd be returning to the station in fifteen minutes or so. Brennan thanked the man and said they would wait outside.

"We have a few minutes, Da. Should we take a walk around? Looks as if the sun will be with us for a while." Brennan felt as if he was babbling. Ah, a nice day, how about a walk? It was in fact a hot June day with very few clouds, so Declan agreed, albeit reluctantly, to go on a bit of a walk around the streets. It would not provide much of a distraction, but they hoofed it over to Abbey Street and walked past the Abbey Theatre and turned up Marlborough Street.

When they arrived at the corner with Talbot Street, Declan made an effort at lightness and said, "Will you be working in the Confession Box today, Father?"

"Ah, no, I think it's more a case of a curate behind the bar in there these days, not behind the confessional screen." The Confession Box was legendary as a place where priests sympathetic to the rebels during the 1919–21 War of Independence had heard the men's confessions and, presumably, given absolution. The rebels had been out of favour with the Catholic hierarchy, but priests apparently came down from that other place in Marlborough Street, the Pro Cathedral, and heard the confessions of revolutionaries such as Michael Collins. Or so the story was told. The place was the Maid of Erin in those days but was now the Confession Box. It was tempting to head up there for whatever sacraments the place was offering, but consulting DI Rynne was urgent. A pint of porter was not.

So they turned on Talbot Street and walked back in the direction of the Garda station. As they passed Guineys department store, they exchanged a glance. This was the location of one of the three car bombs that had caused so much death, injury, and destruction in 1974. That was the bomb that had killed Brennan's friend Paddy Healey. Brennan reflected, as he so often did, that there was history on every corner in this country. And most of it tragic.

They returned to the Garda station and waited outside the building having a smoke. It wasn't more than five minutes before Shay Rynne and a uniformed guard came around the corner of the building. Brennan raised his hand in greeting, and Shay had a word with the other cop, who went into the station. Shay came over and said, "Declan! It's been a while." More than twenty years. The two of them shook hands. "Any news?"

"No good news." Brennan told him about the threatening note.

"Oh, fuck. Did you bring it with you?"

"Em, no, but I handled it as carefully as I could. We've got it tucked away. And then, Shay, there was the phone call." He described the truncated phone call from Terry.

"And you don't know what caused him to . . ."

"No. So what we're wondering is whether the call can be traced."

"It can, as part of an investigation." He looked Brennan in the eye as he said it. "Then it would have to go to the local superintendent, and well, this process can take up to two weeks before the tracing can be carried out."

"Christ," Declan muttered.

"I know, Declan, I know. I wish I had something better to offer you, but that's the way it's done."

"Even so," said Brennan, "we should give it a try, hoping that in the meantime —"

"No!" Declan barked. "No. We appreciate your help here, Shay, don't get me wrong about that. But two weeks sounds like an eternity, and it would be an eternity for a man clapped up in a house with two gougers he doesn't know, for a reason he doesn't understand. We'll have to go at it another way."

Neither Brennan nor Shay asked what that other way might be. Brennan had no idea what to do now, and he was sure Declan had no idea himself.

"Keep me informed, Brennan."

"I will. Thanks, Shay, for hearing us out. We'll be in touch."

And that was that.

CHAPTER VII

Terry

Terry was cursing himself, calling himself down to the lowest, for the way he had bungled that phone call. He had blown the only chance he had of relaying to Dec and Brennan the location of the house where he was being held. He should have started with "East Wall Road, house number forty-something." But no, he'd blown it. Was I always this stupid? He wondered. Is this the kind of message I would relay to Ground Control during an emergency in the air? "Hi guys, I'm in the cockpit and I've got a bit of a tummy ache. And my co-pilot is getting on my nerves. And, oh, by the way, the landing gear —" End of transmission. That would be the equivalent of what he had done here. His brother and father must be going spare, having received a call that had to be cut off because Frank was shifting about in his seat, coming out of his stupor, and Terry had had to hang up the phone and clomp his way back to his assigned place in the room. Had to hang up the phone before the one vital piece of information could be relayed.

Terry's day didn't get any better, but he could hardly have expected otherwise. The next bit of aggro was the arrival of Ger from wherever he was holed up. Terry could see the outline of the gun in the right-hand pocket of his trousers. Ger walked over to the bar, poured himself a small lake of whiskey, not, by the look of him, his first of the day. Then he turned and raised his eyebrows at his co-conspirator and their hostage. They both took him up on his offer, and he handed them each a glass of whiskey.

Ger pulled a chair over to where he was facing Terry and sat down. He leaned towards his captive, causing some whiskey to slosh out of his glass. Again. Either he didn't notice, or he affected not to. "Why is your oul man over here, Burke? Trying to get back into the good graces of the patriots he ran away from all those years ago?" Terry didn't bother to reply. "Made his new life in America and never returned to see his family, his old pals, while all the years went by? What is he trying to do now by coming over here, mend old fences? Build up a reputation as a man who was on the right side of history? Remove all doubts that he's an Irish patriot? A true republican?"

Terry couldn't let that go. "My father has always been a republican, always been a patriot. Time and again, he risked his life fighting for a united Ireland!"

"Ah, did he now? But that wasn't always the case, was it?"

"Yeah, it was."

"Except when he was working *for* the Brits! Things could be pretty rough for old Dec over here if word went round about that, wouldn't you agree? Better for him just to hop on a plane and get the hell out of this country rather than have to explain *that* to his old comrades!"

What the fuck?! It was Terry's turn to lean forward, to the extent that he could, to get right into the rat-like face of his jailer. "To state what should be obvious even to the likes of *you*, he would never in a million years have worked for the Brits. He comes from a republican family with a long, long history of fighting *against* the Brits to end their occupation of this country. And he has carried on that tradition all his life." Terry had never been sure exactly *how* his father had carried on the republican tradition during his years in New York, but he knew that Declan had been working behind the scenes in some capacity as a good soldier of a thirty-two-county Irish Republic.

"I guess he never told you about his time at the Big House, working for the *aristocracy*, the Anglo-Irish Ascendancy. Hoping to raise himself up from his bog Irish roots, maybe. Better himself. What do they call someone like that, a social climber?"

Terry couldn't hold back a laugh at that. "Declan Burke is the last person on the planet to try to ingratiate himself with the Protestant Ascendancy, as it was in the old times. Nothing against people who happen to be Protestants, just against the English and their toadies, the loyalists here on this island." Loyalists were loyal to the British Crown and were determined that Ulster would remain a part of the United Kingdom and would never (never, never!) unite with the rest of Ireland. "My father's fight was against the British Army and the loyalist paramilitaries, not against people who happened to be Protestant. And a social climber? He's seen loads of individuals like that. In New York, for instance. Trying to ape the rich folks on the Upper East Side, trying to eat at the *right* restaurants, wear the right clothes. Declan has been laughing at those pathetic pretenders since the day he arrived on American shores."

"Is that right? Laughing at them the same way the toffs in Shersfoote House in County Wicklow must have been laughing at young Dec Burke with the arse out of his trousers?"

What?! But all Terry said was "Not fuckin' likely. I'm thinking you have the wrong man altogether. You've got my father mixed up with somebody else."

"Not a bit of it. We know what we're about. Tell me this, Burke. Did you ever look through old photos? You know, the kind they have in museums, places like that. I wonder if you'd see somebody with her hair shaved off!" Terry made no reply. "You know, what was done to women in times of, em, conflict."

Eh?! Who was he talking about? And what was this about the hair shaved off? Terry knew that was a punishment often meted out to women in wartime, women who kept company with soldiers for the other side. Well, he wasn't going to give him the satisfaction of asking.

Ger got up from his chair, a big smirk on his rodent-like face, and left the room. Terry was determined to put out of mind whatever the verminous creature had been trying to insinuate. His thoughts turned instead to Declan and Brennan. What must they be going through, wondering where Terry was and what might become of him? And what on earth they could do about it. And that banjaxed, truncated phone call! As if things could not have got any worse for his father and brother. Had that been Terry's last and only chance to effect a rescue?

ↂ

Anyway, it was lockdown time. His third night of this, it felt like thirty. The good news was that he was no longer tied to a chair in the company of Big Frankie and Little Gerbil; the bad news was that he had nothing to keep his mind occupied. No, not another night of that. He turned on his light, rapped on the door, and heard Frank call out, "What do yeh want?"

Terry shouted, "Can you at least give me a book to read or a magazine? Even in a prison cell, surely I'd be allowed . . ."

"Don't be talking about prison cells. I've been there. Back away from the door and I'll have a book for yeh."

What was it going to be? *How to Make Friends and Imprison People*? *Kidnapping 101*? But when Frank unlocked the door, opened it a crack, and slipped a book in, it was *Confessions of an Irish Rebel* by Brendan Behan. Now *that*, he admitted to himself, would be entertaining! He said thank you; it would have been churlish not to, and he put the book on his cot. He headed into the jacks for his nightly bathroom rituals. There was a medicine cabinet over the sink, the glass brownish in places as if the metal behind it had rusted. He had already looked for a toothbrush, and there was none, so he didn't know what he was expecting. At least there was toothpaste and enough soap to — to what? Last him for how long? That was the last thing he wanted to contemplate. He saw a bottle of aspirin. He might need a few of those if his captors got rough. And then, what was that? Another bottle of something. The bottle was half full, the label faded.

Whatever it was, it had likely expired quite some time ago. He held the bottle up and read the name of the medicine: dimenhydrinate. Terry was no chemist, but that seemed familiar. Wasn't that the real name of Gravol, the drug you'd take to prevent nausea or to treat it if you had it? He knew that passengers sometimes took it for air sickness, and it was good on a long flight because it put them to sleep. Put them to sleep! How many of these should he knock back now to give him the blessing of a night's sleep? He twisted the cap open and shook a few into his hand and then it struck him: these tablets could be put to a better use.

Two of the tablets provided something Terry desperately needed, something he'd been denied the night before. He managed to get a few hours' sleep. When he woke up, he thought through the plan he had made for the afternoon. Pray God it would work out. For now, he opened the Behan book and concentrated as best he could, not that it was unworthy of concentration. He flipped through the pages and had to laugh when he read about Behan's grandmother telling another old lady not to mind young Brendan's drinking of stout because, she said, if he had the stuff now, he wouldn't bother with it when he grew older. Behan acknowledged the irony of that prediction! The book provided just the distraction he needed until Frank and Gerry unlocked his door, escorted him to his chair, placed the straps about his right hand and feet, and secured the padlock on his right wrist. He had a couple of trips to the jacks. How sad was that: looking forward to using the toilet so he could have a few minutes not tied to a chair. Once in a while on these occasions, he listened up against the bathroom door and heard Frank mumbling into the telephone. Terry could not make out what he was saying. Was it Ger he was ringing? Where was Ger when he was not in the house? Was he sitting outside in the car, with his gun at the ready?

Terry suspected that Ger was not always outside the house in his car or wherever he stationed himself. He had to eat and presumably get some sleep. Sometimes Terry heard a car start up, and that seemed to coincide with Frank going to the door and taking a look around. Did Ger give Frank a signal when he was going to be off duty for a short (or maybe long) spell? Did he have a pager? For now, though, it was the usual routine. Terry wasn't a man who could tolerate long silences, so even though Frank was his captor, he was Terry's only option for a bit of chat, a bit of normal behaviour. He tried to engage Frank in conversation about sport, current events, or past events, glorious or appalling. This would help pass the time and, he hoped, might cause Frank to look on him as a fellow human being, not just an object to be used for his own ends. Frank responded to a few of Terry's remarks and offered some opinions on various sports figures and other people. But it was clear that he was distracted. His legs were crossed, left over right, and the left foot jiggled nonstop. He kept looking around him and towards the window as if he expected a visitor or a message. Or what? What were these guys waiting for? And then the phone rang. Frank lunged for it as if expecting to hear that he'd won the Irish National Lottery. But no. He grabbed the receiver. "Yeah?" A pause. "Who?" And he smashed the receiver down, end of conversation.

Whoever had called the number, the call was not what Frank had been hoping for. Was this about Declan? Terry knew it might have been something else entirely that Frank had been hoping to hear. But what about the warning letter they had sent to Declan? Did they think Declan would obey their order to up and leave the country? Wouldn't they be frantic to find out that Dec had complied with the order and flown out from Dublin Airport? How did they expect to receive notice that that had occurred? How would they know whether Declan had kept "his gob shut"? Terry could not even guess at whatever plan his captors had. And he was not about to ask. Because he had a plan of his own. He couldn't see himself embarking on it till the afternoon. It was a plan fraught with risk, but it was all he had.

Declan

Brennan was reclining on the sofa listening to what sounded like opera on the radio. Declan knew that some of the music in opera was brilliant, even if the stories were often far-fetched. But were they any more far-fetched than Declan jumping up and claiming he wanted to go out for a little drive? At half ten on a Saturday night? It was obvious from the face on Brennan that he did not buy the "little drive" story his da was peddling. But no matter. "I'm off," Declan said to him, grabbed the car keys, and left the house.

This was the day after the summer solstice and there was still some light in the sky, but it wouldn't last much longer. His hands were shaky on the wheel, his feet shaky on the pedals. Him, a man who owned a transport company and now he had the jitters driving a car. Well, he hadn't become *too old* overnight to drive; it was all the stress and, yes, the fear about Terry that was making him seem like a decrepit oul fossil. He resisted the urge to pull over to the side of the street and take a rest. He might pass out, fall asleep, and be here till sunrise. Was he going to survive this ordeal, the abduction of his beloved son? Or would it kill him after he had survived so many dangers during his long, eventful life? And what did he expect to get out of this quest he had embarked on tonight? He was not looking forward to it, but this was the reason he had returned to Ireland, so he would see it through.

He drove through the docks area and across the Liffey. Continuing in a northerly direction, he soon found himself in areas dominated by large brick apartment buildings known as Corpo flats. This was public housing for the poor, owned and maintained by the Dublin Corporation, that being the council that ran the affairs of the city. He passed by crowds of young people drinking and partying in the streets, many of them shouting at passersby. Some of it was done in good humour, some of it not. One lad pitched a bottle at the car coming towards Declan's; it smashed against the windscreen and shattered, inspiring a roar of laughter. The bottle was in pieces but the windscreen intact, and the driver kept on. Declan was a little leery about leaving his car on Seán MacDermott Street, but he didn't want to spend a lot of time walking about, so he found a spot, parked up, and locked the car. There were a few people out and about. A young couple with a baby in a pram, another couple leaning against a lamppost having a snog. A few rough-looking gurriers as you'd see anywhere. He came to a laneway and peered ahead. Nobody there. Walked on to another and saw a young fella sitting up against a wall, drinking from a bottle. He gave Declan a hostile look but didn't speak. Declan walked farther along and saw a man lying face up on the pavement. The ground around him was littered with rubbish, broken bottles, bits of gauze with blood on them, and a syringe. Declan jumped as a rat scurried past.

It was an idiotic question, but he felt compelled to ask. "Are yeh all right there?" It was like in the films: there was always somebody asking "Are you okay?" to someone whose family had just been killed or to someone sitting bleeding outside a bombed-out building. But Declan asked his questions anyway. "Should I ring for . . ." For what, a doctor, an ambulance? He knew what the answer would be.

"Sure, I'm grand," came the croaked reply. "Have yeh a bit of . . ."

It was money he was looking for, and little wonder. Declan reached into his pocket, first taking a look around him, and withdrew a five-punt note. It wasn't much, and Declan was sure it would go towards something that would make this poor lad even worse off, but to refuse him seemed even worse than that.

"Thanks, man."

"Listen. Would yeh happen to know of a fella by the name of Dennison? Denn or Dinny, something like that?" He thought of something else, which might or might not be accurate. "Sounds a bit like a Brit?"

The lad merely shook his head. Declan felt that he should be doing something for him, but he knew any further offers of assistance would be refused. This poor lad, and so many like him, had no illusions about help being available. Not the kind of help that would have any lasting effect. Declan said, "Try to take care, would yeh?" and left the alley.

He tried a couple more shaded passages, saw the same sad sights, the same unsanitary detritus, and had no luck in finding anyone by the name of Dennison, Denny, or Dinny.

Brennan badly needed something to keep his mind off the kidnapping of his brother and the threat against his father. *What?* Brennan was fretting about *his* needs when it was Declan and Terry who were the victims here? As he so often did, he sent up a mea culpa for his selfishness. But it was Sunday morning, time for Mass. And he knew there was a lovely Mass at Saint Mary's Pro Cathedral. The brilliant Palestrina Choir had a history going back nearly a hundred years. He told his father where he was going and invited him along.

"Thanks, Brennan, but I'll pass on that."

Brennan was about to ask his father where he had gone last night. Then he thought better of it. If Da wanted to tell him something, he'd tell him. "Don't be alarmed," Declan said now. Had he been reading Brennan's mind? But no. "Missing Mass doesn't mean I've lost my faith. At least in the Supreme Being. I don't have much faith in my fellow man these days."

"Little wonder, Da. Let me give you a blessing, and I'll be off." He made the sign of the cross over his father, said a prayer in Latin, and headed for the door.

When he walked out to the car, he took a look around. There were a few people out walking, a few cars on the road. One vehicle captured Brennan's interest: a dark green van parked on the next block over, to Brennan's left. On the side of the van were the words "Conahan Plumbing & Heating." The bodyguards were on duty. He got into his car and headed in the opposite direction, towards the city centre, relieved to know that his father had company. Or would have company if the need arose.

ග

The sixteenth-century Italian composer Giovanni Pierluigi da Palestrina had written some of Brennan's most cherished music. Brennan considered the Renaissance polyphony — a style of music with two or more melodic lines in a piece — one of the greatest achievements in the history of music. In the history of Western culture. Now, he was seated in Dublin's great (provisional) cathedral in Marlborough Street. The place was packed with worshippers, and golden light blazed down on them from the high windows of the domed ceiling. The music lived up to the grandeur of the building. The choir was singing one of Brennan's most treasured settings of the Mass, Palestrina's *Missa Papae Marcelli* and some of the motets he loved best, by Palestrina and Tomás Luis de Victoria. Brennan followed the Mass and prayed for his brother and father. But at times the ethereal harmonies of the choir seemed to lift him into another realm of being, not of this earth. In the words of the Italian patriot Giuseppe Mazzini, "Music is the harmonious voice of creation; an echo of the invisible world." Brennan had often read of the mystical ecstasies of the saints, the elevation of their spirits to God and detachment from the material world. Father Brennan Burke was no saint, but the music he was hearing today could almost lift him into that realm.

If only that joy could last.

CHAPTER VIII

Terry

The endless morning had finally ended, and it was afternoon in the sitting room of the East Wall Road Prison. Afternoon, early afternoon, was the start of drinking time, and Terry was chuffed to note that Frank had already been into the bottles. The man had been asleep, or passed out, for an hour or so, though Terry assumed that the armed guard was outside. Was he out there in a car with his gun at the ready? There wasn't even a slit in the wood covering the window, so this was definitely not a room with a view. Was Ger perhaps on the other side of the road on the bank of the River Tolka? Doing what? Sitting on his arse on the low stone wall, gun pointed at the house, and Ger greeting passersby with a "Fine oul day, isn't it?" Or was he in the next house over? Terry had heard children's voices, and the sound seemed to be coming from the house to the west side of him in the terrace. But what about the house on the east side of him? He hadn't been aware of any sound coming from there. Was that Ger's observation post?

Terry's first concern, though, was dealing with Frank. And what Terry smelled off the man today was whiskey. He had regained consciousness. Good. And now a drop for Terry. "Would you take pity on a thirsty man, Frank, and go over to the bar?"

Frank actually laughed, almost with good humour. The booze had lightened his mood. "What would my guest like today?"

"A bit of that John Jameson would go down nicely," Terry said, playing along with the mood. "Is there any left in the bottle?" Terry knew there was about two-thirds of it gone, because he'd been keeping an eye on the supply. He figured that if Frank had been guzzling it during the nighttime, the bottle would have been tossed away by now.

Frank picked up the bottle and a glass and began to pour. The drinking glasses in this establishment were heavy, fit for purpose, not delicate little crystal flutes.

"Ah, let me pour it myself. The only pleasure I get these days, pouring my own libations." What in the hell would he do if Frank said no? Terry's plan depended on Terry himself doing the pouring.

"Sure, pour some for yourself, if you're able for it. But save a drop for me, would yeh?"

Perfect. "What kind of a guest would I be if I didn't do that?"

Frank brought the bottle and the glass to Terry. "You're going to manage that with one hand manacled, are yeh?"

"I've poured drink for myself when I've been in a far worse condition." His right wrist was manacled, but he was able to move his fingers, so Frank put the glass in his right hand, and Terry took the bottle in his free left hand. He started to pour. But there was something else he had to do: slip something into his drink. And he needed to direct his captor's attention elsewhere while he did it. But first, he had to send up a prayer that a bottle of Jameson resting unsupported on the arm of a chair would stay in place, not crash to the ground. Not yet.

Still gripping the bottle and glass, Terry jolted back in his seat and whipped his head around to the left, to the entrance to the house.

"What?!" Frank cried out and turned to see whatever had startled his captive.

"Is somebody at the door?" Terry exclaimed. On the occasions when the other louser, Ger, came into the house, he seemed to slip in on silent feet. So, if there was a noise, Frank wouldn't dismiss it as Ger coming in. The way Terry saw it, nobody else would be welcome at this address. Frank walked over, opened the door, and peered out.

In the few seconds he had, Terry reached into his shirt pocket, grabbed a tiny piece of paper, brought it out, and poured the contents — ground-up pink powder — into the bottle. He began swishing the bottle around.

Frank came back and said, "What was it you heard?"

"I don't know. Thought I heard something out there."

"I didn't hear anything. And there's nothing happening out there."

"Sorry. I guess I'm a little jumpy these days. Can't imagine why! I —" Now it was time for part two of the pantomime. He turned towards his half-filled glass of whiskey and ah, ah, ah-choo! He sneezed on it.

"For fuck's sake! Give me that bottle before you slobber all over it."

And so he did. Terry kept to himself the glass of sneezed-into, virus-laden whiskey that nobody would want. And handed over the bottle of whiskey and sleep-inducing dimenhydrinate to his thirsty prison guard. The ground-up contents of three tablets of the stuff.

Frank sat down in a chair a few feet away. Then began the long, tense period of waiting until Terry could make his next move.

Frank's conversation opener was not a welcome one. "Your oul fella hasn't taken the hint and left this country yet."

"How do you know?"

Frank gave him a look that conveyed the message *Am I talking to an imbecile?* "We have ways of knowing these things."

Terry stopped himself from putting on a made-for-television German accent and saying, *Ve haff vays*. He didn't want anything to rile the man up. He wanted him relaxed. So Terry started in on his "fascination" with all things Irish. "I think I can pretty well assure you that whatever it is you don't want Declan to talk about, he won't talk about it. If loose lips sink ships, even the *Titanic* would still be afloat if oul Dec had been at the helm. But get this, Frank. When I was in high school in New York, we were putting on a variety show. And just to get a rise out of my dad, wind him up, I put on a big high hat made of green plush with a black band around it. Got it in one of the stores just before Saint Patrick's Day. That's when you'd see those foolish hats, in the bars on Saint Paddy's Day. They're supposed to make you look like a leprechaun or something."

"Leprechauns, for fuck's sake," Frank growled.

"Exactly. I knew what old Dec would think of that! And I made it worse. I grabbed the shillelagh he had brought from Ireland. Started dancing with it with that hat on. And I started singing this goofy song called 'It's the Same Old Shillelagh.' Recorded by that old crooner Bing Crosby. It's awful! It had the effect I knew it would have on Declan. 'Yer not getting up on the stage and lookin' and soundin' like that!' Oh, he was wild!"

Frank got a laugh out of that one, and Terry started to worry that his foolish talk would keep the man awake. So he started acting sleepy himself, fading out and then jolting upright, awake. Decided he'd better keep silent. And so the minutes passed. Had it been an hour since he administered the drug? An hour and a half? The time dragged on, as did the silence from both of them. Good. And then, finally, it happened. Frank slumped forward in his chair. Terry regarded him for a long moment and then took a deep breath and made his move. His original plan was to rock his chair and knock it over. Break his glass that way. But that would be even more likely to wake Frank up than the sound of Terry breaking his glass.

It was now or never. He gripped the glass in his left hand and bashed it against the windowsill. Shit! A sharp fragment of the glass cut into his hand. Blood oozed out of it. Frank started at the noise and lifted his head. "What?"

Terry stayed quiet. He held the remains of the shattered glass in his hand and waited for Frank to pass out again. The seconds dragged on, but finally he did. And Terry got to work. The razor-sharp edge of his glass was his knife. He started with the strap holding his right wrist. Blood dripped from his left hand, but he ignored it. He sawed away at the strap, back and forth. It was leather and it was tough. But eventually it began to fray as Terry kept at it.

"Who's tha'?" Frank was awake? Terry looked at him in alarm, but his eyes were still closed, and liquid was dribbling from his lip.

The sawing went on. Then, yes! He managed to cut through the strap. Both hands were free! Terry's heart was pounding in his chest. Wouldn't that be a fine outcome, he thought, I get myself free of my fetters and then I have a feckin' heart attack before I can get out of the chair. But heart attack or not, he had work to do. He bent over with his trusty glass knife and started slicing away at the left leg strap. Back and forth, back and forth with the glass. Shit! The sharp edge broke off. There was another triangular peak of sharp glass, so he tried with that. Took longer, but it did the trick. His left leg was free. One more to go.

Slam! A car door outside. Was it Gerry? But Ger was always as quiet as a cat stalking a mouse. Or a mouse stalking . . . What did mice eat? Anyway, Ger wouldn't slam a door. Terry knew this room was in the front of the house, but the front window was boarded up. And even if he were close enough to it and it wasn't covered, he couldn't risk being seen. He leaned over and got to work on the final bond holding him in place. And he finally snapped it open.

No time to waste now, not a second to stop and think. He quietly eased himself out of the chair, making sure he didn't scrape or bump anything. He started tiptoeing his way to the door. Two more feet to go, and Frank let out a moan and then a "What? Where?" and he swivelled around in his chair. "You!"

Terry had no more time. He wrenched the door open and jumped to the pavement outside, nearly tripping on his feet. He heard a shout. Looked back. Saw the number of the house, but it barely registered. Frank was in the doorway. A signal to Ger, wherever he was lurking? He heard another door opening. Then "Burke!"

Terry couldn't spare even a fraction of a second to turn again and see whether Ger had a gun on him. He had to run. He took off down the road, running west. It was raining and the pavement was wet; his feet made a splash with every step. An image formed in his mind. From where? A movie? Military training? An image of a man being fired upon and zigzagging left and right to avoid the gunman's aim.

Do it now! He veered to his left. But no, he couldn't do that. Not enough distance from zig to zag. Narrow sidewalk. If he zigged any farther over, he'd bang into a house. Zagging the other way would put him out on the street in the traffic. But traffic was a good thing: lots of cars going by, their tires hissing on the wet concrete. Would a man want to be seen firing a gun with that many onlookers? That many witnesses? Terry ran for his life.

He turned left on the first side street. A good omen, surely. Faith Avenue! But whoa! He leapt out of the way of a mother and child standing on the corner after he nearly crashed into them. The little blonde girl jumped back, her mouth gaping open in shock, the mum's lips clamped in disapproval. "Sorry, sorry!" he babbled. Wise up, he cautioned himself, this is your only chance to get away. Don't blow it!

He ran past a line of pebbledash houses and stucco houses painted in pastel colours. Got to the first intersection and turned right on Leinster Avenue. More terraced houses of brick and other materials. What was that? The tapping of footsteps behind him. But he urged himself to stay on course and not turn around. The footsteps stopped. Had someone paused to take aim and fire? Should he dive to the ground? Or had someone stopped simply because they lived on this street and had arrived home? His thoughts were a jumble, his head pounding with the effort, the stress; he had to clear his mind. Where was he headed?! At the next intersection, he had to wonder whether his brother the priest and mystic was somehow operating behind the scenes, because the next street after Faith Avenue was Hope Avenue! Another good omen, Terry insisted to himself.

Soon he came out on the North Strand Road, a major thoroughfare. Cars and lorries. The roar of a motorcycle cutting across a line of traffic, the honking of horns and the squeal of brakes as drivers swerved to avoid it. As Terry jogged down the street, he barely took in the blur of colours of people's clothing, their faces. But he had to stop, catch his breath; surely everybody in this busy street could hear him gasping for air. He was in good shape, went for runs all the time. It was the fear working on him. He swung about, surveyed the area behind him. Nothing suspicious. For Christ's sake, Burke, get a grip. Nobody's going to come out onto a busy street like the North Strand Road and fire a gun. *Excuse me, ma'am, I have to get over there and shoot that fella.* He started forward again, now at a walking pace. He no longer had the energy to run. Approaching the Royal Canal, he looked to his right to see Croke Park, the famed stadium for Gaelic Athletic Association games. May I live to see a match there, please God.

He turned once more to look behind him. Again, nothing suspicious. Or at least nothing he could recognize as suspicious.

CHAPTER IX

Brennan

After the heavenly Palestrina Mass, Brennan's mind was still on the heavens. And he had an idea for a short trip out of town, a pilgrimage of sorts. It would give him and Declan something else to think about, not that Terry would ever be out of mind. Nor would their family back home be out of mind, not having received a *We're having a grand old time* phone call from any of them. Not that the family hadn't tried to make contact. Sheila had. She'd made a call to Christy Burke's, and Finn rang to tell Declan and Brennan about it. Finn had told her that the "old phone" at the house in Irishtown was not working, but he assured her that everything was fine and she'd be hearing from the lads before too much longer. Declan then asked Finn to ring Teresa to give her the same line and that he'd be in touch again before long. Dec and Teresa did not yet have a phone that provided call display, so she wouldn't see the phone number for the incoming call. But he figured that if he rang her from the supposedly non-functional phone in Irishtown, she'd catch on that he was not calling from the lively, noisy family bar.

Now, father and son were off for a little diversionary trip out of town. The destination was not far from the city centre. The father demurred at first but was soon persuaded to come along. They'd not be away for long. Even so, Brennan wanted to make provision for the possibility — the desperate hope — that Terry would escape captivity. Or make another phone call.

"Here's what we'll do, Da. I'll go out and find Barry or Donal and ask him to stay in the house while we're away. We'll not be gone for more than an hour and a half, I'm sure. And we can find a phone box and ring the house to see if there's been any contact from Terry." So the decision was taken, and Brennan walked out onto the street, looked left and right, and spotted the van he had seen earlier. It was parked a couple of blocks away, and Brennan made his way towards it. When he got close, he raised a hand and waved. He figured the security man would recognize him, and sure enough, the door of the van opened, and the young man got out. This was the fella Finn said looked like the Sinn Fein, former IRA man Martin McGuinness, with the boyish face and head of ginger curls. Now, was this Barry or Donal?

"Thanks for keeping watch," Brennan said. "I'm Brennan Burke." He reached out a hand, and the man shook it.

"I'm Barry. Glad to be able to help."

Brennan explained that he and his father were going to take a little drive, just as far as Clondalkin and back. Would Barry mind staying in the house in case, well, in case there were any developments in the situation?

"I'll do that, sure."

"Do you, em . . ."

"Donal and I have a key. Now you go off and don't be concerned."

"Thank you, Barry."

With that arrangement made, Brennan and his father were off for the twenty-minute drive to the lovely village of Clondalkin. There were white fluffy clouds in the sky, but nothing that threatened a shower of rain.

The first thing a visitor sees in Clondalkin is its great round tower, made of stone with a conical cap, rising ninety feet in the air. It is believed to have been built in the late eighth century, on the site of the monastery founded by Saint Mochua.

"Ever hear of Saint Mochua, Dec?" Brennan asked as they parked up and got out of their car, setting out for their stroll around the village.

"Can't say as I have."

"I don't know much about him myself. Except that he lived in the five and six hundreds and founded the monastery here. He was a soldier who later became a monk. How about you, Da, as a former soldier? Ever think of taking the tonsure?"

"The only one here taking anything is you, taking the piss."

"I'll take that as a no. But we'll have a look at the ruins that date back to those monastic times." They went on to see two ancient stone crosses and what looked to be a baptismal font. Another delightful structure in the village was the tall square tower that likely dated from the sixteenth century and had been part of Tully's Castle.

Declan obviously noted the joy in the face of his son as he gazed upon these remnants of history. He gave a little laugh and said, "It's a good thing you didn't go into architecture as you once planned to do, Brennan. Oh, you love the grand old buildings, and you're knowledgeable about them. Medieval, classical, Gothic, and all the rest. Nobody could fault you for that. But what would you ever design to be built? Nothing modern, to be sure."

"Right enough. I'd just draw up the plans for a Georgian terrace, a Gothic cathedral. It wouldn't be long before I'd be sacked for not producing anything new."

He spotted a phone box up the street and said, "Should I ring the house?" His father merely nodded; he didn't look like a man who expected good news. And no, Barry had not seen or heard from Terry Burke, and nobody else had come near the place. Brennan gave his father the report and said, "Cap off our visit with a look at Saint Brigid's Holy Well?"

"Sure." When they arrived at the old stone structures surrounding the well, they saw statues, photographs, and pieces of clothing that people had left behind. In supplication? Or in thanks for favours granted? Declan and Brennan walked around for a little while longer, then got into the car and started back to the city.

The conversation, as expected, turned to their missing son and brother. "Oh, God, what is Terry going through? I can't —" The normally cool-under-fire Declan Burke couldn't finish the line. There was no more conversation after that.

By the time they arrived at the house in Irishtown, the late afternoon sun was blazing and the temperature had gone up even in the time since they'd left Clondalkin. Brennan walked up to the door and put the key in the lock. He heard a voice behind him.

"Sure, the sun is splitting rocks out here, and you'd leave a lad out of the house without a key, leave him out to get the flesh burnt off him in the sun!"

Terry! Brennan and Declan whirled around and saw Terry walking towards them from the Saint Brendan's corner. None of the Burkes tried to hide their emotions this time; they fell into a group hug that you might see among the winning players after the All-Ireland final in Croke Park.

"Oh, Terry, thank Christ!" Declan said.

Brennan was not superstitious enough to think his brother's safe return was due to the intercession of Saint Brigid or Saint Mochua, but he, too, uttered a "Thank Christ!"

"My Lord and Saviour came through for me, in the form of a shattered whiskey glass, and here I am!"

"Come in, come in," Brennan said, releasing him, "and we'll hear all about it."

"Yer man Barry was here when I got back. Interesting to see that you — we — have a bodyguard."

"We've two of them."

"Good to know that Finn arranged protection for you. For us. Barry and I had a chat, and I thanked him and said I'd be fine waiting for you alone here. But he said he'd be up the street, keeping an eye on things. He let me into the house, but I came outside after a few minutes to enjoy, well, enjoy being outside. I shut the door behind me. Didn't think about the key, and I locked myself out. Didn't go and bother Barry about it. I've endured worse! But now here we are, all three of us, as it was meant to be!"

Whiskey was the word again, as Brennan poured them all a celebratory glass. Terry's clothing was soiled as if liquid had been spilled on it, attracting dust and grime. There were dark circles under his eyes and swelling on both sides of his forehead. Gesturing to Terry's face, Brennan said, "Did they —"

But Terry waved off the question. "Here's what happened," he said, putting his glass down. And he told them a story of being grabbed by two men outside the Vintage Inn and shoved into a car, where he banged his head a couple of times. Yes, they were the two men in caps that they had all noticed that night. They took Terry at gunpoint to a house in the East Wall Road. "I noticed the number when — forty-two A, that's it." Terry described the two men, who called themselves Gerry and Frank.

Brennan interrupted. "Do they sound familiar to you, Da?"

"They don't, not offhand. But you may be sure I'll be going over those descriptions in my mind. And in my nightmares. And in my conversations with Finn. I imagine Barry and Donal will stay on as our security men as long as we're living here in Irishtown."

Terry said, "I wish I could say *Ah, Finn, that won't be necessary*. But after the experience I had with those two shitbirds, I say we need all the help we can get."

He went on to describe his time in captivity. Brennan could hardly imagine how the time must have dragged, particularly for a man as active and full of life as his brother. He would not have adapted well to hour upon hour of boredom. Compound that with an always-present fear. What was the description he had once read of the life of a soldier? Long periods of boredom punctuated by moments of sheer terror.

"Of course, I tried to find out what their beef was against you, Da, but they weren't giving that away. Frank, the bigger of the two, was a little easier to take than that ferocious bastard Gerry. And I tried to work that to my advantage. I 'let it slip' that I had an awful weakness for the drink, and I tended to talk too much after a couple of jars, but

I loved the stuff so I kept on it. And kept asking for more. Much of it I spilled away on my clothes, so I wouldn't lose whatever intelligence I had managed to retain. I just looked like a sloppy drunk. I jabbered away, telling Frank foolish stories, often with the theme of a Yank fascinated by Irish history and lore. I hoped this might make our family appear less threatening to them — nothing to fear from this piss-head, boys. And I hoped this would make Frank open up a bit, him being a man for the drink as well. But I didn't learn what prompted the kidnapping. I did get the impression that it was you they were after, you they'd wanted to grab, but they never got you alone. So they settled on me, out by myself after lifting a few at the Vintage Inn."

As Terry told the harrowing story of his time in captivity and his narrow escape, Brennan could see their father sagging with relief, as if it was the first time in three days he had relaxed any part of his body or mind.

"Well," Brennan said, "one thing we have now is the address of the house."

"You would at least have had the name of the street much sooner if I hadn't made a bollocks of that phone call to you! You should have seen me inching my way across the room in that chair, hoping to God Frank wouldn't wake up from all the drink he'd had, at my encouragement. I finally get to the phone and then start a lot of blather instead of giving you the location immediately! If I can't keep a cooler head than that, should the airline keep the likes of me as one of their pilots?"

"Don't even think about it, Terry," Brennan reassured him. "Nobody can expect perfection in a situation like that. And you managed to get away! That takes brilliance. Finding the drug, keeping it for the right moment, managing to slip it into the other man's drink, and then using your glass as a knife? I couldn't begin to execute a scheme like that. Sure, you're only brilliant, so you are!"

"Ah, now." Terry pretended to be bashful with the praise, and they all had a laugh. He raised his left hand, and said, "That glass knife took a bit of blood out of me, but the bleeding's stopped now. I'm going to have a shower and change my clothes. You'll be relieved to hear, Brennan, that I gave myself a good sponge bath every day at the sink."

Everybody knew that Brennan was a tad fastidious when it came to cleanliness. "You go ahead. Take your time. And then we're going to consult our Garda friend with the new information we have, namely the address on the East Wall Road."

"Good plan."

"I'll ring him at home, see when would be a good time for us to talk." Brennan consulted the little notebook he kept, with addresses and numbers and other useful information for his travels. He found the Rynnes' number and made the call. Allie answered and told him this was one of the rare Sundays Shay had been called in to work, had to meet with another detective about a case. She had expected him home before now, but no sign of him yet. "So that's where you'll find him, Brennan. Store Street."

"We have some good news. Terry is back with us! He escaped without injury, thanks be to God."

"Ah, Brennan. I am overjoyed to hear it!"

They chatted for a bit, then he thanked her and told Declan and Terry they'd be going to the Garda station.

"You two go ahead," said Declan. "I'm going to ring Finn and Leo, give them the news. And ring your mother and *not* give her the news. Then I'll be having a snooze. The last few days have taken a lot out of your oul fella, Terry. Not that my worries come anywhere close to what you went through."

"No, Da," Terry replied. "I can only imagine what it was like for you. I'm going to ring Sheila now and tell her we've been enjoying the craic. End of story. Then I'll have my shower, and Brennan and I will go and seek the assistance of the Garda Síochána. We've got the security men, so you'll be safe here."

When Terry emerged from the shower, he got into the passenger seat, and Brennan drove them to the Store Street Garda Station. They asked for Detective Inspector Rynne and waited for him to come out of his meeting. He stopped short when he caught sight of Terry. Then he ran over and shook his hand, clapped him on the back, and said how delighted and relieved he was that Terry was free and unharmed. Shay led them outside, and they took a walk down to Custom House

Quay. The River Liffey sparkled in the late afternoon sun, as people walked or rode their bicycles along the quay. Terry told Shay all about his captivity, gave him the address of the house in which he had been held, and gave him the names he had been given for the two men who had held him there. He described their appearance in detail. Shay asked about the conversations they had engaged in; were political matters raised? Terry repeated what he could remember and said, "They're accusing Declan of not being a good republican."

"Ha! They're far off the mark there," Shay replied.

"Exactly. So, whatever Declan is supposed to have done, it must be something that pissed off some faction of republicans here in Ireland."

"Where would we even begin with that? Or it may have been only one republican he offended."

Brennan said, "That could be. Now, as usual, Shay . . ."

"I know. Keep this one off the books."

Brennan knew that if this had been an ordinary kidnapping or crime, DI Rynne would have brought the full weight of the Garda Síochána to bear on the case. But Shay well knew that Declan would not want that, would not co-operate with the investigation, especially if it touched upon his republican history or that of his former brothers in arms. And Brennan and Terry made no mention of Finn's security plan.

"What I'm going to do," Shay said, "is check the records to see who owns that house and the houses next to it, see if any familiar names come up. I'll let you know what I find. Can't do that until tomorrow, but why don't we conduct a bit of surveillance tonight?"

"We? You'll come with us?"

"I will. Off the record, at least for now."

"Now, we left our oul man home," Brennan said, "but I'm asking myself whether we should bring him along, in case he might recognize someone, if we see a man or two lurking around the East Wall house."

"But," Terry replied, "the two gurriers calling themselves Gerry and Frank were not of Declan's vintage. There's that word again! In their fifties, maybe."

"You've a point there," Brennan agreed. "The surveillance will be done by the three of us."

They got into the Burkes' car, and Brennan said, "We'll make a little detour to Irishtown. Get into costume."

"Costume?" Shay asked.

"Head gear for my brother here. Don't want him to be recognized if the two body snatchers turn up. And for yourself as well, Detective Inspector Rynne. It's undercover you'll be tonight."

When they pulled in at the house, Brennan sprinted inside. The door to his father's bedroom was closed, and he made a point of being quiet as he rummaged through their belongings. He found a typical Irish flat cap, tweed with a front brim, the kind worn by the two captors and by a large percentage of the male population of Ireland. He remembered it as his father's, though he hadn't worn it yet on this trip. And Terry had a New York Yankees baseball cap. Brennan rarely wore a cap or hat and had not brought one. He took the two caps out to the car. "Terry, the ball cap. The other one's for you, Seamus."

"What about yourself, Brennan?" Shay asked. "Those fellas would have seen you the night they took Terry."

"I don't have one. I'll just keep my head down if we spot anyone of interest."

"Right. Make sure you do."

Terry and Shay dutifully donned their caps, and Brennan started the engine. He asked Shay for the best route to the East Wall Road, an area of the city not all that familiar to Brennan. When he had traversed the roads and bridges and arrived at the East Wall, Terry directed him to a parking spot several blocks from their destination.

Fortunately, the sun god had favoured them with a fine evening and an excuse for three men to be out on the footpath that runs along the bank of the River Tolka. Just a group of walkers in casual summer clothing, two with their faces partly obscured by their caps. The things anyone would wear for an evening walk along the riverbank. And for keeping an eye on the houses across from them on the East Wall Road. They alternated between walking and sitting on the low stone wall between the footpath and the river, looking out for any action around the block of houses. The sun moved across the sky and twilight came and then darkness. And nobody approached the house where Terry had been kept, or the place next door where he believed Ger might have been holed up. No light shone, or seeped out, from inside either house.

The Burke and Rynne surveillance team were frustrated, and hungry, and wondered whether there was any point in staying out there all night. Shay said, "It may be that nobody will show up, but if I were a chancer who used a house for holding a man captive and I had to get back in there for some reason, I might do it in the late hours of the night."

"That may be so," Brennan agreed.

"I'll stay on."

"No, you've done enough overtime work here, Shay," Terry said. "Brennan and I will stay out here."

"Right," Brennan said. "This is what we'll do. We'll go and drop Shay home, then go to a chip shop, get us something to eat. And we'll go to our house and pick up my camera. Yes, it's dark and we can't very well use a flash while working undercover. But if somebody turns up, I may be able to snap a picture. There could be enough light from the houses, or lights from a car coming along the street. Can't hurt to try. And if we get an image that shows up on film, Shay may be able to make an identification. Slim chance, I know."

"Couldn't hurt to try," Shay agreed.

Terry spoke up then. "I'm not leaving. If they show up, I don't want to miss them."

"But, Terry," Brennan began.

"You fellas go. I can run fast if there's trouble!"

So, with some misgivings, Brennan headed off in the car with Shay. "I'll drop you at your place, Shay."

"I shouldn't be leaving you fellas to do all the work, Brennan."

"You have to work in the morning. We don't. And you'll be assisting us tomorrow when you check the ownership of that house."

"But, Brennan —"

"Have you forgotten, young Seamus, that I am a priest of God? That I have a doctorate from the Angelicum in Rome? And that I am, therefore, infallible?"

"Oh, I didn't think it worked that way, Father Burke."

"Let's just say it does, and leave it at that. And leave you at your door on Fitzroy Avenue."

"Thy will be done, Father. And now you have a cap." He handed it to Brennan.

The father's will being done, he left Shay at his door. Shay would be checking the house records tomorrow and would ring Brennan as soon as he had the information.

Brennan stopped and got two boxes of fish and chips, and soft drinks, before stopping in to get his camera. Again, no sign of his father. Door still closed. Good. It was rare that Declan ever admitted to being exhausted or needing a snooze, so Brennan knew this Dublin excursion was taking a lot out of him. He drove back to the surveillance post. Terry had nothing to report but insisted that they would stay on the watch until sunrise. Brennan figured it would be pointless, but he was obviously not about to leave him out there all night and go home for a nice comfy sleep for himself. So the pair of them sat on the stone wall, ate their late supper, turned to look at the tree-filled park on the other side of the river, and took some desultory walks back and forth on the narrow pavement between the wall and the street. No one came near the houses they had under surveillance. They gave up when the sky began to lighten before the five o'clock sunrise. Home they went, and they flopped down on their beds and fell asleep. Brennan imagined that his brother's last thoughts were like his own: what if, by the time we wake up again mid-morning, the culprits have been to the house and gone again? Gone for good.

Brennan

Brennan and Shay had decided to meet for an early cuppa on Monday morning. Shay was going to be on the south side to speak with someone at the Pearse Street Garda Station. So he and Brennan met at Bewley's in Grafton Street. The café's beautiful stained-glass windows by Harry Clarke would be enough to draw Brennan there even without the scrumptious treats on offer. He arrived before Shay and ordered a cup of tea and a Bewley's favourite: a little tower made of rich chocolate, sponge cake, and marzipan. He hadn't bothered with breakfast, so why not? Shay came in a few minutes later, ordered the same cake and a cup of coffee. After Shay had enjoyed his first sips and bites, Brennan took out a pen and his notebook. "I guess I'm the detective inspector now."

"So be it, DI Burke. Here's what I have. Nothing on the car; without the plate number or registration, there wasn't anything to go on besides the make and model. If it was used in other offences, I don't have any record of it. But I've had better luck with the house."

"You have? Good!"

"The house where Terry was held is owned by a widow named Margaret Hannigan. She also owns the house next door, to the east. That's the place Terry thought yer man Ger was staying when he wasn't prowling outside with a gun at the ready. Mrs. Hannigan is not known to the Gardaí. Her husband died many years ago, and she inherited the places. Her daughter lived in one of them and a son in the other until recently. Apparently, the daughter and son moved to other places. So there's a rental agency involved. The most recent tenant is a man by the name of Caoimhin Berrigan. Not Frank, not Gerry. Another name not known to the Gardaí, as far as I'm aware. But I'll be checking into it. Does the name sound familiar?"

"Not to me. What's the spelling?" Shay told him, and Brennan wrote down the name. "But I'd be unlikely to know it, no matter who it was. I'll see what Declan has to say."

"Berrigan signed a short-term lease for four months. Term is up at the end of August. So, it began well before you and Declan and Terry came over." Shay took a sip of his coffee and looked at Brennan. "Did Declan announce his plans to return to this country? Who would he have told?"

"As far as I know — and I think I'm right here, Shay — he told nobody except our ma and siblings. His arrival came as a complete surprise to Finn. I only heard about it myself a couple of weeks before the trip. He was keeping his cards close to his vest."

"As always."

"As always. So this man Berrigan apparently wanted the house, wanted the two places, for some purpose that had nothing to do with Declan. At least initially. Thank you yet again, Shay, for helping us out, finding the name of the renter."

"Now, I can't go the next step, questioning the owner or the renter, without opening a file, starting an investigation. Even if I did the questioning on the sly, there's no guarantee word wouldn't get round. We have some talkative folks in this country! And then I'd have to explain myself at Store Street, and the kidnapping would be revealed. Which, as you know, I think it should be. But your father wants it kept sub rosa, and I'll try to keep it that way. As long as I can."

"I appreciate that, Shay. I know this doesn't sit well with you, keeping a criminal offence off the books."

"Wouldn't be the first time." He looked Brennan in the eye when he said it. Brennan knew of incidents in Shay Rynne's past when he had done things he did not want his fellow Gardaí to know about. But he'd become what he most wanted and deserved to be: a well-respected member of the Garda Síochána. A policeman from a rough background in the Corpo flats, who had confounded his critics and who had an understanding and sympathy for the people in the tenements, an understanding that not every guard could boast.

Shay was also, Brennan knew, sympathetic to the Irish republican cause: to reunite the twenty-six counties in the South with the six counties in the North, for one all-island republic. One independent republic with no more British soldiers or British role to play in the North. Could Detective Inspector Rynne's contacts among the Irish republicans on both sides of the border help solve the question of who wanted Declan Burke out of the country, and why? But Brennan was hesitant to venture into such sensitive territory, unless it became absolutely necessary.

"Are we headin'?" Brennan said to Shay as he put down his empty cup and wiped the chocolate from his mouth. Yes, Shay had to head out. "We'll be in touch, Shay, and not only about this bit of bother. I'll want to see you and Allie and the kids again soon."

"Any time, Brennan. Slán go fóill." Bye for now.

CHAPTER X

Brennan

"There's something I didn't tell you," Terry said to Brennan when he was back in Irishtown. "Didn't tell you when our da was in the room."

The brothers were sitting across from each other at the kitchen table, Brennan with a glass of orange juice, Terry with a cup of coffee. Declan had gone out in the car to fetch some things for a late breakfast. "Well, he's not in the room now," Brennan said, "so let's hear it."

Terry proceeded to recount a story that had Brennan gobsmacked. The kidnappers had claimed that Declan had once worked for the Brits, or at least for the Anglo-Irish Ascendancy, specifically for a wealthy and powerful family who lived at a grand estate in County Wicklow. Ger and Frank had asked Terry if he had ever looked at old photographs, the kind they have in museums. "There was even a remark about some woman with her hair shaven off."

"Say that again, Terry?"

"They asked about old photos and then, 'I wonder if you'd see somebody with her hair shaved off.'"

"Her."

"Right." Everyone knew that was a punishment meted out to a woman for fraternizing with the enemy. "And they mentioned the name of the manor, the grand estate. Shersfoote House."

Brennan tried to take this in. The connection, if any, to their father. Then, "Are you up for a little spin out in the country, Ter?"

"Is the Pope a Taig?" "Taig" was a slur, a pejorative term for Catholics used by Protestant militants in the North of Ireland. The theory was that it came from the Irish name Tadhg, which had long been a common one for Catholic boys.

"I'll take that as a yes. We'll get away as soon as we can, and we'll invent a story for Da about where we're off to."

A few minutes later, Declan returned home and announced that he had all the ingredients for a full Irish breakfast, which would be filling enough to double as their midday meal. "Extra blood pudding for you, Bren."

"Oh, God," Brennan muttered. Even the phrase "blood pudding" had always been enough to turn his stomach. As his father well knew.

"You're looking a little pale there, my lad."

They sat down to eat, and Brennan had the bacon, eggs, toast, beans, tomatoes, spuds, and soda bread. But he drew the line at blood pudding, which was a sausage-like object made with pig's blood, pork, and suet. Someone had once told him that suet was hard fat from around an animal's kidneys. He had never bothered to check whether that hideous claim was true or not. Brennan didn't know or care what went into blood pudding. Here at the table, his brother grinned at him as he speared the unspeakable thing with his fork.

After Brennan had enjoyed a few bites of his mild and bloodless meal, he said, "I met with Shay. We have a name now. The man who rented the two houses from the first of May till the end of August."

"May?! That's well before —" Terry began.

Declan cut him off. "What's the name?"

"Caoimhin Berrigan." Brennan watched his father's face for a sign of recognition.

But no. "Never heard of him."

Brennan wasn't sure whether that was a good sign or bad. It hadn't been a friend or acquaintance of Declan who had taken this action against him, but they were still in the dark as to who was behind it.

"It's time for another chat with Finn."

"Right, Da," said Terry. "He may know. We'll go when we finish up here. Now, what about some of our cousins and old pals of yours, Dec? Should we be planning some visits?"

"No."

"No?"

"We might be putting them at risk. Those fuckers who are out to get me might find out we've paid a visit to somebody, and that somebody could be the next target. To ratchet up the pressure on me."

As painful as it was to see his father finally back in Dublin and feeling unable to renew old acquaintances, Brennan knew he had a point. They simply did not know who or what they were dealing with. Terry must have thought so, too, because he did not pursue the matter.

After they finished their meal, they left the house and walked out to the car. Brennan was about to get in when something caught the corner of his eye. He turned to his right and looked up the street. There parked a couple of blocks away from them, in the direction of Ringsend, was the green van. Brennan could see that both men were in the vehicle this time, and they both got out when they saw the Burkes outside the house. "You haven't met the lads yet, Dec. Terry and I have, or at least we've met Barry. Let's stop and introduce you."

"Let's do that."

When they arrived at the van, Brennan said, "Barry, I've met. So you must be Donal." He was dark-haired, and Brennan noted the facial scar. Finn had advised him not to mention it, not that Brennan ever would.

All the introductions that had not yet been made were made now, and the Burkes thanked their two security guards for their vigilance.

"We've been taking shifts," Barry said. "You won't always see us out here, but one or the other of us — sometimes both of us — will be cruising by or stopped someplace out of sight. We'll be keeping watch. Finn has us set up in Saint Magdalen Terrace, and you can come by there or ring us. And Finn has the telephone hooked up again. Donal, can you write out the number for them?"

"Right, so." He went into the van and came out a few seconds later with the phone number on a slip of paper. He handed it to Terry.

Then Barry said, "Now, can you give us a description of the men who took you? I didn't want to lay this on you when you first got back here. Finn told us a bit, but it would be good to hear it first-hand from yourself."

Terry described Frank and Ger "as they called themselves" and recited the address of the house in the East Wall Road in case that might be of use to Donal and Barry. The Burkes talked to them for a few more minutes, repeated their thanks, and returned to their car.

ல

When they arrived at Christy Burke's, Finn was seated at a table talking to a group of people, and young Nugent was serving at the bar. Finn started to rise when he caught sight of them, but Declan said, "Don't let us interrupt you there, Finn. We'll get our pints and talk to you later."

They greeted Sean Nugent, gave their order, and sat at another table. Finn joined them a few minutes later. They assured Finn that Barry and Donal were carrying out their responsibilities in Irishtown.

"We're seeking your wisdom again, Finn," said Declan.

"Ah, I'm not sure how much wisdom I can offer."

"We've a name. The man whose name is on the lease for that house where Terry was held captive."

"Who is it?"

"Fella by the name of Caoimhin Berrigan."

Finn was shaking his head. "I know a couple of Berrigans, but not a Caoimhin."

Brennan repeated the name to himself. Sometimes, he knew, the last *I* was marked with a fada, an accent over it, making it sound like "ee." Without the fada, it sounded like a short *I*. So there were several pronunciations. Aloud, he said, "Kwee-veen, Kwee-vin, Kee-veen, Kee-vin."

"Kee-vin," Finn repeated. Then, "Vin? Vinny Berrigan? I always thought it stood for Vincent."

"Christ!" Declan exclaimed. "You're thinking Vinny? Would he do something like that to me? To us?"

"Hard to imagine, Dec."

"Well, we're sure as hell going to find out. Where's he living these days? Or is he inside?"

"He's out. Been out for years now."

Brennan and Terry exchanged a look. The man must have been in Mountjoy Prison.

"But I've no idea where he's living," Finn said.

"Where does he drink, do you know?" Declan asked.

"Doesn't drink here." Finn leaned forward then. "I don't know where you'd find him in the ordinary run of a day or week. But if he's the Vinny I knew, you'd be almost certain to find him two days from now. At Hill 16. The pub, not the stand at Croker." Hill 16, Brennan knew, was one of the terraces at the Gaelic Athletic Association stadium, Croke Park. He was familiar with the pub, too, a well-known sports bar here on the north side. "Vinny's people are originally from Wexford, and Wexford played the Dubs a few days ago in hurling. Wexford won the match, and they're going to be showing a rerun of it on the telly. There will be a crowd watching it there in Hill 16, and they'll be all fired up for the Leinster final next month. If the man still walks amongst us, he'll not be missing the gathering at the bar."

"You're a genius, Finn!" Terry exclaimed.

"Ah, now, I'm only a simple barman."

"This is all sounding good," Terry said. "We'll be having a few scoops at the Hill 16 pub two nights from now."

"That's what we'll do," Brennan agreed. "But how will we ever pick Vinny out of the crowd at the bar?"

"Isn't the solution obvious? I'll go with you. Yes, I occasionally take a drink in other establishments. Now, most of the Wexford lads will be wearing their colours, purple and gold. Their jerseys. So it's them we'll be watching. I'll recognize our man if he hasn't changed too dramatically in the last few years."

"Brilliant, Finn," said Terry. "Now we'll be off. Coming, Da?"

Declan nodded yes, and the three of them left the bar. With any luck, Brennan reflected, two days from now they might be face to face with the man who held the lease on the East Wall house and held his brother captive inside.

They didn't see the dark green van when they returned to Irishtown, but they agreed that they would not expect to see it every time they came and went from their house. When they were back inside, Declan went into his room and Terry turned to Brennan. "When are we going to Wicklow?"

Wicklow where, according to Terry's kidnappers, Declan had worked for the powerful family who were the farthest thing from republican Irish.

Brennan didn't hesitate. "We're going now."

ᔕ

The warm sunny weather provided the perfect alibi. Terry told Declan that he and Brennan were going out to Killiney Beach for a swim. As they had predicted, Declan took a pass on the outing, so the brothers gathered their swimming togs and towels and headed out to the car. "We'll have to come back wet, or at least a little dampish, Bren."

"We'll do that. Maybe we really will have a swim. But for now, we set our course for County Wicklow. With a stop at a tourist office first to find out where the Big House is located." So they drove into Dublin city centre, found a tourist information place, and a parking spot.

"I'll be the tourist," Terry said and opened his door.

"Tourist, me arse. Where's your camera?"

"Ah, you're right. I forgot my camera in New York, and I don't have a Hawaiian shirt or a floppy hat. But a camera's not a bad idea.

Another one!" He was no doubt referring to their first night in Dublin, when he'd bought a camera and brought it to Christy's for the aunt of those new little twin boys. "County Wicklow is beautiful, I'm sure," he said, "and we'll probably want a picture of the Big House. I'll see what I can find after I go into the tourist bureau and ask about 'some of those big, fancy houses you have here in Ireland.'"

Terry was back a few minutes later with a map. And a Polaroid camera, so they could see their pictures right away. "The tourist lady says the place is a few miles outside the village of Kilmacanogue. She also pointed out a museum in that area, a little place run by a couple of the local families. She thinks there is likely a display of some kind relating to Shersfoote and other great family estates. So we'll check that out as well. I'll be your navigator."

They left the city and headed south along the coast to Bray and then inland, through the lush green countryside of County Wicklow. As they got closer to their destination, the Great Sugar Loaf Mountain loomed before them. Terry snapped a photo of the mountain. But soon they were in an area of well-tended fields and stands of trees, and then the stately home was in their sights.

"Good God, look at that!" Brennan exclaimed. The house was in the classical style, with a central door and windows placed symmetrically beside it and on the upper storeys. The stone exterior was a light grey.

"You've reverted to your first ambition, Bren."

"I do that occasionally, sure." Brennan had been on the road to a career as an architect before his unforeseen call to the priesthood. "Look at that breakfront. Pedimented breakfront." He meant the triangular structure above the third storey over the central doorway. "I don't think either of us have fallen for the story of Dec working here as a servant of the grand old family. The Brits, as your kidnapper put it. Declan Burke, toiling for the Anglo-Irish Ascendancy. But I'm not sure I'd be able to resist an offer of employment here, no matter how humble."

They motored up the long gravelled driveway, which was surrounded by freshly cut grass and ornamental shrubs. Terry snapped a picture of the house.

"So, what do we do now, Bren? Knock on the door, doff our caps, and ask whether the gardener or the stable boy or the auto mechanic left a trowel or a stirrup or a wrench here by mistake, and we're here to collect it, with all due respect, sir?"

"My dear chap, I wouldn't dream of imposing upon such an imposing property. Let us be off."

"You don't want to have a look around, see the stables, the garage or wherever they kept the vehicles?"

"They'd be round the back."

"Drive over so we can see them."

Brennan drove up to the house and turned, following the gravel driveway that ran along the front of the building. Past the left-hand corner of the house, he had a view of the stables, a row of rough-stone buildings sited along the courtyard.

"Look at that," Terry said, pointing to the other side of the courtyard. "A Bentley. These toffs certainly travel in style. If I didn't have a 747 jet at my disposal, I just might bow and scrape to the lord of the manor here and apply to drive him around in the snazzy car. Maybe our da felt the same way. After all, he's spent his decades in New York running a transport company! Is this where he got the taste for it?"

"Perhaps so, if he was ever really here. Time to investigate the slander perpetrated by that thug who held you captive, and have a look in the museum."

They pulled away from the grand manor and enjoyed travelling through the lovely countryside until they came to the little village where the Wicklow Uplands Museum was located. They cruised along the high street, past a Norman-style church, a butcher's shop, and a pub. The museum was a modest building with a cream-coloured stucco exterior and a light-blue door. "Will we need to explain our interest in the place?" Terry asked.

"It's a museum, open to the public, so I wouldn't think so."

"I'll give them a line anyway. That I'm a tourist and an amateur historian, and my brother has a particular interest in the great old buildings."

They went inside, and Terry approached a middle-aged woman at the desk. Brennan heard him reciting his lines, and the woman gave him a friendly welcome. She introduced herself as Agnes, and the Burkes gave their first names.

Shersfoote House had its own small section in the museum. Paintings of the house, the outbuildings, and gardens adorned the walls, alongside panels outlining the history of the place since it was constructed in the mid-1700s. The family, descended from English nobility, had settled in Ireland in 1695, started off in a modest building with a fair amount of land, and later expanded their holdings and had the grand house built for them. As with so many of the great estates, this one had a number of tenant farmers living in small houses on the lands. When the Great Hunger — the Irish Famine — hit in the 1840s, the tenants could no longer pay their rent. The records here showed that, like so many other landlords, the Shersfootes evicted their tenants, cast them out in the dead of winter. The papers did not show what became of the tenant families, whether they were among the million who emigrated or the million who died of starvation or hunger-related disease.

There was a display of photographs showing the family dining at their table, and another of an evening party. The women were wearing long, slim dresses that flared out at the ankles; their short hair was done in soft waves. The men were in double-breasted suits with wide shoulders. Other photos showed children and adults on horseback. And there were pictures of motor cars. "Bren, look! Cars from the 1920s, 1930s. A Rolls, of course, and a Bentley. And here's a guy in chauffeur's livery. Is that what you'd call it? The driver's uniform. But he's got dark hair; it's not our Declan."

"No such luck. No such bad luck?" They looked through the pictures, and there were no further sightings of a driver until: "Ah. Terry, have a look at this. You don't happen to have a magnifying glass on you, I suppose."

"Not today, no. Sometimes I use one to find the runway when I'm coming in for a landing."

"God help us. I hope you don't announce that bit of codology to your passengers."

"Ha, no. So far, my own eyes and the instruments have done the job for me. What do you have there?"

The two of them peered at the old black-and-white picture of a man in a chauffeur's cap sitting at the wheel of an elegant old car. "What year would that be, Terry?"

"That's the Rolls. Mid-1930s. I'll ask Agnes at the desk if there might be a magnifying glass on the premises." A minute or so later, he returned with a smile on his lips and a spyglass held up to his right eye. "Let's have a look. I don't know what we're hoping to find: Declan or no Declan." He leaned in towards the photo and peered through the glass. "I don't think so, Bren."

Brennan took the glass and reached the same conclusion. It was not the image of their father as a man in his twenties at the wheel of the car. "And I don't imagine there is anything on paper naming the people who worked on the estate."

Putting on an over-the-top British accent, Terry replied, "Not our sort, my dear chap. No, that just would not do."

"So we're no further ahead. We don't know if Da really worked there or that was a fabrication of Gerry's just to wind you up."

"Right. Let's motor. Oh, would you look at that?" He pointed to a picture of a horse rearing up on its hind legs, and a young woman in jodhpurs and a riding cap staring at the animal. "I remember when I was little I always wanted to be on a horse when it reared up like that. Not much chance of that in New York City, Brennan."

"No, now . . . Jesus! Look at the man watching the young one and the horse. It almost looks like —"

"It *is*, Brennan."

In the corner of the photo was a car and a man kneeling beside it with a wrench in his hand, fixing a rear wheel. But the man was distracted by the horse, or the young lady, and that was where he was looking. The profile was unmistakable. Declan Burke.

"Oh Christ! What do we do now, Brennan?"

Terry raised the camera and pointed it at the photo, captured his father on film.

"You'll not be showing that around anywhere, Terry," said Brennan.

"No. All right, Bren, what are we going to do? Return to the Big House, beg her ladyship's or lordship's pardon, and ask if they have any fond memories to share about one of their hirelings? Ask if his pension has been kept up to date?"

"I wouldn't suggest it, even if we suppose any of that generation are still in residence."

"Well, Declan is still with us, so anyone of his age or younger . . ."

"Still, I'd say Dec would not be best pleased if we dug up his past in this way."

"That's a mild way of putting it. He'd likely have our kneecaps! But can you believe this, Declan Burke serving the Anglo-Irish establishment? What was he thinking? He could have earned a few shillings pulling pints at his father's pub."

"And probably did. But maybe it wasn't just shillings he was after at the Big House. Perhaps he was casing the joint."

"Well, we know this much. He didn't burn it down or blow it up. Maybe he's an old softie when it comes to great architecture. Like yourself, Brennan." Terry looked at his brother. "So, what do we do? Confess to him what we've done?"

"That would be the right thing to do."

Agnes noticed their interest and walked over to them. Brennan was fairly sure she could not have heard their whispered conversation. "I see you're interested in the pictures. Some of the family are shown here. Fascinating history, fascinating family. The family line goes back something like five hundred years. In England. That's not something everyone is keen on, of course." She smiled when she said it, and the Burkes smiled back at her. "But it's a shame you missed Verna. She's our genealogist. She comes in on Wednesdays and Fridays. Verna would be able to tell you all about that."

"Oh, that would be great!" Terry enthused. "Maybe we'll come back another time."

"You'd be most welcome."

ᔕ

It was a rare auld time indeed when Declan Burke could be found dozing in his chair early in the evening, but that was how Brennan and Terry found him when they arrived back at the house in Irishtown. Little wonder he was exhausted. He was half asleep in the sitting room, a cup of tea and two cigarette butts in an ashtray on the table beside him.

"Maybe he won't notice that we're not wet from our swim!" Terry said.

"Won't matter. We're going to come clean with him. No pun intended there."

Declan's eyes opened when his sons came into the room.

"Are yeh all right there, Da?" Brennan asked him.

"I'm grand. I went out, walked a bit, saw the green van with one of our bodyguards on duty, bought a newspaper, and, well, here I am."

Terry and Brennan sat down, and Terry said, "We had an interesting little day trip today, Da."

"Did you now?"

"We did. We were in County Wicklow."

Going to the next county over would not, in normal circumstances, be cause for alarm. They could have taken a drive to the lovely coastal town of Bray in County Wicklow for a swim or a walk on the beach. Brennan could see not alarm but a certain wariness in the closed expression on his father's face. The impression of wariness was compounded by Declan's silence. No *Oh, and what did you do there?* Not a word.

"We saw a grand country estate there, a classic Big House of the landed aristocracy."

Declan made no pretence of not knowing which house this might conceivably have been. "What the fuck were you doing there?"

"When I was in captivity, my captors made a point of needling me about you, Da, slamming you for an apparent connection with Shersfoote House in Wicklow." No reply. "I, of course, defended your honour, your lifelong loyalty to the republican cause. And I have no doubt whatsoever about that loyalty. But it had me concerned, whatever those shitheads might have been hinting at. So Brennan and I decided to motor down there and have a look about the place." Terry did not mention their research at the museum.

Declan's eyes went from Terry to Brennan and back. Sounding like a man who dreaded hearing the answer, he asked, "What were those fuckers hinting at?"

"I didn't take them seriously, Dec, considering the source. But they were trying to insinuate that you, well, worked for the lords of the manor, took the king's shilling, that sort of thing."

Declan picked up his cup and took a sip of tea. "Ha! I was looking for a lot more than a shilling in that place. The silver, the art, the treasures in that palace could have funded our lads for years."

Brennan was surprised at his own reaction, the relief he felt hearing that. Him a priest, relieved at — yea, celebrating — the confession of his father, having broken two of the Ten Commandments. *Thou shalt not covet thy neighbour's goods. Thou shalt not steal.*

Terry gave a little laugh and said, "So, what did you get away with, Da? Did you use one of their pricey cars to transport all the loot to your hiding place?"

"How could I do that? Wasn't she deep enough in the soup without —" He jerked backwards in his seat, nearly spilling his tea.

She? Who was *she*? Brennan asked quietly, "Da? Who do you mean?"

"Who's the captive now? You two have me here, interrogating me like a couple of peelers!"

"We're not the peelers, Da. And we have only your well-being at heart. That's why we're in Ireland with you now, and that's why we're trying to find out who has what information that they are trying to use against you."

"Och, I know, Brennan. It's just that there's been so much, so much aggravation," he said, putting his cup down on the table.

"When you said 'she,' Da, who were you talking about?"

"That was before I met your mother, or before she finally relented to keep me company. But she, the one in Wicklow, she went off with another fella. I'm sure they lived happily ever after. Now, I'm going to get out of here for a while."

"Where are you off to?" Brennan asked.

"Not Wicklow." He rose from his chair, went into the jacks for a minute, then emerged and, without another word, walked out of the house.

Declan

Declan had remembered something that had not struck a chord the first time he heard it. It was a few days ago, and he'd been walking along O'Connell Street towards the bridge; there were a couple of women his age walking in front of him. When they reached the corner with Middle Abbey Street, one of the women pointed to her right and said something about the laneways connecting with Abbey Street. "Don't be wearing those summer shoes in any of the laneways along there, Bronagh." She pointed to the open-toed sandals her pal was wearing. "You'd soon have a needle stuck into your toe and you'd die of it before you reached the Mater." The Mater hospital. "Young fellas stickin' needles in their arms. Drugs! All over this city!" They had both shaken their heads at the thought of it and kept walking to the bridge. Declan had laughed it off at the time and forgotten all about it; he didn't see the humour in it now. He was not going to avoid those places but search them for one man in particular, who might be sticking a needle in his arm.

Once again, he walked among the ruins of people's lives. Thin, ravaged faces. Men, boys, and some girls as well in filthy clothes, lying on the pavements or propped up against the gritty walls of surrounding buildings. Discarded needles, pieces of foil that Declan assumed had been used to cook the smack. Bandages, blood, and, oh Christ, a steaming pile of human shite. Again, he steeled himself to ask if anyone knew of a man named Dennison, Denn, or Dinny. And added the "maybe speaks with a bit of an accent. British-like." Declan tried to make it clear that he meant no harm to the man; he was a "relation," and the family were concerned. This met with some remarks, as might be expected. "The family should've been a bit more concerned early in his life if you're thinking you'll find him round these parts!" And "I'll be yer Dinny if the family is concerned enough to come by with a pile of bank notes and a dinner of chicken supreme and a bottle of the finest Chardonnay!" His offers to ring someone to help this or that person were met with everything from indifference to sharp profanity-laced rebukes. He pointed to a man passed out in the middle of the lane and said he would ring for an ambulance. A young lad responded, "Ambulance? Hospital? Cop on to yerself!" Declan got that; they'd not be able to inject heroin in a hospital. "What d'yeh see comin' right after the ambulance, yeh oul streak of misery? Peelers, right? Now fuck off away with yerself!"

He was getting nowhere. He *was* nowhere. Had he misunderstood the letter and the diary pages? If not, what were the chances he would find his lost son, if son he was? He could not go to every laneway in the city of Dublin. He would try a couple more here on the north side and maybe look for a few on the other side of the river.

Another laneway, same result. Darkness was coming down on him. He turned into Saint Michan's Place, walked along between the grey walls of the buildings, looking behind him every now and then to make sure he wasn't being followed. Targeted as an elderly stranger, perhaps perceived as a tourist who had lost his way. A man in middle age came towards him, and he braced himself. The man's dark eyes were focused on Declan's own. Am I in for a fight in a part of the city where I can't expect anyone to come to my aid? Well, he knew from long experience how to use his fists and he would again, if he had to. Though he didn't delude himself that the power of his fists was anything like it had been in his younger years. But the fella looked him over, then brushed past him. What had he been looking for, a wallet bulging out of a pocket, one of those belted packs the Yanks often had? As the man went by, Declan turned to him and said, "Excuse me."

"You're excused. Now sod off."

"I'm looking for a relation of mine. Dennison. Sometimes we call him Dinny, sometimes Denn. Speaks with a bit of an —"

Then it was the stranger in the lane who had an accent. In a parody of an Anglo-Irish voice, the fella said, "Ah, Dennison, yes. Fine fellow all round. You'll find him pissing himself over there at the edge of that wall. Too much of the gin, eh, old chap?" He went on his way.

And there, near the end of the lane, was a man sitting with his back against the wall, an empty vodka bottle in his right hand. The man's hair was grey, dirty, and matted, his face marked by deep lines. He was considerably older than the other people Declan had seen on his odyssey through these hellish pathways. Late middle age, which would be right for the time of that episode in Declan's life. The man looked up with blue eyes at half-mast. Didn't speak. And yes, his khaki trousers were soaked around the crotch.

Declan cleared his throat, then asked, "Are you Dennison?"

"May I ask who is inquiring?" The voice was faint and slurred, the accent Anglo-Irish.

What was Declan to say to that? "Em, someone who would like to help you."

"Here to lift me from my present squalor? Or perhaps to help me pay for my medication?"

Declan leaned down, trying to get a good look at the face. Except for the blue eyes like Declan's own, he saw no resemblance to his own face or those of his family. But that was often the way; sometimes the offspring resembled one side of the family and not the other. "I want to help you," Declan repeated.

"Who the fuck are you? Someone from the Corporation? The health department? A Franciscan, one of the angels of Saint Mary?" He inclined his head in the direction of the nearby church, Saint Mary of the Angels.

Declan tried for a light remark. "I'm no angel. Anyone will tell you that."

"I don't care who the fuck you are. You're many years too late to *help* me."

Years. Declan debated with himself. Should he ask? "When is your birthday? What year were you born?"

"Oh, dear man, are you going to bring me a cake?" The voice was getting fainter, the eyes starting to close.

Footsteps coming. Declan whirled about, saw a hard-faced young man with his hair buzzed off. "Ah," said the fella on the ground. "Here it comes now. The only cake I need. A bit of pure white icing is all I ask." He pushed himself up and held a hand out to the man approaching. But the man kept on walking. "No! Come back!" The sardonic voice was gone; this was a cry of desperation. To Declan, he shouted, "Fuck off and don't come back! I don't need whatever you're peddling!"

He needed what the other man was peddling. Declan walked away so Dennison — if indeed it was Dennison — could get it. That was the only thing in the world the poor soul needed. As he said, nothing Declan was peddling could fulfill that need.

CHAPTER XI

Brennan

When Declan had left to do whatever he had in mind to do, Brennan decided to make a call to the Netherlands. He knew that his friends Monty Collins and Maura MacNeil were in The Hague for a legal conference centred on the International Court of Justice and the International Criminal Court. Maura was attending as a representative of Dalhousie Law School in Halifax, where she was a professor. Monty, as a criminal defence lawyer, was interested in the conference as well. They would, of course, be taking advantage of their time there to do some touring around. They had, in fact, tried to entice Brennan to join them for a few days. He hadn't thought he could get away from work, so he'd had to decline the invitation. But that was before he received the news of Declan's return to the land of his birth and had scrambled to make a much different overseas journey than the one Maura and Monty had in mind. He had told his two friends about the hastily hatched plan for Ireland, and he knew they would want to know how Declan's homecoming was panning out.

They had given Brennan the name of the hotel where they were staying, so he rang the operator, got through to the hotel's reception, and left a voice message on the phone in Monty's room. An hour or so later, Monty returned the call.

Monty Collins

It would be understating things to say that Monty was intrigued, and disturbed, by what Brennan Burke had to say on the phone. Terry snatched by persons unknown and making a harrowing escape from his captors. A threatening note left for Declan. And the efforts by DI Shay Rynne on the family's behalf. Monty was convinced that Declan truly had no idea who was behind the kidnapping and the threat. And he understood that Declan, and his sons, would not rest until they had uncovered whatever secret lay behind this calamity, uncover it and presumably try to ensure that the family would not be targeted again. Brennan had then turned the conversation to Monty and Maura's time in The Hague. Monty said, "The conference is going on for a week, and we've added a few more days to travel around a bit. The presentations, the international context, the tales told by lawyers from all over the planet, it's all fascinating. And, Brennan, you'd love it here. The old buildings, I mean, some of them dating back to medieval times. Gothic structures, Renaissance, gabled roofs and spires all over. Or maybe you've been here?" He had, and yes, he had spent hours walking and ogling the eight centuries of architecture. When they ended the call, Monty assured Brennan that he would stay in touch.

Maura had been trying to hear the voice coming through the phone, but "There's a lot of that I didn't get. Fill me in."

So he told her about all the misadventures endured by their friends, the Burkes.

"Lord thunderin' Jesus! They must be going out of their minds with worry! I don't even want to think what might have happened to

Terry if he hadn't got away. Or what might have happened to Declan if they'd managed to capture him. It seems as if he was their target."

"Oh, I think we can assume that."

"And he really doesn't know what led up to all this?"

"He doesn't. Brennan is sure of that." He paused for a second, then, "Maura, I'm thinking —"

"I know exactly what you're thinking. You want to go over there."

"Support them, try to help somehow."

"How, though? What can you do to help in something like this, buried in Declan Burke's past?"

"I don't know. But I'd like to be there for them. And the conference here — as great and informative as it is — is more in your line than mine. You as the professor, me as a humble little lawyer defending local boys who've been naughty on the streets of Halifax, Nova Scotia. Not that I don't hope for some big international case someday."

"Be careful what you wish for. You never know when that international crime ring will come knocking at the door of Stratton Sommers asking for Montague Collins, Q.C. But I hear you. And you'll be able to get the material for anything you miss at the conference. I know you want to get over to Dublin. I would, too, if I hadn't committed myself to the meetings here. So, go on, get your arse in gear and make your plans. But be careful, for Christ's sake. You don't know what you'll be dealing with over there; even the Burkes don't know."

"You're right."

"But you're going. Well, at least warn those guys to take care of themselves. Tell Father Brennan X. Burke that if anything happens to him, *I* shall take over his choirs. Our accompaniment will be ukelele only. And we'll do only hymns written in the 1970s and '80s. Like that one . . . what was it? Brennan's head nearly blew up when he read the words to it."

"Probably that one about 'fellowshipping.' A new verb? Sounded more like human trafficking across the seas than whatever it was supposed to sound like. I tried to forget it, but some of it has stuck to me like, well, never mind like what." He proceeded to sing in a mawkish voice the lines he remembered, "'Gift is you and gift is me, that is where it is today.' Something, something, then, 'Fellowshipping with each other, in the brand-new sharing way. Oooooo, fellowship in a brand-new way!' Compare that to, say, 'Immortal, Invisible.'

"'Immortal, invisible, God only wise,
In light inaccessible hid from our eyes,
Most blessed, most glorious, the Ancient of Days,
Almighty, victorious, Thy great name we praise.'

"*That* is poetry."

"You're right, so this is what I'll do. Threaten to do that tacky, *that's where it is today* sort of 'music' with his choirs. Can't you just see his reaction? *Sure, you'll have me demented!*" She said it in a perfect imitation of Burke's Irish voice. "That will guarantee his safe and urgent return to Halifax."

So it was decided. After making a few inquiries, Monty found that the quickest and most convenient plan for him was to fly from Rotterdam The Hague Airport to London, and then on to Dublin. He called the Burkes' number in Dublin, and just as he was about to give up, thinking there was nobody home, Brennan answered the phone. Monty told him he'd be flying into Dublin at twelve thirty tomorrow afternoon. "This is brilliant news, Monty. But are you sure you want to interrupt your time in the Netherlands?" Monty assured him that he could easily spare the time for a little trip to Dublin and gave Brennan the details of his flights. Brennan said he would be at the airport to meet him.

ᔕ

The next day, as he flew over the water, Monty thought about everything he had ever noted or heard about Declan Burke and his history in Ireland. And there was a lot of history! He had fought as a soldier — or Volunteer, as they were termed — with the Irish Republican Army. He had made a midnight escape from Ireland with his family decades ago, and that was connected with his IRA history, Monty knew. What he didn't know was the extent to which he had continued to assist the republican struggle from his new home in New York City. He was well acquainted with Irish crime figures in New York, the Hell's Kitchen Irish mob. But whatever had inspired the current threat against him was centred in Ireland. As a lawyer attending legal conferences in Europe, Monty found his mind turning to the courts, and he wondered if Declan had ever faced criminal charges for any of his activities. Yes, he had spent time in the Joy as they called it in Ireland, Mountjoy Prison. But that had been when Brennan was only a toddler. Long time ago. Something rang a bell faintly in Monty's mind; he couldn't remember exactly. He looked out and saw that they were flying over land now. London. Once again, he marvelled at the size of that great city. A few more minutes and the first of his two flights would be landing.

CHAPTER XII

Brennan

Brennan got a call from Shay on Tuesday, inviting him to supper at his sister Francie's place. Shay had told her that Brennan was in town, and she immediately asked Shay to invite him along.

"Kevin will be there, and it's a while since you've seen him." Kevin was Francie's son.

"Great. I'd love to see the two of them." Monty's flight would be landing at half twelve, so Brennan would have time to spend with him in the afternoon, before going to see Francie and Kevin.

"Francie hasn't strayed far from the family homestead, don't you know." Shay said it with a laugh. The family homestead, where Shay and his sister grew up, was in Fenian Street. It was one of the many Corpo flats in buildings owned by the city of Dublin. "She's had work most times over the past years, but with a child to raise on her own, she was never able to afford a place for just the two of them. There was a lovely fella in her life for a few years after Kev's father fucked off.

But her new man died two years ago. Natural causes, I hasten to say. Sad situation. Oh, wait now; you'd have met Davey, I think."

"I did. I met him a couple of times. He was a fine fella. A great loss when he died."

"Anyway, they had rented a place, but again she couldn't afford it alone. Now she's in with her long-time friend Sarah. They were in high babies together, pals ever since." The second year of primary school. "Sarah moved to a good-sized flat a few years ago with her daughter and granddaughter and invited Francie to move in. So that's where we'll be headed. I'll come by to collect you around half five."

"Grand. See you then. Will we have the advantage of sirens and flashing blue lights to bull our way through the traffic?"

"Sorry, no, just my own humble car."

ᔕ

Brennan left for Dublin Airport just before noon to meet Monty's plane. He was there in just under twenty minutes, parked his car, and walked into the arrivals hall. He got to his feet when he spotted Monty coming through with a small travelling case on wheels. "Monty!" he said in greeting. "Anyone would think you're a Dutchman yourself, coming from the Netherlands. You look the part." He could well have been a Dutchman with his blond hair and blue eyes.

"Oh, I've tried to fit in. But they see through me every time, as soon as I try to speak the language."

"Don't they say that Dutch is the language closest to English?"

"Frisian, apparently. Spoken by people in a part of the Netherlands and in part of Germany. But I don't know a word of it. You'd have more of a chance with it than I would, you being a man of several languages. And, of course, at the conference there are people from all over the globe, so lots of work for translators."

They stepped out of the airport and headed for the car park. "How's it going, Brennan?"

"Fuck."

"Ah. Somehow I think that would be understood in several languages, Father."

They arrived at the car and got in. Brennan said, "We're not getting anywhere, not yet at least, trying to track down whoever is behind all this."

"I hope I can help in some way."

"I don't know how, but I appreciate your coming over. Are you staying with us? We've a house in Irishtown. Only two bedrooms, but we can make room for you."

"No, I've booked a hotel. South side, not far from the river."

"Are you sure? The offer stands."

"I'm sure, but thanks, Brennan. Now, tell me more. Have the police been involved? The guards?"

"Unofficially. You've heard me speak of my old friend Shay Rynne."

"Right."

"He's a detective inspector now."

"Well done."

"And he's trying to help. Unofficially, as I say."

"That makes sense, given that you don't know what might be behind this. Something your father might not want brought to the attention of the police."

"You said a mouthful there. I think we're all going on that assumption. Me, Terry, and Shay Rynne himself."

Brennan pointed out a few sights as they drove into the north side of the city, some of which Monty recalled from previous visits. "Have you a thirst on you, Montague?"

"A pint would go down nicely. Will we be stopping in at the family firm?"

"We're on our way." And a few minutes later, the car was parked, and the two of them were walking in the door of Christy Burke's. "Finn! You remember my pal Monty?"

"Monty! Welcome back."

"Thanks, Finn. It's good to be here. Even though . . ."

"Even though. Right. Pint for each of yis?"

"Please."

Finn asked after the family and life in Nova Scotia while he poured the pints, waited for the first part to settle, and began the second part of the two-part pour. Then Brennan led Monty to a table near the back of the room. They raised their glasses to each other and took their first sips.

"So, Brennan, you have a copper involved. I'm wondering if a lawyer can be of any use."

"If you have any suggestions, I'd love to hear them."

"I may be treading on sensitive ground here, but was your dad ever taken to law? In recent years, I mean. Charged with anything? Convicted?"

"Well, you remember the story of him being in the Joy, and our mother moving the family to Rathmines."

"Hard to forget that story!"

"But it's hard to imagine any of that coming back to bite him in the arse now. I was barely out of nappies, it was so long ago. And I don't know of anything in more recent times. I think it's safe to assume he hasn't been convicted of anything since his time in the Joy."

"You're probably right. But something he said to me. A few years ago? I'm not sure when, and I can't bring back what it was. Sorry, Brennan. That doesn't sound all that promising, does it?"

"I'll wait to see if there's more to it."

"It's just that I seem to remember Declan, one of the few times I saw him. It was in New York. Right, that time we were all down there. And he'd been having a few drinks."

"Och, that narrows it down, so it does."

"But he's not a big boozer, as I understand it."

"No, you're right. He isn't. So, if he was on the batter, and that brings up a memory for you, I'd like to hear it."

"It's just that he was talking about a court case. And the way I'm remembering it now, I think he was involved in it."

Brennan was about to take a drink but put his glass down on the table and said, "Involved in what way?"

"That's what I'm trying to recall. Not as a defendant. I'm sure I wouldn't have forgotten that. And something about it had him stirred up. It wasn't way back in history, wasn't back in his time here in Ireland."

What was this? "In New York, you mean? A trial or something there?"

"I'm sorry to be so wishy-washy here, Brennan. Let me think about it for a minute. Or let's change the subject, and it might come back to me later."

They chatted about the conference in the Netherlands, some sightseeing he and Maura had done, the beautiful buildings, the art museum and galleries, and then Monty remembered something. "He was a witness, that was it."

"Eh?"

"Declan. He was grousing about somebody he knew, a friend or . . . an associate of some kind on trial. We were sitting there, wherever we were. I had just come off a trial, and it went off the rails. The witness I had been relying on to support my client, when the witness got on the stand, he was effin' useless. And when it was time for cross-examination, the Crown prosecutor ripped his evidence to shreds. Blew my case out of the water. My guy got convicted, sent to prison. I was going on about this to Declan. I have no idea why I was bending his ear about it. But then it was Declan himself who was griping about court, something that happened."

"When? Where?" Brennan asked.

"Let me think." He paused, looked down at the table. "Declan himself had been a witness. And something about it had him riled up."

"I don't remember him going to court, being called as a witness. At least not any time when I was still in New York. But would I even have known? Dec is a man who keeps his cards close to his vest, as you well know."

"I know. And he didn't go into any lavish detail on this occasion either." Monty's face seemed to brighten. "It was in England! I remember now. England."

"England? How in the hell could he have been . . . He was never in England. Or if he was, it would have been way back in time when we still lived here in Ireland. He might have been up to some . . .

should I say 'shenanigans'? Some operation being carried out on British soil?"

"No, no. It was something much more recent. I definitely had that impression. Not something way back in his Dublin days."

"He went over to England from New York? Not when I was still in New York. Surely, I'd have known about it. And after I moved to Canada, if that had happened, Terry or somebody else in the family would have told me about it."

Monty shrugged. "That's the way the memory is coming back to me. Maybe he went to England and didn't tell anybody. Made up another story about where he was going."

That could be, Brennan thought. He ran the New York branch of Burke Transport. He could have told the family he had to drive a vehicle, or deliver some goods, to some other town or city in the USA and he'd be away for a while.

"So, Brennan, should you ask him?"

Brennan shook his head. "If he was after sneaking off to England for some sort of court appearance and didn't tell any of us he was going, he'll not want to be questioned about it." He raised his empty glass and looked at Monty's. "One more?"

"One more!" It was nearly a shout.

"You're a man in need, are you, Monty?" Brennan laughed. "The pints can't come fast enough for yeh?"

"No! One More Can! That was his name."

"What kind of a name? Whose name? What are you on about?"

"The man your father mentioned, the man on trial."

Brennan stared at his friend as if he'd lost the head. "What the f—?"

"The guy had a nickname. One More Can. His real name was Lorcan, and his friends called him Lorcan 'One More Can' whatever his surname was. Did you ever hear of him?"

"I'd have remembered."

"I'd have thought I would too. It only came back to me now. Maybe one more pint will bring the man's surname back to my memory."

"We'll test that theory. Sit tight."

Brennan got up and got two more pints of Guinness, brought them to the table. He looked at Monty and saw his head bobbing, lips moving. There was no music on in the pub. "A song only you can hear?" he asked as he put the glasses down.

Monty laughed and said, "I'm sure that as a musician yourself, you know that it is easier to remember lyrics, or poetry, if you can put a melody to them. That's what I'm trying to do. Singing the words 'Lorcan One More Can' over and over to myself, trying to hear the next line. The man's surname."

"I get it." And he did. What Monty said was true. Brennan could remember the words to songs he had not heard since his earliest years in school. He knew that if they were just words written down without a melody, he'd not have remembered any of them.

"It'll come to me," Monty said. "If and when it does, it will be time for me to go back to school."

Had he been reading Brennan's mind? "School?"

"Law school, here at Trinity College. If I get the name, I'll hope that the case was reported. And I may be able to find it in the case reports in the law school's library."

"Well! Nobody should ever underestimate you, Mr. Collins, Queen's Counsel."

"I believe the term is *Senior Counsel* over here."

"I should hope so. Wouldn't want to give the impression that the Queen has any jurisdiction here. At least in these twenty-six counties. Oh, before I forget, tomorrow evening we're going to a bar called Hill 16. It's a sports bar where a crowd will be watching television, a rerun of a recent hurling match. Why don't you meet us there?"

"Great. What time?"

"I'd say be there by seven. It'll be a nice break after your day poring over the law books."

"I'm sure it will."

"I don't know if I should be looking forward with anticipation to the result of your researches, Montague. Anticipation or dread."

"That remains to be seen."

ര

Brennan told Monty he had been invited for supper with Shay Rynne's sister and nephew, and Monty assured him that he could keep himself entertained during the evening. Walking around the city, taking in the sights, that would suit him just fine. So Brennan left him at his hotel and returned to Irishtown. At the appointed time, Shay arrived in a dark green Ford Mondeo, and Brennan got in. "Allie's not coming?"

"No, she's at her ma's. The kids are all home; I wonder if our house will become a party scene this evening. Every teenage kid on the north side hearing that the Rynne kids 'have the house' tonight!"

Brennan laughed. "Been there, done that."

"Me too," Shay replied. He started the car, and they were off.

They left Irishtown and soon enough were stopped before a familiar sight. The Corpo flats in Fenian Street, where the Rynne family had been living when Brennan met them, and for many years after that. The building was large and rectangular with balconies running the length of the building, dividers between them. The structure was made of brown brick with white trim around the balconies and windows. "Loads of memories here," Shay remarked.

"And I don't know the half of it," said Brennan.

"Count yourself lucky. Ah, there's a space. We'll park up there and walk over to Sarah's."

It was a short walk to a terrace of two-up-two-down houses. "Sarah's is the second from the end. She managed to convert two bedrooms into three small ones. Francie has one of them, Sarah another, and her daughter and granddaughter the third."

Shay walked up to the door and knocked. A tall, fair-haired young man opened the door. "Shay! Tar isteach." Come in. He looked beyond Shay then and saw Brennan. "Brennan, how's the form?"

"Fine altogether, Kevin. And yourself?"

"I'm spot on! Come in, come in."

Kevin Rynne brought them into a sitting room crammed with well-used furniture and toys; the walls were decorated with a child's crayon drawings. Brennan and Shay cleared pieces of clothing and dolls from a couple of chairs and sat down. Brennan could smell something cooking in the kitchen. A heavy-set woman poked her head round the corner; she had light brown hair pulled back in a ponytail, and a pair of round eyeglasses perched on her nose. She greeted Shay. "And who's this yeh have with yeh?"

"I'm Brennan Burke."

"I'm Sarah. Will yeh be staying on for supper?"

"I will, if I may. Thank you, Sarah."

"I'm sorry you won't get to meet my daughter and her little girl. They're off visiting friends."

"Another time, then. I'll look forward to meeting them." Brennan turned to the young man then. "Good to see you, Garda Rynne." He knew that Kevin had always used his mother's surname; the boy's father, whatever his name was, had abandoned them before Kevin was even out of nappies.

"Ma!" he called upstairs. "Shay's here with Brennan Burke."

Footsteps on the stairs, and then Shay's sister joined them. She had the same black curls as her brother, and like Shay, she was showing a bit of grey now. Brennan got up and gave her a hug, then returned to his seat.

"You must be proud of this young officer, Francie," he said, pointing to Kevin.

"Oh, I am." She smiled across at her son.

"I remember him racing a toy car round your flat, instructing us that it was a Garda car, and that he would be a guard when he grew up. A uniformed guard. He did not think much of Shay appearing in plain clothes when he was moved up to work some serious criminal cases."

"Of course, I didn't think much of him," Kevin responded. "Any little lad knows the guards wear uniforms and caps and drive marked cars; that's how they earn the recognition and respect of all those bowsies on the street! Or so I thought then. The reality is a bit different."

"What? You are not accorded the respect you deserve when you go out on patrol in your uniform?"

"I do my best to educate the young persons out there in the streets. I've a ways to go yet."

"And you, Francie, what are you up to these days?"

"Have yeh ever been to Anois agus Arís, Brennan?"

"I have. I love the name of the shop." The phrase was often used to mean "now and then," but the literal translation was "now and again." Perfect name for a shop selling new and used books. "And I've come away with armloads of books. I read them and then take them back to A agus A because I can't fit them all in my suitcase for the flight home!"

"I'm working there, and you're the kind of customer we love. You buy the books, read them, and return them for us to sell again! I started last year, after putting in a few years working at a grocer's shop and then a laundromat. I love books more than dirty linen so when the job came up at Anois agus Arís, I made the move."

"You could have got on with Telecom Éireann, Ma," Kevin said. "You'd be bringing home a bigger wage packet."

"Ah, that was just Clodagh talking."

"Her friend Clodagh works for the telephone company," Kevin explained. "She's been there a long time now."

"Now, Kev. Clodagh wanting me to work there doesn't mean she does the hiring at Telecom Éireann! But I do appreciate her wanting to help me out."

Shay said, "She's helped some of us in other ways, though, bless her heart." Brennan saw Shay wink at his nephew when he said it.

"Don't be telling anyone that, Shay," Francie scolded him. "We don't want her getting sacked."

No one spoke for a moment, and then Brennan turned to the young copper. "So, Kevin, how are things in Pearse Street?" Meaning the Pearse Street Garda Station, where Kevin worked.

"Nothing going on in Pearse Street, Brennan. Haven't had to nab any of my old mates. All crime has been solved, all miscreants off the streets."

"I would expect nothing less, once you donned the uniform and got to work."

"So I've nothing to do but conduct surveillance on the girls across the way at Trinity." The Garda station was across the street from Trinity College. "Make sure they don't get into any mischief, nothing more than stumbling home from the pub. And I'm yer friendly neighbourhood peeler, always ready to lend a hand if there's a young lady in distress."

"Good man, Garda Rynne."

Francie got up and went to the kitchen, then called out, "Supper!"

She and Sarah served them one of Brennan's favourite meals. Steak-without-kidney pie and a side of colcannon: creamy mashed spuds with bits of cabbage and scallions mixed in, and loads of butter. Cans of ale were offered, accepted, and poured, and it was wonderful catching up with Shay's sister and nephew. He thanked them and said he looked forward to seeing them again before long.

When he and Shay got to the car, Shay asked, "Want to take a cruise by that house in East Wall, Brennan? Not that we're likely to see either of those lousers there now."

"Couldn't hurt, I suppose. Park up and take a stroll along the riverbank, glance over at the house and look for signs of life."

So that's what they did. It was one of those Dublin evenings when the sun was out but the few clouds in the sky managed to produce a shower of rain. Well, they were both accustomed to that, so they set out on their walk. The river reflected the early evening sun in a blaze of gold, and couples and young families were out enjoying the warm summer air. Some had been prepared and brought umbrellas. Brennan and Shay made a couple of passes by the place where Terry had been held. Nobody there. They chatted as they walked along. Shay asked about the Burkes in New York and about Brennan's sister Molly in London. And Brennan commented on the Rynnes he had just met up with again.

"It's great to see young Kevin following in your footsteps, Shay. He's a fine guard, I'm sure."

"Ah, he's had to put up with some grief from his friends in the old neighbourhood, the way I did myself. And it didn't help that he's working out of Pearse Street, which, as you likely know, has jurisdiction over Fenian Street. But he tells me that's eased off a bit now. He can enjoy a drink at Moroney's and not be shunned or slagged too much. And things went easier for him with the other guards. They're a little more open-minded these days."

Brennan remembered how Shay had been treated by his fellow peelers in Store Street during his first years on the force. The other guards came almost entirely from areas of the country other than Dublin, and "Dubs" were looked down upon. That went double for a boy from the tenements in Fenian Street. So Shay had to endure a great deal of slagging, nasty innuendo, and suspicion until he proved himself to be a superb addition to the ranks. He'd also had to put up with aggravation from his old mates in the Corpo flats, who had been treated none too kindly over the years by the peelers. They were not a crowd supportive of their local police. But that had eased off as well, following successes by their old pal in bringing down some of the more privileged citizens of Dublin. It was good to hear that that phase had passed for Kevin.

"Francie must be delighted with him."

"She is. She's been a wonderful mother to him, and her with no support from that piss-head who fathered him on her. When she took up with Davey, he was great with Kevin, was like a true father to him. But he died when his heart gave out on him, and Kevin and Francie were devastated. But Francie's been doing well, all the same. She has a couple of close friends, which is important for anyone. Sarah there at the house, and Clodagh, the one who works for the phone company. Francie would be earning more if she worked there, but she never applied. She loves her work at the bookshop. And I wouldn't think Clodagh would have enough influence in a big outfit like Telecom Éireann to get her mate hired on!"

When they passed the East Wall house once more, Brennan said, "Should we give up on this, Shay? I don't think we're going to see the culprits this evening."

"We might as well. We'll head back to the car. Oh, I meant to ask you: if you're not otherwise engaged on Thursday night, how would you like to attend an engagement party?"

"Who's become engaged?"

"My boy."

"Well, that's news! Who's the lucky lady?"

"Girl by the name of Isabel. We're having a few people over, and you and your brother, your da, you'd all be welcome to come. Don't bring a present! It's not that kind of a party. Just a few bites to eat, a few drops to drink, and good wishes for the young couple."

"Count me in. And I'll mention it to Dec and Terry."

Brennan took another look up and down the East Wall Road. "Those two men may never show their faces here again; they can't be confident that Terry wouldn't call in the guards to investigate."

"As he has done. Well, it was you called me in, so."

"Right. And we're all grateful for your assistance, Detective."

"You shouldn't be. I haven't managed to detect a feckin' thing. Terry got out on his own, so we didn't have to wait two weeks for a trace on that phone. Of course, Declan wasn't keen on us opening an investigation, and me having to go through the superintendent to arrange a trace, so I suppose that wasn't going to happen anyway. But I still want to help you in any way I can." He was quiet as they walked back to the car. Then, "I wonder . . ."

Brennan turned to face him, gave him a questioning look.

"Clodagh. Works for the phone company."

"Right. And?"

"She helped me out a couple of times. On the sly. Traced calls in circumstances where I didn't want anything on record."

So Shay could ask Francie's friend to trace a call without going through the formal process involving his superintendent? This would not be the call Terry had made from the house; they obviously didn't need that anymore. But what about other calls? He waited for Shay to put it into words.

"She could trace calls coming to that house, those two houses. And calls made there as well. That could provide us with some vital information. Names and locations of people those two fuckers are dealing with."

"That would be brilliant. But is that something Clodagh could do? Something she *would* do?"

"As I say, she's done it before. Just between the two of us, now . . . Kevin, of course, knew her while he was growing up. Her being over visiting Francie. And she did some tracing for him on a case a couple of years ago. She helped Kevin put a real psycho into prison. The streets were a good deal safer with him out of action. Kevin was celebrated at Pearse Street, received pats on the back from the higher-ups, was toasted in the pubs, and didn't have to put his hand in his pocket for a week after that!

"Nobody at Pearse Street knows how Kev actually got the information. As far as I'm aware, nobody ever caught on about Clodagh tracing the phone calls. She managed it then; she might be able to manage it again. I'll see what I can do."

CHAPTER XIII

Monty

Monty had enjoyed a long walk around the city, and he had stopped in to hear some tunes and enjoy a drink at the Cobblestone, a pub that brought back good memories of a previous visit to Dublin. Now, in the morning, it was time to get to work. He knew a lawyer here in Dublin. Had known her when she worked for a few years in Halifax. Enya Reynolds had started her law career in Dublin, met a Canadian man, and moved to Halifax with him. The couple were friends with Monty and Maura. Enya practised with a Halifax firm for a few years until her husband died in a car accident, after which she and her two children relocated to Dublin. She and Monty still exchanged Christmas cards, and he was sure she would help him out if she could. So he picked up a Dublin phone directory at his hotel and found her law firm. He dialled her number, got her secretary on the line, and she put him through to Enya.

"Monty in Dublin! What did you do, hijack a plane to get here? And you need me to represent you? I'll need a big portion of my fee upfront, for something like that."

"Now, Enya, didn't they teach you in law school here not to jump to conclusions before examining the facts?"

"Ah, to be sure, they did. How are you, Monty? How's Maura?"

So they caught up on each other's lives. Enya was married again, and all was well.

"Here's where you can help me, if you'd be so kind."

"I would, of course."

"I have to find a case, a matter heard in England, likely in the last decade or so. I'll need to trawl through some case reports to find it."

"No worries. As you know, Trinity College has the School of Law. And stacks full of law books in the Berkeley Library. Och, but you're not a student and not connected with the college, so you'll need a visitor's pass. Is this a pressing matter at all?"

"I'd like to get at it right away. It's to help a friend, and it's, well, I'd like to start today."

"I understand. I'm not sure how long it would take to get a visitor's pass for the Berkeley, but no matter, I can send you to another of the law firms here in the city. A big firm with a much bigger selection of law reports than I have here."

"That's great, Enya."

"And I'd love to see you if you can spare a bit of time. Lunch, maybe?"

"Sounds good. I'll see how my research goes, and one way or another, we'll go to lunch. I'd be keen to get to the Stag's Head again, if that would suit you."

"That would suit me fine. Now, take note of this address for Adelman McReith LLP, and I'll ring them and let them know you're coming. Then we'll meet at the Stag's Head. Say, half twelve?"

So that was the arrangement. He had the address of the law firm, and he obtained a city map from the hotel's reception desk. The place was near Stephen's Green in the city centre, so he set out for the office.

It was a mild day, mostly sunny and not too hot, so he could comfortably wear a shirt and sports jacket, looking lawyerly and not overheated. He arrived at the multi-storey modern building and went inside, where he was welcomed by the receptionist who'd had advance notice of his arrival. She got up and showed him to the shelves of statutes and case reports, including those from England and Wales. He expressed his appreciation and looked over the stacks of books in front of him.

His efforts to trigger his memory by singing the name and nickname he remembered had paid off in the middle of the night. He had awakened with the sounds of *Lorcan "One More Can" MacGillicuddy* ringing in his mind. Of course, he had no idea which court the case had been heard in, or what year, but he decided to start with reports from the early 1990s and the 1980s, given that the event Declan had spoken of had seemed fairly recent. And whatever it was had happened in England. There were several series of case reports from England, so Monty got to work, pulling one volume after another off the shelves and searching the indexes for the name MacGillicuddy. He found a few, and he flipped through the pages to see if the case looked like something that might have involved the likes of Declan Burke. He scanned the reports for his name.

After an hour and a half of searching, his stomach began to growl. He looked at his watch and saw that it was 12:10. Time to take a break and walk to the Stag's Head to meet Enya. He walked out into the sunshine and wondered whether he'd be able to find his way to the Stag's Head from here. Yes, walk to Dame Street and take it from there. And he found it without any trouble. The grand old Victorian pub had stained-glass windows, rich dark wood, and of course the stag's head itself mounted over the bar. Like so many Dublin drinking establishments, it could boast that James Joyce drank there. And some said Michael Collins had lifted a glass or two there as well. So Montague Michael Collins felt right at home. He took a seat, and not two minutes later, Enya walked in. Dressed in a navy-blue suit and with her dark hair tied back, she looked the same as when he had last seen her in Halifax. He stood, and they had a quick hug and sat down to order. They caught up on legal and family news, and she was interested to hear about the conference in The Hague. So it was a pleasant encounter as he enjoyed his shepherd's pie and his pint, before returning to his work.

Back at Adelman McReith's office, he searched through more of the English case reports looking for the name MacGillicuddy, and then there it was. A decision of the Court of Appeal, Criminal Division, in 1985. Two men had been charged with the armed robbery of a jewellery store, which took place when the sole employee was closing up shop for the evening. It was winter, February of 1982, and darkness came early. The Crown's position at trial was that this was not an impulsive action taken when the defendants happened upon the man leaving the shop. It was premeditated. One of the robbers had arrived with a gun. And the jewellery store had been featured in the news in the days before, because an actress from a popular English soap opera had been interviewed on television and had showed off her engagement ring, a pricey ring with several diamonds. She had mentioned Annelise Hendrikx Jewellers, and the place had enjoyed an upsurge in business thereafter.

Two men wearing masks had confronted the employee as he emerged from the jeweller's back door. The back of the shop was in an alley of other businesses that were closed by that time of the evening, so there was little risk of being seen. The robbers grabbed the employee, forced him to re-enter the shop and turn off the security system, and to open the vault where the cash was kept. They got away with eleven thousand pounds. They did not take any of the jewellery; perhaps they were not in the business of trying to sell items that were obviously stolen goods.

The defendants were Lorcan MacGillicuddy and Roderick Daniel Murphy. Because of the masks, the jeweller could not identify the men who had held him up. But the one who gave him the orders to turn off the alarm and open the vault had a strong Northern Irish accent, which the jeweller recognized as Northern because a family who lived close to him spoke exactly like that, and they were from Belfast. As was Murphy, until his move to England in the late 1970s. There were two other witnesses near the shop; they had seen men running out of the alley, one of whom tripped and fell and then pulled up his mask, presumably so he could see better. The men kept running towards a car parked near the alley. One of the witnesses noted the plate number and called the police. The car, of course, sped away. By the time the police found the car, abandoned on a street in Cricklewood, there was no one in it. But the vehicle was registered to Lorcan MacGillicuddy. The police had officers watching the car until, two days later, a man came for it. Not Lorcan MacGillicuddy but Roderick Daniel Murphy. There was no sign of Lorcan, and he was not arrested until two weeks later at his flat in Cricklewood. The money was never found. Both men were charged and sent for trial. Lorcan testified in his own defence and denied everything. He claimed that the car had been taken without his permission while he was on holiday in the United States. Murphy did not testify. The eyewitnesses gave evidence and were able to confirm that Murphy was the man who had fallen and removed his mask.

Both defendants were convicted. The robbers had threatened the employee with the gun but did not use it, did not physically harm him. The sentences would have been more severe if they had done so. Murphy and MacGillicuddy were convicted and sentenced to six years in prison.

Both men appealed. Appeals of the verdict in a jury trial were based not on the jurors' decision as such, but on errors of law supposedly committed in the conduct of the trial, for instance, errors committed by the trial judge. Several arguments were raised by lawyers for both the convicted men, arguments challenging the trial judge's instructions to the jury. But Monty skipped through them until he found a reference to the one witness he was interested in. Declan Burke. What on earth was Declan doing testifying in an English court in a trial about a jewellery store heist? There was no reference to anti-terrorism legislation in the case, so presumably the Crown did not consider this a robbery in aid of, for instance, the IRA. As far as Monty knew, robberies of that kind tended to be of banks, security vans transporting cash, and that sort of thing, where the amount of money was more likely to be worth the risk. Not that the RA would turn down eleven thousand pounds if it came their way. But that was not an element of this case.

Now here was the answer. One of the grounds of appeal related to the testimony of Declan Burke, specifically his answers on cross-examination by counsel for the Crown. The prosecution. And the judge's references to those answers while instructing the jury. Declan was Lorcan MacGillicuddy's alibi witness. He told the court that MacGillicuddy had been visiting in New York City at the time the robbery was committed, that he had met MacGillicuddy through mutual friends by the name of Búistéir. The record showed that the prosecutor repeated, "Booshtare?" And the judge interjected, "What's *that* when it's at home?" And some of the jurors laughed. Declan explained with, Monty assumed, strained patience that it was an Irish name.

There were only two gatherings where Burke and MacGillicuddy were both present. And one was on the night the London robbery was committed, February 17, 1982. Declan testified that both men had been invited to the birthday party for the Búistéirs' daughter Siobhán.

That sounded like quite a casual acquaintance to Monty. Would someone he had met through other friends, met a couple of times, have generated the kind of loyalty that would prompt Declan Burke, of all people, to make a secret trip to London to appear in an English court? And leave him open to questioning that he would not be able to predict? Like the questions posed to him on cross-examination.

"Mr. Burke, have you ever been convicted of a criminal offence? Mr. Burke, please answer the question."

"Many years ago."

"Where did this happen?"

"Dublin."

"What was the offence you committed? Mr. Burke, we need your answer."

"A weapons offence."

"You had a weapon. What kind of weapon?"

"An old gun my father had in the War of Independence."

"War of Independence. By that, do you mean the war that was waged in Ireland against the lawful authority of the British Empire?"

At this point, the case report noted, MacGillicuddy's lawyer rose to object that the question was irrelevant and prejudicial with no probative value to this case. Irrelevant to the question of MacGillicuddy's whereabouts on the night of the robbery. But, of course, that was not the real purpose of the question. The question — the insinuation — was put out there to tarnish Burke's credibility as a witness in the English court. The prosecutor replied that he had merely been trying to make sure he understood the witness's answer. The judge allowed the questioning to proceed.

Then it was "Mr. Burke. Are you or have you ever been a member of the Irish Republican Army, the IRA?"

The defence objected again. And again the judge allowed the question. Declan did not answer, and he was asked again. Finally he said, "No." The prosecutor then said, "Hmm. And were you incarcerated as a result of the *gun* offence?"

"I was."

"How long were you in prison?"

"Six months."

"Where did you serve your time?"

"Mountjoy Prison, Dublin."

Knowing Declan as he did, Monty could well imagine the look of hostility on his face and the sound of it in his voice when he answered those questions. Questions he knew full well would be asked. And that was it for the brief cross-examination, but it made quite an impression on the judge. In his instructions to the jury, he said that the jurors should be wary of evidence given by witnesses whose conduct in the past made their testimony unreliable. The Court of Appeal, rightly, concluded that these remarks were meant to refer to the evidence given by Declan Burke. And his evidence was being put in question for reasons that had nothing to do with the matter of MacGillicuddy's whereabouts or his guilt or innocence of the offence charged. In other words, the judge was instructing the jury to take account of matters that were not relevant to the questions at issue in the trial, and he was not so subtly discrediting details of Declan's testimony. It was clear that the judge was prejudiced against this particular witness and had let that prejudice taint his instructions to the jury. There was more to it, more to the Court of Appeal's findings of error on the part of the trial judge, but Monty had the information he was looking for: Declan Burke's role in the trial of Lorcan MacGillicuddy.

It struck Monty that the evidence against MacGillicuddy was so weak — nobody saw his face at or near the jewellery store, and when his car was found, it was the other defendant who was in it — that a verdict of not guilty should have been the right call. Not guilty, if the alibi evidence had not been tainted by the judge's prejudicial remarks in his instructions to the jury. And the Court of Appeal agreed. Whether MacGillicuddy was really innocent or not, the judge's instructions were such that the verdict of guilty should not be upheld. The Court of Appeal could have ordered a new trial but an acquittal was called for, given the errors committed by the trial judge. So Lorcan MacGillicuddy won his appeal and walked away a free man.

Monty wondered what he himself would have done if he'd been on the jury, with or without the trial judge's ill-considered remarks. When the police had finally found MacGillicuddy at his flat, he made his claim that he had been on holiday in the United States. What evidence did he have? Well, his passport had since expired and he had not yet renewed it, so he had discarded it. Any other papers to show he had been there? Airline ticket? No, all discarded. Photos, souvenirs of the trip? MacGillicuddy said he thought he had pictures and souvenirs and would look through his things to see if he had anything. By the time of the trial, he had come up with a couple of amateur-looking photos of New York scenes, including one of a man who looked like him with a couple of other people in a horse-drawn carriage outside Central Park. He also produced a couple of shoddy souvenirs, which, of course, as the prosecuting counsel stated in his summation, the defendant could easily have obtained in the meantime. But the witnesses in London were not able to give a useful description of the second robber. The fact that his car had been used in the robbery was highly suggestive of his guilt, but nobody could place him in or near the car that night. If he really had been in New York, someone — someone such as Roderick Daniel Murphy — could have got hold of the car and used it for his own purposes. But Monty had not bothered to read all the pages of legal arguments, of defects alleged to have been committed in the conduct of the trial; there was obviously more to it. Monty's natural skepticism, not to mention his years in the criminal courts, made him more than a little suspicious of MacGillicuddy's claim of innocence.

For his purposes, he had what he'd been looking for: the involvement of Declan Burke in the trial on behalf of Lorcan "One More Can" MacGillicuddy. The other defendant, Murphy, had served his sentence and had long been out of custody. Where was he now? England? Ireland? Someplace else entirely?

CHAPTER XIV

Brennan

On a bright Wednesday evening, the Burke brothers, two sets of them — Brennan and Terry, Declan and Finn — approached the crowd of people, mostly men, standing outside the Hill 16 pub with pints in their hands, some enjoying a smoke. Many of them wore purple-and-gold jerseys to show their allegiance to County Wexford's hurling team. Wexford had recently defeated Dublin in the Leinster semifinal, Leinster being one of the four provinces of Ireland. Brennan heard his name being called, and he turned to see Monty walking towards him. The Burkes all greeted him and were greeted in turn.

"Now, I don't want to prowl about staring into faces yet," said Finn.

This brought a puzzled look to Monty's face, and he raised his eyebrows to Brennan. Brennan gave his head a quick shake, and Monty said, "I'll take a walk around, scope the place out. Always fun to be in a new drinking spot."

"Always fun," Brennan agreed and turned his attention to his uncle.

"Our man may be out here," Finn said. "Vinny." The man who had leased the two houses on the East Wall Road. "But we'll go in and get our drinks first. Look around inside. You may be sure it's jammed in there as well, with last week's match being replayed on the telly. If I don't see Vinny in there, we'll come out and do our surveillance here."

The others followed him into the crowded pub. There was hardly room to move among the people standing or sitting, watching the replay or chatting with friends. The Burkes waited their turn at the bar and, in time, had their pints in hand. Now, how to find the man they needed. Finn was the only one of them who knew what Vinny Berrigan looked like, at least what he looked like now.

Reading Brennan's thoughts, the thoughts of them all, Finn said, "We'll find him."

But then they got caught up in the rapid back and forth of the match, and Monty walked over to join them. "I love this," he said, pointing to the screen. "I can't get over how fast the game is, and they're not even on ice!" Hurling was much like hockey but of course was played on grass. "I guess it's stating the obvious that this sport is the predecessor to our Canadian national game. Predated it by many years. But how far back does it go, hurling? Does anybody know?"

Brennan replied, "I've seen some records that say it was being played two thousand years ago."

"That's amazing! We've had our version, with our ice and our skates, for just under two hundred years. That's ancient history in a country like Canada. And if I may boast a bit here, hockey got its start in my home province of Nova Scotia!"

"Right. And it was Irishmen who got it going."

"True. It was Irish immigrants who were playing it. Irish guys were the first to play ice hurling, which became ice hockey. It's great seeing the original here in Ireland."

"Being reminded of all this, Monty, makes me want to don a pair of skates and play with your hockey pals next winter in Halifax."

"You'll be most welcome, Brennan."

The old Irish version was still wildly popular in its home country. Every county's team in hurling as well as in Gaelic football had a loyal following, and the excitement was manic at the inter-county level. But Brennan returned his thoughts to the matter at hand.

"Any sign of him, Finn?" he whispered. Not that he needed to whisper. The noise level was so high he could almost have shouted the question and not been overheard.

"I'll move through the crowd a bit, see if I can spot him. I can't imagine him missing out on this." So Finn made his way around the bodies gathered in the place and was greeted by more than a few of the punters. When he returned to Brennan's side, a man in a Wexford jersey came up to him and said, "Finn, are yeh trying to pass for a Wexford man? Don't want to be associated with the losing side?"

"Ah, Dermot, I'm a Dublin man through and through. I'll never give up on our lads in blue."

"I'd say you'll have a long time of 'never givin' up,' but good on you for your loyalty." He raised his glass to Finn, smiled, and moved on.

"I've looked about the room. No sign of our man in here. Let's head outside." So the four of them walked out to join the big crowd of drinkers standing around the pub. Monty stayed riveted to the televised game.

Finn said, "There's some fellas around the corner I could see from the window, so I'll — Vinny!"

He was looking at a tall, heavy-set man, with thick, greying, fair hair around a monkish tonsure. His face had a ruddy tinge to it.

"Vinny Berrigan!" Finn called out again.

The man peered through the haze of smoke. "Finn?" He reached out and shook Finn's hand. "Brilliant match. My relations down in Wexford town must be over the moon. It'd be great gas watching it again inside there, but how often do we get tropical weather like this?"

"It was a brilliant match, even if not for my home team. How's the form, Vinny? It's been a while."

"It has."

"Come here to me, Vinny, could we have a quick word?"

"Sure."

Finn gestured to a spot out on the pavement, beyond the gathering of revellers. The Burke brothers began walking over to them, then parted to allow Declan to go ahead. Berrigan stared as if trying to place the new arrival. Then he had it. "Declan?!"

"How've you been keeping, Vinny?"

"Stint in the Joy a few years back. Better now."

"All right, here it is. We're not here by accident, though we are enjoying the craic here this evening."

"Not by accident, you said, Declan."

"No. We're here to talk about a house in the East Wall Road."

Berrigan's head moved back, his eyes narrowed. "East Wall Road?"

His confusion looked genuine, at least to Brennan.

Declan said, "Two houses, side by side. Leased to Caoimhin Berrigan."

"A lease in my name? What's this about? I didn't lease any houses. I've my own place in Blanchardstown. What are yeh on about, Declan?"

"My son here, Terry, was snatched by two men and held captive in one of those two houses. Records show they are both in your name. Leased from the owner for four months."

"What the fuck? He was snatched?" He pointed to Terry. "And somebody's using my name? You can be sure I had nothing to do with this at all. And you can be sure I'm going to hunt down whoever the bastard is that used my name in connection with whatever the fuck is going on."

He was telling the truth. Brennan knew it. And he was steaming. Declan had obviously come to the same conclusion.

"Here's what happened, Vin." And he recounted the story of Terry's captivity, the two men's warning sent to Declan to get out of Ireland and keep his mouth shut. Terry's escape, and his description of his two captors who called themselves Ger and Frank. "Sound familiar to you at all?"

"Not right off, but I'll be stewing about this and trying to remember if I've ever met them."

"To state the obvious here, Vin, I'm their target. They've a grudge against me and —"

"Or they're afraid of you. They want you to keep quiet about something they think you know, something that would bring grief or shame down on their heads. Or death or arrest." He waited, as if for Declan to enlighten him. "You really have no idea what's behind this, Dec?"

A pained look crossed Declan's face, and he said, "Well, we all know what accounted for my swift departure from these shores all those years ago."

"That business with Quinn. But I know, and I've known for years, Declan, that nobody's still holding a grudge against you for that." He moved in closer to Declan and spoke quietly. But Brennan heard. "Sure, you well and truly made up for that. It's a closed book now."

Nobody spoke for a long moment. Then Berrigan said, "Whoever these gougers are, they're no friends of mine any more than they're friends of yours, Declan. Using my name like that. Somebody has it in for the two of us, for some unknown reason."

"True enough. Now we'll let you get back to your celebration here. And now that our side is out of it, I wish you and Wexford the best of luck in the next round."

"Go raibh maith agat." Thank you. "Keep me in the loop, Dec. Whatever you find out about this, I'll want to know about it. And if I hear anything, I'll be in touch. I'll pop in to Christy's."

"Thanks, Vinny. And sorry to come up on you like this."

"No need to apologize, Dec. Somebody set you up, set us both up."

Monty

Monty had emerged from the crowded pub just in time to hear a man say to Declan that somebody had set them up, both of them. Of course, Monty had no idea whether that "setting up" might be related to the Lorcan MacGillicuddy case in which Declan had been a witness. Tonight would be his only chance to speak with Declan about the trial. He would be flying back to The Hague tomorrow morning. So, with a tinge of guilt about adding to Declan's distress, he set out to do just that.

"Excuse me, Declan. Could I talk to you for a sec?" Declan looked a bit leery, and Monty couldn't blame him. But this was his only opportunity. "It won't take long. Maybe just over there?" He pointed across the street, where they could speak and not be overheard.

So they crossed over, and Monty said, "Declan, you may be less than pleased when I tell you what a nosy parker I've been." This brought nothing but silence and another wary look. "I'm concerned about you, as are Brennan and Terry." A nod. "So I tried to remember something you said to me a few years ago. About a trial you'd been involved in. Testified in."

The chilly blue eyes stared across at Monty, but then the eyes blinked. Declan took a breath and said, "One More Can MacGillicuddy."

"Yes. And so, with Brennan and Terry trying to find out what might be behind the kidnapping and the threatening note to you, I wondered whether there was anything in that court case that might have, well, come back to bite you."

Declan gave a snort of laughter. "That and all the other things in my past that might have come back to snap me in the arse."

"Right. So, lawyer that I am, I did a bit of research. Off the books, so no charge!"

"Good of you, Monty."

"And I found it."

"Found it?"

"The case against MacGillicuddy and Murphy. The Court of Appeal decision in one of the case report volumes."

"I see."

"You provided an alibi for MacGillicuddy."

"I did."

"And he was a free man after the appeal decision. But Murphy would be out now too. He served his time, and that time was up several years ago."

"He'd be out, yes."

"Where does he live, do you know?"

"He was living in Cricklewood, where a lot of our people live in London."

"Does he have a strong connection with Ireland? Family here?"

"As far as I know, Murphy is originally from Belfast. If he's spent any time in this part of the country, here in Dublin, I wouldn't know. How would I? This is my first time back here in four decades."

"Do you think he might be holding a grudge against you? For helping get the other defendant off? If, for example, Lorcan One More Can was not really innocent and took part in the robbery and was never punished?"

Declan's ready reply came as a surprise. "Of course, Lorcan was in on the robbery. The thing that saved his arse at the trial was that anti-Irish bigot of a judge. You should have seen the face on *his Lordship* when he made a remark about an Irish name I used in my evidence. Some sarcastic line he used. And he told the jury to be wary of putting too much store in my evidence! Me as a convicted criminal. Convicted decades ago for something completely irrelevant. What he was really saying was not to believe a word out of the mouth of this Irish mick, who denied membership in the Irish Republican Army, the same IRA that had made war against the brave British soldiers who were only doing their duty as the troops of the British Empire. And I did hear after the appeal that some relation of his had been injured in a battle or an attack somewhere in the North of Ireland, so you can imagine how he viewed anyone associated with the RA. But he's not supposed to be bringing that personal baggage into the courts. Anyway, his attitude and some other legal errors, whatever they were, got the verdict reversed for Lorcan." Declan smiled then and said, "But to give the oul bigot his due, he was right about one thing. I was lying through my teeth up there on the stand."

Good of oul Dec to acknowledge it, Monty thought to himself.

"So," Declan said, "that must have been burning Murphy's arse. You can understand that. One of them gets off, walks away with the cash, while his partner in crime gets slammed up in the nick."

"He really did it. Lorcan. So . . ."

"Let me see if I can guess your next question, Monty. Why did I go all the way over to the land of the Sasanach, even into their courts of law, to give evidence for a man I knew to be guilty?"

"You got it." Monty would ask about the money later.

"I owed Lorcan a big favour. Well, it was surely a big favour I paid him back with, so it was."

"What had he done for you, Declan?"

"Actually, it wasn't him but his father. And it was way back in time, before I left these shores. Let's just say Mr. MacGillicuddy Senior took a risk for me and did something that allowed me to escape the fate that befell Roddy Dan Murphy all these years later. I won't go into the details, but I told MacGillicuddy that if I ever saw the opportunity to help him or his family, he could be sure that I would do so. And I did."

There was no point, Monty knew, in trying to pry into whatever that long-ago incident was. Declan would remain tight-lipped, as they say. But what about Roddy Dan Murphy? "So. Murphy. Could he be responsible for what happened on your return here? Resentment against you for helping to get the other robber off, leaving Murphy to be the only one to pay the price with those years in prison?"

"But remember, Monty, the note left at the house told me to keep my gob shut." Yes, that was the angle in this that had left Monty puzzled. "There's nothing about Murphy that I know and others don't. It would more likely be Lorcan himself who wouldn't want something told." Declan glanced across the street at the crowd standing outside the Hill 16. Monty resisted the temptation to prompt Declan. After a few minutes, Declan looked about him again and leaned in towards Monty. "I'm opening my gob about this to you, Monty, not to anybody else."

As much as Monty wanted to hear this, whatever it was, he wouldn't feel right if he heard something significant and kept it from Brennan and Terry. "I'll be the one to make full disclosure on this point, Declan. I don't see how I could keep anything from Brennan and Terry if you know something that may explain what has happened here in Dublin."

"I understand that. Fair enough. I'll tell you, and you tell only the two of them, nobody else."

"You have my word."

"All right. Here it is. It was Lorcan MacGillicuddy who got away with the cash after the robbery. Eleven thousand British pounds or whatever the amount was. At some point in all this, he promised Murphy that he would keep Murphy's half of the money safe somewhere and have it for him when he finished his prison term. But guess what?"

"Oh, give me a minute here. Let me think. That money was not available to Murphy when he was released from the slammer?"

"Long years in the legal profession have given you a fair amount of insight into the criminal mind."

"Thank you for that kind compliment, Declan, but anybody over the age of two would have come to the same conclusion."

Declan laughed. "Exactly. But I guess poor oul Murph during all his years of confinement thought that at least he would have the consolation of those thousands of pounds waiting for him when he got out, giving him a good start on his new life. But there was not a shilling to be had."

"I wouldn't want to be Lorcan 'One More Can' MacGillicuddy when Murphy found that out."

"Lorcan came up with a story. Said some of our lads had, em, heard about the heist and the money — heard about the court case — and demanded that Lorcan hand it over."

"'Our lads' being the men fighting for a united Ireland free of British occupation?" The IRA.

Again a nod from Declan. "Demanded that the money be handed over to them for the cause. For the good of their native land. Except that was all fiction. Never happened. The RA never asked for or demanded the money. Lorcan kept it all to himself."

Right, Monty reflected, that's what had Declan grousing about the case during the conversation with Monty years ago. Monty could not recall what Declan had said, but this would explain why he had been vexed at the time.

"Lorcan was clever enough not to go throwing it around," Declan said, "buying flashy clothes or an expensive car. But he kept it, or spent it somewhere."

"And he sure as hell would not want that known."

"He would not."

Declan

Many's the time Declan had told himself he deserved a boot up the hole for that escapade in London, agreeing to appear as a witness for Lorcan MacGillicuddy. Venturing into the courts of the Saxon and giving perjured testimony for a man who had committed the crime he was charged with. Having to listen to that oul Irish-hating bigot, the beak up there on his bench running the trial. And now was that idiotic decision coming back to haunt him? Is that what accounted for the kidnapping of his son, the threatening letter delivered to the house in Irishtown? The house that now had bodyguards because whoever was behind all this knew where he and his two boys were staying.

And then there was that dismal scene in the laneway, one of so many dark places where fellas ended up, having been brought down by their addictions. Picturing the human wreckage he had seen, he felt his head getting heavier, his eyelids closing, as if he, too, had been brought to such a weak state that he could do nothing but lie in the gutter. Was the man he had spoken to really named Dennison? It seemed so. Was that man his son? Declan had seen no family resemblance, but then that might be expected in a face lined by age and by hardship. That Declan was his father seemed to be the implication in those diary pages. The row seemed to be about a failure in parenting in relation to that one son. And Althea's husband's remark about whether Declan Burke would have been "better at this" than he, the husband, had been. A better father, was how Declan read it. Whether the man in the laneway was his son or not, Declan had no illusions about being an angel of mercy able to lift him out of the squalor and carry him to a life of everlasting bliss. It was likely that many well-meaning people, experts in the field, had tried and would try again and again. What that poor fella needed was not the empty words or futile gestures of a father he never knew existed. If Declan was the father at all.

CHAPTER XV

Brennan

The morning after the evening at Hill 16, Brennan was on the phone to Monty about his plans to fly back to the Netherlands. "My flight leaves at three thirty. I'd like to stay longer here, but tomorrow morning, Maura is giving a presentation along with a lawyer from Vienna. Lawyer by the name of Rhea. The subject is the Vienna Conference on Human Rights, which took place a couple of years ago and measures taken by various countries in light of the conference. I don't want to miss it."

"I wouldn't miss it, if I were you, Montague. Herself would have your head on a plate."

"Right you are. She would have no regard for my human rights."

"I'll get you to the airport in plenty of time for your flight. But what say we get together before that?"

"That would be good, Brennan, so I can fill you in on my research. You and Terry?"

"Right, so."

"Where should we meet? A place that serves alcoholic beverages, perhaps? I've been to a couple of places like that. There are others, I expect?"

Brennan played along. "I've heard it told that there are close to eight hundred places in this city where one can go on the gargle. How about we meet you at the Bailey just after twelve noon? It's not that far from where you're staying. It's in Duke Street between Grafton and Dawson. There's an awning over the entrance and an outdoor terrace."

"I'll find it. See you there."

He found it; Brennan and Terry saw him there, dressed in a light-blue polo shirt, standing at the bar and being handed a glass of whiskey. Brennan and Terry said their hellos and ordered their drinks, a pint of Guinness and a Jameson whiskey for Brennan, a pint of Smithwick's red ale for Terry.

When they were seated at a table, Brennan said, "Your grand-uncle Michael used to drink here."

"The famed Michael Collins, you mean? I was in another drinking spot on this visit, and it, too, boasted of Collins as a former customer. The Stag's Head."

"That's exactly who I mean. Mick Collins. Surely by now you've tracked down the connection between his Collinses and your own."

"I think there's little doubt. Nobility and courage run in our family, not to mention brilliant good looks. Though I have to say you look more like him than I do, Brennan."

"I'll take that as high praise indeed. The legend is that Collins used to slip in here to the Bailey for a drink when he was being hunted by the Brits. And some of the most brutal representatives of the British occupying forces, those being the Black and Tans, would be drinking downstairs in this very establishment."

"The man had bollocks of steel," Terry added. His companions agreed.

"Now," said Monty, taking a glance around the room. "I did my research, thumbed through the law reports. Cases from England. It took a while but I found it: the case in which your father gave alibi evidence for a friend."

"Alibi evidence?!" Brennan exclaimed.

Monty went on to recount a story of a jewellery store robbery in London in the early 1980s, two robbers, one of them caught almost immediately, the other away off with the money and not arrested till a couple of weeks after the heist. "The fellow who was harder to find was Lorcan 'One More Can' MacGillicuddy, an old pal or associate of Declan's in the past. Here in Ireland. To be more accurate, it was MacGillicuddy's father who was an associate of your own father."

"And you're saying our Dec hopped on a plane, unbeknownst to the rest of us, flew to London, and testified in an English court!"

"Now, Brennan," Terry said with a laugh, "why wouldn't our da do that? Probably did it every other week."

"That's the last thing I'd ever have expected him to do, appear in an English court. Not in handcuffs, but willingly. Yet another surprise from our dear oul da."

"Declan's evidence didn't do the trick for Lorcan at the trial. And he didn't testify on behalf of the co-accused, Murphy. Both the culprits were convicted and sentenced to several years in prison."

"How many years?" Brennan asked.

"The sentence was six years."

"So, they're out now."

"Lorcan's conviction was overturned by the Court of Appeal, so he's been out since the mid-1980s. The other robber, Murphy, served his time, but yes, he's out too."

"Do we know where they are? The case was in London."

"The appeal decision indicated that they were both living in Cricklewood in London at the time."

"Right. Cricklewood is a big Irish enclave over there."

"Murphy was originally from Belfast, so he may be back on this island now. We don't know."

"Murphy may be two hours from here," said Terry. "And with a grudge against our father for testifying for the other guy and not for him."

"Maybe," Monty replied and paused to take a sip of his pint. "But there's more to it."

"Of course," Brennan muttered. "Isn't there always?"

"Declan's evidence was that MacGillicuddy was in New York City on a bit of holiday when the robbery occurred." That brought snickers from Declan's two sons. "Yeah, I know. A little too convenient, and apparently the jury didn't buy it. And it would not have been the reason for the Court of Appeal overturning the conviction. Appeals in jury trials are based on errors in the conduct of the trial, for example, the way the judge instructs the jury, not on the jury's findings as such. I didn't read all the arguments about the judge's conduct, his instructions, the grounds of appeal. I was only interested in Declan's role. Anyway, Declan's story — sorry, I mean Declan's *evidence* — was that he met Lorcan a couple of times through other friends, and they became friends themselves."

"After meeting a couple of times," Brennan said. "And that was supposedly enough to inspire our Dec to fly over and present himself in the court of the Sasanach."

"That was the official version. But your father told me, and this is to go no further than you and Terry, that he owed the MacGillicuddy family a big favour from years past. Lorcan's father had done something for Declan, and it sounds as if whatever it was, it kept Declan from facing criminal proceedings himself."

"Oh, Christ, do we even want to know?"

"He wouldn't tell you even if you wanted to know. He wouldn't tell me. It's a closed book. So he went to England to repay his debt to Lorcan's family."

"So, we have nothing to fear from Lorcan," said Terry.

"Um, it's not quite as simple as that."

"Of course it isn't," Terry replied.

"Lorcan had promised to squirrel away half the take — they stole eleven thousand British pounds — he promised to keep half of that for Murphy when he got out of the clink."

"Wait, let me guess," said Brennan.

"You've heard many confessions in your day, Father. Has that made you skeptical? Cynical, even?"

"Lorcan kept all the money for himself. Has it all spent."

“Correct. And he came up with a cover story. Put the word out that when the IRA men heard about the heist, they demanded that he hand over the money for the cause of Irish freedom. And so he did. Except that never happened. There was no such demand or request. Lorcan kept it all himself.”

“And if word of this got around, Lorcan would be in fear for his life.”

“Yeah. From Murphy, who spent years in prison while his partner in crime walked free and took all the cash.”

Brennan took last sips from his drinks and addressed his companions, “Another and another?” They both accepted the offer, and Brennan got up and went to the bar. He’d be driving, so he got drinks for the others, no more for himself. When he was back, and the glasses had been distributed, he said, “Thinking about what you’ve told us, Monty. Yes, Lorcan would have reason to fear Murphy, but it might be a stretch to think Murphy would extend that grudge to Declan. Sure, Declan helped Lorcan get off, but Murphy’s resentment would more likely be directed at Lorcan. And the warning to Declan obviously stemmed from a fear that he would reveal something. The note told him to keep his gob shut. That scenario would more likely reflect Lorcan’s fears; if the truth got out, he’d have reason to fear retribution from Murphy.”

“And maybe even from the RA,” Terry suggested, “if they found out Lorcan made up that story about them demanding the take. And them not getting it.”

“Maybe nothing to fear from them officially,” Brennan replied, “but if some rogue member caught wind of it.”

“And Lorcan can be fairly sure that Declan, with his republican connections, knows the truth about the money.”

Brennan and Monty had a lot to talk about on the drive out to the airport.

CHAPTER XVI

Terry

When evening came, Terry and Brennan left the house to go to Shay Rynne's place in Drumcondra. The occasion was the engagement of the Rynnes' son, Brennan Thomas — godson to Brennan Xavier Burke — to his girlfriend, Isabel. Declan had declined the invitation, couldn't get himself into a party mood, but he asked his boys to pass along his congratulations. On the way out of Irishtown, they spotted the green security van and waved to the man inside. Donal, Terry thought.

They were greeted by Shay at the door and went inside. Brennan was in civvies for the occasion, no black clerical suit or Roman collar on him tonight. Two little boys, three or four years old, were chasing a little girl a few years older, all of them squealing with laughter. A couple dozen people, most in their twenties, were standing in the sitting room with drinks in their hands. They chatted and laughed, and some sang along with U2's album *Achtung Baby* playing in the background.

Terry leaned towards Brennan and said, "Which of these young fellas is your godson?"

"Over there," he pointed. "Tall with the black curls like his da. Dark green gansey on him." Sweater. "Goes by Brens. And that must be Isabel."

As Terry watched, Brens looked over and smiled as a beautiful young woman approached him. Isabel. He put his arms around her, gave her a quick kiss on the mouth, then whispered something in her ear and stepped back. She rewarded him with a radiant smile of her own. Her hair was black like that of her fiancé, but straight and cut in what Terry's mother called a bob, just above her shoulders with bangs nearly to her eyes. She was a few inches shorter than her beau, slim and shapely, dressed in a form-fitting sleeveless dress in a colour somewhere between red and purple. Just as Terry was about to go over and introduce himself to the couple, they were hailed by somebody at the back of the room. And a sweet-faced woman with auburn hair walked over to Terry and Brennan.

"Allie, this is my brother Terry. Terry, meet Mrs. Rynne. Allie."

"Lovely to meet you, Terry. Make yourself at home here. Drinks on the sideboard, and you'll find a few things to snack on as well."

"Thank you, Allie."

She reached over and put a hand on Terry's arm. "I am so happy that you are back safe and sound from your ordeal."

"Thanks, Allie. And I am grateful, as you can imagine, to Shay for the help he's been giving us. I'm happy to meet you. I always enjoy meeting new people."

"There's such a crowd here, you probably won't get to meet everyone. But see that huddle of teens over there?" She pointed to a cluster of young people at the far end of the room. "Those are my four youngest. Aisling, Maeve, Liam, and Orla." Two of the girls had their mother's dark red hair; the boy and the other girl were black-haired like their dad. "No doubt they're planning mischief of some kind!"

Terry was about to reply when he heard, "Allie, love!"

He looked across the room and saw a woman leaning on the back of a chair. She appeared to be in her seventies, with a heavily lined face and white hair pulled back in a bun. She was wearing a short-sleeved dress patterned with roses and white track shoes on her feet.

"Yes, Ma?"

"I brought some scones. Did you see them there?"

"I did, Ma. Thanks. I'll set them out on a plate." To Terry and Brennan, she said, "Excuse me, gentlemen. Help yourselves at the bar there." She pointed to an array of bottles and glasses atop a cabinet on the other side of the room, and then she left for the kitchen. Terry and Brennan headed for the bar and poured themselves a glass of whiskey each.

"Mrs. Cotter!" Terry heard a woman's voice and looked into the next room, the dining room. It was the bride-to-be calling out to Allie's mother.

Mrs. Cotter smiled and walked over to Isabel. Terry was surprised at how spry the older woman was on her feet. "I think we've known each other long enough, Isa, that you can call me Mamie!"

"Okay. Mamie."

"Enjoying the craic, Isa?"

"Very much," Isabel replied and gave Mamie Cotter a hug. "It's so lovely to see you. And I want to thank you again for letting me come along with you to visit Mrs. Delahunt."

"She loves to have company, does Claudia Delahunt. In her condition, God be good to her, there's not much she can do. Physically, at least. But her mind is as sharp as it ever was, and she appreciates the kindness of people who take the time to visit."

"And that, em, personal care you give her. It's not everybody who is able for that sort of . . . that sort of thing."

"Ah, now, it's no big effort on my part to help her with her . . . needs. She was very good to my mother. As you know, my mother used to do for her. Kept the house sparkling clean, doing the messages, all that. I like to think I've kept the place up to the same standard when I took over from my ma!"

"I'm sure you did."

"They stayed close until Ma died, and she loves to hear stories from our family, the children, all that."

"Mrs. Delahunt must be so grateful."

"Ah, well, it's just what anybody would do. Hoovering the carpets, scrubbing the floors, changing the linens."

"That's loads of work. Big place like that."

"Musha, loads of work never bothered me!"

"I would love to go with you again someday."

"Sure, pet, we'll go and see her again soon. She'll be delighted."

"Nice to hear," Terry commented to Brennan, "an older lady cheerfully taking on the task of assisting someone even older. And the young bride-to-be wanting to go along as well."

Just then, Terry heard Brennan's name being called. Shay was summoning him over to meet somebody. Terry took the opportunity to look at the framed pictures on the vanilla-white walls of the room; they showed fascinating objects retrieved from Ireland's ancient past. He especially liked the tools and a bog body, the remains of a man over two thousand years old. Then the young groom was at his side. "My ma loves the old artifacts," he said. "Allie the archaeologist. You'll not find any modern art in this house! Iron Age, medieval, yes. 1980s, 1990s, no. I'm Brennan Thomas; everyone calls me Brens or Bren Tommy."

"Terry Burke, brother of your godfather. Does that make me your goduncle? Not a very attractive word, I guess!"

"No, we'll take a pass on that! How are yeh, Terry? Any brother of Father Burke's is welcome in this house. And will be in mine! When I get one."

"Congratulations on your engagement. When's the big day?"

"We haven't quite settled on that yet. And I'm . . . we're hoping that your brother might be willing to perform the ceremony."

"He'd love to do that, I know."

"It was him that married my ma and da. Maybe you knew that?"

"Yes, I knew. And I know how much that meant to him. That, and Shay and Allie honouring him by making him your godfather, giving you the name Brennan. The way I heard it, he was left speechless when they told him the name! Not for long, knowing our Brennan, but for a moment there. That's how moved he was."

"Lovely to hear, Terry. Brennan is class! His music is brilliant. I've made a point of learning the organ parts and the tenor parts to some of the great traditional church music he does. Everything from Renaissance polyphony to Mozart and Handel. And of course Gregorian chant as well. No organ needed for that. Brennan is exactly the kind of priest anyone would want. Dedicated, but never stuffy! And a top-notch intellectual. There's nothing naive about his faith; it is well grounded in reason. I guess all those degrees from Rome would do that for him!"

"Oh, he's a bright spark, no question."

"And yet he's a fine man at a party or down the pub with the lads."

"That he is!"

"And there's nothing formal about him tonight, dressed like the rest of us here. No collar on him for this hooley. I really —"

"Brenny!" That was his intended, summoning him to the other side of the room.

"Och, gotta go. Nice talking to you, Terry."

"Same. Enjoy your evening!"

Terry walked over to his brother, who was in the entryway to the kitchen. But when Terry got closer, he didn't want to interrupt because two young ladies were busy interrupting each other as they gabbed away to Brennan. The conversation consisted of the two of them one-upping each other with stories of the rock bands and trad musicians they had seen. After a few more minutes of this, Brennan caught sight of Terry and excused himself. They walked to the bar, helped themselves to more whiskey, and Terry said, "I just met your godson. I took to him right away. You must be proud of him."

"I am indeed. I've enjoyed the time I've been able to spend with him on my visits home here."

"You didn't snag him for the priesthood, I see."

"Oh, I had to go easy on that. He loves the great Latin hymns, motets. He now has his degree in music, and he's been hired to teach at Waltons. You know, the music school. He has a deep religious faith, regained after a few wild years. More than once he told me he was thinking of taking Holy Orders, becoming a priest. I had to go lightly. Didn't want to, well, didn't want to exert undue influence on him."

Having talked with Brens, Terry knew how much he admired his priestly godfather. If there was an element of hero worship, Terry knew his brother would not want to trade on that. Not, as Brennan just said, exert any undue influence that would see the younger man follow in Father Burke's footsteps to a life in the church. "Whenever that subject came up," Brennan said now, "I cautioned him that he would need a long period of discernment and independent advice. And, well, look at him now." Brennan smiled in Brens's direction. "He's chosen another path, and he looks delighted at what he sees in his future."

The room was suddenly quiet, and Terry realized that someone had turned off the U2 records. Then he heard a guitar and turned towards the sound. A lovely girl with long wavy blonde hair was standing with a guitar in her hands, its strap hanging down. She said, "Somebody asked me for a song. Honest, they did! And on an occasion like this, a love song is in order. As soon as I can get this . . ."

She was fiddling with the strap, and Brennan walked over to her. "Let me help you there."

"Thank you, Brennan!" So, they had already met. Right, she was one of the girls who'd been chatting him up.

"Anything for a young musician, Janey."

She smiled at him and introduced her song, "I'm going to do 'Angel of the Morning,' the Juice Newton version." And she did a stellar job of it, sounding almost like Juice Newton herself. Everyone clapped and congratulated her, and she bowed in response. "I've always thought that nothing says love better than that long, drawn-out *da-ar-linnn* at the end!"

"Amen to that," Brennan agreed.

"Give us another song!" someone requested, but Janey shook her head.

"No, no. It's not my show here tonight!"

Brennan looked at her and said, "No? How about I give *you* a song, dear lady?" And he put his hands out for the guitar; she slipped the strap off and passed it to him. He strummed it a bit and adjusted the tuning. Then he put on the voice of Mick Jagger, sounding so very, very English. He sang "Lady Jane," the song in which the suitor forsakes all others and pledges his troth to his dear Lady Jane. When he finished the song, he put the guitar down and made an elaborate bow to Jane, extending his hand to her in an old-fashioned gesture that matched the tone of the song. Everybody loved it; they clapped and cheered and said Brennan should join the Rolling Stones on their next tour. One of the young fellas called out, "You just proposed marriage to her, mate. You'd better do the right thing now!"

The males of the species were not the only ones to react to Brennan's talents. He was a fine-looking man, no denying it, with that strong profile, those black eyes and the black hair with silver on the sides. Terry knew that his brother had long been admired by the fairer sex, including the younger set, and tonight was no exception. Admiring — some longing? — gazes lingered on him as he laughed and did an exaggerated bow to his audience. Jane herself was hugged and lauded for her engagement to such a talented and dedicated suitor. The way she grinned at Brennan suggested that she might well consider a proposal from him. Was Brennan enjoying a moment of imagining just that scenario?

"Great craic," a man beside Terry enthused, and Terry was in full agreement.

Brennan

"Brennan Burke, I believe! Or is it Mick Jagger?" The bride-to-be had sprinted over to Brennan, nearly tripping on her spike-heeled shoes. "Brennan, I've been dying to meet you; Brenny has told me so much about you!"

He put his hand out, but her hands were occupied, fluffing her hair up and pushing strands of it out of her eyes.

"It's a pleasure to meet you, Isabel." And it had been a pleasure hearing her conversation with Brennan Thomas's gran. Brennan had heard Isabel complimenting Allie's mother, Mamie Cotter, for the way Mamie had been caring for the old lady who was very ill. Was Isabel a nurse perhaps? A medical student?

"Are you in the medical profession in some way, Isabel? I couldn't help overhearing you talking with Mrs. Cotter."

"Oh, no, I'm not. I work in a bank. But people often tell me I should train to be a doctor. I have the . . . Oh, I shouldn't boast to you. It's just that I did very well in school. And I love working with people. But," she said, and she treated him to her dazzling smile, "what I love most is music! Brens has his degree in music, and he tells everybody I'm a better singer than he is!"

"Are you going to give us a song?"

"Ah, no. Janey did her singing, and I wouldn't want to . . . Oh, she was good, no question about that."

There was a little twist to her mouth when she said it. Brennan couldn't quite identify the expression on her face. Was he seeing irony? Sympathy? She wouldn't want to what? Show up the other girl?

"I'd better not sing you one of my songs, Brennan. *Father* Burke. I was in a band for a couple of years. Not here in Dublin. And some of our songs were . . . I shouldn't say it. Not to a priest! But you know how they rate films — not for children under fourteen or whatever the age is?" She moved in closer till they were almost touching. "Well, you could say that about my singing!"

"Ah, I'm well over fourteen, Isabel," he told her, laughing.

She laughed, too, but strangely enough, he did not see laughter in her eyes.

"Even without the music, then, it's a pleasure to meet you, Isabel."

He held out his hand, and she took it. And it was as if a bolt of electricity had shot through his arm; it was all he could do not to snatch his hand away. But it was her eyes that disturbed him, grey eyes that were cold, empty. He tried to banish the first impressions that struck him, the words: callous, uncaring, unsympathetic. Surely, he was overreacting. Could he really make such a judgment on such a brief encounter? It seemed she had not noticed his reaction; she withdrew her hand but kept up a line of chat about her work, the surprising amounts of money that some people in the city deposited, while other poor souls did not have enough even to open a bank account. The remarks about the poor people of Dublin were delivered in a flat tone, as if they were things she felt she should say once the subject of money had been raised.

Later in the evening, Lady Jane was at his side again, and he joked with her about *their* "engagement." Where should she and Brennan have the wedding? Dublin Castle, a fitting place for such a lady? She laughed and agreed that the castle would be grand. At one point in the conversation, he looked over Janey's head and saw Isabel standing not far away. He had a good view of those expressionless eyes. Suddenly there was a scream. A child's high shriek from the direction of the staircase. This was met by cries of "Oh, no!" "Is he hurt?" Brennan turned to the side, intending to go to the stairway, but the archway out of the sitting room was blocked; there were so many of the guests congregated there. The child was wailing now. Fear? Pain? Had he or she fallen down the stairs? Brennan moved forward; he would go through the archway between the dining room and the hall, get to the stairs that way. He started to pray that the child was not badly hurt. He took a couple of steps and found himself facing Isabel. She was staring ahead at something, not in the direction of the stairs. And there were those eyes again, focused on the distance. No expression in them, exactly the way they had been when he had been speaking to her earlier. No emotion, no concern. When he got to the staircase, there was a crowd of guests gathered around one of the little boys, who was sobbing in his father's arms on the bottom step. The man looked up and said, "More of a fright than anything. He tripped and fell but not from a height. Sure he'll be fine. Won't you, Kieran?" There was a collective sigh of relief, and murmurs of sympathy to the child.

"Can I get anything for him?" Brennan asked the father.

"A drink of juice?" a woman asked.

The father shook his head. "Thanks, I'll just let him rest here a minute."

People gradually moved away, again expressing their sympathy and assurances to Kieran that he would be fine.

When the party wound down, Brennan and Terry took their leave with best wishes for the newly engaged couple. Wishes uttered with more enthusiasm by Terry than by Brennan.

As they drove back to Irishtown, Brennan recalled a conversation he had had more than once with Monty Collins. As a criminal defence lawyer, Monty had looked into the eyes of countless clients over the years. And with some of them — a small minority of them, to be sure — where one would expect a reaction, there was none. What was the story Monty had told? He was interviewing a client in one of the jails or prisons, and something terrible happened. A prisoner was being beaten and was heard screaming, and what Monty noted — noted perhaps because of studies he had read — the client's eyes showed no reaction to the screams of the man in pain. The pupils of the client's eyes did not dilate. The dilation, or opening, of the pupils was known to be a common reaction to negative emotional events, sounds, or sights. Pupils not dilating was believed to be a mark of the true psychopath, a lack of emotional connection with other people, their traumas.

Well, Brennan could hardly peg this young woman as a psychopath. What were the chances of that? And hadn't he heard her showing great sympathy for the poor old soul that Allie's mum was caring for with such dedication? Could that be a person without empathy for other people? But Brennan himself, over the course of a lifetime, had had intuitions that a person was . . . evil. Or at least cold, without compassion for others. He could not explain it. Sometimes he had that electrical jolt he'd felt when he touched the hand of Isabel. Sometimes it was an indescribable feeling that, as strange and nebulous as it was, had been proven right. All that being said, Brennan knew what he'd felt when he touched the woman's hand and looked into those emotionless grey eyes. How could Brennan bring this up with his godson? That she was bad; a life with her would mean trouble for the husband. That he should walk away. Run. She brought to mind the old Percy Sledge song "Take Time to Know Her," about a man who gets to the church with his future bride, and the preacher takes him aside and tries to warn him off her. The preacher's intuition told him, as Brennan's did now, that she was bad news.

He decided to share his misgivings with Terry. "What did you think of Isabel?"

"A looker! And your godladdy seems quite taken with her."

"Taken *in by* her may be a more accurate reflection of the relationship."

"What are you talking about, Brennan? I saw her playing up to you there. Good news for us *older gentlemen* if the young ones like the look of us. Or admire the wisdom we must have acquired over the years. But Father, a little bit of flirting is hardly a mortal sin."

"No, Terry, it's something else."

Brennan looked across at him. Terry must have seen something in Brennan's own eyes. He said, "Ah. That bad, is it?"

"That bad."

CHAPTER XVII

Brennan

Brennan Thomas Rynne and Isabel were not the only ill-matched couple on Brennan's mind. Lying awake after the engagement party, his thoughts turned to the young woman his father had taken up with at the Big House in County Wicklow. What had become of that relationship? Had it forestalled Declan's ambitions of looting the grand estate of items that would be useful in the struggle to force the British out of the north of Ireland? Shotguns or rifles the family used for hunting? Jewellery, silver that could be sold to raise funds? Would Brennan and Terry learn anything of value if they visited the museum again, if they spoke with the genealogist there? The woman at the museum said the genealogist came in on Wednesdays and Fridays. Tomorrow was Friday.

Terry needed no persuading. Once again, they gave their father a story. Brennan said he wanted to see the medieval castle and Saint Begnet's Church in Dalkey; there were burial sites dating back as early as the sixth century. Brennan had toured the site on a recent trip to Ireland but told Declan it had been years since he had seen it. So off the brothers went again. Terry brought his Polaroid camera as any sightseer would and again brought it into the museum as part of his tourist schtick. Agnes, the museum guide, remembered them from their previous visit and gave them a warm greeting. After a bit of small talk, she introduced them to Verna, the genealogist. She was a tall, slim woman with greying dark wavy hair and silver-rimmed glasses. She smiled at them when they were introduced.

Terry spun her a line about his interest in a couple of the families featured in the museum, but his brother here, Brennan, was an architecture buff and he was most taken with Shersfoote House. "Built in the 1700s, I noticed. They knew how to build a proper house back then!"

"They certainly did," Verna agreed. "Come have a seat." She led them to a room off to the side, and they all sat around a table. "The 1700s, yes, but the family lineage is much older than that, of course."

"Oh, is that so?" Terry replied.

"Yes, one of the first known men in the family line was associated with the court of Henry the Seventh. So, late 1400s, early 1500s." Verna went on to give them a detailed history of the family through the centuries. Brennan was nearly fidgeting with impatience, although he admitted to himself that the genealogist certainly knew her field. And the information would be of great interest to visitors who were not focused on one of the daughters who lived more than four hundred years after King Henry. The daughter who lived in County Wicklow, Ireland, and consorted with the likes of Irish republican Declan Burke.

Finally, at long last, Verna said, "Now here we are in the present century. These were the sons, Percival and Gilbert. And the only daughter, Althea." She shuffled through some papers. And some photographs. "Ah, here is the wedding party. Althea's wedding. She married well, as they say. Frederick Bonneville Earnshaw. Son of another prominent family, military family from England." Verna held the photo up for them to see. The bride's fair hair was shoulder-length and done in elaborate waves. Brennan recognized the style from the film stars of that era, the 1930s. She wore a voluminous white dress. The groom was a stern-looking man in military dress, the uniform of an officer of the British Army. No grins for the cameras from him.

"A lovely girl," Terry said.

"She was indeed."

Verna peered at the picture. "Does her smile look a little forced, do you think?"

Brennan looked closely at it and thought yes, perhaps it did. Terry looked too. "I'm not sure. Maybe you're right. I wonder why. A little nervous on her wedding day, perhaps, nervous in front of the photographer."

"Oh, I shouldn't descend to gossip here!" Verna said. "But, well, the Earnshaw fella was, shall we say, a little late coming to the altar."

Terry laughed. "Is that right?"

"She was well along in her first pregnancy. But no matter. They went on to have three more children after that first boy. I know we have pictures of Althea's family somewhere here. Just let me dig through the collection."

It would be interesting to see a picture of the Shersfoote daughter when she was a little more relaxed than on her wedding day, but Brennan didn't think there was much chance she'd have been photographed with Declan. Or if she had, that the photo would have been preserved by the family for posterity.

"Here we go. Althea's children. Out on the lawn, hard to make them out."

Brennan saw a boy of around nine and three younger children, two girls and a boy. The kids all stared at the camera. Was that a cricket bat in the older boy's hands, or was Brennan projecting his own expectations onto the scene?

"And here they are, grown up." There was a black-and-white photo of the two sisters, another showing the youngest three together, and another, a colour photo of an army officer. Brennan picked up that one. Oh God, what am I seeing here?! He looked across, caught Terry's eye, and then looked down again at the photo. Terry's eyes widened when he saw it.

Verna noticed their interest. "A distinguished-looking man, isn't he? The oldest of the four, Dwight Frederick Earnshaw. He followed in the steps of his father and joined the army. The British Army. His father is still alive and well. The mother, unfortunately, is not. Althea died a couple of years ago. So, we have Dwight here in full military kit. Someone told me he is stationed somewhere in the North. Northern Ireland."

And Terry, quick thinking as always, came up with a plan. He said, "I have to say I always like looking at those old photographs. Classics, they are. I wonder what kind of a camera was used to take those old pictures. Something a little more sophisticated than this one!" He had the Polaroid camera on a strap around his neck; he took it in his hands and showed it to Verna with a laugh. Then he jerked his head around, looking out to the main room. Had he heard something? Verna turned, too, and Terry looked at Brennan and mouthed the words "Distract her!"

Whatever his brother had in mind, and Brennan thought he knew what it was, he would go along with it. "Verna, there's something I've been wondering about." Now, he'd have to identify whatever it was he claimed to have wondered about. "It's one of the buildings pictured out there." He pointed to the main room. "Could I ask you something about it?"

"Certainly."

Brennan got up, and she did the same.

ᔕ

Twenty minutes later, after thanking Agnes and Verna, Brennan and Terry were sitting in their car, staring at the Polaroid photo Terry had taken of Dwight Frederick Earnshaw, Althea's son.

Terry spoke first. "Jesus Murphy! When I first looked at it I thought, yeah, a Brit soldier. Sort of thing you'd expect coming from a place like Shersfoote House. But on closer inspection, it struck me."

"Right. That's not the face of a Saxon. And that's the least of it! Christ Almighty, can you believe this?"

The man in the photo appeared to be tall, and he had sandy-blond hair, clear blue eyes, and what Brennan thought of as a stereotypical Irish face. It would be an exaggeration to say he looked like a twin, but he definitely looked like a brother. A brother to Brennan and Terry's brother Patrick.

"I find it hard to believe is right, Bren! A Paddy Burke look-alike in the uniform of a British soldier! I'd say that explains why the groom was late coming to the altar! And not looking all that happy about it."

"An arranged marriage? The parents hooked her up with someone much more suitable than porr oul Dec, humble servant that he was? Or was pretending to be. Maybe the groom was someone they had in mind for her all along. A man of good family."

"Perhaps he was already in her life, already a beau, and she played away for a while and had a rollicking good time with Dec."

"And I doubt very much that the parents knew anything about her dalliance with Declan. That sort of thing simply would not do. So her story to the parents would have been that Earnshaw was the father of the child."

"What about Declan? Did he know about the kid?"

"I wouldn't think so, Terry. He talked about her, the girlfriend, said they were together a short time. Then he never heard from her again. He knew she got married, but that would have been public knowledge, so to speak. So it sounds as if when they parted, that was the end of it."

"You're probably right. But *we* know about him. So, Brennan, are we going to find this brother of ours?" No reply, but Terry was not put off. "We can hardly saunter up to one of the army barracks and knock on the door. *Hi, can Dwight come out to play?*"

"No, you're bang on there, Terry. Our sort would not exactly be welcome at any gathering of the British colonial powers."

"Verna did say he is stationed in the North here, so he's only a couple of hours away. Speaking for myself, I'll find the temptation overwhelming. A brother we've never met? I'll want to meet him."

"I know. Or at least see him. I'm not sure meeting him would be in anyone's interest."

"Yeah, I suppose. Now, we need some advice on how to go about this. But anybody we can think of to ask is somebody we can't ask, if we want to keep this mission a secret from our da."

"And that is an order, Captain. Dec must not learn of this. I imagine it would be a very painful revelation. That means we can't ask Finn, can't ask our cousins in Belfast."

"Do you know anybody here in the Republic, Bren? In the Irish Army? Somebody who might know a thing or two about the opposing forces in the North?"

"No. We have our pal who's a peeler, but I wouldn't expect him to have any inside knowledge of the British Army on the other side of the . . . the partition."

"Couldn't hurt to ask, right? Ask him who to ask."

"That's what I'll do," Brennan said. "Of course, with all this going on, we're not going to meet our original departure date!" Their original idea had been to fly home at the end of June. They were only a couple of days away from the month's end, so that wasn't going to happen.

"No, our da won't be ready to leave until he's tracked down whoever is causing him, causing us, all this aggravation. I don't know what he's planning to do if he catches whoever it is!"

"We may not want to know."

"True enough. Anyway, I'll be in touch with the airline, see about flights next month. Mid-July, I guess we'll be thinking now."

ᔓ

When they were back in Irishtown, Brennan put a call through to Shay at the Store Street Garda Station, and they agreed to meet at the Cobblestone. Brennan had been known to sneak off from Christy Burke's to the Cobblestone, which was celebrated far and wide for its trad music sessions. The pub's owners, the Mulligans, poured a more than decent pint as well. There was a light mist as Brennan made his way across the north side to Smithfield; as soon as he got to the market square, he could hear a concertina and a bodhran. Good, a session was underway by the windows in the front area of the pub. Shay had not yet arrived, so Brennan ordered his pint and stood leaning against the bar, enjoying the tunes. Then when Shay came in the door, he got his pint and the two of them moved to the back of the room so their conversation would not interrupt the musicians.

"You're going to find this a strange question, Shay."

"Wouldn't be the first. Ask away."

"Now, this is confidential."

"Confidentiality is something I'm well used to."

"True enough. It's one of several things Declan's enemies may know about him, something they think they can use against him if he doesn't keep his gob shut about the things he knows about *them.* Whatever they are."

"Crystal clear so far," Shay said with a laugh, and he took a good swallow of his Guinness.

"Terry's captors made a point of telling him about an old love of Declan's. I hasten to say that Dec knew her before he started walking out with our mother. So, that alone would not constitute material for blackmail."

"Of course it wouldn't."

"But it's the girl's family, her home and history that make it a painful subject."

"Oh, how's that?"

"Are you familiar with Shersfoote House in County Wicklow?"

Shay stared at him. "The Big House? Well, one of the Big Houses in that county."

"Declan's old flame was a daughter of the house. Althea."

"What? Are yeh coddin' me?"

"I'm not. Declan actually worked for the family at Shersfoote House when he was young."

"Worked for the . . ."

"Worked for a prominent member of the Anglo-Irish Ascendancy, accent on the Anglo. The landed gentry."

"Hard to get your head around that, eh Brennan?"

"Oh, yeah. Worked with their vehicles, did some driving, auto repairs, that kind of work. And that pair of blaggards who snatched my brother when they missed their chance to grab Declan, they are threatening to put it about that Dec was 'working for the Brits' when he was otherwise an upstanding, trusted member of the IRA. And of course, Shay, he was not in any way betraying his brothers in arms or the republican cause. We came clean with him about what we had learned, and he fessed up about the girlfriend. But what he was really doing on the grand estate, as your Garda instincts would probably tell you, was looking the place over, for whatever he might be able to nick for the benefit of the RA. He was, as the saying goes, casing the joint. Any guns on the premises? Almost certainly, as the toffs would be keen on hunting foxes. Money, jewels? What might be there for the taking? I don't know what, if anything, he lifted from the place. Maybe he backed off a bit once he developed a grá for the daughter of the family."

"Mother of God! That man's life. They should make a film of it."

"Oh, he'd not be after that kind of publicity. But come here to me, Shay. There's more to the story. And this part, we're fairly sure Declan doesn't know. She had a child, a boy."

"You're havin' me on! Another Burke? Your big brother!"

"But he wasn't acknowledged as a Burke. I don't know how the young one reacted to this, but we think the family arranged to marry her off to a man much more suitable, don't you know. Eminently more suitable than Declan Burke, a low-life Paddy who tinkered with their cars and drove them from place to place and — unbeknownst to them, of course — answered to his officer commanding in the IRA. So, Althea took as her husband this good Anglo-Irish chap, a young man from the best sort of family. There was a marriage, a birth, and the birth certificate would read Dwight Frederick Earnshaw."

"Jaysus, you have to feel sorry for the young one, the daughter manipulated by her family like that."

"Yes, and was she haunted by it ever since?"

"So, what's the story, Brennan? Where do I come into this? You're thinking the son is behind this threat against Declan?"

"I don't know what to think. The other thing about this Earnshaw, like the man who is on record as his father, is that he's a military man. British Army."

"You're jokin' me! This is like something from the telly."

"I only wish. No, it's the truth. Now, we learned all this at that little museum in County Wicklow, in the village near Shersfoote House. And another piece of the puzzle is that Earnshaw is apparently serving right here on this island."

"He's serving with a unit in the North?"

"He is. That's all we know about him. Of course, I can't see him being behind this move against Declan. That seems to have been the work of some disgruntled republicans. The pair that snatched Terry in place of Declan, they threatened to use this secret love affair as something to hold over Dec's head; they would go public with it, if Dec didn't keep his gob shut about whatever the other secret is. They'd portray him as a traitor who worked for the other side. The Brits. No, our interest in Earnshaw is more personal. Does he know the truth, who his real father is? Would his mother have told him? Somehow I doubt it. Or did the man who he thinks of as his father go through some kind of crisis and tell him the secret of his parentage?"

"I'm sure you're right that you have nothing to fear from this brother of yours, a soldier of the occupying power! At least nothing personal."

"But here's the thing, Shay. Even without any connection to the kidnapping and the threats, Terry and I . . ." He looked at their glasses on the table. "The well's run dry here. I'll get us a refill." He got up and went to the bar, returning a couple of minutes later with two full glasses.

"Go raibh maith agat."

"Fáilte romhat." He took out his pack of cigarettes and lit one up. "Terry and I would like to see him, get a glimpse of him. As I say, as far as we know, Declan was never told about the boy's existence, and we'll not be upsetting him with that news. But here we are, only a couple of hours away from a man who is our brother, or half our brother. Yeah, I'm sure it sounds childish. *We wanna see our big brother!* What good could it possibly do? I can't claim any justification beyond curiosity. We've seen a photo of him. One of the photos at the museum. He looks a lot like our brother Patrick."

"Sure, you'd like to get a look at him. That's only natural."

"And now for the next part. Perhaps I'm being fanciful here, but you being with the Gardaí, maybe you have some information from beyond our border, information about military matters up there. Oh, as soon as I say it, I realize how foolish it sounds. That you, a Dublin guard, not a military man, would have all kinds of inside knowledge of the doings of the British Army in the other jurisdiction on this island. But I don't know. You might hear things from time to time, and well, there you have it."

"It's not all that foolish, Brennan. Of course, we've always received information about the conflict up there, attacks by soldiers or acts in which members of shadowy army units colluded with the loyalist paramilitaries. And attacks against soldiers. We hear names, places where army units are stationed. I, em . . ." Shay turned his head, looked around the pub as if the wrong set of ears might hear his words. He lowered his voice, which made it hard for Brennan to hear him over the sound of the musicians up by the front window. "I have a contact — contacts — know a couple of Nordie men."

Brennan's impression was that there was one contact in particular, and the cop in Shay wanted to gloss that over. He said nothing and waited.

"I could ask a question or two, see if I can find out whether there is any info about a soldier named Dwight Earnshaw."

"I would be very grateful to you, Shay. Again! And Terry would too. I'll leave it in your capable hands. What say we move up to the front and take in some of that music?" By now, there were two guitars and a fiddle, and a young man stood to sing "Dublin in the Rare Auld Times" and sounded so convincing you could believe he'd been alive and present during those rare auld times.

ꟹ

Brennan took a call from Shay the following morning, and they arranged to meet in half an hour's time on Custom House Quay. The weather was kind to them, cloudy but no rain yet. Brennan and Terry waited between the River Liffey and the superb neoclassical building that was the Custom House. Brennan was well familiar with it and had always enjoyed looking at the building's keystones, elaborately carved faces depicting fourteen different river gods, one for each of the major rivers in Ireland. Shay came along shortly after the Burkes arrived. They greeted him, and he told them of a plan for Belfast. "I've a contact for you in Belfast."

"Jesus! You work fast, DI Rynne!" Terry exclaimed.

"Of course I do, Terry. I'm no liúdramán!" No loafer. "You'll meet your man this evening at the Boat Ashore. It's a bar in Sandy Row. The two of you will have to do some role-playing. You're going to be tourists from the States or Canada, and you'd better be Prods. We're talking about Sandy Row, after all." Sandy Row, as Brennan knew, was a Proddy — Protestant — area of Belfast. "The man who is going to meet you will come upon you as if by accident, and he'll decide he'd better try to help these two clueless tourists on their first visit to Belfast. Bring a street map of the city, and be hunched over it at a table in the bar."

"Who —" Brennan started to ask but got a warning look from Shay, and he realized he was not to know who Shay's contact was in Belfast. Was the man a member of the police force there, a pal of Shay's, or was he something else? Shay and the Rynne family were known to be sympathetic to the republican cause; Shay's father, Talkie Rynne, had served time for his rebel activities many years ago. Was the Belfast man a republican; might he even be an informer of some kind reporting to Shay? In Shay's role as a Garda, or in his civilian life? Those were the kinds of questions you *did not ask* in Ireland.

"The man will tell you his name is Reggie, and that's all you have to know about him. You and Terry will be George and Will from, I don't know, Minnesota or Toronto."

"Thank you so much, Shay. Greatly appreciate it. So we head up north today."

"Reggie says that will work as well as any other day for your . . . your outing in Belfast. You'll have no trouble finding the bar in Sandy Row."

"No worries, we'll find it. Sandy Row. The Boat Ashore." Brennan laughed. "Sounds like a song we all know."

Shay laughed along with him. "You'll see when you get there."

CHAPTER XVIII

Brennan

Brennan and Terry announced to their father that they wanted a bit of a break and had come up with an impromptu plan to see the Giant's Causeway on the north coast of Ireland. The legend was that the Irish giant Finn McCool had built a line of stepping stones, a causeway, so he could walk across to Scotland to confront his rival, a Scottish giant named Benandonner. But after they met, the Scot fled back to his homeland and ripped up the causeway, leaving the stones as they are today. The scientific explanation is that the stones were formed by volcanic activity nearly sixty million years ago. It is a stunning sight, composed of forty thousand hexagonal basalt stone columns of varying heights. A few years ago, the Giant's Causeway had been declared a World Heritage Site. So, a perfectly credible reason for Brennan and Terry to go to Connolly Station and board a train for the North. They knew their father well enough to know he'd have no wish to come along on a sightseeing expedition. And they knew that Donal and Barry were on duty as watchmen, and bodyguards, to protect him.

But before they left, the three of them made calls home to wife, mother, and pastor, telling them that they'd be extending their "holiday" a little longer than anticipated. No, not sure how much longer. The original plan had been to fly home at the end of the month. Well, tomorrow was the thirtieth of June, so that was not going to happen. They were now thinking they'd probably stay for another couple of weeks or so. The truth of the matter was that they had no idea how long it would take to sort things out. But Terry had contacted his airline and had come up with a couple of options for the middle of July. That was as close as they could get to a new timeline. They each apologized and came up with a fiction to explain the delay. People they wanted to see, things they wanted to do. After all, it had been more than forty years since Declan had been in Ireland, so he had a lot of catching up to do. Nothing was said about any *troubles* they had encountered during this homecoming visit to Ireland. Father Burke's call to Monsignor O'Flaherty went fine; O'Flaherty could not imagine anyone being in a rush to leave Ireland, his family's ancestral land. Terry and Declan had to undergo a bit of interrogation, but they got it done.

When Brennan and Terry headed out, neither of them mentioned previous visits to Belfast, which, to understate things, had not always gone off without incident. They had a role to play today, and they dressed for the part. They costumed themselves as respectable tourists for the journey or, more to the point, for their appearance in the Boat Ashore bar in Belfast. They wouldn't go overboard, so to speak. Nothing gaudy: just short-sleeved shirts, khaki trousers on Brennan, jeans on Terry. No wide-brimmed hats, no cameras hanging from straps around their necks. And they had decided on mild American accents: not New York, not the South, just what Brennan understood to be Midwestern speech. The world was more familiar with Americans — for too many reasons to count — than with Canadians, so they thought Yanks would draw less curiosity than Canucks. They took an afternoon train from Dublin up the coast to Belfast. Even though it was a Saturday in the summer, the train was not crowded. Not a big tourist destination, Belfast. But the two-hour trip provided lovely green fields and hills for viewing along the way.

They signed themselves in to a hotel in the city centre; there were maps available at the reception desk, so they took one of those and consulted it over lunch. Then they set out walking through the city streets. When they got to Great Victoria Street, they turned left, heading south. They passed by the Grand Opera House, an elaborate nineteenth-century building of red brick and light-coloured plaster work, with onion domes on either side of a triangular rise in the roof. Then there was the Europa Hotel, known far and wide as the most bombed hotel in Europe. Brennan had heard that it had been attacked more than thirty times. They continued walking until they reached Hope Street and turned right.

"Hope Avenue on my escape route from East Wall Road, and now Hope Street?" Terry remarked. "Am I to see a deep meaning in this, Father Burke? Should we take encouragement from this?"

"I'm trying not to say 'I hope so,' but what else can I say?"

"Well, there's Sandy Row," Terry said, pointing ahead, "so we'll have to drop the mysticism and all references to your priestly state."

"So we shall," Brennan agreed as they veered left onto Sandy Row.

"And no making the sign of the cross when we pass their churches." Many people in Ireland, even if lapsed from the faith, made an automatic sign of the cross whenever they walked past a Catholic church. Not that there would be any Catholic churches in Sandy Row.

No one could be left in doubt about which side of the sectarian divide this community was on: red, white, and blue union flags — Union Jacks — were flying everywhere, and there were murals proclaiming allegiance to the British Crown and celebrating the gunmen of the loyalist paramilitaries. Brennan and Terry were in plenty of time, so they strolled along the street past the shops and lanes of two- and three-storey red-brick houses until Terry checked his watch and gave Brennan the eye. The plan was that Reggie would be in place by half past five, after which the Burke brothers — now to be known as Will and George — would happen upon the Boat Ashore and walk in for a refreshing drink. It was twenty-five past the hour, so they made their way to the pub, which sat on the corner of the street and a narrow laneway. A mural on a side wall illustrated the theme of the place:

a boat near the shore of a river, and a man dressed in a tweed jacket and tartan kilt working the oars as the bow floated up to the shore. Terry sang, sotto voce, "Sandy row the boat ashore, hallelujah." When they entered the building, they saw a long mahogany bar with taps and bottles and a few drinkers in place. Some of the tables were occupied, but the place was not full. Another mural reinforced the theme of the bar, and Brennan nudged his brother. In this representation, the kilted man — Brennan assumed he was Sandy — was again rowing his boat towards the shore. But there was more: in another boat farther out in the same direction was a red-haired bearded man all dressed in green, with the name Mick in yellow letters on his shirt. It couldn't be more obvious: this was a "mick," an Irishman, and the full name for Mick was of course Michael. Poor oul Michael was rowing his boat ashore, but he was way behind the Ulster Scot, Sandy, who was destined to reach the shore well before Michael. Reach the shore and presumably lay claim to it. It was a sectarian jibe, no question, but Brennan enjoyed it nonetheless. At least it didn't show a man cutting his hand off and throwing the bloody hand onto the land, making him the first to touch the land and thus assert his claim. That was the legend of the Red Hand of Ulster. But enough of that; it was time for the Burke brothers to get into their act as George and Will, who knew very little about the history or landmarks of Belfast.

Terry started things off. "I wonder if we can get a boat, George, rent one or something. Just for a couple of hours."

"Maybe so. We'll look into it. But let's get a nice cool drink first. I don't want to walk around all day full of beer! So let's order something smaller. Whiskey."

"Good idea." And they each ordered a Bushmills. Good Protestant whiskey. With ice. They chose a table, far from the bar, and Terry pulled the street map out of his pocket. They bent their heads over that, chatting about what they'd like to see next and how to get there.

"Need some help there, lads?" The Belfast voice came from the bar, and they turned towards it.

"We'd really appreciate it!" Brennan replied in his impersonation of a Midwest American. "We want to see as much of this city as we can."

The man was of medium height, stocky, with wavy dark hair pushed back from his forehead. He got up from his bar stool and came to the table. "Mind if I take a wee seat here?"

"Please do," Terry urged.

"Where are you from?"

"We're from Duluth, Minnesota," Terry claimed. "I'm Will, and this is George." They all shook hands, and their contact introduced himself as Reggie.

"So, where d'you want to go from here?"

"Well, we're planning to see the Ulster Museum. It doesn't look that far away."

"Aye, it's a nice walk along University Road there." His finger traced the route on the map. "And the Botanic Gardens are there as well."

"Hey, yeah, it would be great to see that," Terry agreed. "And what's that famous clock? Our dad worked repairing clocks and watches back home in Minnesota. And he was real good at his work. So good, he ended up buying the business!"

"He sure was," Brennan concurred. "Pop made sure we were never late for ball practice. So, yeah, we'd like to see that clock. Memorial clock, is it? Something like that?"

"The Albert Memorial Clock. You'd want to take a bus or a taxi. See here, it's a bit of a distance."

There followed a bit more tourist information, and then, still hunched over their map, George and Will got what they were looking for from Shay Rynne's contact in Belfast. He placed a piece of paper on the map, and they all pretended to be studying the map, as the man said quietly, "Write down the number where I can ring you at half eight this evening."

Good thing George had the hotel's receipt in his wallet. He copied the phone number onto the slip of paper. "That's one thing," Reggie said, sotto voce, "and there's also this. The man you want to see, he drinks in a bar called . . ." The Crown and Sword? The Soldier's Rest? Brennan imagined some likely names for a soldier's local. But when Reggie flipped the paper over, Brennan saw the name Gin Millie's and the address. Reg continued to speak quietly, saying, "Yer man has the rank of major and is posted to Thiepval Barracks in Lisburn. He and his fellow officers drink in this place two or three evenings a week, usually after an early supper on a Tuesday, Wednesday, and Thursday. Even in good, solid loyalist Lisburn, they take no chances, and the place is heavily guarded. Inside and out, armed guards, and you'll be searched with a metal detector on the way in. You'll go in as tourists; I'll leave it to you to come up with a reason to be there. You'll be able to spot him there, but don't try to speak to him. That would draw too much interest."

Reggie stood up and said in a louder voice, "So you've a better idea how to get where you're going now, gentlemen?" The word "now" sounded like a mix of "nye" and "nar."

"Yes," they both replied. "Thanks very much, Reggie." He raised his hand in acknowledgement and returned to his place up at the bar. They stayed on for a few more minutes and then left with another "thank you" and walked out into the light rain falling on Sandy Row.

They took a bus back to their hotel near Saint Anne's, the Anglican cathedral, and had an early supper in the hotel's restaurant. Then they headed out for a walk through the streets of the city centre. The British Army had scaled back its presence in the city; no longer were there uniformed soldiers regularly patrolling the streets. Brennan caught sight of an odd-looking structure, a long triangular building with a rounded corner. "This is obviously the local version of the Flatiron Building," Brennan said. "I've heard about this place, and it's all good. Bittles Bar." So in they went and enjoyed the friendly service and a lovely, creamy pint of Guinness. Then they returned to their room to await the phone call.

It came right on time at half eight. "Here's the other adventure I've planned for you. Thought you might enjoy seeing two aspects of yer man. What I'm going to tell you now is how you can see him in his official role, which he won't be in when you see him later in the club. Get yourselves over to Ballymurphy tomorrow morning, ten o'clock." He gave Brennan the address in the Ballymurphy housing estate, a strong nationalist-republican area of the city. "It's a room used, well, used by fellas I know." Fellas Reggie knows? Brennan knew better than to ask. "There's a key box beside the door. The number is nine eight four two. There's no significance to the number; otherwise, someone would cop on to it. That will open the box, and you'll find the key inside. Go upstairs to the back bedroom where you'll see a television and a video recorder. It's set to the place on the tape where the man you're interested in is giving a wee funeral oration over the grave of a fallen soldier. He only speaks for a couple of minutes, but you'll get the idea. Then turn it off and leave the house. Leave the key in the box and shut it securely."

"We will. Thank you very much, Reg."

"Oh, wait! A correction. I told you that the men from the barracks usually go to Gin Millie's on evenings in the middle of the week. But my information now is that they're going off somewhere next week. Middle of the week. On manoeuvres, I suppose! But from what I've heard over the years, if they're going to miss those regular shifts at the bar, they go on the weekends. So you'll have to try that. Tomorrow night, or maybe they'll be there on Monday."

"You're well informed about the British Army's movements, Reg." Brennan heard a chuckle at the other end of the line. "That's what we'll do. Thanks, Reg."

"Best of luck."

ᔕ

Brennan had not been sure what he and Terry would have done about weekday evenings at the bar. Probably return to Dublin and come back again for one of those nights. Either way, they would have needed another story for their father, in addition to the Giant's Causeway tale. Now, with their assignment in Ballymurphy tomorrow and their only opportunity to catch sight of their quarry being tomorrow night or Monday, it hardly seemed worth the effort to return to Dublin and then circle back to Belfast and Lisburn the next day. Well, they'd wait till tomorrow and come up with another line of bull.

On Sunday morning, they boarded a bus to West Belfast and found their way to the Ballymurphy housing estate. They walked up to the end house in a terrace of brown-roofed, beige-walled houses. They lost no time opening the key box and going inside; they figured it might not be a good idea to linger outside and be noticed. They found the television and VCR in the back bedroom and followed the instructions to see what Reg had arranged for them. The recording showed a scene in a cemetery, with uniformed British soldiers surrounding an open grave. A young squaddy said, "Farewell, Harry," saluted, and backed away.

Then another man stepped forward. He turned his head and looked all around, and Brennan gasped. It was as if his brother Patrick Burke was standing in the graveyard in the uniform of a British Army major. Older, but he had the same bright blue eyes, similar shape to the face. "Sergeant Helmsley, it was an honour to serve with you. You were a valiant soldier in the service of Her Majesty the Queen, in the service of our great empire." Major Dwight Earnshaw spoke in the upper-crust voice of an upper-crust member of British society, or the Anglo-Irish version of it on the island of Ireland. "The men who served with you and fought alongside you appreciated your good humour, your skill, and, most of all, your courage in battle and on the streets of Northern Ireland. You never once let the terrorists intimidate you. In your last moments, in that ambush, you stood facing the terrorists and opened fire on them even as you knew you were outnumbered. You had always stood ready to die in battle; nothing made you hesitate, not for one minute. I promise you, dear friend, your brothers in arms will finish this battle. We will put a stop to the terrorists and restore peace to this province, and it will maintain its position as a valued part of the empire. We shall achieve victory, and we shall always remember your service and valour in achieving that most honourable goal!"

Brennan and Terry were silent for a long moment, then Terry said, "Well, I don't foresee our father and this son embracing after a lifetime apart, do you?"

"I do not. A father who would be considered a terrorist, a son who would be considered an enemy soldier."

"And what about us?"

"We're this close, only a few miles. How can we resist the temptation to have a look at him?"

"If we don't take the opportunity presented to us, Bren, I know I'll be waking up at three in the morning thinking, *We were this close!*"

"I know. Let's clear out of here, and we'll move on to the next scene in our little drama."

They left the house, locked up, and deposited the key in the box.

"You know what happened here in 1971."

"Oh, yes."

Ten unarmed civilians had been shot and killed. It was known that nine of them had been shot by British soldiers, and most likely all ten. An eleventh victim died of a heart attack. A priest, Father Hugh Mullan, was shot in the back after he went forward to attend to an injured man. Shot and killed. Brennan felt the outrage all over again, as he walked through the Ballymurphy housing estate. "One of the victims was the mother of eight children. And Father Mullan had something white in his hand, which he had raised and was waving as a white flag. Isn't that recognized the entire world over as a flag of surrender or truce, a signal saying *I am not going to shoot. I am not going to fight*? And they bloody well shot him! Him and all those others."

Terry replied, "Every time I hear these terrible stories, I think I should have moved over here years ago and joined the fight. Taken up arms against the occupying force."

"I hear you." Then, "We'll walk back through the Falls as long as the rain keeps up." Keeps up and doesn't come down from the clouds. The Falls was one of the main Catholic areas of the city.

"So, Bren," Terry said. He spoke softly, even though there was no one else close enough to hear. "What do you make of our man Reggie? Or whatever his real name is."

"An inside source, inside the republican movement, an IRA man, reporting to Shay? Reporting to a member of the police force of the Republic of Ireland. We can be damned sure he's not reporting to the peelers up here, the Royal Ulster Constabulary!"

"Certainly not."

Brennan wondered, but didn't give voice to it, if Reggie was reporting to Shay not in Shay's role as a copper but as a man sympathetic to the republican cause, sympathetic to the Provisional IRA.

They walked along the Falls Road, with its bars and republican murals, its Irish tricolour flags. They passed the Royal Victoria Hospital and, farther along, Saint Peter's (Catholic) Cathedral. Father Burke said a mea culpa for having missed Mass on a Sunday morning. Then they came up to the twenty-storey Divis Tower. "You know the story of that place, do you, Ter?"

"Yeah. The British Army had the top couple of floors, had to fly in and out of it by helicopter! The only way they could safely get in and out." He turned to his brother. "You know what I'm going to do, Brennan?"

"I won't even try to guess."

"I'm going to put up a new building. Turn it into a café or a bar and bill it as the 'Building Without a History.' Promote it as the only place in Ireland, north or south, with no history, no bad memories."

"And no good ones. No stories. Nobody would bother to come. Nobody would know who to expect inside. It would be the most boring place on the entire island. You'd be out of business in a month, Terry. Stay up in the air, in a jetliner, where you don't want too much by way of excitement."

"All right, that's what I'll do. So, we'll try Lisburn tonight and hope our man — our brother — puts in an appearance. But if he doesn't, do we stay and try again tomorrow?"

"We've come this far; we won't want to give up if staying tomorrow gives us another chance."

"Right. So, what do we tell our dear old da?"

"You're the storyteller, Terrence. What do you say?"

"Well, we've already seen the Giant's Causeway. Except we haven't." He turned to look at Brennan. "How about we go there this afternoon?"

"Good plan. It is definitely worth seeing."

"And then if we stay tomorrow night, we'll say we wanted to see . . . I don't know."

"We'll come up with something. Best idea is to rent a car. Let's see to that now."

ග

So, they went back to the hotel, arranged to rent a car, and drove up the coast to see the forty thousand rock columns along the shore. The weather was fine so they enjoyed stepping out on some of those six-sided stones. Then they returned to Belfast and, in the late afternoon, took the short drive to Lisburn, a few miles southwest of Belfast. The city had a lovely market square, and they stopped at a little restaurant for supper. The waitress was friendly, clocked them right away as tourists, and urged them to explore the Castle Gardens and, if they were still in town tomorrow, the museum and the new Irish Linen Centre. Will and George, avid tourists the pair of them, took in everything she said and thanked her. After leaving the restaurant, they did take a stroll through the lush Castle Gardens, with its old stone and brick walls, mature trees, and chattering birds. Then it was time to head for Gin Millie's. "It's a good thing for us," Brennan said, "that they started allowing bars to open on Sundays here in Norn Iron. Just a few years ago."

"Amen to that, brother. The kindly authorities here in Norn Iron have given us the opportunity to spot our very own *contradiction in terms*, our new older brother."

"Ah, Dwight Earnshaw's age and placement in the family are not the only contradictions in this drama."

When they arrived at the bar, they made note of two very large men standing in the doorway. The men eyed them, looked them up and down, but did not proceed to search them before they entered the premises. Perhaps security had been relaxed somewhat since Reggie had obtained his information. But in Brennan's view, anybody who tried to cross these two guardians would live to regret it. If they lived.

Gin Millie's was like so many other bars in this country, north and south. The long dark-wood bar with taps and gleaming bottles of spirits, stools at the bar, tables scattered around the room. Gin Millie was personified in a metal poster as the quintessential "bar wench" with blonde puffy hair and a puffy-sleeved white blouse cut low in the front. She was pouring gin from a bottle into a glass and giving a cheeky smile to the punters as she did so.

"I'm usually a beer drinker," George the tourist announced to the barman, "but what the heck — if we're in a gin place, we should have the gin." He turned to his companion. "Right, Will?"

"Bring it on!"

The barman greeted the lame humour with a polite laugh and said, "Tonic? Lime?"

"Oh, right," George responded. "Yeah, sure."

They took their drinks to a table in the middle of the room and sat down to wait. It was half an hour or so before the invasion occurred. A dozen or so men marched in, and nobody would mistake them for anything but what they were. The short hair, the confident demeanour, and the British and Scottish accents identified them as the British Army men who colonized the place on a regular basis. They greeted the barman and some of the drinkers and were given enthusiastic greetings in return. This was, after all, Lisburn. Not the Falls Road in Belfast. The men stood at the bar to put in their orders for gin, beer, stout, and whiskey. They then moved off to occupy a table near the back of the room. One of the doormen came inside and sat on the vacant stool at the end of the bar with a good sightline to the soldiers' table. Or, George corrected himself, the officers' table. Officers' club, perhaps. Even the fellows who spoke without the polished voices of the better schools in Old Blighty, those who had made their way up from the lower orders, had the confidence and bearing of officers, not of the squaddies from the lower ranks.

George and Will surveyed them from their watching post, as discreetly as they could, but there was no one in the group who looked like the man they had seen in the graveside video. Their brother was not at the table. The tourists stayed on for another hour and a half, switching to non-alcoholic beverages after pleading a "low tolerance for the stronger stuff!" George imagined the smirks that line would get from anyone who knew the Burke brothers and their far-from-low tolerance for drink. They both tried to maintain the look of men having a wonderful night out, but the disappointment was a bitter one. As they were leaving, Will called over to the barman, "Hope to see you again soon!" Which they would, in their second attempt the following night.

"So, Bren, what will we do tomorrow before we hit the gin mill again? And what's our story for Da this time? How about Derry? You've been there, right?"

"I have, and it's brilliant. But it's too much to take in, if we just have part of a day there. Too much to see, too much history to reflect upon. Saint Columba in the sixth century, the Siege of Derry in 1689, the Battle of the Bogside, Bloody Sunday. Let's just say you'll not be constructing your building with no history in Derry. But I was thinking we could take a drive to Armagh, see where Saint Patrick set up his church in the year 445."

"Sure. And Declan will have no trouble believing that you want to honour the great saint there, Father Burke."

They managed to ring Declan just before he retired to his bed chamber, and Terry gabbed to him about all the things he'd seen and said they'd decided to stay on and see Armagh before returning to Dublin. How was Declan? "Uh, grand, I'm grand." No further trouble? "Eh? What was that?" He had the sound of a man whose mind was elsewhere. Any trouble? "No, no." Barry and Donal are on the job? "They are." Good. They would see him on Tuesday.

CHAPTER XIX

Brennan

They got into the car on Monday morning, the first of July, with Terry at the controls, and drove through the farms and fields of counties Down and Armagh. Terry could not resist breaking into song, and Brennan joined in. It was Tommy Makem's song "Four Green Fields" with its reference to the field that was still in bondage, the one they were in now, the Province of Ulster. When they arrived in the lovely city of Armagh, Terry's co-pilot pointed out the two great cathedrals, both named for Saint Patrick, facing each other from opposite hills. "There are the twin spires of the Catholic cathedral, and across the way you see the square tower of the Anglican one. It's actually the Anglican cathedral that stands where Patrick built his church all those centuries ago. The Church of Ireland cathedral."

"There it is again," Terry replied. "Church of Ireland. The acknowledgement, no doubt unintentional, that these counties are part and parcel of Ireland. The Troubles are over!"

"If only . . ."

They parked the car, walked around the city for a few minutes, then headed up the hill to the Catholic cathedral. Once again, Brennan marvelled at another impressive house of worship. Construction took place over many decades starting in the 1800s, but it was built in the Gothic revival style. The brothers knelt to say a prayer and then walked down the hill and up the other hill across the way where the other — the rival? — cathedral stood. Destroyed and rebuilt several times over the centuries.

"It was on this hill that Patrick built his church. And as if the link with Patrick were not enough, we'll go around to the north side of the church, and you'll see another famous name." They walked around the building, and Brennan said, "Here we are: the burial site of Brian Boru."

Brian was the High King of Ireland in the eleventh century and ancestor of the O'Briens of today. He was famed for his army's victory over the Vikings in the Battle of Clontarf in 1014. In fact, he had some Vikings on his side, and his Viking opponents had some Irish allies. Nothing was ever quite straightforward in Irish history. They saw a plaque, which read "Near this spot on the north side of the great church was laid the body of Brian Boroimhe slain at Clontarf A.D. MXIV." And there was a grave marker with an image of the king engraved on it and a harp. Brian was slain not in the battle but afterwards in his tent. The story that had come down through history was that as the Vikings retreated, they found Brian in his tent. It was Good Friday in the year 1014, and he was at prayer. A leader of the Vikings, Brodir, slew him there. People who have studied Brian say he would almost certainly have reached for his sword and fought for his life. As the Burke brothers stood and gazed at the marker, Brennan once again reflected on the long and turbulent history of the country of his birth.

They descended the hill and took another walk around the city, then stopped for a bite to eat and headed back again to Belfast. Terry, taking on the character of a stage Oirishman, said, "So, Father Burke, the Prods robbed us of another one. They took over the Catholics' first cathedral here, the one connected to our great saint and our high king, just as they did in Dublin, grabbing Christ Church and leaving us with Saint Mary's *Provisional* Cathedral."

"Good thing our oul fella and his comrades in arms aren't with us today. Wouldn't want another round of destruction and rebuilding."

"If you say so."

On the road back to Belfast, Brennan said, "I think we should get a hotel in Lisburn this time, Ter. After all, our base of operations is Gin Millie's, so there's drink involved. Instead of driving back to Belfast, we stay in Lisburn."

"Hard to disagree with that. By the time we get back to our place in Belfast, we'll likely be too late to check out without paying for another night, but who cares?"

"That's of little consequence, compared to what we're trying to do."

So, when they were back in West Belfast, they walked up to their hotel's reception desk, and Terry told the receptionist that they had decided to go to Lisburn for the night. As expected, they would be charged for the night, but the young woman gave them a couple of suggestions for a hotel in Lisburn. She used her computer to print off the names, addresses, and phone numbers and handed them over. Terry and Brennan thanked her and went up to their room. It took only a few minutes, and Terry had a reservation for a place in Lisburn's city centre.

They made the drive and easily located their new hotel. It was a lovely three-storey white building only a few blocks from Gin Millie's.

ᔓ

That evening, Brennan and Terry, back in character as George and Will, passed muster with the doormen guarding Gin Millie's, and they were seated in the bar once again, this time with pints of beer on the table in front of them. "Not that we didn't enjoy the gin last night," Will had assured the barman. "But we're beer guys, and I know it's all good stuff here." And they went easy even on that, not knowing how long they would have to wait for the family reunion, which would be no reunion at all. The other drinkers ranged from solitary quiet sippers to loud, fun-loving boozers well on their way to being langered, calling to each other from one table to another. George and Will made a point of looking amused when someone was being a comical card, and clueless and curious when something was mentioned that American tourists from Minnesota might not understand. Terry kept sneaking glances at his watch as the minutes went by without any British Army presence in the bar.

But eventually they arrived. Half a dozen of them. They were not in uniform, but again their appearance, their bearing, would mark them as soldiers anywhere. The barman greeted a couple of them by rank. And Major Dwight Frederick Earnshaw was amongst them. The Burkes recognized him straight away, looking as he did so much like their brother Patrick. The photo they had seen had been taken years before, and his hair was grey now, a few lines in his face. But it was their man. The soldiers — the officers — marched to the bar and ordered their usual tipple, then headed for their back table. They had to pass Brennan and Terry's table on the way by. Brennan knew his brother — his acknowledged brother Terry — well enough to know he was bursting to get the man into a conversation. But they could not reveal themselves in any way that would disclose the secret of their relationship, biological only as it was, with the major.

The man did not pass them without looking at them though. He glanced at each of them in turn, his eyes resting longer on Terry. Brennan tried to imagine what it would have been like if Patrick was with them; Earnshaw would not have been able to miss the resemblance. But it was Terry here. And being Terry, he could not resist the temptation to speak up. He kept his cover, though, and spoke in the Midwestern American tones he had been affecting during his time in the North. "It's great to see a bunch of soldiers out having a good time! You may not be in uniform, but I know soldiers when I see them. Our dad was an army man, back home. Fought in the Pacific, last year of the war. Second World War. He sure needed a drink of beer when he got home from there!"

"Yes, I'm sure he did." The voice was pure Anglo-Irish, accent on the Anglo. "Americans, are you?"

"Yeah! We're your typical American tourists! Not always knowing where we're going, but we're real interested in learning about new places. It's a real pleasure to be here in Ireland."

"You are in Northern Ireland."

"Oh, I know, I know! Northern Ireland is part of England. I mean, the United Kingdom."

"Quite so. Welcome to Ulster." He gave them a terse nod — Brennan thought it a condescending nod — and went off to join the occupying forces at the back of the room.

When he was out of hearing range, Terry said to Brennan, "Christ, that exchange is all we'll have to remember him by. I know we can't go up to him and tell him that one of his main opponents on the other side of this war in Ireland is his very own father. Father and son, enemies, and they don't know it."

"And they're not going to know it. We can't do this to our da. We have to keep the secret."

"I know, and we'll keep it. But it's fucking painful!"

"It is." But how painful would it have been if the man knew who the two of them really were? Their history and background. Their shared father. They stayed on, had another beer. When the army needed refuelling, it was two other officers who went to the bar for the drinks. Brennan did not want to prolong this non-encounter, so he persuaded Terry that it was time to go. Neither of them could resist taking a last look at Major Earnshaw. But he didn't notice them as they walked away.

CHAPTER XX

Brennan

The hotel room was comfortable and quiet, but neither of the brothers had a good night's sleep, both of them reliving, over and over, the scene in Gin Millie's. They got into their rented car the next morning, drove back to Belfast, and returned the car. Brennan's mind was in turmoil during the scenic train ride back to Dublin. He and Terry had seen the half-brother they'd never known of. Brennan felt guilty; this was really none of their business. But he also sympathized with what Terry had said after they'd left the bar in Lisburn. "I reverted to childhood when I was there, Bren. I wanted to tell our big brother, *I'm not really a dumb tourist! I served in the U.S. Air Force and I'm an airline pilot! And my brother here is Father Burke with a doctorate from Rome!* How pathetic is that?" Brennan had replied, "It's understandable, Terry. It was mortifying to have to keep up our act as a couple of hick tourists."

As far as he and Terry were concerned, this discovery would remain a secret. He knew that Shay would keep it to himself. The only way it would come out was if Terry's captors decided to use it against their father. If Declan revealed whatever it was that the men were so wound up about, they might bring this out as revenge. Though Brennan could not see what they would gain from doing that. The satisfaction of knowing they had embarrassed Declan, that was all. But Brennan's conversation with Shay came back to him; they had both dismissed the notion that it might have been the half-brother himself who would not want his parentage revealed. Would not want it known that he was the "illegitimate" — Brennan himself did not hold with labelling any child "illegitimate" — son of an IRA man. But would the man even know the secret of his parentage? Earnshaw Senior had come "late to the altar," but at the altar he had stood, and he had taken the Shersfoote daughter as his bride. Back in those days, situations like this were not spoken of as openly as they were now. More than likely, Major Dwight Earnshaw had never doubted that the man who raised him was his own flesh and blood. As for the snatching of Terry and the warning note, it was almost certainly Declan's former comrades who wanted something kept hidden. Terry's kidnappers had threatened to reveal the relationship between Declan and Althea, daughter of the family at Shersfoote House, as "proof" that Declan had been "working for the Brits." Did the men who snatched Terry even know of the existence of the British soldier fathered by Declan Burke?

When Brennan and Terry arrived back home, Declan wasn't there. Nothing to be concerned about, Brennan told himself. But he hadn't noticed the dark green van anywhere outside as they drove into Irishtown, so he decided to ring the number the fellas had given them. He made the call and waited. He was just about to hang up when he heard, "Yeah?"

"Hi. Donal? Barry? Brennan Burke here."

"Howiyeh, Brennan. This is Barry. What's happening? I was over there only a few minutes ago . . ."

"No, nothing to be concerned about, Barry. My brother and I were out of town for a couple of days. Da's not home right now. No reason to suspect anything wrong about that, but I only wanted to check in, see if, well, if anybody's been around the house who shouldn't be here."

"No, Brennan. We've been taking our shifts looking about the place. Sometimes in our van, sometimes on foot. Haven't seen anything that had us concerned."

"All right. Thanks for all this, Barry. Much appreciated."

"No bother. Take care, Brennan."

Brennan filled Terry in on the conversation. "Nothing happening."

"My captors must have decided to cut their losses, stay away. May have figured Dec would bring Finn in on it, and they'd likely know that Finn has some, well, hard men in his circle of acquaintances."

"Finn's men and, as far as they know, the Gardaí. They wouldn't be aware that Shay is keeping this off the books, so they could be worried about the peelers coming down on them if they showed up here."

"Let's hope so. Now, where should we go for a bite to eat? I'm a bit peckish here."

Their father walked in the door then. "How was your tour of the occupied territories?"

"Fascinating, Da." And Terry told of some of the places they had been, what they had seen. And not a word of what they were never supposed to see.

"Now, up with yis," their father said. "We're off to Christy's. Finn has something to tell us."

"What is it?" Terry asked.

"We'll hear it from Finn."

"Let's stop for something to eat on the way," Terry pleaded. "Me belly thinks me throat's been cut!"

"No worries; I'll not see you starve, Terrence."

So they headed out in the car, stopped at a convenience store for some sandwiches, and drove to the family bar. Finn invited them back into his office, where they sat with their sandwiches and pints of Guinness and waited for the news.

"First off," Brennan said, "we want to thank you again for the security detail. They're keeping an eye on things. Good lads."

"They are. I take it nobody's been skulking around the house."

"Nobody. I spoke to Barry."

"Good," said Finn. "Now, I've been asking around. Discreetly, as you might imagine."

"We would expect nothing less," Brennan replied with a smile.

"There's a woman who might know of an incident that somebody would not want revealed."

Brennan glanced over at his father. His eyes were narrowed, his lips clamped shut. Wondering no doubt what this latest revelation might be. He didn't ask.

"Who is she?" Terry asked, since his father didn't.

Finn looked at Declan before replying. "She goes by the name Mairead."

Finally, Declan spoke. "Mairead?"

"Cumann na mBan."

"Ah," said Declan.

The organization's name was bland enough. A literal translation was the Women's Council or Women's Association. But in reality, it was more like a women's army. Cumann na mBan was a republican paramilitary organization for women, dedicated to the overthrow of the British colonial presence in Ireland. With some republicans turning towards a constitutional solution, Cumann na mBan stuck to a more hard-line, militant approach, believing that any accommodation with constitutional politics was tantamount to "selling out."

"The Brits don't want to mess with those lasses," Brennan said lightly.

"Sure they're a fierce band of women," Finn agreed. "Mairead is a member. Has been for decades."

"Did they join the IRA, become part of it?" Terry asked.

Finn shook his head. "Some women join the men, but others prefer to stick with their own outfit, where they can set and follow their own rules. Mairead is very much of that breed." Finn got up from his seat. "Here, I'll show you." He walked over to a cabinet and opened a door, rooted around for a minute, then returned with pieces of paper in his hand. "This was before Brid — Mairead's time, but you get the idea."

He laid a black-and-white photo on the table. It showed a group of women in uniforms with skirts and wide-brimmed hats with one side of the brim turned up. A second picture showed women in winter coats and caps with long guns in their hands.

"So, what's the story?" Terry asked.

"You'd best hear it from Mairead. You'll have to go to Drogheda."

"Drogheda. As a matter of fact, we just saw it from the train window. We were up at the Giant's Causeway and did some other touring. Great view of Drogheda from the train. I've always thought that was a scary-sounding name, *DRAW-huh-duh*. Sounds like something on Halloween!"

"It's had its scary times," Brennan agreed, "especially when that old war criminal Cromwell besieged the town in 1649. I've read reliable accounts that say thousands of our people were killed there. Soldiers and civilians, children, women, and men. Cromwell himself wrote in a report back to England that there were three thousand military casualties and 'and many inhabitants.' I've heard people in Drogheda, and Wexford as well, talk about Cromwell as if the murderous blaggard was there as recently as two weeks ago!"

"Well, our trip to Drogheda won't be a day at the fair," Terry remarked.

"No," said Brennan. "And of course, Terry, we'll want to pay our respects to Oliver Plunkett, saint and martyr. To his head, I mean, since that's all we have left of him after the oh-so-civilized English authorities had him hanged, drawn, and quartered. The head is displayed in Saint Peter's Church."

"I think I'll pass on that if you don't mind, Father Burke."

"Other than all that dreadful history, Drogheda is a lovely town."

"Good, then. We'll go and see the town, have tea with Mairead."

Mairead or whatever her real name was. Brid perhaps, according to Finn's little slip of the tongue.

Finn reached into his pocket and pulled out a slip of paper. "Here's the address and directions she added," he said and passed it to Declan. "She'll be expecting you this afternoon. Four o'clock or so."

"Ah," said Declan. "No time to . . ."

"No time to prepare, get used to the idea?" Finn asked.

"No time to lose," Declan replied. "Well done, Finn." He turned to his sons. "Are we off?" And they left the bar.

No more was said about the mysterious woman soldier in Drogheda. At least not until they got into the car. Brennan said, "I'll be the wheelman. So, Da, who's Mairead? Or the woman who goes by the name Mairead."

"I don't know."

"You don't know?"

"What did I just say to yeh, Brennan?"

"Yet she has something to tell you, which may be related to the events that have plagued your visit here in Dublin."

"I met more than one member of the Cumann na mBan during my . . . my active years here."

"Worked with some of these women?"

"There were occasions when our lads and their lasses went out together on an operation."

As they pulled out from their parking spot, Terry asked, "Are we going right away?"

"Why not?" Brennan replied, and off they went.

There was a splash of rain and then, just as quickly, a blaze of sunshine, and it looked as if it would be a fine day for a road trip, going north from Dublin. They had a view of green fields, grazing sheep, the occasional horse or donkey. In less than an hour, they were in the lovely town of Drogheda, founded in medieval times on the River Boyne. They admired its lofty church spires and the sparkling river running through the town. "We have to see a medieval masterpiece," Brennan said. "Saint Laurence's Gate, built around 1250 and still standing." He drove towards the massive grey stone wall with its two high circular towers and crenellated roof. There was an archway for passing under the wall.

"Wow!" Terry exclaimed, sounding like a child with his first glimpse of a castle, which this resembled.

Brennan said, "Now, I'm sure you're saying to yourselves, *That's not a mere gate; it's a barbican.* And it is." A fortified outpost or gateway, built as a defensive structure at the entrance to a town or a castle.

"That's just what I was going to say," Terry replied. "I was also going to say I hope there are lights on top of it at night to protect it from low-flying aircraft."

"We'll leave that up to you, Captain. Now, Da, read out those directions Finn gave you."

Declan read what Finn had scribbled down, and after a couple of wrong turns, they arrived at their destination. It was in the centre of a terrace of two-storey pebbledash houses, Mairead's painted a light greyish blue. They parked up and walked to the house. Before they had time to knock, the door was opened by a woman who appeared to be in her late sixties, or well-preserved seventies, with dark eyes and grey hair pulled back in a loose knot. She stood tall and straight. The words that came to Brennan's mind were "military bearing." She looked past the three men on her doorstep and scanned the area around them, then stood aside and gestured for them to come inside.

"Tea?" she asked.

They all said yes and thanked her.

"Sit yourselves down, and I'll boil the kettle." Her voice was that of a Dubliner.

Declan sat in an armchair, the brothers on the sofa with the window at their back.

Brennan looked around the sitting room. The walls were a dark blue, the floors a rich, dark wood. There were framed pictures on the walls, a couple of streetscapes of Dublin, some of lush fields surrounded by low stone walls. The mantelpiece was graced with photos of young children and babies. There were no pictures of republican men or women in uniform, no Proclamation of the Irish Republic on the wall. The Burkes made no conversation until the woman came in with the tea things and served them. They thanked her again as they settled back with their cups. She sat across from Declan.

"Declan," she said, looking him in the eye, "I remember." Brennan glanced at his father and got the impression that Declan did not remember. "And?" she said, looking from Brennan to Terry. They introduced themselves.

"Thank you for seeing us, Mairead," Brennan said then, using the name Finn had given them.

"I assume that if your sons are here, Declan, I may speak freely in front of them."

"You may."

"Finn told me what happened to one of you. Terry, wasn't it?"

"It was."

"I have the impression, Declan, that you may not recall the occasion when we met."

"I'm sorry," he said, "I don't. But I'm sure it will come back to me."

"I'm sure it will. You'd be forgiven for not recognizing me. I was twenty years old at the time. I was the one brought in by your boys for the job at one of the houses used by Hoofer Crossan." Declan's lips parted; he stared at her. This had obviously come as a surprise. "There were, shall we say, some tense moments."

"Right. Of course, I remember now. Only wish I didn't!"

"Ah, now, we didn't come out of it too badly. We got what we went for. Or a fairly good haul, anyway."

"Good haul of what?" Terry could not resist asking.

"What we needed at the time. This was a couple of years after the Emergency."

"The emergency known to the rest of the world as the Second World War?" Terry asked.

"The very one," she replied. "We weren't in it; we were neutral. But those years were a low point for the lads. Your father's fellow soldiers." The soldiers of the Irish Republican Army.

"A low point it was," Declan agreed. "So many interned in the Curragh, some of them flogged, some executed. A brutal way for men to be treated by the men they'd once fought beside. So, you're right; there wasn't much action for us in the late 1940s."

"But you were given orders to bring in some much-needed funds and to supplement your supply of arms and ammunition."

"We were."

"Any way you could, from whatever source you could find. Which explains why you were ordered to conduct that raid on Hoofer Crossan's place." She turned to Terry and Brennan. "Hoofer was a great man for the horses. Spent a lot of time at the racetrack. He was the leader of a crime family, and he had a gang of associates. A bunch of tossers."

"They were," said Declan. "What could possibly go wrong there?"

"Would I be right in suspecting something did go wrong?" Terry asked.

"Let's just say there were some tense moments!" Mairead said again. "Crossan would rent or take possession of vacant houses. Short-term lets only." She laughed. "This one was a big detached place out in the suburbs. South of the city. Dublin."

Declan turned to Terry and Brennan. "He was a feckin' psycho. He'd slit your throat if he didn't like the cut of you."

"No pun intended, I'm sure, Da," Terry put in.

"From what I recall," Mairead said, "your father here was given some information about the gang, that their fearless leader would not be home at that time. He'd be at the racetrack. And no doubt his little band of followers would be with him."

"Except," Declan said, "for one or maybe two who'd be guarding the place. The goods were in the cellar. We were to, let's say, overcome their resistance to our entry. No violence, just the threat of it. There was myself and Mairead and . . . em, himself."

"Himself, yes." She laughed and exchanged a knowing glance with Declan. "We'll just refer to him as S."

"Good plan. Now, Mairead's role in this was to be a distraction. Should we call it that?"

She laughed again. "What do they call it now, a honey trap? I was to go to the door and hope it would be answered by the man who had been assigned to guard the place. I would give him a sad story. I'd had a drink before we all went there, so there would be a smell of drink coming off me. The impression I was to create was that of a poor, sad lassie who'd been threatened by her brutal boyfriend and was seeking shelter. Seeking the protection of a big strong man, a big powerful gang. And, well, who knew what I might be willing to offer in return?"

"Not exactly the sort of operation you'd drilled and trained for in the Cumann na mBan."

"No, Declan. Far from it." To Terry and Brennan: "We were our own army, skilled in tactics and in the use of firearms. So this was, to put it plainly, beneath me. Let me show you something."

She got up and left the room. She was back two minutes later with a photograph in her hand. She passed it to Declan.

"Ah, brilliant! This," he said, tapping his finger on it, "was no little honey trap."

He handed it to Brennan. It was an old black-and-white photograph of a young woman in a Cumann na mBan uniform and hat: Mairead when she was in her late teens, perhaps twenty. She had a pistol in her hand, and her face was turned to the camera. She was smiling. Terry leaned over to see the picture. "You look pleased with yourself there, Mairead!"

"I was. We were practising, and I had just hit the middle of the target. Oh, yes, Declan. I was no mere honey trap! But I was willing to assist you boys if it meant more supplies and weapons for the republican cause. Which explains why —"

She was interrupted by a loud rapping on the door. "Who's that now? I'm not expecting anyone."

Brennan heard the clicking of the lock, and the door flew open. There was a clatter as something fell to the floor. Brennan's hand jerked, and tea splashed onto his knee. He heard a gasp and saw his father's hand fly up to his heart. What was happening here? Brennan and Terry sprang to their feet and rushed towards the sound. What they saw was a little boy sprawled in the doorway. On the floor in front of him was a small wooden box painted bright yellow. Drawn on the front were stick figures of a boy and girl with grins on their faces. That little scene, the Burkes' startled reactions, spoke volumes, Brennan reflected, about the strain they were under.

A little voice behind the boy said, "Sure, you've banjaxed it for good this time, Rory!"

"I made it for you, Gran!" Rory shouted. "To put your pictures in, all the pictures of us that you don't have in the frames. But now it's in fookin' pieces!"

Mairead reached down and drew the boy up into her embrace. "No, it isn't, pet. It's only the end of it broken off. We can fix it. We'll do that later. It's lovely! Go raibh maith agat, acushla! Come in, Ashling." She hugged the little girl and kissed her. "Come in, the two of you. We have guests today."

Rory looked to be around seven, Ashling a couple of years younger. They both had black wavy hair and bright blue eyes. "These are my daughter's children, up from Dublin." Gesturing towards the Burkes, she said, "These are old friends of mine." She didn't give their names. The boy looked at them; the girl smiled. "Now, where's your ma?"

"She's gone off," Rory replied. "She's out doing the messages."

"But she'll be coming back," his sister assured them.

"Come into the kitchen. I'll get your crayons and colouring books out. And guess what music I have for you on the compact disc player."

"What music, Gran?" one of the children asked.

"The Barmy Bassoons." And she did an imitation of a bassoon and then a trombone going comically off key. The grandchildren laughed, delighted. Then the disc began to play, and everyone heard an orchestra with foolish sounds coming from the instruments.

Mairead emerged from the kitchen and closed the door behind her. "Ah, she's a dote, little Ashling," she said, taking her seat again across from Declan. "And him. Rory's a character, no question about it. They love listening to that CD. The Barmy Bassoons, a group of musicians who play comically off-key tunes for children.

"Now, where was I? Right. At the door of the leading figure in Hoofer Crossan's gang. Distracting the man on guard until Declan and our other lad could come in and put the frighteners on him." To

Declan, she said, "Your task was to clear out the cellar. You knew they had a supply of weapons and, no doubt, some readies in the form of banknotes that could be put to better use than glorifying a shower of wasters like Crossan's boys."

Declan spoke up then. "We got to work down in the cellar. There was hardly the space to move down there, it was so full of stuff. Bicycles, parts of cars, bits of furniture, all of it stolen. It was my job to find the things we needed, those being weapons, and lug them up the stairs and out to our van. Powerful set of arms on this one," he said, inclining his head towards Mairead. "She stepped in to help with the heavy lifting, once the gang's guardian had been sidelined."

"Yes, the third member of our raiding party, S, had a revolver pointing at the gang member, had him up against the back wall of the cellar, keeping him docile while your father and I helped ourselves to the things the republican movement required. But our heroics were interrupted, weren't they, Declan?"

"They were. We heard a clatter above us, and who came stomping down the stairs but the much-feared leader of the gang. Crossan himself. The face on him! Shocked he was, that someone would resort to thieving. And him with a cellar full of stolen goods. In a house he had taken over. Colonized, you might say. But gougers of that sort don't like to share the wealth."

"They're not ones for sharing. So Crossan comes storming down to the cellar. A fearsome-looking fella. Tall with powerful muscles on him, and his hair cropped in a military kind of style. I remember a nasty twist to his mouth. As Declan told you, he had a reputation for brutality. And he had a gun."

"And I didn't," Declan recalled. "There I was, carrying rifles and pistols out to the van. And then I was inside again with not a weapon to defend myself."

"No, we had left that up to S."

"Fine lot of good that did us. The man he had cornered, Crossan's lieutenant, as soon as he saw the crime boss coming down, he lurched towards S and tried to get his pistol. He didn't manage it, but he knocked it out of S's hand. So our only defender was defenceless. But only for a second or so. S spotted a knife or a tool of some kind with a sharp blade. And he got his arm around his captive, Crossan's man, and held the knife against his throat. Strong he was, S, and him barely into his twenties."

"Then Crossan looked at the three of us, one after the other. Pointed his gun at me and at Declan and ordered us to get over beside S. But our Declan didn't move. Just stared at him with those unwavering blue eyes of his and stayed where he was. I remember my thoughts racing. Wondering what to do. Would I be safer standing apart from everyone else or safer obeying the gunman's commands?"

"I remember it all too well," Declan said. "I thought we'd be better off staying apart. If we were all together, he could fire a volley and get us all. If there was distance between us and he fired at one, another of us might have a chance to run to him, overpower him."

Mairead laughed and pointed her finger at Declan. "Cool under fire, this father of yours."

"That's a fair description of him, all right," Brennan agreed.

"But that could not be said about the third member of our raiding party. S. Remember, Declan?"

Declan made no reply.

"S was petrified. And who wouldn't be? He was the closest to the gunman, and like everybody else, he knew Hoofer Crossan was a vicious fucker. He'd shoot S or any one of us without a moment's hesitation. And it looked as if that was what he was going to do. He stepped closer and pointed the gun right at S. And poor S, what did he do? He begged for his life. 'Please, no! Don't do it! I'm leaving, you'll never see me again! Please!' He was crying. And Crossan basked in it, in the young man's fear. He moved in closer again. And poor S, he . . . pissed himself. You could see the liquid coming out the cuffs of his trousers. It was awful!"

"It was," Declan agreed.

"But Crossan loved it, loved the poor lad's terror, his humiliation. He started to mock him, imitating a baby crying, making remarks about him wetting himself. He was enjoying it so much, he missed what else was happening. Declan here had seen a garden spade, a shovel.

He grabbed it, and as quick as a flash of lightning, he raised it over Crossan and brought it down on his head. Knocked him to the ground, knocked him out. Then I was able to reach over and get S's gun off the floor and point it at Crossan's lieutenant."

"I thought you were going to fire it," Declan said.

"I almost did! But I didn't. Couldn't bring myself to do it, to kill someone who . . . I guess I'll say someone who was not on the battlefield, not our sworn enemy in the republican wars. Anyway, the three of us hightailed it out of there, got into our van with our stash of guns and ammo, and sped off to safety!"

"Jesus!" Terry exclaimed. "What a life you've led! Is that a story you tell the grandchildren at their bedtime?"

She laughed. "No, I'm just kindly little old Nana who tells them fairy tales."

"So," Terry asked, "what was it like in the van, the three of you driving off? The guy who was afraid, who p— What was said about it all?"

"Nothing. We didn't mention his . . . his fear."

"Not exactly the image of the bold Fenian man!"

"No, but I'm sure we can all put ourselves in his place. We can all imagine the same thing happening to us."

That was kind of Mairead, Brennan reflected. How humiliated the young fella must have been, particularly in the company of two stoic, unwavering soldiers like Mairead and Declan.

"Whatever became of S?" Terry asked. "Didn't stay with the 'physical force' side of things, I don't imagine."

"That's the thing," Mairead replied. "He did." She exchanged a look with Declan. "He is, and has been for many years, on the Army Council."

"Army Council?"

Brennan filled in the answer for his brother. "If he's a member of the Army Council, that means he's one of seven men very high up in the Provisional IRA. On the council are the chief of staff, the adjutant general, the quartermaster general. You get the idea."

"This guy is up that high in the RA!" Terry was astonished.

"He is," Declan said. "He made up for his . . . his moment of weakness. Made up for it many times over the years."

"But there's more to the story, unfortunately," Mairead said. "S was so wound up about his shame at the Crossan place that he went out that night and had lashings of drink. And then that same night, he went back. To Crossan's. Drove there, I guess, with all that drink on him. Anyway, he got to the house, put on a balaclava, and broke in to the place. Somehow. He was going after Crossan. I don't know what his intention was: Threaten him if he told of the incident? Kill him? But he was out of luck. Crossan wasn't home, nor was his wife. S went upstairs. Turned out there was somebody there after all. Crossan's young fella, twelve years old. I have no idea whether he was the only person in the house or not. But he heard S, started shouting, ran up to him. Leapt up at him and tried to wrench the balaclava off him. S grabbed him, shoved him off. And the poor child went flying down the stairs. Landed on his face." Mairead cleared her throat. "This is terrible. The boy hit his eye on something, suffered serious damage. Blinded in that eye."

The Burkes all murmured their agreement that this was a terrible outcome for the child.

"There's very few of us that know this," Mairead said. She gave a brief smile. "And never you mind how I know it. The few that have the information have kept quiet all these years. Well, I'm after telling you lot! But you're here for a good reason, given what happened to you, Terry."

Declan was shaking his head. "You may be sure I'd never heard about this till now, the injury to the young lad."

They were all silent for a good long moment, then Brennan spoke up. "Sure the Crossan gang would come for S and kill him if they learned the truth of it."

"Or blind him," Terry put in.

"And not just the Crossan gang," Mairead replied. "If the current members of the RA knew what S had done to the man's son, a child, they'd have taken him out themselves." She looked Declan in the eye and said, "They still might, if they got word of it now.

"He is still a powerful figure after all these years, powerful and respected. And he won't want to lose that. Do you think this awful story is what accounts for the actions taken against your family here? Did S lie awake at night after hearing you'd come back to Ireland, Declan? Terrified that you might reveal his moment of cowardice? And his injury to the boy? The shame would be unbearable for a big man like that. A man on the Army Council!"

"I've never told anyone. Not in all these years. Why the fuck would I? And I didn't know until now what he did to that poor little lad."

"He wouldn't know that you didn't know. The shame and the fear may have overwhelmed his reason. When he heard you were in Dublin, it all came back to him. And he lashed out in a moment of fear, thinking *I'll put a stop to his gallop*. Tried to get you; grabbed your son instead. Had his subordinates do it."

"If it was him at all," Brennan said. Then, "If it was him, do you think you yourself are in danger for having this knowledge, Mairead?"

"Sure, no one has come for me yet!"

CHAPTER XXI

Brennan

After returning from Drogheda and having enjoyed a takeaway supper of steak-and-Guinness pie, Brennan, Terry, and Declan were sitting around their table playing a casual game of poker when they heard a knock on the door. And in walked Finn. They greeted him and invited him in.

"The place is looking good," said the owner of the house. "Would yis like to sign a lease, make this a more permanent stay?"

"Ah, now, that all depends on how things go over the next little while," Declan answered. "Sit down and have a drink, Finn."

Brennan got up, poured everyone a glass of their preferred libation, and they all sat down.

"We missed an opportunity," Finn told them.

"What opportunity was that?" Declan asked.

"A few of our men get together once in a while for a little commemoration. Something like Bodenstown." Brennan knew that an early hero of the republican movement, Wolfe Tone, was buried there.

Republicans held a ceremony every year at his grave in Bodenstown in County Kildare.

"Didn't he get a French fleet to try to overthrow the Brits here?" Terry asked.

"You're right. He made several attempts, but the invasions failed. For Tone and other rebels, it all came to an end in 1798. Tone was arrested, tried, and convicted of treason. Sentenced to be hanged. He died before that could happen. Many of us have never been convinced that he cut his own throat. Anyway, he died in Provost Prison, his body taken for burial in the family grave in Bodenstown."

"You were saying, Finn, that you and some of the other men gather for another ceremony, not in Bodenstown?"

"Oh, we go to Bodenstown in June every year, Terry. Wouldn't miss it. But we also have a commemoration here in Dublin, at Arbour Hill Cemetery. Provost Prison where Tone died was at Arbour Hill."

"I never knew that."

"We've never had a fixed date for our gathering at Arbour Hill. This time it was this past Friday."

"So, the missed opportunity?"

"One of the men who always attends these commemorations is the Army Council man you heard about from Mairead."

"Mairead just referred to him as S and wouldn't give his name."

Finn said, "We'll just keep calling him S. He was at Arbour Hill on Friday."

"Shit," said Terry. "We could have seen him there. But, well, we couldn't very well have gone up to him and said, *Excuse me, sir, but weren't you the fella who, uh, had a failure of nerve at that gun raid?*" Then in a more sombre tone, "And caused injury to a young boy."

"No, that wouldn't do at all," Finn said.

Terry outlined another scenario. "But if we could have seen him, and he could see us — me and Da — would he have reacted in some way that looked like fear? Fear of being remembered for that long-ago incident, or fear of being caught for trying to capture Declan, and capturing me instead? But we missed our chance."

"You missed it on Friday, but that's not why I called this meeting." Finn laughed when he said it, and the others laughed along with him.

"There's another purpose for your visit here? You're not just the landlord checking the place for dirt or damage?" Brennan asked. He smiled and took a good long sip of his drink. He lit up a smoke and offered the pack to his father, who took one and fired it up.

"There is another purpose. As I say, there's a group of us who meet at Arbour Hill Cemetery every year to honour Wolfe Tone, and also the fourteen patriots of the 1916 Rising who are buried there." After being executed by the British, Brennan knew. There were sixteen who were executed, two buried elsewhere. "Sure, there's an official ceremony in May of every year, put on by the Minister for Defence, but some of us don't attend that one. We have our own tradition. And we also gather at Glasnevin Cemetery to honour some of the people buried there. Including Parnell and the Liberator, Daniel O'Connell, and Countess Markievicz."

"We mustn't forget Brendan Behan," Brennan said. "His grave is there too."

"Brendan Behan will never be forgotten. Anyway, that event will be happening the day after tomorrow."

"Brilliant!" Terry exclaimed. "But what are you thinking? We stand there in front of a gravestone, and S catches sight of me and Dec, and we look for a startled reaction?"

"We can see S at the graveyard or in the Gravediggers afterwards."

"The pub," Brennan said. Kavanagh's pub was known as the Gravediggers. Plenty of lore had attached itself to that place. Men who'd be digging graves at Glasnevin would, of course, work up a thirst. And they'd knock on the wall of Kavanagh's to signal what kind of a drink they wanted. And they'd get it.

"The pub, yes," said Finn. He turned to Terry. "But I don't think two of you should make an appearance there. If S is there and he recognizes Declan, he might react to seeing him. But that could be a reaction to the embarrassing incident itself, a fear that Declan might remember it. And might know of the injury to the young lad. It would not necessarily be a sign of guilt relating to the plan to grab Declan, the kidnapping of yourself, Terry. We wouldn't know one way or the other."

"True enough. So you and I will go. As far as I know, if S was in on the kidnapping, he never actually saw me. Wouldn't recognize me. And if he was in on the threats and the kidnapping, I'm in no more peril now than I was when this all started. I hope. But whatever the case, I should use another name."

"But it will have to be a Burke name, because at some point we'll be dropping Declan's name into the conversation to look for a reaction to Dec being here in Ireland. A reaction by S."

"Right," Terry agreed. "I'll be Patrick. Well, I won't be Patrick Burke the psychiatrist; that won't be my role. But I'll use my brother's name, and I'll use my own talkative personality! It should be obvious to S that Patrick would not be aware of his involvement in the scheme, if indeed he was involved."

"That settles it," said Finn. "You and I will go, just the two of us. We won't want too many new faces to distract him. But I'll have to think up a reason for having you with me. Some of these people might be a little wary of strangers!"

"I'll try not to look like a peeler or a spook from Special Branch!"

"You've got the right idea."

"Here's a suggestion, Finn. When I was in captivity, I did a bit of acting. Pretended to be the kind of Yank who is fascinated by all that wild Irish history and conflict. Fascinated but woefully ignorant of what it's really like to have lived through it. Or to have fought in it. Naive and wide-eyed, that sort of a thing."

"Good one, Terry! I've no doubt you'll be able to pull it off."

"Your role, Finn, will be one of strained patience. *This nephew is a feckin' eejit, but I'm stuck with him on his visit here on the Auld Sod.* A bit of eye-rolling when I go over the top about my love of the Emerald Isle and my insatiable curiosity about the bold Fenian men."

"I've got my eyes rolling already."

"Good. I'll make a good showing. And you'll also reassure them that I can keep my gob shut. For all my blathering in the Gravediggers,

I'm known as someone who doesn't repeat everything he hears from other punters in a pub."

"Right, so. That will help."

"I'll use the name Pat. And at first it won't be known to them that I'm the son of Declan Burke. We'll have S under close surveillance when we pull that bunny out of the beret. When we mention that Declan is back in Ireland."

"Assuming the man won't recognize you on sight, that he didn't see you when those two men had you in captivity."

"Yes, we'll have to watch for any sign of immediate recognition."

Declan said then, "Your hearts are in the right place here, but any reaction by S — if there is a reaction — will be devilish hard to interpret."

"It will," Finn agreed.

"Not to mention the fact," Brennan interjected, "that you may be putting yourselves in danger."

Finn's eyes went to Brennan and then to Declan. "They won't try anything with Terry, not now. They'll know he's under my protection."

Not for the first time, Brennan wondered what exactly Finn's role was in the Provisional IRA. Did the men on the Army Council have reason to be wary of him?

Terry wasn't put off by any of this. "We'll give it our best."

"No failure of nerve on your part, eh Terry?" Finn asked with a smile.

"Have you ever flown a Boeing 747 in a blizzard, Uncle Finn?"

∽

Brennan would have to miss that performance, and he'd be anxious to learn how it turned out. The next morning, he walked out on the Irishtown Road to buy a newspaper and came back, sat down at the kitchen table, and began to read. A story on the second page was about a murder trial in the city. That brought him back to Monty's research into the case in which Declan had testified. Had taken a flight from

New York to London to give alibi evidence for a man he knew to be guilty of robbing a jewellery store.

He looked up from the paper and said to his father, "I'm wondering about something, Da. That Lorcan fella. Mister One More Can MacGillicuddy."

"Mm."

"Your testimony saved him from a long spell in prison. Surely he'd be delighted to welcome you into his home after all these years."

Declan snickered at that. "Somehow I suspect he'd not be wanting a reminder."

Terry walked into the room then. "Ever the cynic is our da." He laughed. "But I like the idea. Where does he live? Where does he live it up as a free man who beat the law and walked away with all the cash?"

No answer from Declan.

"Think about it, Dec. It might be useful in our investigation to see the face on him when he spots you on his doorstep. Will he beam with joy at the sight of you, or will the nerves go on him? Will he have the appearance of a worried man? A man who is looking into the face of Declan Burke, who saved his bacon years ago but who, no doubt, later learned about the money he was supposed to hold for his partner in crime. A bundle of cash that would have provided a real boost for the man who did serve the time. He'd have needed a few quid to get started on a new life when he was released from the nick."

Declan looked less than enthusiastic, but Terry was keen. "I doubt you know where he's living now. Would he be in the telephone directory? Maybe not, but you could do some asking around. Maybe come up with his address and —"

Their father surprised them then. "I've done the asking. I know where he is."

"Really!" Terry exclaimed. "You sly oul divil, can't put one past you. Where is he?"

"Balyer." Ballyfermot.

"We'll drop in for a visit, see how he greets you. We'll be on the lookout for anything less than a fulsome welcome for his old mate who flew over three thousand miles across the ocean to testify to his good character." Terry looked thoughtful for a moment, then asked, "Did you fly into England on your own passport, Da?"

It was a good question. Declan Burke's name may have been on the records in the United Kingdom as well as in Ireland, as a result of his activities on both sides of the disputed border between the Republic and the British colony to the north. But all Terry got by way of an answer was that familiar frosty glare. He wasn't put off. "Let's motor."

"We're not going to land on him at this time of the morning."

That wasn't an outright refusal. "This afternoon then. Or what does he do? Work of some kind during the day? Or commit robberies under cover of night?"

"The man has had a sporadic employment history. But I'm told he's working these days in a hardware shop. Daytime hours."

"You've done your research, Declan. Well done."

Terry didn't ask where he got his information; neither did Brennan. The fact that their father had made the effort to discover MacGillicuddy's address suggested that he had considered paying the man a visit.

ᔕ

Just after five o'clock that afternoon, Declan was at the wheel and they were driving to the city centre and then beyond, to Ballyfermot in the western part of Dublin. A soft rain was falling, and everything looked grey. Ballyfermot, nickname Balyer, was generally known as one of the poorer areas of the city, and many of the houses bore this out. Grimy exteriors, the odd window boarded up, front gardens full of muck and leaves. The MacGillicuddy residence was an attached pebbledash house at the end of a terrace. The door and the window frames needed a coat of paint, and the front garden had patches of grass with nothing else growing. A small Ford sat in a rocky, uneven drive.

"Old One More Can obviously didn't *move up* when he came into that money," Terry remarked. "Didn't put his money into property renovations or into a flashy new auto. That little Ford must be ten years old. Maybe the money all went down his throat; I don't imagine the nickname One More Can came out of nowhere."

"It didn't. More often than not, he'd have drink on him, from what I heard," Declan replied. "Now, let's get on with it." He opened his door and got out, the others following.

As they approached the entrance, Brennan saw the classic twitch of a net curtain in the front window. Then, when they were on the front step, he thought he heard rapid footsteps inside the house. Declan knocked at the door. No response. Knocked again and then there were footsteps coming their way. A woman opened the door a crack and stared out at the visitors.

"Mrs. MacGillicuddy?" Declan asked and got "Mm" as his answer. "Lorcan and I were mates some years past, and I'm back in the city. Wanted to call in and see how he's doing. It's been a while." Her pale blue eyes went beyond him to his two companions, and he said, "These are my boys, Terry and Brennan. Could we come in for a sec just to say hello?"

This was not a role that came naturally to Declan, the shy visitor on the doorstep pleading for entry. But Mrs. MacGillicuddy was even less likely than Declan to be offered a role on the stage of the Abbey Theatre. Her quick, nervous glance to the left and back at the Burkes did not match her assertion that "He's, em, not home right now."

Terry took over then. "Oh, that's fine. We'll just come in for a second, and my da here will write him a little note. Won't you, Da?"

"I will, sure."

At that, she opened her door to the three strangers and gestured for them to come inside. Mrs. MacGillicuddy was dressed in a flowery summer frock; she was middle-aged, her thin hair a mix of brown and grey, a little extra weight on her. Yes, Brennan thought, Lorcan and his wife would be in their forties or early fifties; it was Lorcan's father who had done a favour of some kind for Declan, prompting Declan to give assistance to the son. And outside appearances to the contrary, the son had done fairly well for himself. A large television had pride of place in the front room, and a new up-to-the-minute stereo was flanked by shelves bearing dozens of compact discs. The furniture looked Scandinavian and new. Was Lorcan keeping his luxuries hidden inside, and leaving the outside looking shabby to curious passersby? Was this his way of not flaunting the money he had kept a decade ago?

Now, what kind of a note was Declan going to write for the man?

"Will you have a cup of tea?" the wife asked, clearly hoping the answer would be no.

Declan complied with that wish and said, "Ah, no, we'll not be stopping for long. Perhaps another time."

"Em, right, sure, another time," came the nervous reply.

"But," Terry said, "would you have a slip of paper and a pen for him?"

"I would, yeah, sure I would."

"And an envelope?"

She shuffled off into another room. In her bedroom slippers. The soft soles of the slippers had not made the sound Brennan had heard when he'd been standing outside. The sound of those rapid footsteps had been made by harder soles. The other occupant of the house had hurried off to the back or the upper floor. Mrs. MacG was back a few seconds later and handed Declan a scrap of paper and a pencil, and pointed to a side table where he could write. She asked no questions, made no comments about the weather, just stood aside and waited for the scene to end.

The scene ended when Declan had scribbled something on the paper, slipped it into the envelope, and sealed it. He said his thanks, and they left. They got into their car, and all three of them looked to the upper-storey window. Were they being observed from up there by the man of the house who had no desire to welcome a man who had so suddenly materialized from his past?

"Well, what do you make of that, Dec?" Terry asked as they drove away.

"He was there, no question in my mind. Car in the driveway, nervous look about the missus, and the sound of somebody walking away from the front room when we appeared on the doorstep."

"Ah, you heard that too," said Brennan.

"I did. The ungrateful fucker wouldn't give me the time of day. Why would that be, I wonder?"

"Because he figures you know about the money he kept?"

"More than likely, Brennan."

"And that story he concocted about where the money went, that the RA had demanded that he hand it over to them, to help finance the fight against the Brits. We know that didn't happen at all. But is it possible he thinks the boys might really be after that money all these years later? And that you, with your republican connections, had turned up to collect?"

"He'd have to have been fretting about that all along if that's what sent him scurrying from the door."

"Or," Terry suggested, "he thinks you became sympathetic to his partner in the robbery. Murphy? That you're on Murphy's side now and you came to confront him about that."

"We just don't know," said Brennan. "But the question is: Whatever is going through his mind, whatever might be keeping him awake at three o'clock in the morning, did it motivate him to call in a couple of thugs to try to abduct you? To send you a warning to keep your gob shut and get out of the country?"

Declan didn't answer, just shrugged his shoulders.

"So, what did your note say, Da?" Terry asked.

"A bit of codology is all it was. I wrote: 'Footsteps. Either you have an intruder, your wife has a shy visitor, or you are not giving me the welcome I might have expected.'"

Brennan and Terry snickered, and Brennan said, "Good way to take the piss out of him. But will your last line be enough to scare him off if he's the man behind the actions against you?"

"You said it yourself, Brennan. We just don't know."

CHAPTER XXII

Terry

Thursday afternoon found Terry and Finn standing in Glasnevin Cemetery as a gentle rain fell on the gravestones. In spite of the rain and grey skies, Finn was wearing the dark glasses he so frequently wore. Terry had never been sure why he wore them, but everyone had grown accustomed to seeing Finn Burke in shades. Terry looked around him. He estimated the size of the cemetery to be more than a hundred acres. He'd read somewhere that it held the remains of more than a million people. Many of the graves were marked with grey stone markers, some with Celtic-style crosses, others looking like elaborate church steeples. And, of course, there was the high round tower for Daniel O'Connell, known as the Liberator for his achievement of Catholic Emancipation in 1829, which removed many of the restrictions the British government had enacted over the years against Catholics. Terry and Finn stayed to the back of the republican contingent on the walk from grave to grave. There were enough people in the group, men and women, young and old, that it had not seemed rude or unusual for Finn not to introduce his nephew. Members of the group took turns reciting or reading short speeches at the graves of people they were honouring. Some of the gravestones stood over the places where the bodies were buried; other stones had been erected to honour people who were buried elsewhere, like several men who had been executed by the British at Mountjoy Prison. The names were familiar to Terry, to all the Burkes. The group stopped by the grave of Cathal Brugha, who had been killed by Free State troops during the Civil War of 1922 to 1923. And Countess Constance Markievicz. He had heard and read enough about her to know that she had been sentenced to death for her role in the 1916 Rising. The sentence was commuted, and she went on to fight for Ireland and its people, in particular the women, the workers, the poor.

Something else Terry knew: two of the most prominent figures in Irish history were buried here. Michael Collins and Éamon de Valera, who took opposite sides during the Civil War. Collins was assassinated by the anti-treaty side in the war: those who could not accept the treaty he had signed with the British, setting up the Irish Free State. Even the republican Burkes had expressed admiration for Collins and were of the opinion that he had achieved as much during his negotiations with the British as they would ever have given up. De Valera had stayed on the anti-treaty, republican side in the war, but when he got into government, he eventually turned on his former republican comrades and had many of them interned, some executed. Neither of their graves were on the agenda today. If Terry had been alone, he would have said a prayer over Mick Collins's grave, but that would not be the act of the IRA wannabe he was about to portray. On a lighter note, he would like to have visited the grave of Ireland's legendary "drinker with a writing problem," Brendan Behan.

The last plot they went to as the gentle rain turned to a downpour was that of Jeremiah O'Donovan Rossa, a prominent Fenian leader who died in New York in 1915. His body was sent home to Ireland and buried here in Glasnevin. His marker was a square stone, lying at an angle to the land. One of the most famous speeches in the history of Ireland was made here by Patrick Pearse, who was executed after the Easter Rising the following year. Finn and his fellow republicans recited part of the speech, ending with these ringing words: "The fools, the fools, the fools! They have left us our Fenian dead, and while Ireland holds these graves, Ireland unfree shall never be at peace."

The members of the group then headed into the Gravediggers pub and shook the water off themselves. They greeted the barman and a few of the drinkers at the bar and tables. It was a classic Irish bar, lots of dark wood and sparkling bottles. As they stood at the counter with the others while they all ordered their drinks, Finn leaned towards Terry and said in a voice only he could hear, "Don't look now, but that fella with the brown jumper and the shirt collar turned up, that's yer man S, and we'll want to be at his table." Terry took his time looking all around the pub, made a point of being wide-eyed and smiling, the gawping tourist. He took note of S. His white hair was thin and his face lined, but he moved like a man much younger than seventy. S got his pint, put it on a table, and then pushed another table towards it, making room for a few of his comrades, men and women. But there was only one vacant seat at that table. Finn walked over and claimed it before anyone else. Terry would have to figure out how to insinuate himself into the gathering. Shouldn't be a problem; his new persona would provide the excuse.

"Excuse me, Finn," he said, standing beside his uncle. "Do you mind if I pull a chair over here?"

"Sure, Pat, I'll make room."

"I don't know anybody else, and you know how shy I am!" He said it in a way that left no doubt; this was no shy wallflower. Finn looked at the others and said, "Shy, me arse. You'll find he's anything but."

"Who would this be now?" a hard-faced man asked.

Finn made the introductions. Well, introduction singular. "This is my nephew Patrick from across the water." That could mean North America or the U.K., but any confusion would be cleared up before too long. The other people said hello or raised their glasses in greeting. Terry could read nothing in S's quick nod of the head.

Terry then grabbed a chair from a nearby table and pulled it in beside Finn. "There. That's better." He lifted his pint to the others at the table and said, "Sláinte!" He deliberately mispronounced it as "Slayn-ta" instead of the correct "Slawnch-eh." Then he gulped down nearly a third of his pint and went into a fit of coughing. From the looks on the faces of the others at the table, he was succeeding in playing the arsehole, the naive blow-in.

"I'm from New York!" Terry beamed at the assembled company. Was that a little twitch of the mouth of S? Would the man immediately associate New York with Declan Burke?

"This isn't my first time in Ireland. I was here a few years ago. I love it here!"

One of the women said, "Good on you."

"And I'm really interested in the history of this place, what the Brits did to the Irish for all those years. Centuries! So I understand why, well, people . . . did the things they did here. For Ireland's freedom. Some colonial powers don't listen to reason, do they? So the only way to get rid of them is . . . Oh, sorry, guys. And ladies. Sometimes I get a little excited."

A man across the table laughed. He was looking at Finn when he did it, so Terry thought Finn might have made a face about his eejit of a nephew. There wasn't any conversation at the table. A couple of people got up to refill their glasses, then sat down again.

Finn broke the silence. "Don't worry about him." He jerked his head towards Terry. "As he says, he gets a little excited. About our *history here*." He said it in a mocking tone. "But let me assure everyone that he does know how to keep that mouth shut. Do you know what he does for his living? He runs a limousine service. He owns the company, but sometimes he drives the cars himself." Terry kept a straight face. His limousines were jetliners making intercontinental flights. But he listened to Finn's version of his life behind the wheel. "And we know from news reports coming from America that he has driven some very important men — important people — around the United States. I've heard over the years from family members over there, who were curious about some of the important passengers. Political men, film actors, celebrities. Where they were going, and why. But much of what his passengers did was confidential. And our man here kept his lips sealed about whatever they did, and where they did it. Didn't breathe a word. Believe it or not." He finished with an ironic look in Terry's direction.

Terry hoped the group would be reassured that the blow-in would not be gossiping about the people here in the Gravediggers, would not be repeating anything he heard from this group of republican stalwarts. But he and Finn were on a mission here. And maybe it was time to see whether the name Declan Burke would prompt a reaction from the man known as S.

He picked up his pint, drained it, and said, "Ahhh! It's so great to be back in Ireland. It feels like home in a way. My dad's from here."

"Your da?" one of the men asked.

Finn provided the answer. "My brother Declan."

There were murmurs and comments around the table from those who were of an age to remember.

"Ah, Declan. It's been a long time."

"He's back now?"

"Good man, Declan."

"That bit of business years back, all straightened out now, I've heard."

But Terry's eyes were on S. And S was the only one of the older crew who had showed no reaction at all.

"Enjoy your pint there, Pat," Finn encouraged him. "Ah, I see you've enjoyed it."

Terry got up then. "Anybody else? It's on me." Two of the men took him up on his offer, and he went over to the bar and ordered the drinks. A bit of conversation started up at the table as he stood waiting. When the pints were decently poured, he brought two to the table and placed them before the men who had requested them. He went back for his own and sat down.

When there was a lull in the conversation, Finn said, "I'm sure we're all wondering where Cormac and Aidan were today."

"We are," one of the men replied. "I've heard nothing from that quarter for a couple of weeks now."

Someone else said, "I heard that Aidan was in the other day for a visit with our friend in the Joy. So he's not gone far away."

"I know Cormac has a cousin who's been active in the North. Would he have gone up there, d'yis think?"

"Risky, if he'd be recognized."

Terry, of course, had no idea who they were talking about, but at least they felt confident enough to say a few names out loud in his presence. First names only, but that was better than the earlier silence. Not too often you had a table full of people in an Irish drinking hole and nobody talking. Terry had been in pubs numberless times and had enjoyed hours of conversation with people he had just met. Terry's reputation as a spinner of tales, a bar-stool bon vivant, was well earned and apparently genetically determined!

Now he had a job to do, but he'd need a couple more strong drinks in him before he embarked on that. Not to build courage but to create the impression that he couldn't hold his drink as well as many of those he'd met in Ireland. After a bit of time had passed, he rose from the table and offered again to buy a round. A few took him up on it, and he delivered the goods. Then he got another pint and a double Jemmy, a Jameson, for himself. When he was seated again, he decided to turn the talk away from the republican soldiers to something more ethereal.

"I'm trying to remember what I heard about this place. Kavanagh's here. Wasn't there a ghost story?"

The woman who had spoken earlier said, "You heard right. There's a ghost who sometimes comes in here. Many people have seen him. He comes in, and you can see him enjoying a pint. He wears one of those old-fashioned collars. What do they call them? Butterfly collars, I think. And a waistcoat and a watch chain, like they wore in the old times. And the people who have caught sight of him, they give the same description. Same description given by people who've never met each other before."

"Let's hope he comes in today! I love a good ghost story."

"It wouldn't give you a case of the janglers, a ghost appearing in front of you?" She laughed when she said it.

"Nah, I don't think so." This presented Terry with an opportunity. "There are a lot of living creatures that are more frightening than anything from the spirit world. Only a few days ago I nearly had the shit scared out of me. Sorry, ladies."

"Och, we've known rougher times." The woman snickered and shared a smile with her female comrade.

The friend said, "It was rough in Armagh, right enough."

"Armagh?" Terry inquired, feigning ignorance. He assumed she meant the women's prison in Armagh. The women said no more, so he returned to the story he was making up on the fly. "I was out for a walk, and it wasn't the most genteel neighbourhood in this fine city. The place wasn't much better than a dump. What do you say here, a kip? This was a block of flats, and rubbish was strewn all around. Now, I admit I was a little over my blood alcohol limit when this happened. Anyway, I was strolling along. Maybe staggering a bit. Not looking where I was going, and I tripped over something and fell on my knees. There was a clattering sound; I had hit some old rotting boards, knocked them out of place. And what came skittering out from under the boards but a great effin' rat! The thing was as big as a tomcat, I swear. And it was coming right for me, giving me the evil eye, with its whiskers twitching. I thought, Christ, if the thing gets its claws into me or its teeth, I'll catch a disease. The plague!"

The story gained him a few smiles, a few laughs. And then he got on to what he really wanted to do. "And it's not just rodents who look like rats." He reached over and snatched the dark glasses off his uncle's face, put them on his own. "Remember, Finn? When Terry told us about that ordeal he went through, he warned us to be on the lookout for a creepy guy who looked like a rat! Skinny face, skinny little lips on him, and a long, pointy nose. What was his name? There were two of them, the ratty one and a bigger one named what? Phil? No, it was Frank. And the rat-faced guy was Ger. Sorry about the glasses, Finn. But I need them in case those tough guys come in here and see a family resemblance between me and my brother! In case they think I'm Terry. No worries for you, Finn; you'd be less recognizable *without* the shades!" There was method to Terry's madness here. He wanted his eyes obscured so he wouldn't be seen watching S when he said the names Ger and Frank.

And a reaction there was, though not a vehement one. When Terry said the names, he saw S turn to look at one of the other men, lips forming the words *What the fuck?!* The names Frank and Ger had, for some reason, hit home.

Had Finn noticed it too? Maybe so, because after downing the last of his pint, he said, "It was grand to once again honour our dead. But now I must get back to my place of employment. I'll be seeing some of yis next week." He turned to Terry and said, "Up with you, Pat. Time to be headin'." They said their goodbyes and left the pub.

When they were in the car and on their way to the Irishtown Road, Terry asked, "So, Finn, who was the man S looked at? Who did he direct that 'What the fuck' to?"

Finn was silent for a moment, then said, "It was Tadhg Finlay Bohanan."

"That's a mouthful!" Terry exclaimed. Tadhg sounded like the first syllable of tiger.

"Is Tadhg a member of the Army Council?"

"No."

"Just one of the lads then, is he?"

"He is." Another member of the RA.

"And it looks as if both of them, S and Tadhg, are acquainted with Frank and Ger."

"Acquainted with them or recognized the description. Even if Frank and Ger are only the names the pair of them use while out on an operation. Or it might just have been a question, meaning *What is this Burke fella on about here?*"

"Hmm." Terry didn't find that a very convincing explanation of S's reaction in the pub.

CHAPTER XXIII

Brennan

Brennan and Terry had received an invitation from Shay and Allie Rynne to accompany them to the Gaiety Theatre on Friday night to see *Borstal Boy*, the play based on Brendan Behan's novel. Allie had already seen it and wanted to see it again. "Sure, it's fabulous. The actor who plays Brendan, you'd think it was Brendan himself come back to life." Well, who could resist an invitation like that? It was a bright, fine evening and the brothers went early for a walk around Stephen's Green. Then they waited outside the theatre, chatting with other Behan enthusiasts until it was time to go inside. When Shay arrived, he was alone. Brennan raised a questioning eyebrow.

"Allie sends her regrets."

"What?" Brennan asked. "She was dying to see the play again."

"She was. But she's gone over to see Mamie, her ma. Mamie's all upset. Something about the old lady she takes care of."

"Right, the one in Ballsbridge," Brennan said.

"Yeah. Mrs. Delahunt. Ah, time to go in."

When they went in, showed their tickets, and found their seats, Shay said, "I hope Allie will get another chance to come. She's always been a fan of Behan. He grew up not far from where we're living now. Any time Allie walks past the Behan house on Russell Street, she gives the place a little salute. Well, more like lifting a glass to him."

"I know he'd appreciate it. We'll hope Allie gets another chance to be here. Her mother — Mamie — is very good to that lady, Mrs. Delahunt."

"You're right, Brennan. She is. Mamie has been trying to smooth out some troubled waters there. Mrs. Delahunt was widowed at a young age and never married again, never had children. She and her brother were the only two in her own family, and the brother died some years ago, leaving a wife who now lives in Spain. I don't know how many children the brother had. But anyway, there's bad blood between Mrs. Delahunt and her sister-in-law. I've no idea what it's about. Allie started to tell me one time, but it went in one ear and out the other, one of those family rows that are all too common. Whatever it was, Mrs. D finally wanted to straighten it out, put it all behind them. And it was Mamie who encouraged her to make the first move in that."

"Good to hear. Any time I'm told about these family rifts, I want to take hold of the participants, give them a good shaking, and tell them to settle it, come to terms, don't let it fester until it's too late. Does anyone listen? Not often enough."

"I hear you. Somebody in the family pops their clogs, and it's too late then."

Brennan twisted in his seat to look around. The place was filling up; Behan had always been a big draw in Dublin. More than thirty years gone now, but pub owners all over the city were still boasting of Behan having patronized the places. Brennan tuned back in to Shay and the tension in Mrs. Delahunt's life.

"Well, Claudia Delahunt is trying to make sure that doesn't happen, one of them dying without this being resolved. And Mamie Cotter has been cheering her on with this. She helped Mrs. D write a long letter to the sister-in-law in Spain, apparently apologizing for her own part in the squabble. The sister-in-law had sent the occasional letter to Mrs. Delahunt over the years, not friendly letters! Mrs. Delahunt ignored the first couple, but then wrote some kind of bland reply to one of them. That was a year or two ago. She feels bad about it all, so she is determined to put things right between them. That's what her recent letter is meant to do. As I say, she apologized for the part she had played in all this, and expressed forgiveness for the other woman's part, and suggested that they patch things up. Maybe the house in Ballsbridge is a factor in all this; Mrs. D has no immediate family to inherit the place whenever she dies."

"That will be a valuable piece of property, to be sure."

"Oh, yeah. Worth millions. So, whatever she wanted to say to the one in Spain, she wrote it all out. She sent it by registered post to make sure it arrived. And what happened? Mrs. D recently received a nasty note from Spain, igniting the entire thing again. She realized that her letter had never arrived; the woman never got it. Mrs. D knew the address was right, so that wasn't the problem."

"What a shame, after all the goodwill Mrs. Delahunt tried to extend to her."

Shay gave a little laugh. "And good on the part of Mamie herself, spurring the old lady on to make things right with the sister-in-law. If things are left as they are, the in-law may not inherit the house when Mrs. D dies. And get this: Mrs. D has hinted more than once that Mamie might be a beneficiary, after Mamie being so good to her all these years. A beneficiary, you know, in her will. Maybe not the house in Ballsbridge, but something." Shay laughed then. "Or maybe the house after all. Who knows? And here's Mamie, working against her own interests to bring the sister-in-law back into Mrs. D's good graces! Ah, here we go."

The lights went down, and the curtain opened. The setting was a flat in Liverpool where Brendan Behan was lodged with the ingredients for a bomb. The young actor with curly dark hair looked convincing as a sixteen-year-old Behan, who was soon joined by a posse of men who came to arrest him for his activities on behalf of the IRA. His plan had been to bomb the Liverpool docks. How many of his fellow Irishmen worked on those very docks? Brennan wondered. And as he so often did, he reflected on what is right and just, and what is most definitely not right and just, when engaging in a war. Even a war that itself is justified. But he settled in to enjoy the play. It was brilliantly done and rewarded with thundering applause.

When the Burkes and Shay left the theatre, Terry said, "Where to now? There's something about Behan that puts a thirst on me."

Shay replied, "McDaid's, where Behan practically owned one of the tables?"

"Could do McDaid's," Brennan agreed, "or if all the Behan fans are headed there tonight, we could go to Neary's. I remember hearing that's where Patrick Kavanagh would escape to in order to get away from Behan at McDaid's!"

They decided on Neary's and enjoyed a couple of pints there before calling it a night. When they parted ways, Brennan remarked to Shay, "See you again soon. I hope Allie gets to see the play."

"I'll be happy to see it again, if she does."

Thinking back to their earlier conversation, Brennan said, "You should check with An Post about that registered letter. See if they can explain why it wasn't delivered."

"We should do that. It was Isabel who offered to post the letter. Said she'd take it to the GPO on her way to work. We'll ask her to check into it." And he waved goodbye.

Isabel. As Brennan walked with Terry to their car, he thought back to that electrically charged meeting he had with the bride-to-be. The feeling of what? Malevolence? The feeling she gave off, which had put Brennan immediately on his guard. What had he just heard now from Shay? That Isabel had offered to post the letter Mrs. Delahunt had written to mend the broken relationship with her brother's wife. The letter that never arrived. Mrs. Delahunt, the widow with no children. The house and gardens in Ballsbridge, which must be the poshest, priciest neighbourhood in Dublin, home to several embassies. The reference to Mamie Cotter perhaps benefitting under Mrs. D's will. Isabel, about to marry Mamie Cotter's first-born grandson. Isabel, whom Brennan had overheard at the engagement party praising Mrs. Cotter and asking to come along to visit Mrs. Delahunt "again."

Brennan knew he could not keep this to himself. Well, he could, but he would never feel right if he did not issue a word of caution before the marriage could take place. And he could not imagine himself conducting the wedding ceremony; he could not be party to it. He did not want to open this can of writhing serpents with Shay; the painful conversation had to be with his son. But Shay would surely hear about it, Shay who had been so helpful in so many ways to Brennan and his family on this ill-starred visit home. And Brennan could not begin to imagine the younger Rynne's reaction. Would Brens perhaps see this as a sly attempt by Father Burke to lure him to the priesthood? The very idea nearly made Brennan ill; he would never do anything so underhanded. But the besotted groom-to-be had to be warned.

ᔕ

He could not put it off any longer, not with the short time he had left in Dublin. So the next day, Saturday, he rang Brens, said he'd like to get together with him, and suggested a stroll along the Royal Canal. The Grand Canal ran along the city's south side, the Royal along the north side. Brens said that sounded like a fine idea, so they met at the bridge near Croke Park. It had been raining but the sky had cleared, with the lovely rainbow that was so often seen shining over Dublin.

"Hey, how's the godfather?" Brens spoke like the film version of a tough-guy New Yorker.

"I'm on top of the world. And don't you forget it!" He wished, momentarily, that he could play the tough guy with his godson for this encounter, but no. Gentleness was called for. "We'll stroll out that way," he said, pointing west.

"I know you're a good walker, but you're not going to take us all the way to Mullingar, are you, Father?"

Mullingar was a town on the canal, about forty-five to fifty miles away. "No, I won't impose that much of a penance on you. As lovely as Mullingar is, the walk would be a tad too long. We'll just enjoy a stroll. Maybe have a pint at the Brian Boru."

"Good plan."

Brennan made small talk for a few minutes, then, "Great craic at your parents' place, your engagement party."

"Yeah, and a good turnout."

"How long have you and Isabel been together?"

"Nearly two years now."

"What does she do, her work?"

"She's just started at one of the banks. Before that, she was an administrative assistant with a firm of accountants. And when I first met her, she worked in a solicitor's office." Hardly a stable record of employment. But Brens apparently didn't see it that way. "That's one of the interesting things about her. She keeps being hired away from her jobs. Word gets round about how good she is at whatever work she's doing, and some other outfit offers her a job!"

Was this an accurate accounting of her frequent changes in employment? Brennan wondered.

"Right. Where is she from? A Dublin girl, is she?" Brennan recalled the Dublin intonations in her voice. Not the sound of a working-class Dub, something a little milder.

"Rathmines, born and bred." So, South Dublin. "It's funny, bless her heart. When we first met, she kind of hinted that she'd had a rough upbringing. Father an alco, and a bad temper on him whenever he'd get stocious. But here's the funny part: it wasn't true. She's actually — what would you call her? A middle-class girl all the way, nice family, no troubles on the home front. The father was rarely stocious, rarely took a drop at all."

The poor lad was making Brennan's task easier by the minute. "Why would she make a claim like that about her upbringing?"

Brens turned to face Brennan, smiling. "It was all to spare my feelings, or so she thought. Me coming from a Fenian Street family, my da brought up in the tenements. She said she didn't want to boast about the easy time she had growing up, the nice house, and all that. But . . ." The smile faltered a bit.

"But?" Brennan asked.

Brens flapped his hand in the air to signify that it was nothing important. Brennan decided to let it go.

They strolled along beside the canal, noting the occasional white swan gliding on the water, the occasional drinker sitting on the banks. "Circle back and stop in at the Brian Boru?" Brennan suggested.

"Let's do that."

The pub had been in place since the mid-1800s just north of the canal. It was named for the legendary Brian, the High King of Ireland whose place of burial Brennan had so recently visited. Now, entering the pub named in his honour, Brennan cast an approving eye on the warm wooden panelling and stained glass in the windows.

When they were seated at a table with their pints, Brennan didn't bother to use small talk as a way to mask his interest in Isabel. "Brens, when you told me about Isabel's reason for giving you a false history of her family life, you started to say something else. You said 'but' and then didn't finish the thought. What was it you were going to say?" Or not say.

Brens turned his head away from Brennan and took a sip of his pint.

Brennan started to go for his cigarettes, then resisted the temptation. He prompted his godson, "Can you tell me?"

Brens took a deep breath, exhaled, and said, "That story, about the harsh upbringing, came up after one of her . . . Once in a while, she loses her temper. She'll be shouting, practically screaming, at some little thing I said or somebody else said or did that offended her. Set her off. I was thinking maybe she gave me the tough-upbringing story because that might explain her loss of control." The young man looked distinctly uncomfortable. He avoided Brennan's eye.

"Brens, I have only your best interest at heart. I don't want to hurt you with this conversation, but I'm concerned about you. Specifically about your planned marriage to Isabel."

Brens turned towards Brennan, stared into his eyes. "What do you mean?"

"You say she loses her temper, screams at you. You've told me about her unstable work history, going from one job to another. And the lies about her family. Surely, that has caused you some concern."

Brennan could hardly hear him as he replied, "Yeah. It does. I met her family, and they are lovely people. Nice house, good schools; everything was fine."

"All these workplace changes, do you really think they resulted from people recruiting her for her abilities, or was it something else?"

"Brennan, I've tried to overlook this stuff, tried to put the best gloss on it. Because she's always told me it was love at first sight for her, when she met me. She was mad about me from day one. Makes me feel as if I'm, I don't know . . ." He looked about him in this shrine to Brian Boru. "As if I'm the new High King of Ireland!" He managed a laugh when he said it, and Brennan laughed along. "See, I didn't walk out with very many girls because, well, because I was trying to discern whether I had a vocation. To the priesthood, as you know. But then this one comes along, with her spectacular good looks, and she kind of . . . overwhelmed me, I guess. And part of that was, em, when she'd have one of her screaming fits, throwing things around and all that, she'd say afterwards that it's because she's" — his face flushed red as he said it — "such a *passionate woman.* And she'd, you know, she'd be all over me to prove it!"

Brennan smiled at him. "Sure we'd all be chuffed with that."

As they sipped their pints, Brennan thought things over. A stable, loving family. No traumatic or violent past to explain her behaviour; it was all Isabel herself, not her family. Brennan tried not to label the woman on the basis of this information and Brennan's own brief encounter with her, tried not to pin a label on her. It seemed preposterous to call his godson's beloved out as a psychopath! Over the course of his life, Brennan had met a few — very few — people who met the criteria for that designation. He had certainly met them in his ministry to prisoners. He remembered something he'd heard from Monty Collins. Monty quoted one of the judges he knew who referred to the very worst of the people who appeared before him as "the ungodly five percent."

Surely, Brennan Thomas Rynne's bride-to-be was not a true psychopath. But look at what had been revealed about her in this short time: the loss of control, the lying, the erratic work history.

How likely was it that she was constantly being recruited by new employers, based on the high quality of her work? How would the new employers know all this about her? More likely, she'd been sacked from her jobs. For performing below expectations, or perhaps for stealing, committing fraud? Whatever the case, she must have put on a convincing performance to get hired by other places of business. One of the oft-cited traits of a psychopath is the ability to be charming and convincing.

Brennan chided himself; surely, he was exaggerating. But then he pictured the scene at the engagement party when the other girl, Jane, had been applauded and cheered for her song. Jane was the focus of everyone's attention again when Brennan sang "Lady Jane" for her. Right after that, Isabel had made a beeline for Brennan; she had not at all appreciated the focus leaving her for another woman, however briefly. A desperate need for attention? Brennan was no psychiatrist, but thinking over conversations he'd had with his brother Patrick, who *was* a psychiatrist, it seemed that at least some of the markers were there. And he could not deny what he had felt when she touched him; he knew what he had seen in her eyes. What he had *not* seen. Brennan's good friends Maura MacNeil and Monty Collins sometimes slagged him, called him a Druid, for those insights he occasionally had into the souls of other people, for his ability to see or intuit things on the "other side." The other side of the thin veil separating this earthly life from the eternal. But they believed him, did not think he was hallucinating or making things up. And they knew, as well as Brennan did, that their little daughter Normie had the same gift. Gift or curse, depending on what might emerge out of the mists.

What did this all mean for Brennan Thomas Rynne? Father Burke had told Brens about some of his occult or spiritual experiences, and Brens knew he was being truthful. So, how much should he tell Brens now? If the young fella went ahead with the marriage, what kind of a life would he have? What about children? Women of this personality type were known to be neglectful of their children, physically and emotionally. And sometimes worse: the mothers would hurt their children or abandon them.

Brennan took a good long swallow of his Guinness and prepared himself to deliver a sermon that his one-man congregation had no desire to hear. "Brens, you're not going to like what I'm going to say, but I can't keep it from you."

Brens turned to him, a wary look on his face. "Keep what from me?"

"I have very great concerns about Isabel." No reply. "It's more than a feeling, although I did have a bad feeling as soon as I met her."

"What do you mean, Brennan, a bad feeling?" There was a sarcastic tone to it, and Brennan could hardly blame him.

"You know I've had intuitions about people from time to time." Brennan knew that the young man had never doubted Brennan's sincerity about those experiences.

"So, what kind of feeling did you get from Isa, or should I even ask?"

"You should ask. She's not good news, Brens. I'm sorry. I'm not getting any pleasure from telling you this. And her eyes; there was a look in her eyes that I've seen in people who . . . who are not all that sympathetic to other people. It's called a lack of empathy."

"Oh, come off it, Brennan. How could you know that?"

"When the little boy fell on the stairs and was screaming with the pain and fear — and nobody knew yet whether he was badly injured — there was no reaction from her. She didn't turn to see what had happened, and her eyes didn't react at all."

"How do you know that, Brennan, unless you didn't turn to see what happened to Kieran yourself? If you were gazing into Isa's eyes, you didn't look over either!"

"Good point, Brens, but I did look. I started for the staircase and that's when I looked at Isabel, who was in front of me, and those eyes of hers hadn't changed. No reaction." He wasn't going to get into the studies about pupil dilation or lack of it; he would move on to the other things that disturbed him about her. "But there are more immediate, more practical things that concern me." He spoke as tactfully as he could of the sudden temper tantrums, the screaming, the lying about her family and background, the unstable work history. "Those are all symptoms —"

"Symptoms?"

Brennan wanted to avoid the word "psychopath," or "sociopath"; he knew how over the top that would sound. "All elements of a condition that some people have, people who are extremely self-involved, with not much care for others."

Brens surprised him then, not by objecting but by remaining silent. Had Brennan at last struck a chord? Was selfishness something the groom-to-be had noted already in his fiancée's personality? Then he thought about Allie's mother and the elderly widow in Ballsbridge. "I overheard Isabel talking to Allie's ma about the work she does for Mrs. Delahunt, Isabel asking to go along again on another visit."

Here Brennan expected an interjection along the lines of *So, now you're finding fault with Isabel wanting to help care for an old lady?* But it didn't come. "Your dad told me — and let me emphasize that there was no reference at all to Isabel in the conversation — told me that there was some kind of family strife between Mrs. Delahunt and her brother's widow. And that Allie's mother, your grandmother, was trying to help her sort it out, repair the relationship. This in spite of the fact that there'd been some indication that Allie's mother might be named in the Delahunt will, might stand to inherit something."

"That's true," Brens acknowledged. "There has been some talk of that, that she might reward Mamie for all her dedication over the years."

"Yet Mamie, God love her, is trying to help heal the rift with the sister-in-law in Spain. Even though that might mean the sister-in-law will cut into the inheritance. Perhaps inherit everything, whatever the arrangement might be."

"Our gran's a good soul, no question."

Now, to less-than-exemplary souls. "Do you think the will, the possibility of inheritance, might have something to do with Isabel's interest in spending time with Mrs. Delahunt?" He saw no need to add that Brennan Thomas, as the first-born son of Mamie Cotter's first-born daughter, might do well out of this in the years to come. As would the wife of that first-born son.

"That would be a stretch, wouldn't you think, Brennan?" The sarcasm was back in Brens's voice.

It was not a stretch at all, in Brennan's view. Then he remembered what else Shay had told him: that Mamie Cotter had helped the old lady write a letter to her sister-in-law, a letter designed to mend the fences between the two family members. But Mrs. Delahunt had received a letter from the sister-in-law, which made it clear that she was still on hostile terms with her. And it was obvious that she had never received the registered letter Mamie had sent. That *Isabel* had supposedly sent. Shay told Brennan that Isabel had offered to mail the letter at the General Post Office on her way to work. A few minutes earlier, Brennan had assured his godson that Shay's conversation about Mrs. Delahunt had not touched upon Isabel at all. Too late, Brennan remembered that it had. He'd better not contradict that now, so he said nothing about the posting of the letter.

Brennan tried the Irishman's equivalent of the English lady at table when something unpleasant came up in the conversation. Instead of *Tea, anyone?*, he pointed to their empty pint glasses and said, "Have another?"

"No, I don't think so, Brennan. I think I'll head" — and he made to get up.

Brennan put his hand on his godson's arm. "Brens, the last thing I want is to see you hurt. I didn't want to hurt you with this conversation, but I couldn't stay silent and see you perhaps make a big mistake by marrying someone who . . . Maybe you should at least allow more time to get to know her."

"I don't doubt that you mean well, Father Burke. But you can imagine, I'm sure, what it's been like for me listening to all this. From you, my godfather and, I could say, a lifelong friend." And he got up and left the bar.

Brennan sat there, devastated. He loved his godson, had loved him ever since he had first held him as a little baby in his arms. And they had grown closer with every visit. Now, he had wounded him deeply. The idea of a rift, an estrangement, between them was too painful to contemplate. But look at the alternative if Brennan had stayed silent, kept his thoughts — his knowledge — to himself. If the marriage went ahead, and it turned into a disaster, which it surely would, and Brennan Burke had remained silent. How would he feel then, knowing he might have prevented it? He went up to the bar and ordered a whiskey. "Make it a double, will you?"

CHAPTER XXIV

Brennan

On Monday morning, Brennan went out for a walk. As he strolled along the bank of the River Dodder, he found himself brooding about the painful confrontation he had brought about with Brennan Thomas Rynne. Brennan knew his intuition was right: marriage to Isabel would be a mistake that the young groom would soon regret. But Brennan recoiled from the memory of Brens walking out on him after their conversation in the Brian Boru. It was agonizing to know he had hurt his beloved godson. And this after everything Shay Rynne had done for Brennan, his father, and brother during this tumultuous visit. Brennan had the young man's best interests at heart, without question, but how would this be received by Shay and Allie? This had kept Brennan awake the last two nights, and it didn't look any better in the light of day, light filtered through a quilting of grey clouds covering the sky. He would have to speak to Shay. Better to face whatever had to be faced than continue to obsess over it. Or so Brennan hoped.

So he returned to the house and rang Shay to see when they could meet for a "short chat."

Shay said, "I've some business to attend to in the Liberties later this morning." That was a working-class area of the city south of the River Liffey and to the west of the main shopping district. "I have to speak to somebody at Kevin Street." The Kevin Street Garda Station, Brennan assumed. "Won't take long. I should be out of there by half eleven."

"What say we meet then at Saint Patrick's Park?"

"Grand. See you there."

Brennan arrived at the Liberties well before his meeting time with Shay. The clouds had not yet spilled their contents, so he took a little walk along Francis Street, noting all the antiques shops, and then he headed for Saint Patrick's Cathedral. It was one of two Church of Ireland — Anglican, to be more accurate — cathedrals in the immediate area, the other being Christ Church. He could not resist taking a peek inside Saint Patrick's, the magnificent thirteenth-century building, even though he had seen it often. As always, he gaped at the soaring interior, the vaulted ceiling, elaborate stone carvings, and beautiful stained-glass windows. And of course, the several artifacts in memory of a man who was witty, curmudgeonly, and not always complimentary about the land of his birth, that being Ireland. Jonathan Swift, dean of the cathedral. A plaque in the floor marked his grave.

After a few minutes, Brennan went out to the adjoining park and stood before a grey stone slab that read, "Near here is the reputed site of the well where St. Patrick baptised many of the local inhabitants in the fifth century A.D." Father Burke made the sign of the cross in honour of the great saint. As if in heavenly approval, the sun broke through the clouds. A fine summer's day. He walked around the park until he spotted Shay coming in from the street. They greeted each other and sat down on a bench.

Shay said, "Here. Have the rest of this." And he handed Brennan the remaining half of a big bar of Butlers dark chocolate. "I'm pals with a ban garda at Kevin Street, and she was kind enough to give me a treat." He laughed then. "There'd have been no treat if she heard me calling her a ban garda!"

That was the name for a female cop, Brennan knew, taken from the Irish word for woman. Bean, pronounced "ban." There were frequent spelling changes in Irish words, for various grammatical reasons. The term was a little outdated now; all guards were guards, be they male or female.

Brennan thanked him, saying, "A great cathedral, Patrick's holy well, and now Butlers chocolate. My day is complete."

He took a bite, swallowed the first delicious square, then took a deep breath and said, "Em, Shay, has Brens said anything to you about . . ."

"About?"

"He and I had a drink together." If only that had been the beginning and the end of it, the alpha and the omega.

"No, he didn't mention it. When was this?"

"Saturday. At the Brian Boru."

Shay shook his head. Well, now, it was up to Brennan to mention it.

"This is painful, Shay. For me, but especially for Brens. And I'm sorry, but it will be painful for you as well."

Shay frowned. "What is it? What's happened?"

"It's about Isabel."

"Oh, Christ, what has she done?"

That was not the reaction Brennan had expected. He was about to ask what Shay thought of her, but he stopped himself. That would be unfair. So he said, "I'm a little concerned, Shay, about the marriage. About Isabel herself."

Shay's face now was expressionless. Unreadable. Am I losing a friend here? Brennan fretted. He waited for a response. Finally, all Shay said was "Go on."

"I met her for the first and only time at the engagement party. And the feeling I got . . . I have a bad feeling about her." Brennan expected a sharp riposte at this nebulous, meaningless statement. But he was met by silence. Grow a pair, Brennan admonished himself. Say what you came to say. "I think she's bad for him, Shay."

"What makes you say that, Brennan?" Shay the detective was going to get the facts from his witness, not taint the evidence by suggesting other answers.

"I got the impression that she needs an inordinate amount of attention. And doesn't like sharing that attention with others. Other girls. Women. There are some people like that, as we all know. And it's not just women, to state the obvious. But it's more than that, unfortunately, Shay. It's there in her eyes."

"What is there? What did you see in her eyes?"

Brennan could not interpret his friend's placid demeanour. Was this his Garda training? Or was Detective Rynne saving his response? Was he going to blow up at Brennan? Walk away as Brens had done. But Brennan had started this, and now he had to finish it. "She had the expressionless look in her eyes that I have seen in, em, people I see in my ministry to prison inmates in Canada. Not all of them, by any means. A minority."

This brought about a reaction, a quick intake of breath. "You saw that in her?"

Not a denial, not a dismissal as if what Brennan said was ridiculous.

"Do you remember, Shay, when the little boy fell on the stairs and was screaming? Was he seriously hurt? All the guests started for the staircase. But Isabel didn't even look over in that direction. I moved ahead to get to the stairs via the dining room archway. And I found myself directly in front of her. She was staring at me, and nothing about those eyes reacted. I know I'm speaking way above my pay grade, as they say, but I've seen that before, and I've heard about it from people who work with . . ."

"With criminals."

"I'm sorry, Shay. Please believe me when I say that. I thought about this all yesterday, stewing about it. I wanted to put it off." Shay looked wary but did not respond. "You've known me for donkey's years. And you know I sometimes have intuitions."

"Sure I know you're a seer, Brennan. A Druid!"

"And I got one of those intuitions — a jolt of alarm, it must be said — when I touched her hand. Coming down closer to earth now,"

Brennan said then, with a little laugh, "there is the matter of her keen interest in Allie's mum's care for Mrs. Delahunt. And the registered letter that was meant to heal the rift with Mrs. Delahunt's sister-in-law. The letter that apparently was never posted."

They fell silent as a woman passed by, leading a group of children to the holy well. The kids were in yellow T-shirts that read Saints and Schoolers Summer Camp. Brennan and Shay smiled at them and raised their hands in greeting.

When they had moved off, Shay sighed, looked Brennan in the eye, and said, "I know, Brennan. I've had the same doubts about her. I've been a guard for a quarter century now, and I've seen some of the types you've described. But . . . but I tried to raise this with Allie. Suggested that we have a word with Brens. And she shut me down. She doesn't want to think badly of our boy's future bride. Allie thinks Isabel is just immature, and she'll grow out of it. I said to her, 'Allie, you're an archaeologist. Should you be digging a bit deeper?' And she came back at me with 'Oh? I'm not being enough of an archaeologist here? What about you yourself — are you being too much the peeler?' So, you get the idea."

"I do, sure."

"Allie did acknowledge to me that she'd wondered about Isabel's keen interest in the wealthy widow."

"Mrs. Delahunt."

"But she said, Allie did, that she chided herself for being too cynical. Not cynical enough, I'd say. Brennan, you and I have been round the pitch a few times, and we know better. Isabel is what she is. What she is and always will be."

"Right. You know it too. I've been so distressed about it. And about raising it with you."

"I understand. And I'm glad you did. I appreciate your concern about it. So you spoke to Brens himself?"

"I did. And it did not go well, as you might imagine. No wonder the poor lad was offended and upset."

"How can he not see this himself, Brennan, and him so intelligent? He didn't just sprout from the seed yesterday. His reaction to you could mean one of two things. One, that he'd never had a doubt in the world about her and thinks you're way off base. Or two, he has had doubts, and it is too painful for him to face them."

"I don't know what to say, Seamus. I'm relieved that you're not ready to baton me to the ground but very sorry that you've seen the same thing in her, which reinforces my opinion that this marriage should never happen."

"And," Shay smiled, "it won't happen with Father Brennan Burke blessing the union!"

"I just couldn't. All this being said, Shay, can we keep this conversation between the two of us? Not let on to Brens that we discussed it? Or is that being too disingenuous? I'll leave it to you to decide."

ꟹ

Later that day, just after four in the afternoon, Shay was at the door of the house in Irishtown. Oh, Christ, Brennan thought, was he here to give him grief about Brens and Isabel after all? But he would wait and hope it was something else that brought Detective Inspector Seamus Rynne to the door. "Come in, come in, Shay. Have a seat." Declan and Terry rose from their seats to greet him. "Will you have a cup of tea?"

"Thanks, but no, Brennan. I can't stop for long. But I've some news for you." He looked around and took Declan and Terry into his glance. "The information you've been waiting for."

They all remained silent and waited.

"This, again, is unofficial. Not on the books. My . . . contact was able to trace the phone calls to and from the place on the East Wall Road."

Brennan heard a sharp intake of breath and looked at his father. He looked like a man awaiting his verdict in a court that was not at all a court of law.

"There were a number of calls over the months to and from the house being leased by the man using the name Berrigan. One of the numbers may be that of the person who really leased the place. As I say, calls going in and out of that house. There are a few names that came up, for one or two calls. But one name was a frequent caller and receiver of calls. That name is Alice McKribban."

"McKribban!" Declan exclaimed.

"The name means something?"

"It does. But not Alice."

Shay raised his hand and said, "No. I looked up her name. She's long dead, if it's the same Alice McKribban. So someone was using her name to set up the phone. Declan? You know the name?"

"Albert McKribban. I thought he was dead!" Declan looked to be on the verge of death himself.

CHAPTER XXV

Brennan

Brennan and Terry stared at their father, who was wordless for a long, tense moment. Then he said, "I'll, em, have to think about this, Shay."

Shay took that as a hint and rose from his chair. "I'll leave you to it. If you need me, you know where to reach me!"

They all expressed their gratitude as Shay took his leave and shut the door behind him.

Declan sighed and looked at his sons. "Now I know. Here's what happened, and it's not a story you'd want to be telling to the children at the choir school, Brennan."

Brennan's thoughts were in turmoil. What was he going to hear now?

"Albert McKribban, who has recently risen from the dead . . . I'd heard he was dead, and so he never came to mind as a suspect in what's happened to us here. McKribban is a Dublin man but was working with our boys in Belfast." "Our boys" needed no introduction; they were the Provisional IRA. "And Albert was quite chuffed with himself when he managed to recruit a tout in the UVF in Belfast." The Ulster Volunteer Force, a paramilitary group celebrated in murals all over the loyalist neighbourhoods in Belfast and other parts of the North, celebrated for the war it was waging against the IRA, the nationalists, and anybody else who wanted Ireland united and the Brits booted off the island.

Declan looked about him as if representatives of the many paramilitaries might be within hearing range. "The tout's name was Mackasey Ward. Ward had not agreed to inform on his fellow members of the UVF out of any kindred feeling for the Irish Republican Army. Not at all. He hadn't switched his loyalties."

"Still a loyalist," Terry could not resist saying.

His father ignored that. "Ward had not become a friend to the RA. McKribban was able to turn Ward because of what he, McKribban, knew about him. McKribban blackmailed him into becoming an informer. And what he had on the man was dangerous information, indeed. He knew that Ward had been closely involved with the Shankill Butchers."

"Fuck!" exclaimed Terry.

"No!" exclaimed Brennan.

"Yes."

The Shankill Butchers were a murder gang who abducted Catholics, just Catholics picked at random when they were going about their daily, or nightly, lives. The gang's idea was *If you can't get an IRA man, get a Taig.* A Catholic. Their hatred took them far beyond just eliminating their victims. They beat and tortured them before killing them. The gang went to places where they knew Catholics could be found, or cruised the streets at night in a car, knowing there were some streets where only a Catholic would venture out late at night. They'd spot their victim, snatch him off the street, pull him into a car, and take him away. The stories about the Shankill Butchers were some of the most horrific, most soul-destroying accounts of suffering Brennan had ever heard. Victims were kicked and beaten. At least one man had some of his teeth pulled out with pliers. The gang were known for using butchers' knives to cut the victims' throats, inflicting several cuts while the victims were still alive, then finally slashing their throats almost to the spine, at times nearly severing the heads from their bodies.

Brennan returned his attention to this father, who said, "This brutal psycho was never prosecuted. Was never identified as one of that gang. Somehow, McKribban had come across this information and used it to threaten Ward. If he didn't pass information — genuine intel — to McKribban for the IRA, McKribban would reveal what he knew about him. And that would get him killed or arrested and sent to prison for life. And of course, McKribban used the old *if anything should happen to me, that information is in an envelope in a secure place and will be opened for all the world to read.*"

"I'll be our ma now," said Terry. "I think a cup of tea would be in order." He got up to make the tea, and they waited for it. When they all had their cups, Declan resumed his story.

"So, the UVF had a tout working against them. And as time went on, they started to suspect that information had been leaked. They started looking around for suspects. And woe betide any man who was caught informing on that or any other paramilitary group. So Ward came up with a plan. He set out to direct suspicion elsewhere. Nothing blatant, like 'D'you know where so-and-so goes after his meetings at the Orange Lodge? He heads right to the Falls Road to whisper in the ear of the Shinners and the Provos.'" Sinn Féin and the Provisional IRA. "No, he was a little more subtle than that. He pointed the finger at a man named Edison Colyear. I never knew why Ward singled Colyear out for this dishonour. Some personal grudge, some other kind of history with the man? Did Ward think Colyear suspected him? I simply don't know. Like Ward, Colyear was a member of the UVF. He was an Orangeman and soldier for the pro-British side of the conflict. There are always some members of paramilitaries who see themselves primarily as, well, as terrorists; others see themselves as soldiers for a cause. Colyear was a soldier. And he was not a tout; he was loyal to his own side. But the rumour got about, and it got him killed. Eight years ago. Shot by his fellow loyalists, gunned down in his house in front of his family."

"That's dreadful."

"It gets worse, Brennan. A stray bullet hit Colyear's little girl, Ailsa, his youngest child. Nine years old. She died instantly."

"Oh, Christ! To take the life of a child!"

"How do they put it so callously nowadays? Collateral damage. She wasn't the target, but she lost her life. And it was Albert McKribban who set all this in motion. This catastrophe would bring shame on McKribban, but that was the least of it. If his involvement became known, he'd be a target for the loyalist paramilitaries. And they would not handle him with care! So McKribban was desperate to get away. He tried to immigrate to the USA, to New York. He heard that I, well, I knew people in New York who could help him resettle. But I'd heard the story. So when he came to me, I told him to get the fuck out of New York and never show his face there again."

And now, Brennan reflected, McKribban had told Declan Burke to keep his mouth shut and get the fuck out of Ireland. When he couldn't get hold of Declan to warn him — or had he planned to do more than warn him? — he had a couple of his goons take Terry captive and tried to pressure Declan that way. But it hadn't worked. "You had no idea that McKribban was behind the kidnapping of Terry, did you?"

"I thought the fucker was dead. I do know that Mackasey Ward is dead. But here's McKribban still alive. And now we know he's been using another name. Berrigan. It never entered my head that this was the sordid history behind the kidnapping. If I'd known, I would have . . ."

"You would have what, Da?"

All Brennan got by way of an answer was the death stare from his father's cold blue eyes.

"It's a fine day out there. Why don't you take yourselves out for a little walk," Declan said. "I need time to think all this through."

"Sure, that's what we'll do," Brennan agreed, and he and Terry left the house for the light of the sun.

∽

"I'm of a mind to go up there," Declan announced when his sons were back inside.

"Up where, Da?" Brennan asked, but he had an idea of what the answer would be.

"Belfast."

"I think you've had enough excitement for one day, dear," Terry said in the voice of a mother speaking to a rambunctious child. "Enough for a year of days, a lifetime of days."

"And so have you, Ter," his brother countered. "What is it you'd want to do there, Da?"

"Give that family an explanation. The Colyears. Reassure them that their husband and father was not a tout, did not betray his own people. They've been living with that slander for far too long."

"Why you, though, Da?" Terry wanted to know. "Why should you be the one to go to Belfast and tell the family what happened?"

Declan leaned forward in his seat. "Because nobody else ever did. Not as far as I'm aware. And now that I know it was McKribban behind the threats against us here, I feel as if . . . well, as if the Colyear family and our family are both victims of that fucker, McKribban. And the Colyears deserve to hear the truth."

Brennan felt a rush of love for his father. Declan wanted to give solace to the family of a soldier for the other side, a soldier who would not have hesitated to blow Declan Burke off the face of the earth. Declan knew, though, that Edison Colyear had been a good soldier, loyal to his cause, however it differed from Declan's own. "But," Brennan said, "you'd be putting yourself in danger, Da, a Dublin man turning up on their doorstep and talking about all that bother. If anyone overheard . . . this would be a classic case of *what would the neighbours think?* And in this case, the Colyears would be justified in worrying about exactly that. They'd be afraid of more retribution against the family."

"They deserve to know the truth."

"They do," Brennan agreed. "But isn't there some other way you can get the message to them?"

"Like what, Brennan? Send them a little card through the post? Signed *A Secret Admirer*. I sure as hell couldn't sign my name to it.

And why would his widow or anyone else in the family believe something like that? They have to hear it in person."

"Well, isn't there anyone you can contact," Terry asked, "to pass the message along?"

"Who, Terry? I don't have any *contacts* on the loyalist side up there. And I don't want anybody on our side of things, our boys in the North, to get wind of this. If they know already, they'll be as determined as McKribban is to keep this shameful catastrophe under wraps. And if they don't know, I have no intention of playing the role of informer, giving away the secret."

"No, I suppose not!"

"The only person who's going to hear this from me is the man's widow. She'll want to spread the news to other members of the family, but I'll be back on this side of the border by the time the word gets round. And she'll not know me by my real name. I'll introduce myself as, well, I'll figure that out."

Brennan tried to picture the scene, his Dublin-born father at the widow's door in Belfast, claiming to be somebody else and telling her he has important news to impart. *Would yeh mind if I stop in with yeh a while, missus?*

He thought for a moment. Then, "If a kindly Protestant minister came to her door, she'd surely invite him in, offer him a cup of tea, and hear what he had to say."

"What are the chances of that?" Terry asked. "Unless . . . Sure, amn't I the bar-stool bullshitter in the family? Haven't I always been able to spin an improbable tale? If I —"

"No, Ter. I see myself in that role. You, like our oul fella, have been through enough. More than enough. And I can talk Belfast. I can *sined like a mon from Kynety Dyne.*" (Sound like a man from County Down.) "Would ye ever doubt me for a wee minute now?" It sounded like *Would ye aver dyte me for a wee munnut nye.*

His father and brother laughed, but Declan was quick to dismiss the plan. "I don't intend to see either of yis take the risk."

"The risk would be greater for you, Da," Brennan countered. "If this were to go sideways somehow, and someone caught on to who you are, connected your name to your . . . history here on this island, it could go badly for you. Not a problem for me, a visitor from right there in Norn Iron with no present or past membership in any illegal organization."

"What did I just say, Brennan? I can't have you taking the risk."

"O ye of little faith. The Lord's representative here on earth has spoken, and his word is law," the Lord's representative declared. "Now, let me figure out the best way to appear at their door. Do Presbyterian ministers wear the collar? Yes, sometimes. Some do. Or I could be Church of England. Excuse me, Church of *Ireland*."

"*Church of Ireland*," Declan remarked. "If there is a Proddy church in Belfast calling itself the Church of Ireland, which there is, then they're admitting the North *is Ireland*. Hasn't anybody copped on to the significance of that? Should we be seeing this as a breakthrough, a step towards a united Ireland at long last?"

"I know. I was saying the same thing the other day," Terry replied. "But I wouldn't suggest putting all your Easter Rising eggs in that basket, Dec."

"I'll go with that, nonetheless," Brennan asserted. "A little closer to us papists liturgically, maybe easier for me to fake."

"Brennan, for fuck's sake, don't be putting yourself in the way of harm."

"You mean, for *Christ's sake*, Da, and I'll be putting myself under His protection for the mission."

Declan merely shook his head, obviously well aware that once his oldest (acknowledged) son had his mind made up, he was going to go through with whatever he was minded to do. "Ceart go leor." Right enough. "But the two of yis have seen a calendar, have yis? You know what's coming up."

"We're only four days away from the Glorious Twelfth," said Terry. The twelfth of July was the biggest day on the calendar for the loyalists of Northern Ireland. Their loyalty was, of course, to Britain, not to Ireland. The Twelfth was observed by members of the Loyal Orange Order who still commemorated the victory of William of Orange — their beloved King Billy — over the Catholics in 1690 in the Battle of the Boyne. They were still crowing about it now in the mid-1990s. The Orangemen held marches throughout the summer every year, but the Twelfth was the high point. Brennan had on several occasions seen them marching through the streets dressed in their orange sashes and bowler hats, playing their flutes and banging their lambeg drums. They often marched past Catholic churches singing and playing anti-Catholic, anti-Irish songs like the "Famine Song." That would not be the time for Dublin Irish Catholics to be wandering the loyalist neighbourhoods of Belfast.

"So, lads, we'll have to get our arses on the road tomorrow and get back here before all that carry-on."

"And how are we going to find the right house, Da?"

"I know the address."

"*How* do you know the address, Da?" Terry asked.

His father gave him the Declan Burke death stare. "I *know*."

"Ah."

"Eighty-four Irwin Avenue. In East Belfast."

"We'd best be leaving tomorrow, to get ahead of the Orange crowd and their marches."

"And their bonfires," Terry added. Loyalists lit bonfires all over their areas of Belfast the night before the big marches.

Declan got up then and walked to his room. Brennan heard the sound of a zipper being opened or closed, and then it was a drawer being opened and closed.

Declan returned to his chair in the sitting room and said, "I believe you know how to use a gun, Brennan?"

Jesus wept! Brennan stared at his father. What now? Brennan was not a man for guns. How many people had died by gunfire in the United States in the years he had lived there? He remembered seeing a figure for one year, the death toll for gun deaths, including murder, suicide, and accidents. Nearly forty thousand in one year. How many sermons had he given, where he had worked in a plea for gun control? But, in fact, Brennan did know how to use a gun. It wasn't his father, the (former?) republican warrior who had given him the lessons. To be sure, Declan had taught him early in his New York years how to handle himself in a fist fight, an attack in the street. But it was brother Terry, when Terry had joined the armed forces of the USA. He had signed up with the Air Force with the intention of getting his flight training there and then moving on to become a commercial airline pilot. The plan had unfolded exactly as he had hoped.

At the time of his military training, Terry had brought brothers Brennan and Patrick to a gun range, and when their young sister Bridey got word of the plan, she insisted on being included. Terry taught them how to fire a rifle and a handgun and hit a target. Brennan took little satisfaction from his unforeseen skill with a handgun, a skill almost equal to that of Airman First Class Terrence Burke.

CHAPTER XXVI

Brennan

The next afternoon found the Burkes checking into a hotel in Belfast city centre. They wasted no time lounging about in their room; they had a quick supper and then they wanted to see where their mission would be taking them the following morning. They had decided on morning as a time when a woman might open her door to a stranger, albeit a stranger decked out as a cleric of the Church of Ireland.

They set out in their car, Terry at the controls, for East Belfast. They were going to scope out the neighbourhood where Father Brennan Burke, in the guise of the Reverend William Henry Hanna, would seek admission to the home of the widow Colyear. They drove from the city centre and over the bridge crossing the River Lagan. And saw a tower of wooden pallets that must have been fifty feet high. All to be consumed by fire on the Eleventh, Bonfire Night. Every year, the loyalists lit bonfires the night before the Twelfth, and every year, the fires were bigger, more elaborate, and more dangerous to their surroundings. There were several of these towers to be seen as the Burkes drove through this loyalist enclave of the city. Attached to the stack, to be consumed by the flames, were the flag of the Irish Republic, a picture of the Pope, another of republican hunger striker Bobby Sands. Sands was a hero to Irish republicans, one of ten prisoners who died on hunger strike in the early 1980s to protest the loss of their status as political prisoners. Here in East Belfast, murals on gable walls portrayed men in balaclavas, with guns pointed out, along with the insignia of loyalist paramilitary groups like the UVF and the UDA, Ulster Defence Association. In the Falls, of course, republican walls honoured their own gunmen; Brennan was well aware of those and how they would strike terror into the heart of anyone from this area wandering into that one.

The Burkes had the Colyear address, but they wanted to see in advance what the neighbourhood was like. Was it isolated? If trouble arose, would they be on their own? Or were there many neighbouring houses where they might be observed from windows overlooking the street? Which of those scenarios would be to their advantage? Or disadvantage? They didn't know, but they wanted to check out the terrain where they would be carrying out their operation. They had family in Belfast, as they did in Dublin, but again, Declan had put the kibosh on any suggestion that they visit them. He didn't want any of his relations to know about his return and the events it had unleashed. At least not until it could be sorted once and for all.

So, here they were in Belfast shortly before Bonfire Night in their Opel Astra with its Dublin licence plates. They were wise to get to the city before the fires were actually lit. Brennan didn't want to think of the reaction they might have provoked among the throngs of people in the streets of Belfast, all psyched up by those towers of flame. And the Irish symbols being burnt in effigy. Even now, two nights before the event, there were crowds of people standing around the towers.

"As you fellas know," said Terry, "I witnessed Bonfire Night that time I was here with Conn. And I remember quite a scene in the Shankill Road."

"I can only imagine it," Brennan replied.

"We were driving along, and those wooden pyres were towers of flame and smoke. Even with the car windows closed, we had the overpowering smell of woodsmoke and the chemical stink of burning tires. And Jesus, the crowds! They were all around the fires clapping and roaring with approval, and leaping aside to dodge the objects that came tumbling down from the stacks to the ground. It was a primitive scene, no question, with people cheering and shouting, their grinning faces lit by firelight."

Terry's description of Bonfire Night, the pumped-up atmosphere of gleeful hatred, gave Brennan the chills. He was overtaken by a feeling of disquiet, of foreboding. And sometimes his feelings, his intuitions, were borne out by later, disturbing events. No, he scolded himself. Catch yourself on, Burke. Look around you. Who wouldn't have a feeling of foreboding? Us being Taigs in the days before this infernal hate fest. He could all too easily imagine a frenzied mob surrounding the car if the mob learned there was a papist priest and an old IRA veteran on board. Brennan and his father and brother would be torn to pieces. His fear ratcheted up when he saw two men turn away from their tower and glare at the car, at the Dublin licence plates; they knew a pack of strangers — *Fenians* — when they saw them. Oh, Christ, here they come. The two men, one with a square face and a shaven head, the other with long wavy fair hair and an unkempt beard, started towards the car. But they were distracted by loud cheers behind them and they turned away, as someone pointed to an effigy of the Taoiseach — the prime minister of the Irish Republic — being nailed to one of the pallets. Terry drove past the scene with no harm being done. Deo gratias! Brennan told himself again to shake off the fear and loathing and concentrate on their mission of mercy in loyalist Belfast.

Tonight's goal was to scope out the Colyear family home. They found the street, Irwin Avenue, and Terry made a left turn off the Newtownards Road. He drove a short way up the street, and Declan said, "There it is." It was a three-storey red-brick house at the end of a terrace of houses with front-facing gables and bay windows. This was a residential neighbourhood with rows of houses along Irwin Avenue and the surrounding streets. There could be many eyes on their appearance tomorrow morning, but Brennan figured that would be better than doorstepping the Colyear family in an isolated area where anything could happen, and no one would see it. What film was it where they said, "No one can hear you scream"? Well, somebody would hear your screams in this neighbourhood.

CHAPTER XXVII

Brennan

The Burkes got back to their hotel unscathed and took to their beds. In the morning, they decided to make their move early. If no one answered the door in Irwin Avenue, they could try again. Brennan did a little work on his black clerical shirt: made little tears in the collar and folded the material back on each side of the notch, making the white a little wider. That seemed to be what he had seen on Church of Ireland clergymen. There was a bit of a debate about Declan's insistence that Brennan arm himself with a gun for the encounter. Brennan knew Declan had brought one for himself as well, for this incursion into enemy territory. He tried not to imagine a scenario where one or both might be needed.

"We don't know how many members of the family might be at the house," Declan said. "Mrs. Colyear and who else? Of course, we're hoping they'll listen and be thankful for your explanation. But there's no telling how they'll react, after what they've been through. If I really thought they'd take it out on you, Brennan, retaliate against you, I'd be insistent that you step aside and let me handle it."

"And I'd be just as insistent, Da, that I do this and not put you in the way of any more aggravation. Terry and I have said it before and I'll say it again: you've been through enough. It's my turn now."

"Then you'll be taking this with you." Declan reached into his suitcase and drew out a Browning 9-millimetre pistol.

"Oh, Christ."

"Put it in your trouser pocket. And never mind that it is summer: wear that jacket, the blazer you brought with you. It will hide the bulge of the gun. It's loaded. We've already established that you know how to use it. Pray to God you won't have to. And you probably won't. When this is all over, you may laugh at me all you like, as I treat you to a celebratory pint in some lovely bar on the west side of town."

Terry took the wheel again, and they headed to Irwin Avenue. The Colyears' place was a bit rundown; the white paint on the window frames was chipped and stained, and one of the upstairs windows had a sheet of plywood covering the bottom half. The black front door had been defaced by something in orange paint. Graffiti? Whatever it was, it had been smeared or scuffed beyond recognition. Other graffiti on nearby buildings, and the union flags and murals, announced to the world whose side the residents were on. No pictures of the Pope here, except for those placed for burning on tomorrow night's bonfires. But that would be of little concern to the Reverend William Henry Hanna, formerly known as Father Brennan Burke, whose doctorate in theology from the Angelicum in Rome would never be mentioned here, when he made his surprise visit to the family of Edison Colyear.

Terry parked the car on a side street a block away from, and out of sight of, the house. Brennan — the Reverend W. H. Hanna — got out and made to close the door. "Remember, you're a Proddy minister," his father instructed him, "so don't be invoking the BVM" — the Blessed Virgin Mary — "in your chat. And make sure the door doesn't lock behind you. We'll be lurking near by. In case we decide to join the party. Or in case we hear a lambeg drum in there and cop on that they're getting ready for Orangemen's Day!" Declan could not quite pull off the effort at humour.

"I'll see what I can do," Brennan answered.

"We'll find a place to stand, close but not close enough to be seen," Terry said.

Brennan parted with them and walked around the corner and along the block to the doorstep of the Colyear house. He rapped on the door with the knocker and waited.

Faded, that was the word that came to mind when Brennan faced the woman who answered to his knock. If, as expected, this was the widow Colyear, Brennan knew she could not be as old as she appeared to be. Rebekah Colyear had had a daughter who was only nine years old when she was killed by the hitman's stray bullet eight years ago. The years following that horrendous time had not been kind, leaving her with a pallid, lined face, greying fair hair, and a look of resignation in her light hazel eyes. As she stared at the clerically collared stranger at her door, her eyes seemed to say *What fresh hell is this?*

Brennan put on his best Belfast accent, albeit a refined version, and said, "Good morning, Mrs. Colyear." She waited, didn't dispute the identity. "I am the Reverend William Henry Hanna. But that sounds rather formal, doesn't it? People just call me Mr. Hanna. Or Bill."

"What is it I can do for you, Mr. Hanna?" She sighed as she spoke, sounding exhausted. "Are you sure you have the right person, the right address?"

"I am. And I apologize for being a stranger standing at your threshold. But I'll explain myself, if I might come in?"

She turned and walked back inside. She did not close the door, so he took that as an invitation, or at least as permission, and followed her in. He took it upon himself to close the door behind him but did not click the lock into place. He saw the family's kitchen straight ahead, and there was a staircase on the left. And there, sure enough, was a lambeg drum on the bottom step. The drum the Orangemen played during their marches. To Brennan's right was the sitting room, painted a nondescript beige, which had perhaps once been pale yellow. The room was sparsely furnished with mismatched pieces, a sofa upholstered in a green-and-gold pattern, a bright blue armchair with the arms and head area worn to a shine. On the floor near the side window was a pink-and-white quilt, and a little blonde-haired baby curled up asleep.

"Ah, what's her name?" the Reverend Mr. Hanna asked in his Belfast voice.

"Elspeth, my son's wee girl," Rebekah replied. "We call her Ellie. Have a seat there." She pointed to a brown upholstered chair, covered in a maroon-and-white afghan, so he sat down. Across from him was an open entranceway to the dining room. Brennan could see a chipped wooden table piled with placemats, dishes, and cups.

"Would you like a cup of tea?" The ritual of tea was offered even to an unwelcome stranger.

Brennan reasoned, as he often did, that the familiar, homely routine might relax her, so he said, "Tea would be lovely, thank you."

"How d'you have it?"

"A wee bit of milk and sugar, thank you."

In less than a minute, she brought him his cup and sat across from him, waiting.

"I won't keep you long, Mrs. Colyear. Here's the reason for my visit. I know that your husband . . ."

Before he could continue, there was a little cooing sound from the baby. Brennan heard footsteps approaching from the hallway, and a man appeared in the room. He looked to be in his mid-twenties, tall and muscular with light brown hair brushed to the side of his forehead. He was wearing jeans and a white T-shirt.

"Ed, love. Come in. This is the Reverend Mr. Hanna. Our son, our oldest. Edison, named after his father."

"Nice to meet you, Ed. Now, it's about your father that I'll be speaking to you."

"My *father*?"

The baby cooed again, emitted a little sigh, and Brennan said, "Ach, what a lovely wee baby. May I?" Brennan started towards the quilt and nobody protested, so he stood and looked down at the baby. Her blue eyes fastened on him, and she reached her little hands out to him. She gave him bright smile, and his heart began to melt. "Ah, isn't she a dote?" Without thinking, he raised his hand to bless her, make the sign of the cross over her. Remembering where he was and who he was supposed to be, he stopped himself from completing the Catholic gesture. Instead, he reached down and lifted the baby in his arms. He was rewarded with another adorable smile, and he smiled back.

"Put her down." *Dyne.* It was a command.

Brennan looked up from the dear little face and into the face of Edison Colyear. The look in Colyear's eyes gave Brennan a chill. It was suspicion he was seeing in those eyes; this was a man on full alert. Before Brennan could think of anything to say, Colyear dashed from the room. Brennan heard what sounded like a drawer being wrenched open and then slammed shut. He was back in an instant. With a gun in his hand, pointed at Brennan.

"I said put her down. Who the hell are you, you fuckin' Dub?"

Brennan's heart pounded in his chest, his mind raced. What had he done? Distracted and charmed by the baby, had he dropped the Belfast accent? He played back his words; yes, he probably sounded Dublin. Whatever the case, Colyear had him pegged as a Dublin man. His cover was blown.

"Did you not hear what I said? I'll give you something you'll hear!"

The man's mother cried out, "Ed, put it away! This man will leave!"

Brennan couldn't turn to look at Rebekah, but her voice revealed how petrified she was. Colyear didn't reply to his mother, didn't take his eyes off Brennan.

Brennan knew that Colyear would not shoot him as long as Brennan was holding his baby girl. But Brennan was not going to hold a child as a shield, a hostage. Edison had lost his little sister to a bullet all those years ago. Brennan would not use baby Ellie as a shield. He would take a bullet first. He slowly bent forward and laid the baby down. Then gradually straightened up. Never taking his eyes from the gunman, he eased himself away from the quilt.

"Who are you, you fuckin' Dub? Coming into a family's home, disguised as a man of the church! What are you, a fuckin' Fenian? You're not going to —"

“I mean no harm. Let me explain. I came to reassure you that your family —”

“This family has suffered enough! You’re a dead man!”

Colyear was going to shoot him, Brennan knew it from the look in the young man’s eyes, the tone of his voice. Brennan had to put an end to this, and he saw only one way to do it. He had to take a chance and take his gaze off Colyear. He jumped in place, like a man startled, and jerked his head in the direction of the door. Colyear reacted with alarm, turned his head, and Brennan made his move. He knew he’d be striking fear into the heart of Rebekah, but he couldn’t take the chance of not doing this. He withdrew the Browning pistol Declan had forced upon him. He pushed the thumb safety down, moved the slide back, and released it to chamber a round. Ready to fire. He aimed it at Colyear. Colyear turned again to face him, eyes opening wide at the sight of the gun, and he started to raise his own. Brennan had no option; he took aim at his opponent’s weapon and fired. His bullet hit the target, Colyear’s weapon, and the gun flew to the floor. His mother screamed. The baby let out a cry of alarm. Colyear kept Brennan in his sight. Had Brennan’s perfect aim convinced him that Brennan was indeed a dangerous element let loose in the house? Brennan could almost see Colyear’s mind working, wondering whether he dared reach down for his gun. Brennan’s mind was working too. Keeping his eye and his aim on Colyear, he stooped to pick up the empty cartridge case that had been ejected from his pistol. He shoved it in his pocket. He could put an end to this right now: shoot Colyear and wound him, render him harmless. But he couldn’t bring himself to do it, to shoot the man whose family had endured so much, the family Brennan had come to relieve of the infamy they had lived with for so long. But if he didn’t . . .

A sudden bang to Brennan’s left. The door. He didn’t stop to think; he whirled around.

Declan and Terry had burst into the house. Must have heard the shot. Was there now a third gun in the room? Declan’s? Declan and Terry looked at Brennan, saw him pointing his weapon across the room. They turned to Colyear, who had retrieved his pistol from the floor.

"Ed, love, don't!" Mrs. Colyear pleaded.

"Mum, take her and go upstairs!"

"Drop it!" Declan shouted, as he reached into his pocket. Colyear clearly saw Declan Burke as the threatening figure he was, as he had been in the past and was now again. He took aim at Declan.

In moments of extreme danger, time slows down. Brennan had seen the gun pointed at his father. He had to protect him, the only way he could. He had to move. Now. He felt himself drifting through the air, almost suspended in the air, as he threw himself in front of Declan. Brennan knew what was coming. He felt fear like a stab to his heart. He was in the path of the bullet. He began to pray, silently but in song. "Hold Thou Thy cross before my closing eyes. Shine through the —" A flash of light. Intense pain. Then . . .

CHAPTER XXVIII

Terry

Flight Captain Terry Burke had always been calm in an emergency. Emergencies in the cockpit of a 747, crises set in motion by stormy weather or by unruly or threatening passengers. But this was his brother, beloved brother, lying wounded on the floor of a house in East Belfast. Terry's mind flashed back to himself and Brennan cavorting in the waves at Killiney Beach, and to the words Brennan had quoted from Yeats: "Soon shall our wings be stilled, and our laughter over and done." Tears sprang from Terry's eyes. Had Brennan somehow known? No, of course not. Terry was nearly paralyzed by fear and grief, but he had to act. Had to call for an ambulance. Only when he started for the phone did it register with him that the shooter — Mrs. Colyear's son — had fled the scene, run out the back of the house. Terry could tell by the look of Rebekah Colyear that she was not up to the task of calling for help; she sat unmoving in her chair, eyes and mouth wide open with horror. Terry saw the telephone, rushed to it, and called 999. "We need an ambulance! East Belfast." He gave them the address. "Gunshot wound, fell back, hit his head, knocked out, urgent!"

Then Terry dropped to his knees beside Brennan, begging him not to die. Declan Burke, kneeling on the other side, was white with shock. "Terry, keep him alive, keep him with us!" It was the first time Terry had ever heard a begging tone in his father's voice. Declan knew Terry had learned first aid in the military; if ever there was a time to step up and meet an emergency, it was now. Blood was seeping through Brennan's black clerical shirt from a wound high up on the left side of his chest, and from his left arm as well. Terry had to stanch the bleeding. What could he use? There were white cotton cloths on the arms of two of the chairs; he got up, grabbed them, and bunched them up. He pulled Brennan's shirt up towards his neck, tried to wrench it off his arm, but he couldn't manage. He knew from his training that he had to apply as much pressure as he possibly could to stop the bleeding.

"Da," he said, and looked across the room at Rebekah Colyear.

Declan took a deep breath and started to speak. "Mrs. Colyear, my son here, he came to offer you comfort. About your husband. We have information . . ." She reared back in her chair at that. "Information that will clear your husband of the suspicion he was under." Declan Burke could be cool-headed in an emergency too. His old training as a soldier in the Irish Republican Army came through for him now, and he managed to wrench his attention away from Brennan as Terry ministered to him. He told Rebekah the whole story of the real informer inside the UVF, one of the Shankill Butchers by the name of Mackasey Ward, and of her husband's innocence in that respect. He explained why one of them had come to the door in the guise of a Protestant minister, figuring that she would admit him to her home.

"And as for your son" — the son who had shot Brennan Burke and run from the scene — "we'll not be identifying him to the authorities."

Terry looked up at his father and was about to protest, but stopped himself in time. Young Colyear — Ed? — must genuinely have thought that his family was under threat again from strangers who had entered the house without giving their true identities. Men armed with guns.

He was justified in taking action to protect himself, his mother, and the baby — his daughter?

Declan spelled out the cover story that they all should adopt. "We'll say that a man came in, that we have no idea who he was. A stranger who may have seen a man with a clerical collar and thought he was a Catholic. A Catholic here in East Belfast. A stranger followed my brother into the house, fired a shot, and ran away."

The woman stared at him. Terry desperately hoped she was listening. Hoped that, despite the trauma of the moment, she was taking in what Declan was saying and would remember it. Recite it, as given, to the police.

Brennan was not moving. He was bleeding, but still breathing, and Terry could feel a pulse. He prayed to God to spare Father Burke from death. Please, please, God. And when Terry's mind turned to what his father had just said, he found himself in agreement. He could not even imagine the complications and the uproar if Declan Burke had to reveal to the Royal Ulster Constabulary — the Northern Ireland police — the sordid history of the real informer working against the UVF and for the IRA. Declan's own history would surely come out. It didn't bear thinking about.

To Rebekah Colyear, Terry said, "To make sure no suspicion falls on your son, your story is that you have no idea who the shooter was, had never seen him before. He barged into the house before we were able to tell you why we had come to call on you. Whatever you do, don't reveal to them what we told you. About your husband or any of that." Terry thought for a minute. "Say the gunman was middle-aged with, I don't know, thinning dark hair, and that's all you noticed. If they ask whether he was wearing a mask or a face cover of any kind, you'll have to say no. We'll say the same. A sudden impulse to shoot a stranger would not have afforded him time to put on a balaclava or anything like that."

Where was the fucking ambulance? And with Terry reporting a gunshot wound, the police would be sure to come as well. "Mrs. Colyear, go upstairs and take the baby with you. Remember we didn't have time to tell you why we came. A stranger, middle-aged with thinning dark hair, came flying in and opened fire on . . . on this man here." He pointed to Brennan. "As far as the police are concerned, that's all you know. Up you go, now. We'll take care of things down here." Even through her shock and fear, Terry could see the relief in her face as she went to pick up the baby girl and take her upstairs. The little one stared at Brennan lying there and whimpered a bit, as if in sympathy.

Now it was time to think, think clearly. And sanitize the crime scene. Terry and Declan had both seen the Browning pistol in Brennan's hand, and another gun at the feet of Ed Colyear. Terry knew that he and his father would have reached the same conclusion: the shot they heard had been fired by Brennan to knock the gun out of Colyear's hand.

"Da! Look around, see if there's anything that —"

"I don't want to leave his side!"

"But anything that might show —"

Declan got it then. He went back into soldier mode, illegal paramilitary mode, and examined the scene for evidence. Looked around where he and his sons had been standing and across the room where Colyear had been. "Christ!" He crossed the room and bent down, and Terry saw him pick something up from the floor. "Bullet," he said and scraped his shoe across the floor where the bullet had grazed it. Yes, that was the shot they had heard, which had propelled them into the house. The shot fired by Brennan.

"Terry, take the guns and get into the car and drive away from here!" his father commanded.

"I'm not leaving his side!"

"D'yeh think I want to leave him, for the love of Christ?"

"I'm checking his heart, his breathing. I have training in this, Da. And I can come up with a more innocent-sounding explanation for my presence here than you can for yours. Please, Da, get the guns and leave. Here are the keys." He handed the car keys to Declan. "Meet us at the hospital."

"It'll likely be the Royal," Declan said. Then he muttered something Terry couldn't hear.

"What was that, Da?"

"The Royal Victoria Hospital and British Army post." Yes, Terry remembered, Conn had told him that the Brits had some of their men stationed at the hospital complex. And had snipers on the roof of one of the buildings.

"I imagine we'll be safe from the British Army, arriving in an ambulance. Meet us there and say your prayers!"

Terry dug into his brother's pocket and retrieved the gun, and a spent cartridge case, and handed them to his father. Declan took them and said, "Give his hands a thorough washing." Brennan's hands, right. To remove any trace of the gun. What was it called? Gunshot residue. "Yours, as well. And wipe a cloth through his pocket there." Where the gun had been.

Declan then leaned over his unconscious son and spoke urgent words into his ear, words that Terry couldn't hear. Then he put his hands on Brennan's face, leaned down, and kissed his forehead. Terry saw the tears in Declan's eyes before he turned and left the house.

It wasn't five minutes later when Terry heard the sirens. He turned and saw the reflections of flashing blue lights in the front window. He got up and ran into the kitchen, found a washcloth and a bottle of washing-up liquid. He poured some onto the cloth, wet it under the tap, and brought it back to the sitting room. He washed his brother's hands and his own and swiped the cloth around Brennan's pocket. He returned the cloth to the kitchen counter. Just in time. Then he realized he needed something to remove the evidence of the attempt to remove the evidence! He saw a kitchen towel, snatched it off the rack, and proceeded to dry his hands and Brennan's, everything he had made wet. The door flew open and two men barrelled into the room, uniformed police. The ambulance crew followed them in. Four new people in the room. What they saw when they came in was Terry wiping his brother's forehead with a towel and uttering soothing words. Nothing more than that.

The paramedics, a young woman and young man, rushed to Brennan's side, performed some checks on him, and, at the same time, asked Terry what had happened. Terry gave the spiel he and his father had agreed on.

One of the police officers asked, "Your name?"

"Terry Burke."

"And?" he asked, turning to the man lying silent and still.

"My brother, Brennan Burke." Only then did he remember: Brennan had entered the Colyear home under a false name, Reverend William Henry Hanna. Too late to undo the damage now. But that false ID would not have stood up for long, not in a situation like this. That bit of theatre was of no importance now, with Brennan lying wounded from a bullet and unconscious from a fall on his head.

The cop was speaking again. Terry had missed part of it. "Sorry, what did you ask me?"

"What do you know about the man who did this?"

Terry shook his head. "Nothing. Never saw him before."

Just then, the baby let out a cry from the floor above. Shit! Now the cops would be going up to question Mrs. Colyear. Please, please stick to the script, Rebekah! Before heading upstairs, one of the coppers said, "We'll be coming to the hospital to speak with you."

There was a flurry of activity as the paramedics lifted Brennan onto a stretcher and carried him out to the ambulance. Terry grabbed the incriminating cloth and towel, bunched them up in his hand, and followed. He sat with Brennan for the race to the hospital, with the blue lights flashing and siren screaming. As they roared through the streets of East Belfast, Terry peered out and saw the towers of wooden pallets for Bonfire Night. He saw again the flag of the Irish Republic and photos of the Pope, all of which would be incinerated tomorrow night.

The ambulance rattled over the bridge across the River Lagan, the water shining in the sun, and they were in the city centre. Before long, it was the republican murals of West Belfast that caught Terry's eye as he glanced out: the Irish tricolour, references to the Easter Rising of 1916, IRA gunmen. But all he wanted to see was his brother, wanted to see some movement, however slight, to show that he was still together, body and soul.

Finally they pulled in at the hospital, the ambulance came to a stop, and — God be praised — Terry saw Brennan's eyelids flickering. Terry hopped out to let the paramedics remove his brother from the vehicle and carry him into the building. He saw a bin of some kind and stuffed the towel and cloth into it, then followed the emergency team inside. If there were soldiers on the premises, they were out of sight. And if there were still snipers on the roof of one of the buildings, Terry couldn't spot them. But they'd keep themselves hidden, wouldn't they?

Terry lost track of the time that passed after Brennan was admitted, presumably to the emergency room, and then wherever the doctors would be working on him after that. Terry refused to admit to himself any notion that the doctors might not be working on him. Declan had come running into the waiting room, fear engraved in his normally placid face. "What's happening?" Terry had nothing to tell him.

After what seemed like days, and was only hours, a doctor came down the corridor and said, "Mr. Burke?" Terry and his father stood. Terry was sure his own face was as white as his father's.

The doctor gave them the news. "Bullet grazed the outside of his chest, went into his arm. We operated, were able to remove the bullet. Dressed the wounds. He's been moved into a room. Once we set him up with a cardiac monitor and fluids, you'll be able to see him."

"So," Terry began, "he's —"

"He's going to be fine. Lucky man."

Terry felt his whole body slump with relief. It was as if he had been unconsciously holding himself upright. "Thank you, thank you!" he babbled to the doctor.

Half an hour later, he and Declan were standing beside a hospital bed as Brennan lay there motionless. Not quite motionless, thank God and Mary and all the saints. Brennan was breathing, and a monitor beside his bed showed the up-and-down peaked lines, which Terry knew represented the heartbeat. Brennan's left upper arm was bandaged; there was a tube in his right arm, delivering IV fluids. Terry did not speculate about what else might be attached to him, out of sight. He and his father stayed by his bedside as the doctors and nurses came and went and tended to their patient. They offered reassurance whenever the patient's father and brother asked about Brennan's condition and his prognosis. Yes, it seemed that Declan's and Terry's prayers would be answered.

CHAPTER XXIX

Brennan

What was he doing still in bed? Whose bed? This wasn't . . . Where was he? What time? He tried to raise his head, get up. Arrggh. Burning pain high up on his left side, his arm, an ache in his head. How long had he been asleep? Whose bed? Ah, the hospital. Oh, Christ. Man aiming at Declan, ready to fire. And then up in the air, himself in the air. Sideways. And a sharp, intense, stinging pain. He was still in pain. Had they . . . A picture formed in his mind, a man standing over him, looking down, talking. Quiet voice. Who? Ah, the man was a doctor. They were going to operate on him. When? He moved his right arm. A sting! He looked over. Something was stuck into the arm. A tube. He turned his head. Left arm bandaged. And bandage on his chest. They did the surgery. When would he be out of here? He started to push himself up in the bed. Gasped with the pain and settled himself down again. He was overcome with drowsiness, started to pass out. But no, he had to stay awake, find out what the fuck was going on, what was going to happen. He twisted his head to look around. On a table beside him there was a box with a screen. A television. No. A monitor, it would be, with lines spiking up and down. Showing what? His breathing? His heartbeat? There was a white curtain around his bed. Where was his father, his brother? Outside the curtain? Should he call out for them? Where were his cigarettes? He needed his cigarettes! He started to call out, but somebody came into the room, said something, looked into his eyes. He started to speak but felt himself drifting back into sleep.

The light looked different in the room. How much time had passed since he'd woken up earlier? He heard a laugh out in the corridor, a delightful feminine laugh, and there in the doorway was a sweet face and a head of short blonde curls. A nurse. She came over to his bedside.

"How are you doing now, Mr. Burke? Or Father Burke; forgive me, Father."

"I . . . Te absolvo, my dear." He could hear the weak croaking of his voice. He'd have to do better if he was going to get himself discharged from this place.

"My name is Jill."

He cleared his throat. "Forgive me for not standing to greet you, Jill."

"You, too, are forgiven, Father. I hope I haven't committed any mortal sins in your presence."

"I wasn't really present here, I don't think, if being conscious and intelligent is what we mean by present. How long was I out of it?"

"For a while, Father."

Her voice was not that of a person born and bred in Belfast. The west of Ireland, perhaps.

What had they been talking about before he got distracted by her voice? Sin, was it? He played along. "If you haven't killed anybody, Jill, your soul is probably clear of mortal sin." He peered at her. "You haven't killed anybody, have you? You've kept me among the living. I hope the same can be said of your other patients."

"They call me the Saint of Lourdes here, Father, for all the miraculous cures I have performed! And you'll be one of them."

"Ah, bless you, darlin'."

"Actually, I must confess there is nothing miraculous about me. I've been well trained here at the Royal. We are known throughout the world as experts in treating gunshot wounds."

"You would be, given all the bullets flying here. Now, I know the doctor explained this to me, but I wasn't at my best when he spoke to me. The bullet that hit me?"

"I'm sure you don't feel like a lucky man right now, Father, but luck was with you. The x-ray showed that the bullet just grazed one of your ribs and lodged in the muscle of your left arm. There were no difficulties extracting it. There were no sharp bits of bone from that rib, and there is no irreparable damage to your arm. You're all patched up and dressings applied. You'll have some pain for a while, but it won't be anything to worry about."

"Buíochas le Dia." Thanks be to God.

"Now, I just have to check your fluids here."

She examined the tube and the needle in his right arm and the bag of fluids, whatever they were, that were being fed into him.

"All good, Father."

"Call me Brennan, would you?"

"Brennan, it is."

Terry came into the room then, with a steaming cup of coffee. Declan was right behind him. "Jesus!" Terry exclaimed. "You're back in the world with the rest of us!" His hand jerked, and some of the coffee spilled to the floor, but Terry paid it no mind.

Then it was Declan. "Oh, thank God! Brennan, you're . . . you're awake."

"I am, Da. Alive and awake. And how are you yourself?"

"I'm grand. I'm not the one lying in a hospital bed."

"When did it happen?" Brennan asked. "How long have I been in here?" *And when can I get out?* Brennan was not a man for hospitals.

Terry replied, "The . . . the injury happened at around nine thirty this morning. There was a bit of a wait for the ambulance. Heavy traffic. But you were brought across town and in here not long after ten. We're now into the afternoon."

"Can I just —" He tried again to sit up and grimaced with the pain. He lay back down.

"I imagine they'll want to keep you in for a bit," Terry said. He looked over at the nurse. "He's looking a lot better, isn't he? Sorry, what's your name?"

"I'm Jill."

"And I'm Terry, his wee brother. And this is our da, Declan."

They said their hellos, then Terry claimed, "I'm the talent in the family. Would you like me to sing a song for you, Brennan?"

"Jesus, no!"

"Shit. He's blown my cover already. He's the musician in the family, Jill. Great singing voice, runs a choir school. Saint Bernadette's over in Canada."

Brennan replied, "I don't know, Ter. I may lose my position there. I'm asking myself did I convert to Protestantism? There I was, brought near to death in East Belfast, and what went through my mind? Not the 'Ave Maria' but that grand old Proddy hymn, 'Abide with Me.'"

"It's a beautiful hymn," Terry said. "And I'm sure we were all calling upon the Almighty in words from that very song. And will be again someday; we know not when." There was nothing jocular in the tone of his often-comical brother when he sang the words: "Fast falls the eventide. The darkness deepens. Lord, with me abide."

Brennan blinked and started to speak, but his father walked over to the bed and put his hand on Brennan's shoulder, on the uninjured side, and gave it a little squeeze. "Brennan, I don't know whether to get down on my knees before you or give you a boot up the hole. You saved my life. You risked your own life and nearly lost it. I'm near the end of my time in this world, only a few more years left to me, if even that much. And you have decades more to live, and to give as a man and a priest. And you nearly cancelled it all for your oul man." Declan turned to Jill then and said, "It's true. He saw the man aiming his gun at me, leapt up into the air, and came between me and the bullet."

"Oh my God!" Jill exclaimed, her gaze turning from father to son.

"Da," Brennan began. Coughed and began again. "Terry and I came to Ireland to try to keep you out of trouble, keep you safe, on your return to your homeland after four decades of exile. We could hardly have let you be killed."

"What a failed mission that would have been," said Terry. "What would we have said to our dear mother?"

"What am I going to say to your mother about *this*?" Declan pointed to the hospital bed and the room. "She nearly lost her son. When she finds out, you'll be hoovering bits of me up off the floor."

"Don't be troubling yourself about it, Da. We'll come up with a prepared statement. What do they say? A communications strategy to make the story as palatable as we can for our dear mother Teresa."

"Good luck with that, Terrence!"

Terry leaned over the bed then and said, "So, Bren, what did you see when you were out? Did you have a near-death experience, as they say?"

Brennan shook his head. "I guess I wasn't near enough to death to experience anything like that. You know the line, Ter: 'He is not dead but sleepeth.'"

"Well, *I* had a near-death experience when I saw what happened to you!"

"Who's this now?" Jill said, turning to the door. "Ach, the constabulary."

There were two big men in the doorway. One was hefty with a bullet-shaped bald head; the other was younger, tall and muscular with close-cut light brown hair. The older man pulled out a card of some kind, held it out and said, "Police."

"I hope you won't be exhausting our patient here, officers."

They didn't give Jill the courtesy of a reply, just waited for her to leave, and then moved towards the bed. Didn't ask after Brennan's health. They rattled off their names, but Brennan didn't catch them. The younger one took out a notebook and pen, and the interrogation began.

Terry peered at the card the copper held out. Royal Ulster Constabulary. The older of the two introduced himself as Detective Inspector Wilson and his partner as Detective Constable Hamill.

"Your names?" Wilson asked.

Terry had given their real names to the police who arrived at the Colyear house, so their real names it would have to be. "I'm Terrence Burke and that's my brother, Brennan."

"Brendan?"

"No. Brennan."

"And?" The cop turned to Declan.

"That's our father, Declan." Their father stared into the distance, as if the peelers weren't even there.

To Terry, "Where are you from?"

"New York."

"And them?" The peeler pointed to Brennan and Declan.

"New York, originally from Dublin. Brennan is working in Canada now."

"Passports?"

Terry willed his father to exercise his right to remain silent. Did they even have a right to remain silent in this woeful wee state? But Declan had never needed any incentive to keep his mouth shut in the presence of the police. "We left our passports in Dublin," Terry replied.

"I see." The cop gave him a narrow-eyed look, then said, "Tell us what happened."

Oh, Christ! Terry was worried enough about Mrs. Colyear sticking to the story they had agreed upon. But at least in her case, she had all the incentive in the world to report that an unknown gunman had come barging into the house. That version of events left her son entirely in the clear. But what would Brennan say? He had been unconscious when Terry and Declan had come up with the "stranger" story.

Brennan started to reply, but Terry overrode him. "A man came running into the house! I never saw him before in my life. Well, I wouldn't have. I don't know Belfast. He didn't even say anything, or if he did, I was too frazzled to take it in."

"And then?"

"Did the guy say anything, Da?"

Declan was trembling, which he had not been doing before now. In a faint, shaky voice, he said, "I don't know . . . I can't . . ." The frail old man couldn't continue. In spite of the terrible situation, Terry had to admire his tough old boot of a father acting the part of a delicate, confused old man. In other circumstances, Terry would have laughed.

"So, this man you say you didn't know entered the residence and what? What did he say?"

"I don't r-remember," Declan stammered. "I don't know if . . . if he said anything at all. Just had a gun, and well, he shot . . ."

"Maybe he saw the Dublin plates outside!" Terry suggested then, without letting on that he had parked the car out of sight of the house. "This wouldn't be a Dublin-friendly neighbourhood, I know, so . . ."

"So, what were yis doing there?" The big stern face and the rapid-fire questioning suggested — confirmed — that this was not a Dublin-friendly police force.

Brennan spoke up then. The weakness in his voice was not feigned. "I was there on a bit of a, well, an ecumenical mission."

"What d'you mean by that?"

"I thought while I'm over here in Ireland —"

"*Northern* Ireland," the peeler corrected him.

Terry didn't risk a glance at his father, who had taken up arms to make this region of the island part of *Ireland* and was no doubt steaming over this political dinosaur.

"Yes, Northern Ireland, of course," agreed the blessed-are-the-meek priest from his hospital bed. This new meek and mild Brennan Burke deserved an Academy Award, in Terry's opinion, for his performance here today, and their father would be in the running for best supporting actor. But Terry urged whatever lieutenants the Lord commissioned for His people to keep their stories straight that Brennan would not, in his weakened state, reveal the real reason for the visit.

Brennan resumed his performance. "I had read or heard somewhere that the lady, Mrs. Colbert?" Ah, the poor man was confused.

"Colyear."

"Right. Sorry. Mrs. Colyear's husband had been killed during the Troubles, the conflict here. And well, I saw myself on a bit of a mission, to her and perhaps some others who had suffered. I wanted to express my sympathies and do so from a Catholic perspective. Show her that our sympathies are not only limited to, well, one side of the conflict. You know?"

"No. I don't know. How many of these missions did you plan to undertake? Have you never read a newspaper over here? D'you not know how many thousands of people have been killed or wounded by the terrorists?"

Terrorists on all sides, Terry thought but kept it to himself.

"What did you think you were going to accomplish?"

Father Burke shook his head sadly. "I guess I was a little, em, naive."

"No shit, Sherlock."

"Perhaps I should have realized there could be trouble. I know that part of Belfast is, well, a Protestant area, loyal to the British Crown, so . . ."

"Aye, you should have. Did you not take a look around you and see the wee Union flags, the kerbs painted red, white, and blue?"

The humble priest bowed his head. "I know. You're right, of course, officer. But you know," Brennan continued, "Church of Ireland priests wear a collar, too, so why would anyone assume I'm a Catholic priest?"

"Your brother here said it. Were you not listening? Dublin plates on your car."

The junior copper glanced down at his notebook, flipped a couple of pages, and showed the book to his superior officer, who looked at the three Burke men in turn. Then he said, "We spoke with Mrs. Colyear."

"Wha—" Terry began and changed course just in time. Avoided what could have been a major slip, asking what she had said, what story she had told. "What a terrible experience for the poor lady!"

The cop merely stared at him. Terry had no idea what a shaken Rebekah Colyear might have said to the police, or how it would or would not have matched the story Terry had instructed her to tell. At least Brennan had now heard that an unknown gunman had burst in upon them.

"I hope to God you catch the man," Brennan urged from his bed. "The idea that this gunman is out there. Who knows when he might strike again."

"I know, Brennan. My fears exactly," Terry responded, playing along. "And were you the first victim? Have there been others? A man his age with a gun, middle-aged man like that; he may have had a long history of this sort of violence."

"Describe him for us."

"Middle-aged, I'd say, or a bit older." There, he got it in again, that the gunman was not a young man. Nothing like Mrs. Colyear's son. "He was getting thin on top. His hair, I mean. I think it was a dark colour. But it all happened so fast, I couldn't tell you much more than that. He shot Brennan, and he ran out of the house."

"What was he wearing?"

Oh, no. Had they covered that detail with Mrs. Colyear? Terry couldn't remember. He'd better come up with something. Something common or typical. "I think it was a track suit. Dark grey, or black maybe. I'm sorry, I just . . ."

"When our officers arrived at the house, there were just two men at the scene. From their description, that was the two of you." Brennan and Terry. The investigator turned to Declan. "You're the father?"

"I am."

"You were present when the shooting occurred."

Terry felt a jolt of alarm. They knew Declan had been there. Mrs. Colyear would have told them; she had no reason not to. So . . .

"But you weren't there a short time later when our men and the ambulance arrived. Where were you?"

He had left the scene to dispose of the guns he and Brennan had been carrying. And to move the car even farther out of sight. Please, Da, come up with a harmless explanation.

"Where d'yeh think?" was Declan's reply in that old-man voice he had put on, with a touch of belligerence added. "I went out to try and catch that fucker."

That brought a skeptical look to the face of his interrogator. "*You* went out after him. The age of you. Why didn't this fella go?" He pointed to Terry.

And Terry provided the answer. "I have first aid training. I couldn't leave my brother."

The two cops looked at each other then, and the senior man said, "The two of you will be making a wee visit to the station. Now." *Nye.*

"What?" Terry exclaimed. "We're not leaving Brennan here!"

"This is a hospital. They have better *first aid training* here than you have. And one of our officers will be posted outside the room."

A guard against a future attack. Surely, Terry thought, the Colyear lad would not be making another attempt on Brennan's life. But wait — Colyear had not been aiming at Brennan. His target was Declan. There was a reason for that: Declan had come flying into the house and was reaching for his gun when Colyear fired his shot. Terry told himself to settle down. Ed Colyear would not come walking into the Royal Victoria Hospital to attack Brennan, Declan, or anyone else. No doubt the young guy was living in fear of being identified as the shooter. Terry hoped Rebekah Colyear had reassured him that he and his family had nothing to fear from the men who had come from Dublin and made their ill-fated appearance in East Belfast. Of course, Terry breathed not a word of this to the police officer.

CHAPTER XXX

Terry

So, just when Terry thought the evening couldn't be any more surreal, he and his father were in a police car and then were taken into a police station surrounded by what looked like a bomb wall. He tried to imagine the reaction of his wife, Sheila, if she could somehow watch this scene playing itself out. He longed to hear her calm, reassuring voice. Longed to be back home in New York with all of this behind him. But no, this wasn't over yet. There was some rigmarole as they were brought inside, and DI Wilson consulted quietly with another officer. Then Wilson said to Terry, "You're coming with me. You," he said to Declan, "are going with him." He crooked his head towards the other cop.

"What's going on?" Terry demanded. "Are you fucking arresting us?" No reply. "We're being treated like suspects here!"

Again no reply. Just a narrow-eyed stare from Wilson. DC Hamill grasped Terry's arm and led him down a hallway and into a nondescript room where he was placed in a chair on one side of a table.

There were two empty chairs on the opposite side. The only other item in the room was the recording device. Declan had been taken away in the opposite direction. Terry was left alone to simmer and stew. What did the police think happened? What theory were they working on that they wanted to question him and his father separately? Did they think Terry and Declan were guilty of something? What was that law about organizations? Forbidden groups? Proscribed organizations, he remembered; that was it. They had Declan's name. Could they run his name through a file or a system somehow and find out he was an IRA man? And arrest and charge him for being a member? Terry told himself not to let his mind wander off into those roiling waters. But there was no comfort to be had in dwelling on the crisis facing them now. Surely they didn't think one of them had shot Brennan! So, what was it? Were they hoping to break apart the story they had been told? Why else would they put them in separate rooms? And what was keeping them? How long was Terry going to have to wait here?

He looked at his watch. He'd been in the station for nearly twenty minutes. He shifted in his seat, then stood up and walked around. Once again, he was confronted with something he found hard to endure: boredom. He always had to be doing something. But what he didn't do here in this room — he made a point of not doing — was pay any attention to that mirror or window on the wall. He assumed it was one of those windows where the cops looked in at the robbers. All they would see was a man, restless with boredom, pacing the floor as he waited for his interrogators.

They arrived around fifteen minutes after that. Wilson and Hamill. They all sat down.

Wilson began the questioning. "Mr. Burke, tell us again why you paid a visit to that woman and her wee grandchild."

Terry repeated the fiction Brennan had cooked up, about his mission to express sympathy and understanding across the sectarian line.

"Sectarian line, eh? But your brother did not go in as a T— a Catholic, did he? If he wanted to promote some idea of what?

Solidarity between Catholic and Protestant? Why did he not go in as a Catholic? Why the false identity as a Protestant minister?"

That was an easy one to answer. "He knew which side of the line Irwin Avenue was on! East Belfast, a Protestant loyalist stronghold. He figured he might not even get in the door if he didn't reassure the lady that he was a Protestant! His plan was that he would reveal his true identity once he got into the conversation."

"Then some man you say you don't know, this man just marches into the house with a gun and shoots your brother?" Wilson assumed a B-actor expression of skepticism.

"That's what happened. He saw the Dublin plates on the car, I guess, and maybe watched us going inside. Went somewhere to get his gun?" Terry shook his head; he couldn't possibly speculate.

"What did he look like?"

Be careful here, Terry warned himself. They had to stick to the description they'd all agreed on, but to recite it word for word would imply that yes, they had all agreed on a story to peddle. He thought back to what they had come up with. Thinning dark hair, so don't say that. "He was an older fella. Well, older than me. Fifties, early sixties maybe? A little extra weight on him, starting to lose some hair."

"But swift on his feet."

Another shake of the head; be it not for Terry to explain how the middle-aged attacker got away.

"What did the man say when he entered the house and confronted yis?"

There would be room for some variance here, given how fast everything happened. "He was shouting something about Dublin, fucking Dubs, something like that."

"And he targeted your brother."

Shit. Here it was again, another aspect of the story that might have varied in the telling. Young Colyear had aimed at Declan, but that was because Declan had rushed into the house, had seen what was happening, and reached into his pocket for his gun. Terry worried that Mrs. Colyear might have told the police that Declan and Terry had come in only after hearing a shot, the shot fired by Brennan. A shot the Burkes had covered up by getting rid of the evidence. But would she be afraid that revealing this might bring her son into the story? Her son instead of the stranger? The Burkes had assured her that they would not mention the son at all, but who knew what she might have said when questioned by police in the wake of such a traumatic incident? And had Rebekah told the police that Brennan was shot trying to save his father's life? The angle of the shot, the bullet wound, might have indicated that Brennan was not standing upright when it happened. He had thrown his body in front of Declan and was no doubt at an angle when the bullet hit him.

With all this whirling through his mind, he had lost the thread of the conversation. "I'm sorry, what did you ask me?"

"I said the stranger targeted your brother. That's what you're telling us?"

"He did, yeah."

Wilson looked down at his notes, then up at Terry. "Now, when our officers arrived at the Colyear house, when the ambulance arrived, the only people there were you, your brother, Mrs. Colyear, and her grandchild." He paused. "Your father was not there. Not there with his badly wounded son." Another pause and a stare across the table. "Where was your father?"

"He just took off, went after the guy! Tried to catch him."

This was met by an ostentatious look at the notebook, then a skeptical raised eyebrow. The kind of gesture Brennan himself often made. "A man well into his seventies runs off to try and catch a gunman? Is that what you're telling us?"

"That's what he did. He was outraged! Who wouldn't be?"

"What about you? You're a much younger man. Why wasn't it you who ran off in pursuit of the gunman?"

"Da didn't want to leave Brennan, of course, but I told him I couldn't leave because I have first aid training. So I tried to tend to Brennan as best I could."

"Oh, right, your first aid training. Where did you learn that?"

Now they'd be getting much more information about Terry than he wanted to give. But he knew they could get it anyway, now that they had his name.

"I was in the U.S. Air Force."

Then, it seemed, they'd had enough. They told him he could go. But was it a good thing or not that they *had enough*? Enough evidence? Of what? Had they bought into Terry's version of events or not? What steps would they take to try to find the unknown shooter?

Terry was snapped back to the present when Wilson asked, "Where are you staying in Dublin, in case we want to speak to you again?"

The house in Dublin. Can't mention the owner, Finn Burke! "We were lucky to find a house available to rent."

"Telephone number?"

He shook his head. "I'm sorry, I don't remember. Didn't use the phone much."

"Where are you staying here in Belfast?"

"The Donegall Street Inn and Suites."

"Detective Constable Hamill will give you a lift." Was this a courtesy or regular procedure? Most likely a ploy to check up on their location.

Sitting in the police car ten minutes later, Terry and his father didn't utter a word. When they arrived at the hotel, they made a point of walking casually into the building, giving no appearance of two men who desperately wanted to know what the other had said under questioning by the Royal Ulster Constabulary. But it came out in torrents when they were alone in their room. Terry recounted what he had told the police. And his relief was immeasurable when Declan repeated what he had said in the hospital room: that he had run out of the house and gone in search of the gunman. What he had really done, as he described it now, was something else entirely: he had run to their car with the two guns, got into the car, and driven it to the River Lagan, found a spot out of sight, and thrown the guns into the water. Then he had driven to the hospital. The car was still parked at the hospital, so once they were confident that the peelers had gone off to their station, they started walking from their hotel in Donegall Street to the Royal Victoria Hospital. It was a bit of a hike, but a good walk to work off some of their fear and frustration.

As they walked along, Declan gave voice to his feelings about the local police force. "Those fucking Brit toadies! It was all I could do to hold my temper in check."

"Now, Da, we can hardly criticize them for investigating a shooting."

"I know, but wouldn't I love to investigate some of *their* shootings? Shooting at unarmed peaceful protestors. Colluding with the loyalist paramilitaries in the murder of some of our people!"

"Yes, I've heard some of the stories," Terry said, but he understood his father's need to expound on the subject.

"It's a well-established fact, collusion between the Royal Ulster Constabulary and the UVF, UDA, UFF, the lot of them. They make a point of not charging some of the killers, letting nationalist deaths go unsolved, in order to protect their sources in the paramilitaries. And they've gone much farther than that — they've been known to stand back, or even assist, when our people are targeted for assassination. Them and some sinister elements of the British Army."

The British Army! Terry was not about to let it slip that his father had a son in the British Army right here in the North. He limited his response to the cops. "Right, the police! Upholders of law and order."

"Like fuck they are."

CHAPTER XXXI

Brennan

Brennan was feeling a bit better by the morning of his second day in hospital, sitting up in his bed enjoying a smoke. The bullet had been removed, and the tube taken out of his arm. He had undergone a neurological assessment to check out his cognitive abilities, memory, reflexes, motor strength, coordination, and other things, and he passed the test; they told him he would not need a brain scan. They had obviously concluded that he had not suffered a serious brain injury when he was knocked back and knocked out. So, his own diagnosis was that he was ready to be released from his confinement in hospital. He would be careful not to show any signs of pain or weakness that might banjax that plan.

Now there was something else. With all the trauma that had ensued as a result of the Burkes' goodwill mission in Belfast, one of the quandaries that beset him today was *What do we tell the folks?* Brennan's older sister, Molly, was a university professor in London, which would be only a short flight away. But she was spending this summer in Mexico, teaching courses there. She was, Brennan knew, planning to stop in New York for a visit with the family before returning to London when her summer term was up. So no need to cause her concern about this now. How much should they tell their mother? Patrick and his other siblings? Terry's wife, Sheila? Brennan remembered Declan and Terry calling home to say they'd be extending their visit, and even that innocuous statement had been met with questions. What on earth were they going to tell the family *now*? And what about Brennan's friends Monty and Maura? His fellow priests in Halifax? Well, he knew the answer to that one: he would not be ringing Saint Bernadette's parish office and telling any of this to Monsignor O'Flaherty or anyone else there. At least not now. He would give Mike O'Flaherty a watered-down version at some point after his return to Nova Scotia.

But the most pressing question on Brennan's mind now was what to tell Shay Rynne. The heart-scalding conversation with Shay's son, Brennan's godson, was very much on Brennan's mind. On his conscience. As was the debt of gratitude the Burkes owed to Shay for all his attempts to assist them and for keeping the details to himself. Brennan felt he could not keep from Shay — Shay as his close friend, not Shay as Detective Inspector Rynne — the fact that he had been shot in Belfast. Inevitably, the news would come out someday, and it would look strange indeed if Brennan hadn't mentioned it to his friend. *Oh, yes, by the way . . .*

But there were aspects of this that he did not want to reveal to Shay: the identity of Edison Colyear or any of the Colyear family, or the past shooting at the Colyear house when Ed Colyear, senior, and his nine-year-old daughter had been killed. That was still an unsolved murder — two unsolved murders — and Shay might feel remiss if he kept that information from the Northern Ireland police force. He was no fan of the Royal Ulster Constabulary, with its history of collusion with the loyalist paramilitaries. But still they were the police, and those murders had been committed in their jurisdiction and never solved. Declan truly did not know who had killed Colyear and his little girl — it was not the tout Mackasey Ward, but unnamed loyalists who had believed the slander that Colyear was an informer — so that made Brennan feel a little better about keeping it from his detective friend. Now, what to tell Shay? He was sure of one thing: he would not string his friend along by telling him a total stranger had come flying into the house and shot him. He would tell him about Declan trying to provide some comfort to a family in Belfast, and that "someone" was on the scene and felt himself to be in danger, and the shot fired at Brennan was in self-defence. Brennan would be honest enough to say that he himself had a gun.

Brennan outlined his plan to his father and brother, then arranged to make a phone call from the hospital and rang Shay at home. Shay was gobsmacked when Brennan gave him the pared-down version of the Belfast saga. He insisted on leaving for Belfast immediately to visit the patient, and Brennan then said that he had been worrying over the situation with young Brens and his fiancée and wanted to put things right.

Shay arrived in Belfast early in the afternoon. And young Brens was with him. Brens stared down at his godfather, opened his mouth as if to speak, but was apparently at a loss for words.

"Jaysus, Brennan!" Shay exclaimed. "I've come across men who've been shot, but I never thought you'd be one of them!"

"I hear you, Shay. It came as a bit of surprise for me too. Thanks for coming, both of you." He looked at Brens and Shay in turn. He flinched with the pain as he made his way up to a sitting position in his hospital bed. He was thankful that his guests affected not to notice. Then he proceeded to tell them the Burke-approved version of the story.

Shay was looking into his eyes as the recital went on. When Brennan finished, Shay said, "Somehow the detective in me thinks there is more to the story than I'm hearing."

"Isn't that always the way, Detective?" Brennan countered.

"It is. And it is now. But I'll have to accept it as given, and I won't be passing any of it over to my less-than-esteemed colleagues in the Royal Ulster Constabulary."

"Thank you, Shay. All we want to do is get the hell out of here with no more complications."

"That's understandable. Complications in the North of Ireland could keep you tangled up till the day all of Ireland is united, and we're all one big happy family."

"I'm not expecting that to happen in my lifetime."

Then there was something else he had to bring up with the policeman, another matter that was not to be brought up with Shay's fellow Gardaí. "You won't be surprised to hear, Shay, that Declan does not want to press charges over the snatching of Terry and the threatening note the kidnappers sent." Shay made no reply, and Brennan tried to think of the best way to claim that police involvement would not be necessary. "It seems that Declan and Finn will be able to, em, express their displeasure to the men involved and discourage them from any further actions or threats."

There was a wry twist to the detective's mouth then, and he said, "I think I can assume that your little adventure here in Belfast is related to the events in Dublin."

"You may make that assumption."

"But I must warn you, Father Burke. If any dead bodies turn up on Dublin soil, and I suspect they might be related to this series of events, I shall have to take action."

"Be assured, Detective Inspector Rynne, that there will be no men turned into corpses as a result of all this." Brennan prayed that he was right about that.

Shay turned the conversation to less contentious matters and told Brennan that Allie sent her love and wishes for a quick recovery. And the three of them chatted for a while until Brennan said, "Brens, if I could have a word?"

Shay took the hint; after all, Brennan had confided to him about the painful conversation he had had with his son. Shay said, "I'll leave you two to talk, and I'll see you again before we leave, Brennan."

When it was just godfather and godson, Brennan began, "I've wanted to speak to you again after the way we . . . I left things last time. I'm sorry —"

Brens raised his hand to cut off what he was going to say. "I hardly know how to begin this, Brennan, so I'll just dive in headfirst. Last time we were together, I left as a wounded man." He laughed self-consciously then. "I shouldn't be saying that to a *really* wounded man!"

Brennan waved away the apology. "I know, Brens. I can't imagine how you felt."

"I felt as if I'd been stabbed in the heart."

"I'm so sorry, Brens. I didn't want to hurt you but —"

Again, Brens put up his hand to silence Brennan. "But you were right. What made it so painful was that I already had my doubts about her, and what you said left me no way out. No way out of confronting what I feared was the truth. I wanted to meet with you again. To finish the conversation you started and that I didn't want to hear. But now, well, I've heard it, and I've had to admit to myself that you were right."

"I take no pleasure in being right about something so distressing, Brens."

"I know. I know you well enough to understand that. All those things you mentioned, the lying about her family and, yes, about her work history, the contradiction between her charm and her screaming fits of temper, they all hit home with me. I can't deny any of it. And she absolutely craves attention, can't stand it if somebody else is getting all the attention. I'll bet that's a *symptom*, too, is it?"

"Mm," Brennan conceded.

"Of course, I didn't let on to her that I'd heard any of this, didn't tell her about my conversation with you. But I started asking some questions. About her work, about some other things. And the stories changed yet again. She didn't even seem embarrassed at giving completely new explanations, which contradicted the earlier ones."

Yes, Brennan had seen that in some of the bad characters he had met. Knew it was typical in many of the worst of the breed.

They were silent for a few minutes, and then Brens said, "Da took me aside and told me something. About my gran, Mamie, trying to help Mrs. Delahunt repair her relationship with her brother's wife. His widow living over there in Spain. Mamie assisted Mrs. D in writing a letter to the sister-in-law, apologizing for anything she had done and offering to get the two of them reconciled. But the letter never got to Spain. Mamie knows this because of an unpleasant letter the one in

Spain sent to Mrs. D. It was clear that she had never got the loving letter from Gran in Dublin." Brens sighed then and said, "I hope to God you'll be up and out of here soon, Brennan."

Brennan smiled at him. "I will, sure."

"And get this: about that letter. It was Isabel who so kindly offered to post it. She took it in hand, said she'd take it to the GPO and send it as a registered letter. And yet" — he raised his hands in a comic imitation of a magician — "it never got to Spain."

Brennan did not let on that he had known this. He waited.

"So I asked Isabel about it. And I have to say it was fascinating watching her work, watching her decide what kind of story to give me. I'd started off by saying, 'Whatever happened with that letter you went to post for Mrs. Delahunt?' 'What letter?' That was her first response. So I reminded her, not that she needed reminding. 'Oh, right. I posted it.' And I said, 'Well, it never arrived.' 'How do you know that?' she asked. 'Never mind how I know.' And she insisted again that she had posted it. Where? She had to think about that. Then she remembered. She works in the city centre, so it would have made sense to take it to the General Post Office in O'Connell Street. 'The GPO,' she claimed. I said, 'Let's get the receipt and take it to the GPO, ask them about it.' Of course, she claimed they hadn't given her a receipt. Obviously, she painted this as the fault of the people behind the counter at the post office. 'Well, we'll go ask them about it anyway. Gran said it was the fourteenth of March when she wrote it.' This went on for a while, her making excuses and me knowing none of it was true. Finally, I said, 'You're lying. You never posted it. What did you do with it?' And at that, she stormed off with some choice words for me that would never be uttered on any operatic stage! And me standing there, knowing the whole thing was a performance, knowing from what Da told me that she had never posted it. Did she throw it in a bin somewhere? Burn it? I don't fucking know.

"So, with all this, Brennan, I'm really sorry for the way I acted when we met at the canal, had our drink at the Brian Boru. I've been regretting it, you may be sure. I *know* you've always had my best interests at heart, including about this. So, Brennan, I'm sorry!"

"No, Brens, no apologies required. You handled the whole thing better than anyone else would have. You were remarkably calm. And I'm sorry that it has to be this way, that she's the way she is, and that I had to tell you." Brennan's throat was dry, and he coughed, winced with the pain in his left flank.

"I ought to let you rest, Brennan."

"No, I've no need of rest. I've had enough of that to last a lifetime. A can of beer would go down nicely though."

"You're every bit the tough man my da says you are!" Brens laughed as he said it. "But no beer on me today, Brennan. Sorry."

"No worries. Maybe I'll have my brother smuggle some in for me. Doctors have been known to prescribe Guinness for their patients, as you may know."

"I hope you'll have one of those wise physicians taking care of you here." He looked away for a moment, then said, "But about Isabel, I should have known, should have seen through her. Well, I did, but wouldn't admit it to myself. I can't look at her the same way now. Still, it's going to be painful ending it. I loved her for two years, ignoring what I suspected about her. I definitely want to end it, but I'm not sure how to go about it."

"It might be best if you rig it somehow so that she's the one who ends it. That way, maybe she won't keep harassing you about the breakup. It shouldn't be hard to get her angry, work her up against you!"

"That's for sure, but I won't be looking forward to those scenes of drama!"

"Perhaps it can be something about money. Something that suggests a future with you will not be a life of luxury."

"Not a grand house and garden in Ballsbridge! Truth be told, she's already been after me to get a better job, something that pays better than teaching music at Waltons. But I love Waltons and I love teaching there, making music with the students. I've no intention of giving it up. Unless . . . Maybe it's time for me to think again about becoming a priest. That idea never entirely went away."

"Maybe so, Brens, but this would not be the time, not after a breakup. It might just be a reaction, and something you'd regret later."

"Something *else* I'd regret later!"

Brennan smiled. "Right. You'd need a period of quiet reflection. Not all this drama."

"Oh, there will be drama. You can go down to the betting shop and place a good-sized wager on that. But I think your idea is a good one: spin it so that she's the one who dumps me, rather than have her screaming about me dumping her."

Brennan leaned over, ignoring his pain, and put his hand on the young fella's arm, gave it a little squeeze. "I wish you all the best in getting through this, Brens. Any time you want to talk, just ring me in Halifax. Any time, day or night. You have my number."

The younger man blinked as tears formed in his eyes. "Thank you, Brennan. You know how much I appreciate that. Have always appreciated your guidance and support. Not to mention the good times and the laughs we've enjoyed! And drink taken, on occasion. I nearly suffered an early death myself when I heard what happened to you here! Thank God in Heaven you're all right." He looked around him. "I don't see any of that prescribed Guinness here in the room. But how about this? I'll go out and get my da, and we'll smuggle something in. Would you like that?"

"There's no word in the Irish language for yes. But I think we can take it as implied here. There's no word in Irish for no either! A glass of something would go down nicely. Or one of those little bottles that are meant to be slipped into a pocket."

"Let thy will be done, Father." Brens grinned as he stood and headed for the door. He went out. An hour or so later, the Rynnes returned and slipped a little bottle of whiskey under Brennan's pillow. They raised their hands to Brennan as if raising glasses, wished him well, accepted his thanks, and took their leave.

CHAPTER XXXII

Brennan

After two days in the hospital, Brennan walked out on his own two feet, with bandages on his chest wound and arm and a prescription for some drugs to lessen the pain. Terry was with him. It was cloudy but warm, and it felt glorious to be out in the air again. He looked around at the massive hospital complex and noted its location between the Falls and the Grosvenor Roads.

"Declan is waiting in the car over there on the Falls Road. How are you for walking? It's not far."

"I'm grand." Brennan held his arm steady to avoid aggravating it. It was only a few minutes before he spotted the Astra parked on the side of the road.

Terry stopped and held up a hand for Brennan to do the same. "Hold up a second, Bren. What are we going to do about our father's first-born son?"

With all the other commotion that had beset the family during this trip, Brennan had tried to push from his mind the question of his lately discovered brother and what effect the discovery might have on his father. The question could no longer be avoided. And he now felt as if he had known the answer all along. And it was not the answer he and Terry had been going with till now. If anyone had the right to decide what to do, or not to do, in this situation, it was Declan. Not Brennan and Terry.

"Do you think our dear old da will want to take a trip to Lisburn?" Brennan asked.

"I guess that will depend on how well he takes the news we're about to hit him with. *If* we hit him with it."

"Will he hit *us*, do you suppose?"

"Would we deserve it if he did? Are we going to reveal our secret to him?"

"It's not our secret to keep, Terry. That seems obvious to me now. Going behind his back to find the man, that was our secret. The fact that he is our father's son — that's for Declan, not for us. Our da has a right to know."

"I'm with you on that, Bren. But what about —" His voice was drowned out by a bus passing by. "But what about approaching Dwight Earnshaw? You and I held back, didn't reveal the connection, that time in the bar. But now that Da is here with us, should we come clean with him too? With Dwight, I mean?"

Brennan shook his head. "No, I can't see us doing that. We don't have the right — in fact, I think it would be morally wrong — to tell Dwight, in case he never knew. If he grew up thinking Earnshaw was his father, it would be too painful for him to hear that his father was in fact another man, and that his mother and . . . and her husband had deceived him about this all his life. He would be in pain and might well be enraged. And it would be painful for the man who raised him as his own." Verna at the museum had told them that Earnshaw Senior was still alive. "It would be hurtful for the entire family if they found out they had been lied to all this time. And perhaps the worst outcome of all would be the members of the family disillusioned about their mother. And her no longer alive to defend herself. The hurt would come not from the fact that she had a relationship with another man back in the day, but that she had misled the family about Dwight's parentage all this time. If in fact that was the case. And somehow I suspect it probably was."

Terry took a deep breath, released it, and said, "So maybe we just offer to take Dec to have a look at the guy and leave it at that. Anyway, let's get moving." They walked to the car.

"Welcome back to the land of the living, Bren," his father said when they were all seated in the car.

"Sure, amn't I delighted to be back?"

"Now, there's a man we have to see before we return to the hotel."

"Oh?"

"Yeah," Declan said. "The peelers have been nosing about. We've caught sight of them outside the hotel. Only a couple of times, but still . . ."

"Why aren't they out marching and banging their drums with all the rest of the Orangemen on this Glorious Twelfth of July?"

"They have other ways to show who's in charge up here in this Northern statelet."

"So they do," Brennan agreed.

"Da has been in touch with Finn," Terry said, "and Finn has arranged for us to see a man here in Belfast. I have the directions." He held up a slip of paper.

Declan said, "I'm a little concerned about getting away across the border and out of here."

"The border you don't recognize."

"But unfortunately, there's a whole crowd here that do recognize it. And I want to be well clear of it before that shower of shites get any ideas."

Brennan assumed that the shower of shites were the Royal Ulster Constabulary. "Ideas about what?" he asked.

"It's against the law here to — how do parents and schoolteachers put it? — to hang around with the wrong crowd."

Terry put it plainly, "The Provisional Irish Republican Army is a proscribed organization."

"I'm well aware of that," Brennan replied.

"So Dec here is worried that the peelers might stumble upon some information about his background."

Declan started the car and pulled out into the road. "I want to get the fuck out of here in case they dig up information about me and haul me back to their barracks, even lay charges against me."

"Unlikely, though, wouldn't you say?" Brennan asked.

"Everything about this wee statelet is unlikely," Declan said. "Its very existence is unlikely and yet it's still here, still separated from the other twenty-six counties to the south."

"But even in the twenty-six counties, if we're talking about a certain organization being illegal, that's the situation in the south too. Amn't I right? You could be at risk in Dublin as well as in Belfast." *If you are still a member.*

"I'll take my chances at home in Dublin. I want to get clear of this city before they know we're leaving. And I intend to do that in a way that will foil any plan they have to follow."

"What do you mean?"

"You'll see."

They drove along the Falls Road, past the shops and the bars that Brennan knew to be republican drinking spots. Brennan saw his father checking in the rear-view mirror from time to time, concerned no doubt about being followed by the police. Soon they were passing the Milltown Cemetery where a great many republican heroes were buried. Declan asked Terry, "What does my note say? Where do I turn?"

Terry the navigator replied, "You're going to Andersonstown. Keep right when you get to the Glen Road. There will be a blue Peugeot 205 parked just outside the house. Keep on . . . There it is." A Peugeot with Monaghan plates. "Pull in behind it."

"Are you going to fill me in on this little excursion?" Brennan asked.

"All will be explained," Declan replied. "I'll go inside." The message was *And you lads will wait out here*. "You two gather up anything you have in here." In their car. But all their belongings were back in the hotel; Brennan hadn't had anything with him but the clothes on his back when he was transported to the hospital. The clothes on his back and the bullet in his arm.

Declan got out of the car and walked to the door of the corner house. He rang the bell and waited. A tall, heavy-set man in his early fifties opened the door. His eyes surveyed the street. Apparently satisfied, he gestured for his visitor to come inside.

A few minutes later, Declan came out and walked to the Peugeot. He inserted a key into the lock, opened the door, and got into the driver's seat. He beckoned to his sons, and they joined him in the car, Brennan in the back, Terry in the front. Declan opened the glove box and took out a piece of paper, looked it over, and put it back in its place. He started the engine and drove away. Any peeler looking out for a black Opel Astra with Dublin registration would be sorely disappointed. Unless they happened upon a house in Andersonstown, Belfast. As for a Peugeot registered in Monaghan, the county right on the south side of the border, that would surely draw no official interest.

"What's going to happen with our old car?" Terry asked. "Finn's car."

"Our man will hide it for a while and then drive it to Dublin for Finn, and he'll get this one back."

"Who is he, the man in there?" Brennan inquired of his father.

"Brennan, there's a saying here in Belfast. *Whatever you say, say nothing.*"

"So that's how it is?"

"That's how it is."

ഗ

"Da," Terry said, "there's something we have to talk about, before we go back to the hotel."

Declan glanced over at him. "I don't know what you're on about. But why don't we check out of the hotel now? We'll have lots of time to *talk* on the way back to Dublin."

"For one thing," Terry said, "if the peelers are still keeping an eye on our hotel, we don't want them seeing this car." Declan gave a quick nod of his head. "And when you hear what Brennan and I have to say, we're thinking you may want to stay here in Belfast another night."

"Why the fuck would I want to stay in Belfast for another night? It's not as if we've been enjoying the craic, is it?"

"I've got an idea."

"So you have. Let's hear it."

"It's a beautiful day. Let's take advantage and enjoy some sun and fresh air."

"Why do I suspect I'm being set up here?"

"I know fresh air and grass and flowers aren't the usual amenities we enjoy when we're in Ireland, but let's break from our usual practice and spend some time in the great outdoors while we have our chat."

Terry proceeded to give his father directions to the Belfast Botanic Gardens in the lovely part of the city near Queen's University. Declan gave a snort of derision but followed the prompts to their destination. When they arrived and parked up, Brennan saw the magnificent Palm House, an enormous glass building with a rounded roof over the central part and two great wings to the sides, where plants of all kinds were kept. Flowers of every colour in the spectrum were on display outside as they walked along. Even Declan looked intrigued as he gazed about him. By way of habit, Brennan reached into his pocket and pulled out a pack of smokes, then chided himself. The scent of the flowers was intoxicating; he would not desecrate it with clouds of cigarette smoke.

"Let's have a seat here," Terry suggested, pointing to one of the benches. When they were seated, the conversation began. "Da, I told you about the two low-lifes, Frank and Ger, making those insinuations about the Big House in County Wicklow, and you told us you had a relationship with a young woman there."

"I did." He didn't elaborate.

"Well, we did a bit more . . . research."

Declan sat up straight, as if ready to meet a challenge. But he didn't speak.

"Da, she had a child. A boy."

His reply took them by surprise. "I know." Ah, so he knew all along. But no. "I got a strange letter in the post. A few weeks ago."

"A letter! Who from?" Terry asked.

"Someone in that family. Althea's family. Her granddaughter. She found Althea's diary after Althea died. That's, em, that's what spurred me on to come back here now."

Was that the piece of paper Declan had snatched back from Brennan on the plane? That seemed like years ago.

"Jaysus, Da!" Terry exclaimed, "You're a man full of surprises. Who all knows about this?"

"Nobody."

"Not even —"

"Not even your mother. I'll . . . I'll be telling her when I get home."

"Have you met him? The . . . your son?"

Declan didn't answer right away. Then it was a quick "No."

Brennan was about to repeat Terry's question, but he knew his father well enough to know that no as expressed by Declan Burke meant *No, and don't be asking me again.*

"Well," Terry said and looked over at Brennan. At Brennan's nod, he said, "We have."

"Christ Jesus! You've met him? How did yis do that? Let me guess the rest of it. You met him lying in a laneway in Dublin."

"A laneway?" Brennan asked. "Why would he be lying somewhere like that?"

"Drugs. The hard stuff. He's addicted. I, em, I went looking for him in some of those dirty old laneways. Saw many a poor young and not-so-young fella lying there, destroyed by the stuff. When I said no, well, I'm not sure it was him. But maybe it was." He paused then, "It likely was."

What the —? Brennan stared at Terry in amazement and got the same wide-eyed look in return. Brennan asked, "Are there two of them?"

"Two of them?!" Declan exclaimed. "There aren't two of them. I was only with her for a short while. Oh, fuck, did she have twins?"

His two present-and-accounted-for sons shook their heads. Brennan said, "No, there was one boy, Dwight, born 'not long enough' after her wedding. So, that's where you come in."

"Came in," Terry could not resist adding.

"Dwight?!" Declan exclaimed at a volume they rarely heard from him.

"That's his name," Brennan continued, "she had two girls and another boy over the next few years."

"I knew she got married to a fella *of the better sort.* I was never in touch with her again. But I did hear that they moved to England shortly after the marriage. Returned home after a couple of years." He looked thoughtful for a moment, and his sons did not disrupt the silence. Then he said, "In her letter, the granddaughter makes reference to two pages she found of Althea's diary. Althea and her husband were having a row, and he brought up my name. Not in flattering terms! Called me a 'grease monkey'!"

"No!"

"Yes, Terry, in some quarters your dear old da is not held in high esteem. And then there was the row about the son, Dennison, and it seemed she was calling the husband out for not being a good father. He countered with something like 'the rest of them turned out fine,' or were successful. I'm thinking now that the granddaughter read that diary, the husband's remarks about me, and she came to the wrong conclusion — that the boy Althea had with me was Dennison. And since I had fathered this poor lad Dennison, I should step in and try to help him. Which I thought I should do." Declan stopped speaking and looked about him, nodded in greeting to an elderly couple walking through the gardens. Then he returned to the conversation, "So that line in the diary about 'the rest of them' was just a reference to the other son and daughters, who had not got into trouble with drugs. And the husband made a crack something like *You think Declan Burke would have done a better job of it?* But that must just have been a general remark about me: if she had stayed with me and never married him. It wasn't about me specifically being a better father to Dennison, because if the first son was named Dwight, the man knew perfectly well I wasn't *Dennison's* father."

Declan's gaze intensified as he looked from Terry to Brennan. "And you lads say you've seen him! Dwight?"

"We have," Terry replied. "Up close."

"*What?* Did you two have a talk with him? Tell him who we are? What the fuck did you do?"

"We, well, had a brief conversation with him. I maintained my cover."

"Your *cover*?"

"Bren and I were posing as American tourists, and I spoke to him in an accent from the American Midwest, playing the dumb tourist. He replied in a voice much more posh than mine!"

"I can't believe I'm hearing this."

"I know, I know, Da. But we didn't hint at anything else, anything personal."

"Where did you see him?"

"Would you like to see him yourself?"

"Where did you see him?" Declan asked again.

"In Lisburn."

"Lisburn!"

"That's where he . . ." Terry hesitated. "That's where he's living now."

"He's living there because — would my first guess be correct?"

"I suspect so," Brennan replied.

"The barracks."

Terry said, "He's Major Dwight Frederick Earnshaw, British Army, Thiepval Barracks."

"Jesus wept!" Declan moaned. "I thought my newly discovered son was a drug addict lying in a puddle of piss in a Dublin laneway. Now I'm hearing he's a British soldier!" Brennan kept his thoughts to himself and thanked God Terry did the same. After a few seconds, their father said, "Maybe it's a good thing we emigrated out of here after all."

It took Brennan a moment to catch the meaning. Then he had it: if they had stayed in Ireland, Declan might have joined his IRA comrades doing battle here in the North. And he might have killed his own son. Or his son might have killed him.

"It's a helluva lot to take in, Da," Brennan said. "But we're here, so do we take the next step?"

"Turn up at the barracks and get the same kind of welcome our Dublin voices got us in East Belfast earlier this week?!"

"Not the barracks. We saw him with a few of his fellow soldiers at Gin Millie's. A bar in Lisburn."

Declan turned to him in astonishment. "Youse were drinking together in the same bar?"

"That's where we saw him. Now, the question is, do you want to do the same?"

His father made no answer. They sat quietly for a while, Brennan staring in admiration at the wonderful glass house and breathing in the scent of the blossoms.

Then Terry said, "If we decide to stay another night, we should move to another hotel. Here in Belfast, I mean. Somewhere the police won't find us. And, as I said, we don't want them seeing our new car. So I'd suggest that once we're back in the city centre, we park at some distance from the hotel. Brennan and I will take a taxi to the Donegall Suites and get all our stuff. Check out, if it's not too late. Well, even if it is, we've got to get out of there. If we have to pay for an extra night, I'll take care of it. And we find another hotel. Take our little jaunt to Lisburn and come back here to Belfast. Then home to Dublin."

"I don't know what to do about this," Declan said. "After all your talk about seeing him, how can I just leave the country, knowing he's nearby, and not take the opportunity to see him for myself? The three of us sitting on the plane flying back to New York and me knowing you met him and I didn't. But if we go there, see him in the bar, what then? Will I feel a temptation I can't overcome, to go over to him? Spill out the truth to him, that I'm his father? We can't possibly predict what his reaction might be. I can't see any good coming out of it, can you?"

"No," Brennan agreed, and he repeated what he had said to Terry about the hurt it would cause to Dwight Earnshaw and other members of his family. Not to mention what Major Earnshaw's reaction might be if he were to discover who Declan Burke really was and what he had done over the years in his fight against the British Army and its Northern allies.

In the end, they decided that this would have to be a look-and-see event for their father, not an evening of revelation. But Brennan wondered, and he was sure Terry did, too, what would happen if and when they were all in the bar together. Dwight Earnshaw had already met them, met them as George and Will, yokels from Middle America. Brennan's imagination failed him when he tried to picture Declan Burke playing the role of father to George and Will, their "Pop," as they had put it during their performance in Gin Millie's. Declan acting like an *Aw shucks, I'm real excited to be in Ireland* bumpkin? Unthinkable!

ᔓ

Not all the plans were finalized, but they did collect their belongings and check out of their first hotel, keeping the Monaghan-registered car out of sight. And they found a little family-run bed and breakfast in republican West Belfast. When they had unpacked their gear, Declan said, "I'm going to ring your mother. And you, Terrence, will you be ringing Sheila?"

"I will, but I'll put it off for a bit. With everything that's happened, it'll be difficult even for a barroom bullshitter like me to act as if *Oh, nothing happening here. Nothing to see here, folks*. I'll be in for a bollocking when I get home, for keeping her out of the loop all this time. You go ahead, Da. We'll all talk to Ma."

So they made their long-distance call to New York and told Teresa Burke they were having a grand old time seeing their homeland again. Only a few more days and they'd be on North American soil again.

When the call was over, Terry said, "Something to show you here, Da. There was a photo of him, of Dwight, at the museum in Wicklow, and I snapped a picture of it."

Declan stood in the centre of the room, unmoving. Then he held his hand out. "Give it over." He stared at it, eyes growing wide. "Holy Christ! He's the spit of our Patrick!"

"He is," Brennan agreed. "We were gobsmacked when we saw the picture."

"I'll likely be regretting this. But let's be off to Lisburn tomorrow."

CHAPTER XXXIII

Brennan

"So," Terry asked the next morning, "is there a good chance the Army men will be at Gin Millie's today, d'you think, Brennan?" The three of them were in the car on their way to Lisburn. "The day after Orangemen's Day. Surely anyone who exerted himself doing all that marching on the Glorious Twelfth would need to relax with a drink the day after."

"Don't forget, though, Terry, he is a soldier, well practised at marching."

"True enough, but might all the Orange lads and their pals in the British Army want to look back fondly on their big day and celebrate it in their local? And this being a Saturday, I'd say the chances are good."

The only response from Declan was "Let's get on with it. And feck off with the Orange blather, would yis?"

The symbols of the Loyal Orange Order were on display when they arrived in Lisburn, the orange flag and a banner showing King William of Orange astride his white horse, alongside the union flags and other loyalist emblems. Nobody mentioned it; the only acknowledgement was a wink from Terry to Brennan. They parked up and walked to Gin Millie's bar. Terry, once again taking on the role of Will the American, greeted the barman. "We were here before. We like this place, so here we are again!"

"Aye, I remember yis."

"And I remember that this is a popular spot with soldiers who are stationed around here. They were a friendly bunch!" They weren't, but that would not have fit in with Terry's narrative. "I wonder if they'll be in today. Or tonight."

"There's a big ceremony of some kind up at the barracks this afternoon, so —"

"So they won't be in?" Brennan could hear in Terry's voice the effort to hide his disappointment. Disappointment shared by Brennan himself. As for Declan, relief perhaps?

But the barman hadn't finished. "Ach, they will be in, if they do what they usually do after an event like this. Sure, they'll have their supper and a glass of wine or a drop of whiskey with the higher-ups." The barman laughed. "Then they'll make their excuses and leave for here. Come in here so they can chat about whatever went on today, and whatever was said or done by their superior officers! They wouldn't be able to speak that freely over at the barracks! Now, what can I get for you?"

The three of them ordered pints and bags of crisps and peanuts, then Terry said, "We may see those Army fellas when we come back. We're having a big supper too!" What? Ah, it was Terry making things up on the fly. "Friends we met on our travels here in Ire— Ulster. Friendly folks in this part of the world! They live just outside the city, and they invited us over. But we'll be back here after we clean our plates at our friends' place! Sorry, I'm gabbing on and on here. I'll let you get back to work, pouring pints for your thirsty customers."

The Burkes took their own pints and snacks and found a table near the front of the room. "So, Terry," Brennan asked, "what is the plan you've concocted for us?"

"Simple. We have our pints here now, then we go off to that supper with our imaginary friends. Or at a restaurant. After that, we station ourselves somewhere to keep an eye on this place and see if it's invaded by the armed men of the British Empire. We wait a few minutes, then we come back and *Oh, hello, haven't we seen you chaps before?*" Terry looked across the table at his father. "You're awfully quiet, Da. Is there something about this little scheme that doesn't meet with your approval?"

That was met with a muttered "Fuck." Nothing more from the man at the centre of this drama. But Brennan could hardly blame him; the prospect of coming face to face with the son he never knew he had would be traumatic for anyone. Or for most people, Brennan assumed. And for a man like Declan, who did not wear his heart or his history on the sleeve of his gansey, this would be particularly painful.

When they had finished their drinks, they said goodbye to the barman and headed outside. A lovely July day. Brennan said, "They've a nice market square here, Da, and the Castle Gardens are lovely."

"Ah. A sightseeing tour. Well, that will likely be more pleasant than whatever awaits us if we return to that pub."

If they returned. Was their mission now in doubt? Time would tell. For now, Brennan led the way along the city streets, through the market square with its attractive shop fronts, some in brick red, some in white, with colourful awnings and signs. When they reached the gardens, which had been the site of a seventeenth-century castle, Brennan once again enjoyed walking by the old stone and brick walls, the towering trees and the blossoms in cheerful colours: pink, yellow, a deep reddish orange. What was it called? Vermilion? They walked to the edge of the park and looked out over the River Lagan. After spending a few minutes enjoying their surroundings, they headed off to find a restaurant and have their supper.

They lingered over their meal and drinks until they thought it might be time for a squad of thirsty soldiers to make their way to their local. But when they got to the bar, there wasn't a soldier in sight. Brennan wondered whether his father was disappointed or relieved, but he didn't ask. They ordered drinks again and found a table, engaged in desultory conversation.

Half an hour passed, then Declan said, "Should we scrap this plan?"

"Let's give it a bit more time," Brennan replied.

And the wait paid off. In they came, the soldiers from Thiepval Barracks. The group was led by an officious-looking tall man Brennan had not seen before, but a couple of others looked familiar. They were all in their khaki uniforms. Brennan and Terry nodded at them in greeting, then made a show of returning their attention to their pints. Until Brennan heard footsteps approaching. What was this? It was Major Dwight Earnshaw walking towards them, uniformed and bemedalled. Brennan could see his father — *their* father — making an effort not to react, determined to maintain his stoic expression.

"Mr. Burke, I presume?"

All stoicism fled at the English-accented words. Declan's jaw dropped as his eyebrows rose. Terry looked like a little boy who had just heard a rattling in the chimney on Christmas morning and was waiting for the treasures to appear.

"I know who you are, Mr. Burke. And I believe you know who I am." He looked from Terry to Brennan and said, "These are your sons, I assume. Your *other* . . . Shall we go into a snug for a bit of privacy?" He pronounced it "privv-acy," the *I* short as in "kin."

Declan had turned to stone or the equivalent; he didn't move a muscle in face or body. Brennan took hold of his arm. "Come on, Da. Let's all sit down and have a chat. Bring your pint."

"There's a snug over there," Terry said, pointing to the far wall. "Door's open, nobody in it."

Earnshaw gestured for the Burkes to go ahead. Perhaps didn't want to risk turning his back to them. Then they were in the snug, Earnshaw on one side of the table, the three Burkes crowded on the other side. Terry was on the outside, but he got up. "I'll sit over there." And took his place beside Earnshaw.

Major Earnshaw

What was the protocol for a situation like this? How to begin this embarrassingly personal discussion? Who should speak first? Declan

Burke was sitting there looking into the distance, saying nothing. The austere black-haired, black-eyed bloke kept his own counsel too. Ah, the livelier-looking one started things off.

"I'm Terry. And I'm curious, as you might imagine, curious about how you know who we are."

"And I am curious as to how you know who *I* am. To answer *your* question, let me say first of all that I am not overcome by curiosity every time a new face appears here in Lisburn. But one of our sergeants lived in the United States for some years, in Chicago. And he recognized the accents in which you spoke — spoke on *that* occasion — as typical of that area of the USA. The sergeant commented on the fact that there are quite a few Irish Americans in the Chicago area. This was a part of the world known to be sympathetic to the Fenians back in their day. And, our sergeant suspected, perhaps to the Fenians of our present times. Which could mean trouble on our doorstep."

Terry Burke obviously found this amusing, smiling with his mouth and with his eyes as he replied, "So, you and your men embarked on a mission to find out what these rabble-rousers were up to."

"Up to, yes. I myself thought you were here for reasons other than a pint of plain. Though I have to say you did a fair job of presenting yourselves as naive American tourists. But you seemed to be showing quite a bit of interest in our men that night."

"Fair dues to you. We were."

"And when I was provided with the information that your name was Burke, well, that opened up an entirely new avenue for research."

Terry again was the family's only spokesman. "How did you find our names?"

"My sergeant again. The men I was with that night, our curiosity was aroused, and it was decided that we would do a bit of digging to find out who you were and why you were here. The sergeant asked the barman if you had paid by credit card. But no, you had paid in banknotes. He wasn't put off by that; he set out to do a bit of reconnaissance at hotels, lodgings, here and in Belfast. And found your names that way. The room was in the name of Terrence Burke."

"Well done, Major. Can't put anything over on the British Army!"

"If only more men would come to that conclusion, this country would be in a far better state." No reply to that.

Not that he would expect a reply. Declan Burke was IRA, as Earnshaw had learned. But what about the other two? Terry. His charm and humour could be valuable to their side, perhaps in recruiting neophytes to the cause, after spending an evening with them in a pub. And the black-haired, black-eyed chap, Brennan. Earnshaw could easily imagine him as the OC of this or that brigade of the IRA, or as the man you most feared if you were identified as an informer for the other side. And Declan. Earnshaw's own, well, his biological father. One look into those ice-cold blue eyes, and you'd know you were facing a fearsome opponent. It was men like him who made the Irish Republican Army such a formidable enemy. Officers at the top of the British Army had been known to describe the Provisional IRA as highly skilled and disciplined, not the wild-eyed fanatics some British soldiers liked to portray them as. Would it make more sense to acknowledge their skill as a fighting force rather than dismiss them as a pack of undisciplined extremists? If that's all they are, why have we not yet defeated them? Yet. Oh, it will happen, Earnshaw was convinced, but it hadn't happened yet. A highly skilled opponent.

Pity the same could not be said about so many of the paramilitaries allied with the British. That bunch of cack-handed ninnies, prats, and muppets the British forces had to work with here in Ulster. That riff-raff, their murders as often for reasons of sectarian bigotry as for patriotism. But needs must: we have no choice but to work with them, such as they are. *Collude* with them. The republicans and nationalists accuse the British Army and security forces of collusion with the rabble here, the loyalist paramilitaries. They don't know the half of it.

Earnshaw returned his attention to present company in the bar. "Now, my question for you: how did you come to know about me?"

He didn't miss the glances exchanged amongst the three of them. Again, it was Terry who provided the answer. Or part of the answer.

"Someone who is not friendly to our family caught my attention and made a few accusations against us. One of those accusations was that our father had not been a loyal, um, a loyal Irishman. That he had worked for the Anglo-Irish aristocracy at a grand estate in County Wicklow. But we knew that his loyalty to Ireland has never been in question, so —"

Earnshaw could not resist interrupting whatever Terry Burke was going to say next. "How would working at a property in County Wicklow make a man a *disloyal* Irishman?" As if Earnshaw didn't know. He had done his research on the Burke family, iron-willed Irish republicans, one and all. But he thought it might be entertaining to hear the answer.

"Well, as you know, Major — could we put ourselves on a first-name basis here?"

Earnshaw gave him the nod. "Dwight," he said.

"As you know, Dwight, many Irish did not have the advantages in life that the Anglo-Irish enjoyed. The landed gentry, I guess we'd call them. So, it might have appeared that Declan was working for the privileged, and in the opinion of some, that meant not working for, or with, his own people."

Point to Terry. Smoothly done. Real answer avoided. Dwight could not resist a follow-up question: "How did he remain loyal to his . . . to Ireland? Was there something he did whilst employed at Shersfoote House that signalled or proved his loyalty?"

Ah, the three of them were wily enough not to answer that one.

After a moment of silence and sips of pints all round, Brennan Burke spoke up. "The name Burke struck a chord with you when you heard it, Dwight. That, of course, tells us that you knew of the connection between yourself and our father here."

There was no avoiding it now. "This happened a few years ago. I was visiting home, and I overheard an argument between my mother and fa . . . my father, in which the name Declan Burke was mentioned. My parents had been a little testy with each other around that time, the time I overheard them. From the context of the argument, I knew that whoever Declan Burke was, there was some history there, and it produced intense feelings between the two of them. When I got my mother alone, I questioned her. And that's when she revealed the secret of my birth. Or, should I say, my conception." He looked into

Declan's eyes. "I must confess I don't quite know how to act in a situation like this."

Finally, he heard from Declan himself. "I know all too well what you mean."

Dwight waited to see if he would say anything more. The silence dragged out, and glasses were drained. Terry got up and ordered another round. When they all had fresh drinks before them, Declan said, "I myself only learned of it a few weeks ago, in a letter from her granddaughter. Althea's granddaughter."

What? "Which granddaughter was this?"

"She didn't give her name. She learned about me from a couple of pages of a diary she found. Althea's diary. She wrote in the diary about an argument between herself and her husband. My name came up in connection somehow — well, a connection in the granddaughter's mind — between myself and another member of your family. Dennison."

Dennison. Dwight Earnshaw could not remember the last time he had laid eyes on that useless article. But wait — had Declan Burke come into Althea's life a second time? At a time that would account for the birth of the family's drug addict? No, surely not.

"She had things arseways, obviously," Declan said. "Was mixed up as to which son I had, em . . . Althea in her diary referred to his addiction to drugs and said she had gone searching for him in some of the rough areas of the city. Dublin. The poor man, God help him."

Poor man? That wasn't Dwight's view of him. Dennison Earnshaw had had every advantage life could offer and threw it all away.

"The girl who wrote me the letter was obviously wrong in the timing. She thought my connection with her grandmother was a later one, a connection with Dennison, and that maybe I could help him. I did in fact try to find him."

"You what?"

"I took myself off to some of the laneways where those unfortunate fellas gather to get their fix."

"Oh? And did you find him?"

"No." That reply came a little too quickly. Had Declan perhaps found him in one of those heroin alleys? Dwight had no desire to hear about it, if he had.

Declan said, "But now here we are. Not Dennison, but Dwight."

Declan

There was silence for a few seconds. Declan observed the man sitting across from him in the Lisburn bar. No question, he had the look and the bearing of a fine soldier. If I had raised him, Declan reflected, what a soldier he'd have been for our side! Declan spoke to him then. "I'm sorry that you had to hear about it, about me, the way you did."

Terry broke in to say, "It must have been painful for your mother to have to reveal it. What was your reaction when you heard it?"

"Well, I didn't whinge about it. I like to think I took it in good grace."

"Right, so," Declan replied. Here was the famed English stiff upper lip. What was the other phrase? *Keep calm and carry on.* A gene obviously carried by the Anglo-Irish on this side of the Irish Sea. Dwight Earnshaw was keeping calm in these trying circumstances; would he be just as cool under fire? *Had* he been cool under fire? And who accounted for those exchanges of gunfire? Men like Declan himself.

"I was not about to berate my mother," said Earnshaw, "about something she had done in her younger days. She had always been a good mother to me, and to the others."

"I'm sure she was. I'm glad to hear it."

Terry again: "What did she tell you about our father here?" Terry glanced over at Declan, and Declan was not sure he wanted to hear whatever it was.

"Very little" was Earnshaw's reply. "Just that he had done work about the place, and that's how she knew him." Nothing else worth saying about me, Declan remarked to himself. Declan Burke? Oh, him. Right. Nothing but a mere hireling, a servant about the place. When Declan cast his mind back to those days, he recalled a much more enthusiastic attitude towards him on Althea's part; she couldn't wait to sneak off to meet him in their little hiding place. But no, this was not the time to dwell on the images that came to his mind, memories of the two of them together.

Again, a long stretch when nobody spoke. Typically, bless him, Terry broke the impasse. "We all know there are things we're not going to talk about, subjects not to be broached. But perhaps, Dwight, you can tell us a little about your life. Personal life, I mean."

Not without the hint of a smile, the major said, "How much will I hear about *your* lives? Yours in particular, Declan?"

Declan started to reply, then stopped himself. He was about to say *Ah, there's nothing to say about me, just a humble servant, a grease monkey tinkering with his Lordship's motor cars*. Or *Look across to the other side of the battlefield; you'll see me there*. But that hint of a smile, Dwight's tone of voice, suggested that he knew very well what Declan's life had been about, particularly his earlier life. Irish Republican soldier Declan Burke kept his gob firmly shut.

Terry saved the day by telling Earnshaw about his own wife and family. Then Terry sent a pointed look at Declan, and Declan got the message. This was a wife-and-kids conversation.

"And your own family, Dwight?" Declan inquired. "Em, your family now, I mean," Declan stumbled and could have kicked himself.

But Dwight stayed in the spirit of things and told them he was married and had a son and a daughter, and a grandchild on the way. Nobody asked whether the son, or maybe the daughter, had served in the British Army. Terry then told Earnshaw that Brennan was a priest, Father Burke, and that brought a look of astonishment to the face of Major Earnshaw, the face that clearly identified him as a brother to the Burkes.

Now, how were they going to end this little scene? Here was Declan looking into the face of a son he'd never known he had, a son who looked very much like his half-brother Patrick. Declan could use some of Patrick's psychiatric wisdom now: how was a man supposed to *feel* when confronted with a son he didn't know?

All he felt right now was confusion, uncertainty, and, as a result, embarrassment. This was nothing like a meeting he'd heard about years before. A woman who was a close friend to Declan and Teresa has been adopted as an infant. She had always known that she was adopted and was grateful for it. When she was well into middle age, she met the woman who had given birth to her. The friend described the meeting as "emotional," with hugs and tears and promises to stay in touch. The daughter knew her mother had "given her up" so she could have a better life, two loving parents who very much wanted their new baby daughter. But the situation here in Lisburn was nothing like that. The father here had not known of the son's existence; the son had spent his life until recently assuming his mother's husband was his father. There had been no lifelong wondering about his biological father. With all this, Declan was simply poleaxed. He had no idea what to do. What did Terry and Brennan think should happen?

Major Earnshaw saved them the trouble of having to decide. "Well, duty calls, so I'll say my goodbyes now. I don't know quite what to say after this extraordinary meeting."

"Maybe I'll give a little . . ." Terry began, but his voice faltered and he didn't finish what he was going to say. What was it going to be, one of his recitals? But it seemed that even Terry Burke was incapable of capturing this moment in one of his pub performances.

Then to Declan's surprise, Brennan rose to his feet with his near-empty pint glass in hand and started to sing what had become, in a way, his own party piece: "The Parting Glass." He glossed over some of the words Declan knew to the song, about "comrades" and "all the harm I've ever done," and gave them a shortened and heartfelt version of the song.

> So fill to me the parting glass.
> And drink a health whate'er befall
> And gently rise and softly call
> Good night and joy be with you all.

When he finished the song, the others rose to their feet. Major Dwight Earnshaw nodded farewell to his father and his newly met half-brothers. His expression was unreadable. Brennan looked at his da and got the impression he was on the verge of tears. A rare sight to behold. Brennan felt tears coming, too, but held them back. Terry felt no such compulsion to hide his emotion; a tear rolled down his cheek. He said, "Maybe we'll meet again before too much more time passes."

"Yes," Major Earnshaw replied, "perhaps we shall."

They both knew it was a lie. But nobody made a point of saying that this was a final parting.

CHAPTER XXXIV

Terry

They drove back to Belfast in silence, said little as they bunked down in their West Belfast B & B. The following day, they made the trip to Dublin in under two hours, and never was the city centre such a welcome sight. The crowds of shoppers and tourists in O'Connell Street; the grandeur of the General Post Office with its columned facade; the statue of the Catholic Liberator, Daniel O'Connell; the broad expanse of the bridge over the River Liffey. Then they were home in Irishtown. As soon as they were settled again in the house, Brennan walked over to Saint Patrick's Church in Ringsend. To give thanks, he said, for his survival and that of his brother and father. And to pray for the Colyear family. And maybe for their brother in Lisburn? Terry and Declan knew they had some calls to make. Terry rang his airline and made flight reservations for the middle of the week. Then he rang Sheila at home in New York and gave her a mild version of what had occurred. A couple of men had "grabbed hold of me" trying to find out what Declan was up to.

Brennan had been caught up in a bit of a struggle and had some mild injuries, but he was fine. He'd tell her more when he got home.

"You're damn right you'll tell me more! And you'll tell me now, not when you get home! There's way more to this than you're saying, Terry." You have no idea, Terry said to himself. Sheila continued, "Terry Burke the storyteller clams up and doesn't tell the whole story! You were grabbed; Brennan had 'mild injuries.' Now what the hell happened?"

"Sheila, my love, I can't get into it now. But I can assure you that everybody is fine. And you'll hear the whole story when I get home. Three more days. I'll see you on Wednesday."

"You're effin' right I'll hear the whole story. And you'll also explain to me why you *can't get into it now.* Be prepared to be interrogated as soon as I meet you at the airport!"

"I know, I know. I shall submit willingly to your interrogation!"

"You shall indeed. Now, take care of yourselves, all of you, and I'll see you soon. Love you!"

Declan rang Finn and Father Leo Killeen and, on these calls, was a little more forthright about what had happened and who had set it all in motion.

When he had finished those calls, Declan said, "Between the two of them, if Finn and Leo had their way, they'd be heading an army to march on Belfast. But as you heard, I explained why the Colyear lad did what he did and that we were going to let it go. And that the Royal Ulster Constabulary — Finn calls them the Royal Ulster Colludulary — would never find anyone to arrest for the shooting. Mrs. Colyear is certainly not going to turn in her son!"

"No," Terry agreed, "and I suspect this case won't be at the top of the RUC's list. Now, listen, Da. I'm thinking about Monty Collins. He'll be back home now after the conference in The Hague."

"Good man, Monty. Sound. And I don't hold it against him, doing research into my past! He was trying to help, and I appreciate that."

"That's why I think we should ring him. He tried to help, and he'll be wondering how it's going here. Brennan doesn't want to call. I guess he can't quite picture himself ringing his friends and saying, *Hi. We blew it. I got shot.* But I imagine they thought he'd be home in Halifax by now. They shouldn't be left out of the loop when something serious has happened to one of their closest friends."

"You're probably right. That Maura, I can just see her flying over here, hunting down poor young Colyear. She'd tear him to ribbons, with no weapon but the harsh words coming out of her mouth. I remember what Brennan once said about her: she has a tongue on her that would slit the hull of a freighter."

Terry laughed. "Exactly. If she gets wind of this, there could be an international incident."

"But all codding aside, you should probably ring them, let them know. While Brennan's out at the church. What time is it there, five hours earlier than here?"

"Four hours. It's ten a.m. there."

So Terry picked up the phone, went through the process of finding a Canadian number and making an international call. It was Maura who answered. Now, how to break the bad news. How to phrase it. "Maura, how are you? It's Terry Burke calling."

"Oh, God, what's happened?"

That stopped Terry short. "Uh, something did happen. He was injured, but he's fine and he'll be with you soon over in Halifax."

"Jesus, something's happened to Brennan."

Terry heard another voice then, the voice of a child. "Mummy, is it Father Burke?"

"Yes, darlin', it's his brother. But Father Burke is fine, and we'll see him soon." To Terry, Maura said, "That's Normie. You remember our daughter."

"Of course I do." She was a student in Brennan's choir school.

"Mum, I *told* you something bad happened!"

What was this? "Maura, what did Normie say?"

"She . . . she has what we call 'the sight.' She intuits things or sees things that the rest of us don't. My grandmother in Cape Breton, she's the same way."

Brennan had told Terry about Normie, referring to her as "the little Druid" for her ability, like that of Brennan himself, to experience what he called the other side. The Burke family called Brennan *their* Druid.

"What happened to Brennan?" Maura's voice was little more than a whisper.

"He was in hospital, in Belfast. He had a chest wound, and also his arm. But, as I say, he is recovering. No lasting damage."

"Belfast. Chest wound. Please tell me it's not what it sounds like."

"It is."

"He was shot! God help him!"

"Mum!" Normie cried out. "That's what I saw! It must have been. When I got upset and I knew something bad happened!"

He could hear the little one sobbing. But she cleared her voice to ask, "Is he really all right, Mum? Did the doctors fix him?"

Terry answered, "Tell her that he really is all right. The bullet grazed the outside of his chest and went into his arm. He fell back and hit his head and was knocked out. The doctors took the bullet out and did a scan for the head injury. He's all fixed up, and you'll all see him soon."

"Oh, thank God! And how about you, Terry?" Maura asked. "Being kidnapped! Monty, of course, told me all about it when he came back to The Hague. I wanted to fly over to Dublin and kidnap all three of you and knock some sense into your heads and put you on a plane out of there!"

Terry laughed then. "I can just picture it. You'd have had us all cowed into submission."

"I wish I had! But what in the hell happened that Brennan ended up with a bullet in him?"

"I won't get into the details, the background now. You'll hear it all from Brennan when he gets home. But it happened because Bren jumped in to save our father's life." Terry was surprised to hear the break in his own voice when he said it.

"Oh, Christ, Terry! He told us before he left that you and he were going along with Declan on his first visit back to Ireland since that midnight voyage out all those years ago. Brennan even joked a bit, saying he hoped Dec wouldn't have to face any demons over there. Or something. And now this!"

"Yeah, there were demons. But this was something else, or at least another . . . A mission of mercy, you might say, which went south. Or, to be accurate, north."

"A mission of mercy involving your father somehow?"

"It's all related. Too complicated to get into now. And there's another story too."

"Another story? The shooting and whatever accounted for it wasn't enough for you fellas?"

"Oh, just a nice little family story. You'll hear it all from Bren when he gets home. Over drinks at — where is it? The Midtown Tavern? O'Carroll's Pub?"

"Could be either of those places. Tell me this: Has he told his fellow priests? Anybody at Saint Bernadette's?"

"No, he hasn't. So I know you'll keep it to yourselves. You and Monty. Well, you and Monty and little Normie. Who knew it already!"

"Yes, apparently she did."

Terry would save the story of Normie's remarkable experience, her clairvoyance, for her to tell Brennan when he got home. He said goodbye to Maura and assured her he'd have Brennan back in his home parish before too long.

"Bless you, Terry. You have a safe trip home, and we'll have a warm welcome for Brennan when he returns to us in Halifax."

CHAPTER XXXV

Brennan

A lovely clear day, and Brennan suggested that the three of them go for a stroll along the riverbank. So that's what they did. The water reflected the azure blue of the sky, and the seagulls flew back and forth in a state of apparent excitement. The Burkes walked for a few minutes, then stood at the stone wall lining the riverbank and looked about them. Brennan felt a stab of pain when he moved his arm with the walking, but he didn't let on. They had a view of the city centre roughly to the west of them, the docklands to the north, and the Lansdowne Road rugby and football stadium to the south.

"A nice peaceful scene," Terry remarked. "But not everyone is at peace, to understate the situation on this island."

"And in much of this world," Brennan added.

"So true. Now, Da," Terry said then, "the name of Edison Colyear, the *senior* Edison, still bears the infamy of him being a tout, an informer for the IRA. When in fact he had been no such thing. The loyalists in East Belfast still think he was a traitor to their cause."

"I think we can assume that his widow will get the word out that he was innocent of that charge. That she heard it from someone who knows the inside story and who took a considerable risk to let her know. She'll tell the son, and despite what happened at their house —"

"Isn't there an expression *Don't shoot the messenger*?"

"I guess not everybody is familiar with that. What is it, the Eleventh Commandment, Father Burke?"

"It is now."

"Right. Anyway, young Colyear will make sure the true story gets around, to clear his father's name. And to put that vicious fucker Mackasey Ward in the frame where he belongs, as the man who really was the tout. He's in his grave now. I hope he died roarin' for a priest, as the saying goes. Or the Protestant equivalent."

When they had returned to the house, Declan said, "I'll boil the kettle. Have we any biscuits left?"

"We've some digestives with the dark chocolate on them," Brennan replied. When the tea had been poured, they all sat down at the kitchen table. Brennan decided to let his father enjoy a biscuit and a couple of sips before raising the subject of Albert McKribban.

A few minutes passed. Then it was time. "It's a relief to know that the reputation of Edison Colyear will likely be restored amongst his loyalist friends and comrades."

"It is," Declan replied. Brennan noted a wariness in his voice.

"Now, what is to be done about Albert McKribban, who sent us all down the rabbit hole? Had Terry kidnapped and sent you that threatening note." This was met with silence across the table. "Da?"

"Finn has a . . . an idea."

"An idea? I've never seen Finn as a man to just sit on his arse and discourse about ideas, Da. He's more a man of action, is he not?"

"All right, all right. He has a plan."

"Yes? Go on."

"Finn and a couple of . . ."

"Couple of what, Da? Who?"

"Friends."

"Friends who play bingo with him at the church hall? Friends who come over for tea and biscuits and watch *Fair City* on the telly?"

"Friends who are well able to take care of themselves."

"Take care of themselves in, say, a tense situation? Would this be Barry and Donal, our security men?"

"No, Brennan, these would be fellas a little more . . . a bit more senior, experienced, higher up in the ranks. Don't be concerning yourselves about it."

"Da, we've all been through this together. Now, fess up. What's the plan?"

Declan pressed his lips together, obviously wanting the lips to stay closed but knowing he had to open up to his sons who had been through this together. "Finn has a couple of the men, hard men, who'll be coming along to . . . make sure that Albert McKribban won't be causing any more trouble for me or for anybody else on this island, north or south. Ever again."

Christ, what did these hard men have in store for McKribban? Not that he deserved much in the way of consideration. But . . . "How are they going to make sure of that, Dec?"

"I know one of the two men Finn has in mind. He can be very persuasive."

How persuasive, how dangerous was this man if he could "persuade" the likes of Albert McKribban never to step out of line again? Brennan knew there was no point in asking his father for that sort of incriminating detail. But if Brennan and Terry came along on the mission, surely they would act as a deterrent to anything too . . . too what? Intense? Frightening? Blood-curdling?

"So, when are we meeting with McKribban?"

His father gave him the dead-eyed stare. "*We* are not meeting with him. Finn was very clear on that."

"Is that so? None of us will be along for McKribban's lesson in proper etiquette?"

"*I* will certainly be there."

Terry broke in then, stating the obvious. "It was *me* his men took captive. And it was only by my own wits that I got away from them."

"I know, Terry. I know. And Brennan in Belfast . . ."

"Right. Brennan shot in Belfast trying to make amends for what McKribban and his men did to that family. So we should —"

"Finn was very clear on the subject, Terrence. The men who are assisting in this matter will have no one else involved but myself and Finn. End of story."

They didn't want any more witnesses than necessary, Brennan reflected, or any more casualties if things spiralled out of control, which was understandable. The Burke brothers knew their father well enough to know there was no point in arguing the point any further. They would have to go at it another way.

Brennan's thoughts returned to something mentioned a few minutes before. "Our two bodyguards, Barry and Donal. I've been thinking we should do something for them. A gift of some kind to thank them. Finn's other house, where they're staying, is just a few blocks away on Saint Magdalen Terrace. If we can think of something to give them, we can take a walk over, see if one or both of them are there and —"

"They're not there," Declan broke in. "They're gone."

"Gone? How do you know?"

"Finn called them off."

"Their services are no longer required?" Terry asked.

"Something like that."

"Their services have been taken over by more senior men," Brennan said.

"Don't be concerning yourself. I've made sure Finn will pass along our thanks and appreciation."

"Still, it would be good to get something for them," Brennan said again. "But what?"

Terry laughed. "Somehow I don't think a bouquet of flowers or a box of chocolates would be the right sort of gift for the occasion."

"A gift card for something maybe? I don't suppose the off-licences have gift certificates!" The liquor stores. "But we could get a few bottles for them."

They were all quiet for a minute, then Terry said, "I've got it. When I'm back in New York, I'll write to Finn and have him pass this along to them. I'll write out a promise to make reservations for the two of them for short-haul flights to wherever they'd like to go in Europe. I'll write it on the airline's stationery to give it a bit of cred! And I'll keep the promise. They'll have those flights as a thank-you present from all of us."

"Good plan, Terry," Brennan and Declan both said.

Half an hour later, when the three of them were having a game of poker, the phone rang. Declan got to it first. "Hello. I am, but . . . No, I'll ring you later. Right." Click.

Brennan and Terry exchanged a glance, but neither of them spoke. What was that about? Dec wanted to make a call later? He turned back to his hand of cards, and not a word was spoken about the brief phone conversation. A silence that, in itself, spoke volumes. As did the fact that neither of the Burke brothers made a move to go down the pub for a few jars before retiring for the night.

When the clock struck eleven, Brennan and Terry could plausibly head for their beds. Neither of them put on a show of yawning or expressing their exhaustion. They went into their room to feign sleep. Declan, too, headed for bed as if he had forgotten all about his intention to ring whoever had rung earlier. Brennan assumed it was Finn. Dec waited for nearly an hour before creeping out to the telephone. Brennan and Terry did some creeping too. Over to their closed door. Terry winked at Brennan as he took an empty glass and placed it against the door, an old trick they had done as kids when they wanted to eavesdrop on a conversation happening in another room. They heard Declan punching the numbers into the phone.

A few seconds later, he said, "Yeah." A pause, then, "Sooner the better. Good. Has to be late. Where? Right, so. Might just as well, since it was him that . . . No, I don't imagine. They'd all be steering clear of the place now. Time? Grand."

Neither of the eavesdroppers made a move until they heard their father walk back to his bedroom and close the door.

Then Terry asked, "So, what do we make of that?"

Brennan thought over the few words they had heard during the cryptic conversation. "Well, they were discussing where this encounter is to take place. And we can be sure it's not here, not with you and me looking on, not in a house owned by Finn."

"What about that 'might as well'? That sounded as if, I don't know, something obvious had come to mind. Obvious at least to Dec and Finn."

"If only it was obvious to us!"

"Yeah. What else did we hear? 'They'd all be staying away now'?"

"Something like that. 'Steering clear of the place.'"

"Now, as opposed to an earlier time. Or they're referring to an incident. Steering clear after something happened. Well, Brennan, we all know some places where *something happened*! And this McKribban, from what we've heard, is a Dublin man. So, I don't think our father and uncle will be heading up to Belfast. Maybe it's where the other thing happened. My captivity!"

"That could be it, Ter. Dec said something like 'he was the one who' or 'it was him.' They were discussing the place to meet. That house? It was McKribban who leased the place under a false name. Berrigan's name. Can we assume this confrontation is going to take place at the house on the East Wall Road?"

"That would make sense, Brennan. Well, as much as anything could make sense in this clusterfuck."

"It's all we have to go on. And Da said 'late,' so he must have meant late at night. Fewer people around. I guess we'll have to wait till we see Da head out late at night. He said 'sooner the better,' so he's not waiting long for this to be done and dusted. Tomorrow?"

"We'll see what he comes up with as an excuse for going out tomorrow night, or whatever night. If he goes out without us, we'll assume the mission is on. So, what is our plan of action?"

"You're the military man, Terry. How would you go about this operation?"

"My training didn't include undercover work, spying, any of that. But somehow we have to see what is going to happen there on the East Wall Road."

"We can't very well sit on the stone wall across from the house and spy on it from there."

"That's right. Not even if we tried to disguise ourselves by wearing some kind of outlandish garb. We'd never live that down!"

"*If* we live." Brennan thought for a moment. "You saw how close Fairvew Park is to the East Wall Road. It's across the road and the river, but the distance is not great at all. And there are trees at the edge of the park across from East Wall. That could be our observation post. We could pick up a pair of binoculars."

"It'll be dark though. Declan said 'late.'"

"True, but we'll be able to see if . . . see how many men go into the house and how many come walking out on their own two legs."

Terry was silent for a moment, then said, "I'm trying to picture it, Bren. Us in the trees, spying on a house through our binoculars. If anyone sees us, will they report us to the Gardaí for being a pair of voyeurs?"

"O ye of little faith, Terry. Surely you of all people can come up with a cover story."

It didn't take him long. "Birdwatchers!"

"Good one, brother. But at night?"

"We're not country boys, I know, but there must be birds that fly around at night."

"That rings a bell," Brennan said. "Or it quacks, caws, or screeches. I'm trying to think — yes! I cracked up laughing when I heard this one time on RTÉ." The Irish national broadcaster. "Scréachóg reilige!" It sounded like "SHCRAY-a-hoag RELL-ig-geh."

"What in the name of God did you say?"

"It means graveyard screecher!"

"You're having me on."

"Not at all. It's the Irish for barn owl. It's white and has a ghostly look about it. The creature got its name from the fact that for some reason, it spends a lot of time in graveyards. I'd rather not speculate on that. It flies around and gives out this long, drawn-out, eerie-sounding screech."

"That would be feckin' scary!"

"Oh, yeah. And scréachóg reilige is one of my favourite expressions in the Irish language. Another of my favourites is snagcheol for jazz."

"SNAG-k'yole, great word! And somehow it's fitting for jazz."

"Well, little brother, we have our plan." He interrupted his own train of thought and said, "I'm a little brother now too. No longer the first-born son!"

"You'll always be my one and only big brother, Bren."

"Go raibh maith agat, Terry, to speak in the language that our other brother wouldn't understand. Now, back to our plan. We'll go to a shop and buy a pair of binocs. Then tomorrow night, assuming tomorrow will be the night, we'll take the bus to Fairview Park. The sun goes down at around quarter to ten, but we know the sky stays light for quite a while after that. We'll stay well out of sight until it's dark. Then position ourselves in the trees and be on the lookout for graveyard screechers."

And hope, Brennan said to himself, there won't be any graveyard screeching from the house on the other side of the River Tolka.

ᔓ

So there they were the next evening after sundown in Fairview Park, Brennan and Terry with their binoculars, lurking behind the trees. They had told their father they were going to the Cobblestone for a session, a session of traditional music. They'd be taking a taxi "just in case" they exceeded the legal blood-alcohol limit for driving. But they instructed the driver to take them to Fairview Park, not the Cobblestone pub.

"What do we look like, Bren?" Terry asked as they stood behind the trees. "A pair of voyeurs, as I mentioned? A couple of scofflaws, hiding out and watching for the police?"

"We are two respectable birdwatchers, Terrence, waiting for those screeching owls to come swooping over our heads."

"Dropping bombs of shite on our heads, you mean."

"Better than what might be in store for yer man McKribban."

"True enough."

There were a few couples strolling through the park, two families with children running about, playing hide-and-seek, enjoying the chance to be out late. The Burkes' focus, though, was not on fun in the park, but on whatever might occur whenever Declan, Finn, and their unidentified co-conspirators made their appearance across the river on the East Wall Road. Brennan and Terry stayed quiet in their hiding place, quiet except for the occasional slap and curse at the cloud of midges that hovered around them. Brennan heard the twitter and squeaks of other nocturnal creatures, and he saw a bat fly low over the trees. As spooky as they were, there was good in them, he knew: they were known to eat midges. A bat, a bat, my kingdom for a —

"Bren! Look!" Terry raised the binoculars to his eyes. It was just past eleven o'clock, and a van had pulled up a couple of doors down from the house where he had been held captive. "Here," he said, passing the binoculars to Brennan.

"No, you keep them, see if you recognize whoever shows up with Dec and Finn."

Five men emerged from the van, one of them with his arms gripped by two of the others. "They're heading for the house. Dec, Finn, and three others. I don't recognize them; they're not the guys who kidnapped me. They're at the door. Opening it. Must have got the key from McKribban. I assume he's the man who's shuffling along in the grip of the two unknowns. They're going inside, light switched on. The windows aren't boarded up now. Only a dim light in the living room. No sign of them in there. Maybe they're taking him to my living quarters in the back. The bedroom."

"So, no familiar faces apart from our da and uncle?"

"Right. Here, take these. You can have a look in case they make an appearance in a window."

Brennan lifted the binoculars and felt a little twinge of pain in his arm, but it was almost negligible. He held the spyglasses up to his eyes and focused on the house. He saw shadows moving, but no one came near the front window. Suddenly there was a loud screech, and both the spies started at the sound.

"What the —" Terry began.

"Incoming!" Brennan announced. Terry ducked for cover, and Brennan laughed. The sound carried on and became almost like a high-pitched wail. "Either it's the banshee, or it's the graveyard screecher!" Something white swooped over their heads. An owl uttering its eerie graveyard screech.

There was no movement to be seen in the house. "What are they doing?" Brennan whispered. "Are we going to see all five walk out of there?"

In the dark silence, the watchers waited. And waited. If anything was happening, it was happening out of sight. "How long have they been in there?" Terry asked, trying to see his watch in the gloom. "The better part of an hour. It's nearly mid—"

Crack! And a shout, more like a yelp.

The brothers spun about and stared at one another. "What the fuck?!" Terry exclaimed. But they knew; they were all too familiar with the sound of a gunshot. The sound had come from across the river. From the house? Brennan could not have pinpointed the exact location, but the odds were on the house. Would there be another shot? Was the man being kneecapped? But there was nothing but silence. What would happen now? How many men would walk out of there? The brothers waited. Nothing. Occasionally a car drove by on the street, but there was nobody out walking. Nobody, it seemed, in the park behind them.

Then the door opened. Brennan raised the binoculars and saw his father and uncle walk out the door. They were followed by one, now two, yes — three men. "Thank Christ!" Brennan whispered. When the five were all outside, two of them again gripped a third, and they walked in the direction of the van. The motor came on, the lights came on, and the van drove off down the East Wall Road.

"All right, the show's over, folks," Brennan said.

"Is it over for McKribban?"

"In some ways it is, I suspect. But they let him live. We'll see what we can find out from Da. Let's get over to the North Strand Road and hail a taxi."

"What will we say to our da, his boys staying out so late?"

"We'll tell him how good the music was at the Cobblestone."

"You'd better light up a smoke then, if you want to be credible claiming we were in a pub!"

"I'll do that. Where there's smoke, there's a drinking hole. Where there's no smoke, there's a night of healthy living in a tree-lined park."

"And the spyglasses?"

"I'll drop them out of sight before we go into the house. Leave them by the side of the road. Some kid can pick them up and make them his or her own."

ꕤ

The taxi left them on the Irishtown Road. There was a small bush outside the house, and Brennan shoved the binocs between its branches. They walked inside and saw Declan sitting in an armchair with a glass of whiskey in his hand. "Where were you fellas tonight?"

Had he forgotten what they had told him, or was he checking to see whether they would change their story?

"Down the pub with the lads," Terry replied. "Cobblestone. And yourself? How did things go with McKribban?" Terry and Brennan sat down on the sofa across from their father and waited. "Da?"

Declan let out a sigh, and then said, "I learned a bit about what's been happening."

"He talked, did he?"

"He did."

That certainly raised a question in Brennan's mind, but he would put that aside for the moment. "What did you learn?"

"That McKribban was not best pleased with his two hooligans for banjaxing the operation, failing to grab me and taking Terry instead. Then letting Terry escape, and us starting our investigation. Things had not gone exactly as McKribban had planned."

"To put it mildly," Terry remarked.

"Frank and Ger, not their real names, as we found out, have been used from time to time by McKribban and other . . . republicans to do various jobs. That would have been why S reacted to your description of Ger when you were in the Gravediggers, Terry."

"All that doesn't reflect well on the *other republicans*, does it, Da?"

"It does not. Fighting for a legitimate cause, fighting against the Brits' occupation —" His voice came to a halt.

"What is it, Da?" Brennan asked.

Their father shook off the question. Had he formed a picture of his newly discovered son in the uniform of the British occupiers? But he resumed his narrative. "Fighting against the British Empire and the Ulstermen who are its bootlickers in the North, that is a rightful cause. And that cause is not helped by the likes of those two clowns, Ger and Frank.

"And McKribban acknowledged that he had leased the East Wall house for a few months, leased it in the name of Caoimhin Berrigan. Unbeknownst to Berrigan. It was to be used as a safe house or a hiding place, a location for other activities he had undertaken. I couldn't be arsed to ask about any of that. McKribban was living somewhere else, in a place he registered in his mother's name. And he was still hoping to emigrate. Where to, I don't know. I'd made it clear all those years ago that he'd better not show his face in New York."

"So, Da," Brennan asked then, "how were you able to obtain all this information from McKribban?"

"The two hard men Finn brought along, they put the fear of God into that fucker."

"How did they do that?"

"You'd only have to look them in the eye, either of them, to be put in fear for your life."

"So that was it? They just stared him down and warned him to behave himself from now on?"

"From now to eternity. And no, it wasn't just a stare. There's a tiny spot in the wall, one of the rooms in the back. There might have been something stuck on the wall, or a picture hook, and now the paint is off it. Less than half an inch, showing the bare white plaster. One of the men pointed it out to McKribban, then walked to the far end of the room. 'D'yeh think I can hit that?' he asked and pulled a pistol out of his pocket. The other man took hold of McKribban and positioned him right beside that mark in the wall. It was just beside his head. McKribban was shaking with the fear. 'You'd better hope I've a good aim,' the gunman said. 'No, please!' McKribban begged. But the gunman took aim and fired. McKribban let out a squeal and crumpled to the floor. But he hadn't been hit. The marksman hit the spot on the wall as intended, an exact hit. Then he said to McKribban, 'If you step out of line, ever, I'll hear about it. And when I see you, wherever I see you, I can get you. D'yeh understand?' And oh yes, he understood. He'll not be messing with anyone ever again."

CHAPTER XXXVI

Brennan

Two days after the birdwatching adventure, Brennan parted with his father and brother at Kennedy airport in New York. There was little left to say about their dramatic sojourn in Ireland, except for this cautionary note from Declan: "I'll let you both know how I've framed the story — the *stories* — for your mother, and you'll stick to that version whenever the subject comes up." The Burke sons agreed to accept those terms, with regard to their mother, though Brennan knew that he and Terry would be much more forthright with Patrick and the other siblings when they had a chance to converse in private. About the events in Belfast and in Lisburn. The goodbyes were emotional, but typical of the Burke men, they kept all that in check and said they'd be in touch again soon. Brennan left them to catch his connecting flight to Canada.

Brennan had rung Monty about his return flight, because Monty had offered to give him a lift home from the airport whenever he arrived. Yes, he would be there. The flight was not direct, went through Toronto, but eventually Brennan had his feet back on the ground in

Nova Scotia. When he emerged into the arrivals hall after his evening flight, it was not only Monty who welcomed him home but Maura and their little daughter, Normie, as well. Monty busied himself by grappling with Brennan for his suitcase. "Enough heavy lifting for you. An injured soldier home from the wars."

"Ah, no worries. I'm grand."

Maura threw her arms around him and burst into tears. "Thank God, thank God, you're home in one piece, Brennan!"

And then it was Normie, she of the sweet face and the red — auburn, he corrected himself — curls. She was looking up at him, her hazel eyes huge behind her glasses, her lower lip quivering. "I *knew* something bad happened!"

"You *knew*?"

"Early in the morning just before the sun came up and I was still in bed and was trying to get back to sleep, I got all upset because I had a bad feeling. That something happened to a big person, a man . . . somebody I love." Her voice faltered. Then, "Is it okay for me to say that, Father?"

"It's more than okay. And I love you, too, Normie."

"Thank you!" She was in tears now. "So, yes, somebody I *loved* was in danger."

Brennan crouched down and took her in his arms. "What day was that, darlin'? Do you remember?"

"It was Wednesday. Last Wednesday. I remember because we went to the beach in the afternoon, but I kept worrying and thinking of that song."

He gently released her from his embrace, and stood. Last Wednesday. The tenth of July. In the early morning. It was morning when he'd been shot. With the four-hour time difference, it was very early for Normie.

He looked at the family gathered around him. "That's when it happened, the shooting."

"Oh, my God!" Maura exclaimed. Monty was staring at him.

Normie merely nodded her head. "I was crying, and that song kept going through my mind."

"A song, Normie?"

"It was one I've heard before. 'Help of the helpless, o, abide with me!'"

It was a rare moment indeed when Brennan Burke was stuck for words. Now Normie was not the only one in tears. His own eyes filled up as he stood staring at her. A long few seconds passed before Maura said, "Brennan, are you all right?"

He started to speak, had to clear his throat and start again. "At the moment of the shooting, when the bullet came for me, these words and this melody flashed through my mind." He sang, "'Hold Thou Thy cross before my closing eyes. Shine through the gloom.' Except I don't think I got to the word 'gloom' before I lost consciousness. Normie, that's the same hymn you heard. At the same time. 'Abide with Me.'"

"Christ Almighty!" Maura cried out. They all stood there, dumbfounded.

Then Normie said, "You were helpless, and so was I because I couldn't help you! I should have been able to see it before it happened and see for sure that it was you, and called and warned you! But . . . but I didn't."

The poor, dear child had always had an overdeveloped conscience. "There was nothing you could have done, pet. Or maybe there was; maybe you were my guardian angel looking out for me and enabled me to move just right so I only got hit in my side and arm. And not my heart."

"Oh, God! Do you think so?"

"God and his angels work in mysterious ways."

He leaned down and kissed her cheek. They all fell quiet once again.

Monty was first to break the silence. "Never a dull moment with you, Brennan."

"I could use some dull moments."

"Maybe you'll hear of a nice quiet retreat with a group of monks somewhere, Brennan," Maura suggested. "But not before we hear all about the latest Burke family adventure in the land that spawned them."

"You'll be hearing all about it."

"And we have whiskey for you at the house, Father," Normie assured him. "Mum and Dad bought a new bottle, not yet opened."

"You know me all too well, my little angel. All too well."

AUTHOR'S NOTES & ACKNOWLEDGEMENTS

I would like to thank the following people for their kind assistance: Joe A. Cameron, Joan Butcher, Rhea McGarva, retired Garda Detective Liam Browne, and a nurse who was on hospital duty in Belfast during the troubled times. Again, thanks to my sharp-eyed and astute editors, Cat London and Crissy Boylan, and proofreader Shannon Whibbs.

This is a work of fiction and my characters fictional. Any liberties taken in the interests of the story, or errors committed, are mine alone.

Gin Millie's and (Sandy Row) the Boat Ashore are fictional bars, as is Christy Burke's, though in the case of Christy's, I've been writing about it for so long sometimes I forget that!

Real pubs in the story are the Cobblestone, Hill 16, the Stag's Head, Kavanagh's/the Gravediggers, McDaid's, Neary's, the Brian Boru, and the Vintage Inn. The Seapoint now goes by the name the Irishtown House. Clarke's is now the Merry Cobbler. And in Halifax, at the time of the story, the Midtown Tavern and O'Carroll's were lively drinking spots.

Irwin Avenue in Belfast is a real street, but number 84 is fictional. East Wall Road in Dublin is a real street, but number 42A is fictional.

Wexford did defeat Dublin in an important hurling match around the time this novel is set. But, for the purposes of the story, I have not necessarily adhered to the real schedule.

In November 2025, Pope Leo XIV designated St. Mary's Pro-Cathedral as Dublin's official Catholic cathedral — it is no longer "provisional"!

And, by the way: yes, you could still smoke in a hospital in the Republic of Ireland and in Northern Ireland at the time this story was set!

Entertainment. Writing. Culture.

ECW is a proudly independent, Canadian-owned book publisher. We know great writing can improve people's lives, and we're passionate about sharing original, exciting, and insightful writing across genres.

Thanks for reading along!

We want our books not just to sustain our imaginations, but to help construct a healthier, more just world, and so we've become a certified B Corporation, meaning we meet a high standard of social and environmental responsibility — and we're going to keep aiming higher. We believe books can drive change, but the way we make them can too.

Being a B Corp means that the act of publishing this book should be a force for good — for the planet, for our communities, and for the people that worked to make this book. For example, everyone who worked on this book was paid at least a living wage. You can learn more at the Ontario Living Wage Network.

This book is also available as an eBOUND Digital Certification (EDC) ebook. ECW Press's ebooks are screen reader friendly and are built to meet the needs of those who are unable to read standard print due to blindness, low vision, dyslexia, or a physical disability.

This book is printed on FSC®-certified paper. It contains recycled materials, and other controlled sources, is processed chlorine free, and is manufactured using biogas energy.

ECW's office is situated on land that was the traditional territory of many nations including the Wendat, the Anishinaabeg, Haudenosaunee, Chippewa, Métis, and current treaty holders the Mississaugas of the Credit. In the 1880s, the land was developed as part of a growing community around St. Matthew's Anglican and other churches. Starting in the 1950s, our neighbourhood was transformed by immigrants fleeing the Vietnam War and Chinese Canadians dispossessed by the building of Nathan Phillips Square and the subsequent rise in real estate value in other Chinatowns. We are grateful to those who cared for the land before us and are proud to be working amidst this mix of cultures.

ecwpress.com